Herbert Kastle was born and brought up in ~~~~lyn. He has been an English teacher, ~~~~ ~~~~ ~~~~rtising copywriter, but he ~~~~ ~~~~ g. Mr Kastle is the a~~~~ ~~~~nding *The Movie M~~~~ ~~~~Dirty Movies* and *Sun~~~~*

By the same author

HERBERT KASTLE

Camera

GRAFTON BOOKS

A Division of the Collins Publishing Group

LONDON GLASGOW
TORONTO SYDNEY AUCKLAND

Grafton Books
A Division of the Collins Publishing Group
8 Grafton Street, London W1X 3LA

A Grafton UK Paperback Original 1987

ISBN 0-586-06578-4

Printed and bound in Great Britain by
Collins, Glasgow

Set in Times

Morden Photos, its photographers, models, other employees
and assorted visitors are not based on actual studios or living
people, nor are the events here described intended to portray
actual events.

For Theron W. Raines

Now am I an outcast. I loathe my own
country. A very drunken sleep on the beach,
that is best.

– A Season in Hell
by Arthur Rimbaud

Book One

1

Marie 'Riposta was fond of saying, 'I'm a native New-
yawka.' It gave her an edge, she figured. It showed the
characters at the studio that she knew the score.

'What she actually did when she said this to either
photographers or models was to hide her frightened,
insecure, unhappy femininity behind a veneer of skyline;
give herself the façade of sophistication which, she hoped,
out-of-towners would accord to anyone born and bred
within the New York City limits.

'She was neither hopeful enough nor stupid enough to
believe this with all her heart, but it helped her keep the
sixty-five-dollar-a-week job as secretary-receptionist at
Morden Photos; helped her maintain equality, as a
woman, with the models who otherwise would have filled
her with unbearable bitterness – they and their beauty
and easy camaraderie with men and, she suspected,
exciting hours of passion.

Not that Marie was ugly or even plain. At twenty she
had a certain dark, thin, intense good looks which, with a
vibrant intellectual personality, would have brought her
the desired amount of personable male attention. However, as her mother once said to a friend, 'My three boys
got all the push and go. Marie's the quiet one.'

The 'quiet' masked a deep inability to believe in herself
as a woman.

But at the studio, she managed to smile a lot and
even wisecracked a little when she felt it was absolutely
necessary – which was any time she had to walk into the
studio proper while one of the four photographers was

shooting cheesecake. Seeing those beautifully built women wearing almost nothing . . .

But if Marie was quiet at home and on her rare dates and at her job, she made up for it when she was with her girl friends. Marie lunched with several girls, none of them from the studio, none of them models or in any way connected with photography. They were friends from her Brooklyn neighborhood – two from President Street, where she herself lived, and one from Eastern Parkway, a few blocks away. These three had one unhappy thing in common with Marie: they were generally unsuccessful with boys. There was another girl, Stella Lago, who lived on St John's Place, but she came along only once in a while, and Marie didn't really like her. Stella was a tall, full-bodied redhead who worked the switchboard in a dress-manufacturing house. She had lots of dates and laughed all the time and boys kept talking to her whenever she was in the Automat, or a luncheonette, or just walking along the street. She talked 'hip,' like some of the people at the studio, and she'd even asked Marie to introduce her to one of the photographers. 'Maybe I could make it in modeling,' she said, giggling, and quickly added, 'I don't dig the real hot stuff – just fashions.'

Marie had managed to put her off.

When Marie was with her three close friends – June, Roberta and Carrie – she would discuss the studio in a vastly superior manner. 'Imagine, a girl taking off her clothes and letting a guy move her around, even touching her here and there. How low can you get?'

'Well, it's their *business*,' June had once suggested, more to draw Marie into the soul-sustaining criticism they all needed than to defend anyone.

'Business! Sure, monkey business! The advertising work and illustration work and other work's okay, I guess, but don't tell *me* about that cheesecake! What sort of girl would let a man see her naked?'

She would continue in the same vein, and then return to her desk on the second floor of the narrow, three-story, Fifty-second Street building, and remember her own words, and so manage to end the day feeling only slightly inferior to everyone else. Not that she actually knew anything about what went on between the models and photographers.

Occasionally she'd mention Henny Girado to her friends, but here she'd drop her critical ways. 'Only really decent fellow up there,' she'd say. 'That Henny Girado I was telling you about. And even he isn't from the city. Comes from Cleveland, or down South, or someplace. I wonder how he ever got into that crazy business. Nice guy.' Her eyes would turn wistful. 'About thirty-five, good-looking. Talks nice, only not like the boys in the neighborhood.'

That Tuesday morning in May, Henny Girado got to the studio at nine-thirty, earlier than usual, and he didn't talk nice to Marie. She'd been feeling confident, happy, because on the way to the Utica Avenue subway station in Brooklyn a boy had looked her over and said, 'Mamma, buy me one of those!' He'd been nothing, really – one of those seventeen-, eighteen-year-old kids with club jacket and long sideburns and a big mouth – but anyway, she'd begun feeling good. So when Henny came in, she screwed up her courage and said, 'Morning, *paisan*.'

She'd picked the worst possible time to remind Henny that they shared an ethnic heritage. He stopped, looked at her and said, 'Okay, so comb the spaghetti out of your teeth and call Eugenia Randolph, Lobar Agency. If you don't get fast action out of her service number, let me know. I've got her home number.' He almost always smiled. He didn't smile this time. He took a step past the

11

desk, toward the door leading from the reception room to the studio, then stopped. He seemed to stoop a little. His long face grew even grimmer. 'Did I get a telegram, or long-distance call, or anything?'

'No,' she said stiffly.

'Get that model over here pronto.' He went into the studio and shut the door behind him.

Marie sat at her desk a moment, stunned. Then her eyes filled with tears and her heart with rage. Finally she blinked away the tears and thought it over and said to herself, An Italian boy can't mean anything bad by that. Not an Italian boy. She called the Lobar Agency, and they said Miss Randolph was booked for today but was available tomorrow, Wednesday. Marie hung up and walked to the door, to go into the studio and tell Henny. But she changed her mind. She returned to her desk and picked up the phone and pressed the Number One extension button. When he answered she said, 'Your model can't make it today, Mr Girado. She's available tomorrow.'

'Tomorrow! I want her here in half an hour! I have a shooting in Brooklyn at three and I need a few hours.'

'Don't shout at *me*,' she said, intending it to be a sharp-voiced rejoinder, but instead whispering thickly. 'I don't . . .' Horrified, she heard her voice breaking, the sobs starting, and quickly hung up. Before she could leave her desk and run to the stairs leading to the third floor – which held darkroom, offices and bathroom – Henny came out of the studio. He put his hand on her shoulder, and she sank back into her chair.

'I'm sorry,' he said quietly. 'I've got a lot on my mind, honey.'

He used the words 'honey' or 'chick' or 'doll' all the time, yet now it struck a too responsive chord in Marie, a

12

would-that-it-could-be-so spot in her brain that set the tears to flowing even more freely.

Henny kept his hand on her shoulder a moment longer, then withdrew it. 'I didn't do all that, did I?'

She shook her head and didn't understand why.

'Sure,' he said, voice still quiet. 'It's like we've got the reasons to cry, and then something sets it off and we cry. It's like we were made for crying, doll. All of us. And I'd just love to join you. I'd just love to sit down beside you and let go and wipe it all away with some free-flowing salt. I dig it.'

She looked up then, afraid somehow, ashamed somehow. 'Don't talk stupid,' she said huskily and dried her eyes.

'Me? I'm Mr Stupid himself.' He smiled, and his irregular teeth gave him that sad, sympathetic, human look that she saw sometimes when she tried to visualize the perfect boy, the boy who would take her away from the five-room apartment on President Street and away from her three loud-talking, confident brothers and away from the mother who looked at her quizzically and said, 'Maybe you're no Gina Lollobrigida, but why don't you go out with that nice Anthony Macri on Church Avenue?'

She had herself under control now and was terribly embarrassed. She kept her eyes away from his funny, wonderful, ugly face and said, 'I mean, don't use that "it's like" and "doll" and "dig it" stuff on me. *That's* crazy.'

'Words,' he said, and smiled and moved back a little.

She sensed his withdrawal then and knew he didn't want to get too close to her, and, like every young girl, and especially an unsuccessful young girl, she blocked the knowledge. 'I wasn't feeling good last night,' she said, and took a tissue from her bag and blew her nose. 'I didn't sleep so good.'

13

'I never sleep good,' he said and smiled again. 'No one ever sleeps good. We just slip in a few winks between worries.'

She answered his smile.

He said, 'Okay, now that I'm forgiven, get me an outside line and I'll talk to Miss Big – ' He cut himself short. 'I'll talk to Eugenia Randolph myself and have her over here in half an hour, or else I'll get another chesty blonde for next year's Clairscent Haircream calendars.' He went back inside the studio with his swift, loping walk.

She gave him the outside line. And in a moment she was telling herself he couldn't possibly understand why she'd cried, because she herself didn't understand it.

Henny Girado walked through the long, white-painted studio room, furnished with an old, black-leather couch and a half-dozen straight-backed chairs along the walls. He went past the shooting area with the huge roll of pink paper hanging high on the wall, extending onto and over the floor. He glanced at the rack of similar rolls, twenty different colors, and passed under the bank of lights fastened to the high ceiling by pulleys, pointed at the shooting area. He looked at the four-by-five Graphic View on its stand, the studio camera he used for calendar shots, and muttered, 'Hope we got enough film to feed you.' He reached the north end of the forty-foot, window-less room and a marble-topped counter extending the length of the wall. He picked up a phone and dialed quickly. 'Hello, Miss Big Tits,' he murmured under his breath. 'Hello out there in big-tit land, this is Henny Girado, and I need some quick cash, as always, and I want to take some pictures of your very big, your very firm . . .'

'Hello,' the high, sweet voice said.

'Hi, doll. This is Henny. Put something on the magnificent frame and trot it over and let me shoot it.'

'Oh – Henny. What time is it?'

'Late. Very late. The sheriff is at the door and the baby is crying for new shoes and the wolf howls loud at the gate. Aah, me darlin', and begorrah – '

'Shut up, idiot. I'm sleeping.'

'Sure, it's like you were dreamin' of Saint Patrick's Day and you paradin' down green-striped Fifth in your altogether – right into me camera. Aah, mavournin, if I could only capture your altogether. What a fortune it would make us in *Playboy*, or if *Playboy* wasn't willin', in the market place – say, the calendar mart.'

'*Crazy!* But do I have to get up now?'

'Honey, you live on Sixty-fifth. I expect you in fifteen minutes. I mean, it's like you were flying.'

'I'm hip, man. See you tomorrow.'

'Hey, I'm serious.'

'Now listen, Henny, you call at the last minute, and I've got another appointment.'

His face hadn't once lost its grim cast throughout the conversation. Now it looked very much like Marie's before she'd begun to cry. 'Doll,' he said softly, 'I've got to make that four hundred bucks before noon. Then I've got to eat, get my car and take pretty pictures of a religious rally at the stamping grounds of the late Brooklyn Dodgers. Then I've got to beg, borrow or steal an assignment to keep me in chop-chop for the rest of the week. It's like I was drowning and you were floating by on a raft. I need you, Irish baby. I need you, phony name and all.'

She was quiet a minute. 'What do you do with your cash, Henny?'

'You like martinis, don't you?'

She groaned. 'Don't remind me. I forgot to take my two aspirin before falling into bed last night.'

'Well, I like money. I drink it, doll. I eat it. I wallow in it. I dig it the most. It's like I'm putting it in the mattress. I'm a miser.'

She giggled. 'Man, you're wild.'

'If Jayne was still poor I'd call her.'

'You couldn't make it with her, daddy. Anyway, like I said, I got another call on the service number. Guess who?'

'Please, Irish. I'm in a jam.'

'Guess who?'

He sighed.

'In your own pad,' she hinted.

'Now that I'm forced to think, it occurs to me the studio is reserved from twelve to two. So who else but.'

She gave a long mock sigh. 'Yeah. The big man hisself. I get all sniv-sniv just thinking of it.'

'Les Bogen,' he said.

'*Crazy!*'

'What time and what act?'

'I don't know the act, but I figure it must be his department store account. And he wants me at noon.'

'I can finish at noon,' he said.

She laughed. 'He promises a long run.'

'He's older than I. Much, much older than I.'

She laughed again. 'I'll get on the road right now, Henny. But it bugs me, the way you play now-you-see-it-now-you-don't with your money.'

'Fifteen minutes?'

'Maybe half an hour.'

'Okay.' Henny Girado hung up and rubbed his eyes. They were ringed with dark circles of exhaustion. He'd had only six hours' sleep in the last forty-eight. He was dead. But it was past the first of the month and the big bills were due and he needed a grand fast, very fast.

Eugenia Randolph was five feet six, had danced at the Latin Quarter as a sub during the first two months of the year, had decided that her 39-24-36 measurements were worth more than a lousy hundred bucks a week and spangled costumes, despite the big-time Johns who waited out front for an intro and a date. She could make at least that much doing cheesecake; and besides, she hated Johns, squares, boys on the make with wallets. She liked the people she met at Morden Photos and other photography outfits in the city. She liked the hip characters and the no-crap talk and the cool way they tried to make it when they tried to make it. Man, it was the most, and the hell with garment manufacturers and oil millionaires.

She walked up to Marie at ten-fifteen and yawned and said, 'Hey, the man wants me.'

Marie nodded quickly, too quickly. 'I'll tell Mr Girado you're here, Miss Randolph.'

The tall blonde smiled and stepped toward the door. 'Why bother, honey? He's got film in the camera.' She yawned again. 'Only I wish he slept more.'

'I'll tell him,' Marie said firmly and picked up the phone and pressed Extension One.

Eugenia said, 'Sure.' She looked at the receptionist and understood for a minute and felt she should say something. Then she opened her bag and lighted a filter and kept her mouth shut. It was like telling your grandmother she was going to live forever, she thought. It was impossible.

'You can go in, Miss Randolph,' Marie said.

'Thank you,' Patricia O'Conner, alias Eugenia Randolph, said. 'Say, is Lester Bogen in there?'

17

'He won't be in until noon,' Marie answered. 'Are you the model he's shooting from twelve to two?'

'Yes.'

'I hope you can finish with Mr Girado before then. Mr Bogen doesn't like to have a model late on a job. And besides, he's reserved the studio for himself.'

'And he pays off in solid gold, doesn't he, honey?'

Marie didn't look up to see the model's grin. She merely said, 'He pays on time, and that's something around here.'

'Check.' The lush blonde swayed into the studio.

Henny was dozing in a chair against the north wall.

'The big thing in modeling's here, man,' Eugenia called, and walked to a door on the left. 'Hey! Get cracking! I want to know what you don't want me to wear.'

Henny came awake in an instant. 'Birthday suit,' he muttered. 'Didn't I tell you? Black-and-white calendars. You want to wear a Mother Hubbard, maybe?'

Eugenia shook her hips. 'You don't know what I do to a Mother Hubbard, man. They call it an Auntie Mame when I get through.'

Henny laughed dutifully as she entered the dressing room, then went to a cabinet over the marble-topped counter and took out a stack of cut-film holders. He set them down, counted them, pursed his lips. Enough for the present job, but he'd need more if anything came up in the next day or so – color too. And he was tight on cash.

He shrugged, carried the film to the camera and bent for an inverted view of the south-wall shooting area through the ground-glass back. He decided to leave the pale-pink paper. On his left was the studio stand, a cranelike affair used to place cameras in high and unusual positions. He studied it a moment, planning a few gimmick shots, then returned his attention to the camera.

When Eugenia came out, wearing high heels and a shabby towel robe, he said, 'Let's work fast.'

She nodded, stepped onto the apron of pink paper and took off her robe. Henny said, '*Oy vay*,' as he studied her lush figure. There was more than just professional appreciation in his voice, and Eugenia smiled, striking a lewd pose that thrust her magnificent breasts and nicely-rounded hips forwards. Henny muttered, 'Work, baby, work,' and went to a portable hi-fi on the counter beside the phone. He looked through a stack of long-play records, selected two, put them on.

'The Bird,' Eugenia said as sick and solid jazz filled the room.

'And Diz,' Henny muttered. 'Don't forget old Diz. Just because he made some loot and stayed alive, people forget old Diz.'

'What do I do?'

'I got a fur piece here, piece.' He picked up a white boa from the shabby leather couch near the dressing-room door and tossed it to her. 'Around the shoulders and into the valley.' Eugenia obeyed the instruction, draping the boa over her shoulders so that one end curved beneath her left breast, undulated around the line of her hip, and settled demurely between her legs, hiding her pubic thatch. Henny went to the camera, set up his shot, slipped a cut-film holder into place, jerked the dark slide so the exposure could be made, held it in his left hand as he picked up the cable release. 'And away we go.'

2

Henny was still shooting Eugenia at eleven forty-five when Lester Bogen walked in, a Rolleiflex dangling at his belt buckle from a strap around his neck. Lester said, 'Good morning,' in a rather thin but carefully trained and modulated voice. He looked at Eugenia. She smiled, arched backward while straddling a chair, and said, 'I singe the customers' hair, Les. The barbers cut it.'

Lester Bogen was just about five feet eight, stocky, handsome in a round-faced, small-featured, mustached way. He was forty-six, looked a few years younger, except in the eyes. His eyes were small, dark, ancient, underscored by a web of fine wrinkles. He wore a greenish-brown tweed jacket, white shirt and old-school tie, brown tweed slacks, thick-leathered oxblood shoes shined to a dull gloss, and carried a green Tyrolean hat in his hand. Everything about him looked good, solid, expensive. He smiled – a neat, cool smile – and said, 'Singe quickly, dear. We've got a twelve-o'clock appointment.'

Henny straightened from the Graphic View. 'Hi, Les.'

'Morning.'

'I may keep Eugenia a few minutes overtime.'

'I wouldn't like that.'

'That, Rembrandt, would be rough.'

Lester Bogen walked to the couch, tossed his hat on one end, sat down at the other. He ran a pinkie over his pencil-line mustache in what was a habitual gesture. 'I could press the point, with the usual results, but I won't interfere with your artistic endeavors.'

'Thanks. Let's try a deep breath, Irish.'

The model straightened, pushed her breasts high, froze with a soft, inviting smile. Lester Bogen shifted weight on the couch. He flicked his ancient eyes over the twenty-three-year-old girl and dampened his lips.

Henny shot the pose, slipped the dark slide into the holder, pulled the holder, placed it on the floor, bent to the ground-glass view, inserted a fresh holder and pulled its exposure guard – all in a matter of seconds. 'Drop the chin a bit. Yeah.' He shot again and put the dark slide back into the holder. 'Tell you what, Les. I'll give you Irish right now if you'll give me three, four dozen Ektachrome sheets for the Graphic.'

'No,' Lester Bogen said, and irritation entered his smooth voice. 'You're in me for too much right now.'

'Ah, but isn't that the price of fame, and of Irish?'

The model said conversationally, 'Henny, you're beginning to bug me.'

Henny's gray eyes narrowed. 'Listen, I can get a dozen top-heavy chicks . . .' But then he sighed and smiled boyishly. 'I'm broke, Irish. It makes me scratch hard. Anyway, I'm finished.'

'Then take off,' Lester Bogen said. 'I've reserved the studio from twelve to two.' He smiled at the model and she smiled slowly back at him. She sat on the straight-backed chair, and the middle-aged man covered her with his eyes and murmured, 'Go on, Henny. Take the film from my desk. I've got about seven boxes of four-by-five in the big right-hand drawer.'

'Thanks,' Henny said. He yanked his last holder and picked up the two stacks of twenty each and placed them in an old briefcase kept around for that very purpose. As he did this, he watched Lester and Eugenia. The middle-aged photographer and youthful model looked at each other. The model got slowly to her feet and walked to the end of the pink-paper apron and picked up her robe. She put it on, not hurrying, still looking at Bogen.

'A funny thing happened to me on the way to the studio,' Henny said.

The model laughed, then stepped up close and murmured, 'Run along, boy. *You* sipped honey from the honeycomb three, four times, didn't you?'

'I didn't live off it,' Henny replied, experimenting, wanting to see what she would say. Actually, he accepted Les Bogen's lechery as part of the man, as a natural thing. Besides, he liked Les.

'Big deal,' the model said. 'Maybe I'd rather you did live off it. Maybe every woman'd rather the man did.'

'Aha,' Henny said, and turned to Lester. 'Now I've got the secret of your success, Mr Bogen, sir.'

'What're you two talking about?' Lester Bogen asked.

'Nothing, Les,' the model said. She looked at Bogen, and he wet his lips, and she became still, heavy-eyed, expectant.

Henny Girado walked to the door. As he opened it, Lester Bogen said, 'Mind if I shut off the noise, Eugenia?' And she said, 'I sort of like it, Les.' And he said, 'Well, of course, I didn't realize, dear . . .'

Henny left. He stopped near Marie's desk and waited. A few seconds later the phonograph went off. 'Always gets his way,' Henny muttered, smiling. A second after that the door lock snapped. 'And that kills any studio work until after two.'

The secretary said, 'He had it set up early last week. He told Mr Morden.'

'And Mr Morden never refuses his star boarder.' It was said without rancor.

'You didn't want to use the studio, did you, Mr Girado?'

'Still mad at me?'

She flushed and shook her head. 'Henny,' she murmured.

'No. I've got to leave in about half an hour. But you must have noticed there's room for more than one photographer to work in there, and Van Roberts had some stuff for *Ebony*.'

'He knows too. I told him, and I told Mr Drake. So everyone knows.'

'Including Eugenia.'

She looked at him, eyes questioning.

He shook his head and grinned. 'What a change you are from the last secretary we had. She saw *more* than there was and had to get in on the act, and finally began believing every photographer belonged exclusively to her, and so we had to send her back to Staten Island. I think it was Lester who flipped her completely.'

'You mean, Mr Bogen . . .' She colored violently.

Henny laughed and took the briefcase up to the darkroom.

Lester Bogen was Morden Photo's elite, the big man, the most successful photographer using the studio. He had several very lucrative advertising accounts, two house-organ accounts, and the rest of the time did slick, pseudo-journalistic photography for the more sophisticated general magazines. His technique had elicited comments such as 'approaches genius' (from a picture editor on the late-lamented *Collier's*) and 'as brilliantly interpretive as a Lautrec' (this from a rather impressionable young lady on a very posh woman's magazine). Earlier in his career, he had won many prizes of the camera magazine and *Life* variety, and only two years ago had been given the signal honor – plus royalties – of having a collection of his photographs put between hard covers. It was titled *The*

City Is a Woman and had text by Marvin Weister, a sensitive if financially unsuccessful young writer.

Lester no longer belonged in a studio like Morden Photos, as did the other three photographers and Morden himself. The studio was a clearing house for girlie-magazine jobs, small general magazine assignments and a rare advertising job. Bogen didn't need jobs that came through the studio and didn't take them, except for an occasional cheesecake assignment. And if it hadn't been for a desire to maintain some degree of legitimacy in his dealings with models, he would have written off their fees and his film as 'entertainment.' As it was, he sold every cheesecake set he shot, and Dennis Parish, a little-seen but very active agent, had within the past year placed two with *Esquire* and one very 'delicate' job – a girl trying on spring hats wearing nothing but net stockings – with *Playboy*.

Lester had made well over thirty thousand dollars a year for the past fifteen years, without working hard at all, and owned a big split-level home some fifty miles from the city, in Peekskill. But money and possessions were, of themselves, of little importance to him. He needed the prestige of a solid income, to impress women. He needed the reputation as a top photographer, to impress women. He needed self-confidence and clothes and health and everything else that men want, to impress women.

Nothing in life was as important as having women, many women, to Lester Bogen – except for one thing. And that one thing was *more* important than women, which placed it on a par with hope of eternal life.

The thing was a person: his daughter Sandra. He loved her with all the emotion he was capable of feeling, and that was a great deal. He gave – and had given all through the nineteen years of her life – love and guidance and long hours of companionship, concentrating on her what other men give to a family of wife and several children and perhaps brothers, sisters and parents. His parents were dead; he had no other children; he and his wife had never been in love and were now strangers. Sandy was his family. She was his only unselfish love. He cared nothing for pets and movies and books and people. She was his life.

Yet he had never spoiled her; never forgotten that the obedience to authority taught her as a child would stand her in good stead when Society took Father's place as dispenser of dos and don'ts. She had always listened to him. And the few times she hadn't, he had forced himself to punish the small, golden-haired child – severely in the rather serious cases of childhood thefts of playmates' possessions; lightly when she tore out a carefully planted tulip or killed a frog after he'd explained how useful they were around a country home in controlling mosquitoes and other annoying insects.

So when he'd told her she must not ask to be taken to his place of employment (another studio farther uptown at the time), she'd accepted it. Later, at the age of fifteen, she'd again asked to be allowed to see his studio, meet his co-workers, go along with him on a job. This time he'd had a very careful answer ready, having prepared it, literally, years before.

'The people I work with aren't, well, very *nice*, sweetie. Certainly not the kind of people a young girl should know. Not that they're dishonest or anything like that, but they haven't very high moral standards. Of course, there are exceptions.'

'Like you, Daddy,' she'd said, and kissed him, and waited to hear more.

He'd gone on, explaining that it was a fault inherent in the business itself – catering to a public which required

25

photographs of nude women to satisfy its prurient tastes. And when he'd finished, she'd nodded, accepting his word as she always had.

As she always would, he hoped and prayed. Because he couldn't allow her to learn about his life away from their Peekskill home. She would never be able to forgive his lechery; never be able to understand that it was a drive outside himself and not connected with love or hate or good or evil. He certainly couldn't *tell* her about it. He couldn't tell anyone; he barely told himself. An appetite, that's all. A ravenous appetite for women, as some men have for alcohol or food or money.

Sandy was nineteen now. She attended Columbia University, here in the city. She dated and certainly knew as much about life as any well-adjusted nineteen-year-old; and only a month ago she'd casually stated she intended to 'drop up to the studio.'

'I'd rather you wouldn't,' he'd said.

'Why? I'm old enough now to resist contamination – or temptation – by any immoral characters.' She'd smiled.

He'd answered the smile and shaken his head. 'I'd still rather you wouldn't.'

She'd raised her eyebrows, and he'd tried to re-evaluate his position. If she did come up, *with him*, she wouldn't learn anything embarrassing. He'd introduce her as his daughter.

No. He couldn't take the chance. She might return another time, alone. She might hear things.

Then he might lose her; and he couldn't face that prospect. She wasn't serious about any boy yet; dated them all and discussed them all. And gave him, her father, her love. He was sure she'd go on this way for many, many years.

'No,' he'd said, firming his voice. 'I've explained it before. I don't want you to come to the studio.'

She'd shrugged, and they'd dropped the subject.

But he'd worried about it. And, on the couch with Eugenia, he couldn't prevent the worry returning. Maybe it was the model's blonde hair, or the closeness of their ages. Maybe it was the thought that some day Sandy might walk into the studio and find him like this.

Like this was naked on the couch with the blonde kneeling above him, working on him with her mouth. *Like this* was the aspect of his life that he would always keep hidden from Sandy, the hours spent behind locked studio doors using his position as Morden's top photographer to enjoy any model to whom he took a fancy. Which meant – because all the models were attractive in one way or another – all his models. Les Bogen's appetite was insatiable. And what harm was there in it? The models enjoyed themselves – Les prided himself on his accomplishments as a lover – and the photographs he turned out furthered their careers. They were old enough to know what they were doing. Which, of course, meant that in a few years the same stricture would apply to Sandy. But Sandy would never do anything like this, of course.

He looked down at the blonde head moving between his legs and reached down to cup her breasts. He spread his fingers, clutching the globes, and lifted her gently onto the couch, putting his arms around her.

Eugenia drew him closer, murmuring thick little words, but her eyes were open and showed disappointment. (So *this* was the great Les Bogen!) Lester Bogen looked at her, at her beautiful face and body, and stopped worrying. Lester Bogen's appetite reasserted itself, and his technique, a truly refined one, returned. He made the disappointment leave the model's eyes.

* * *

Victor Bloom, the regular darkroom man, was out to lunch, but that didn't concern Henny. It had been more than a year since he'd employed a man to do his developing, printing and enlarging (except on occasional jobs where saving the two-fifty-an-hour fee was less important than having finished work reach a client while he had another shooting to handle). He worked quickly on the cut-films, passing them through the three stages of development and hanging them up on clips to dry. He'd print sometime tonight, or tomorrow. (If the shots had been color, he'd have sent them to one of several labs in town – or at least to the one which was still accepting his stuff on credit. If it had been 35 millimeter color – Kodachrome – he'd have sent it to Eastman Kodak. Only on very rare occasions did a commercial photographer process his own color film, and never Kodachrome. It was usually more trouble than it was worth, even to a man in Henny's financial situation.)

He left the dimly lighted room with its sour smell of hypo and walked past Richie Morden's office. Ahead was the door to the staircase and the two lower floors. Around the right-hand turn the foyer broadened into a true hallway with two offices, a storeroom and a bathroom opening onto it. The offices each held two old desks, and the studio's four photographers (not counting owner-photographer Morden) – Lester Bogen, Van Roberts, Laird Drake and Henny – used them.

Henny entered the first office which was shared by Les and Van Roberts. He opened Les's desk, took four boxes of Ektachrome from the big drawer and went through the connecting door on his left into the second office. He placed the film in the big drawer of his own desk, sat down and lighted a cigarette. He had the entire floor to himself, but that wasn't very unusual. The photographers were rarely there, drifting in and out as assignments dictated. For example, he hadn't seen Laird Drake, who shared this office with him, in almost two weeks, and at that time had merely passed him in the hall and exchanged a brief nod.

The phone rang. Henny looked at it, dragged deeply on his cigarette and let it ring four more times. Then he picked it up.

'Mr Girado?' a high-pitched male voice asked.

'Who's calling?'

'Is this Mr Girado?'

'No,' Henny said. 'He's not around.'

'Can you tell me when he's expected?'

'Late next week. He's out of town on a shooting assignment.'

There was a moment's silence, and then the high-pitched voice said, 'If you happen to be a friend of his – by the way, I didn't get your name.'

'I didn't offer it. And I still don't know who's calling.' (But he did know, or at least he knew the classification of the stranger who was calling: Creditor; Representative of Creditor; Collection Agency; or What Have You.)

'My name is Laurence Raymonds. I represent the Grayson Collection Agency of Greater New York. A client has placed Mr Girado's delinquent account – '

'That's none of my business,' Henny said sharply. 'I don't discuss Mr Girado's affairs with him.'

'The girl said Mr Girado was in,' the high-pitched voice interrupted. 'She said she'd ring him. You answered. I strongly advise you – if you are Mr Girado – to contact us within the next week or so to discuss payment of our client's delinquent account. Our client has threatened to take legal action.'

Henny wanted to hang up. He couldn't do anything about the 'client' right now. He didn't know if he'd be able to do anything about the 'client' next week or next year. But there was that threat of legal action.

'Who is your client?' he muttered and added quickly, 'So I'll be able to leave a message for Mr Girado.'

'Charleston-Hedges Laboratories. The account is for three hundred sixty-two dollars and eighteen cents. It's been delinquent seven months.'

'Partial payment was made six weeks ago,' Henny said wearily. 'At that time Mr Girado paid almost a hundred – '

'Paid fifty-five dollars,' the high-pitched voice interrupted. 'The amount I mentioned is still to be paid. I think you'd better take care of this quickly, Mr Girado. Our client is somewhat embittered.'

It wasn't a very warm day, but Henny's face was shiny with perspiration. 'I'll tell him,' he said, and hung up. He dragged on his cigarette and looked at it and put it out. He picked up the phone and punched the button until Marie came on. 'Can't you hold my calls and query me before ringing?'

'I'm sorry, Henny,' she answered. 'We went through this once before. Mr Morden insists that all calls go right through.'

'Yeah,' Henny said. 'But I'm a special case, doll.'

'You'll have to get special permission, Henny. Anyway, why do you want – '

'It's a long story,' he muttered. 'Forget it.' He hung up.

He lighted another cigarette and closed his eyes and winced as he thought of that high-pitched voice. Well, he'd just have to make another payment – a big one – on the Charleston-Hedges Lab bill. Maybe something would turn up.

The phone rang. He got up and left the office. Whoever

it was, Marie would get the number. Then he would either return the call or forget it.

He headed back toward the darkroom, thinking he'd check the negatives or examine some prints he'd made last night. But when he reached the door to Richie Morden's office, he stopped. He smiled as if apologizing to someone and stepped inside.

Morden's office was large and square and had a picture window facing Fifty-second Street. There were pull drapes, now open, of a soft beige color and the floor was carpeted in deep broadloom. The desk was light walnut, the walls were pastel green, and there was a tan leather couch on one wall siding the desk and two matching armchairs on the other wall. Three prize-winning photographs – two by Bogen and one by Girado – hung above couch and chairs. Just inside the door and to Henny's right was a closet, and to the right of the closet was what seemed to be a second closet with vented folding doors. Henny went to this second closet and smiled his apologetic smile and pushed the vented doors apart, revealing a portable dark-wood bar holding a dozen or more bottles of liquor. Above the bar, on a wall shelf, were glasses.

Henny mixed himself a five-ounce 'martini' – Bols gin with just a dash of vermouth – carried it to Richard Morden's desk and sat down in the heavy swivel chair. He sipped, lighted a cigarette, sipped again. Then he checked his watch and squinted in thought. He should call Denver. He knew he should call Denver. Elsa was probably sick with worry by now, wondering if he'd come through. Not that she'd ever call him. Not that she'd ever ask. But he should call Denver.

He sipped again and didn't want to call Denver. He wanted to relax. Christ, he wanted to talk to someone who wouldn't expect money! Money; God-damned money!

He felt himself beginning to sweat again and said, 'A

pox on money.' It wasn't funny enough. It didn't bring him back to happy.

He picked up the phone. There was an immediate dial tone; Morden had one of the three separate lines – the other two being Marie's (who could switch in the studio and the four phones in the two small offices, but not more than two at a time). He dialed Marv Weister's number. He didn't owe Marv a dime – mainly because Marv'd never had an extra dime to lend. He liked Marv, and Marv liked him. They were friends.

'Who is it?' Marv asked, almost shouting. 'Who is it?'

'Whoops,' Henny said. 'Don't tell me. I hit you at the wrong time again.'

'Damn it, Henny. I just had a decent page going. I just had the lead character coming alive. Damn it!'

Henny had heard it before. He didn't let it bother him. Marv Weister wrote slowly, painfully, and then discarded much of what he'd written. But whenever anyone called him, *that* was the time he 'just had a decent page going.'

'Sorry, Marv. I'll hang up.'

'No. Hold it. Long as you pulled me away from the typewriter, I might as well have a smoke and shoot the breeze. Wait'll I light up.'

Henny waited.

'Yeah,' Marv said. 'How are you? And don't tell me about your lousy money problems.'

'I won't. You wouldn't happen to have two, three hundred bucks to spare your dearest friend?'

'Ha! I wouldn't happen to have two, three *single* bucks to spare. And that's probably due to guys like you calling me when I'm just getting going. Listen, what do you think of this for a scene in the novel.' (He'd been talking about his current work-in-progress for months now, and Henny had a pretty good idea of what the book was about.) 'Mich is back home in his parents' Bronx apartment and his mother insists he go with her to a wedding. You know, a real Jewish wedding with all the trimmings. He's sitting at what they call a "young people's table," trying to make conversation with several very bourgeois characters, and suddenly finds he can't remember anything that's happened to him in the past two years – the year in Paris, the months cycling through Italy, France and Switzerland, the women he's screwed and the food he's eaten and the intellectuals he's pumped dry . . .'

Henny listened, interested, but not just in the story. Marv's conversation was ragged, colloquial, almost tough. And this wasn't the way he generally spoke. He was *living* his character at the Bronx-Jewish wedding.

'. . . begins to panic,' Marv continued. 'What the hell have his experiences abroad – the artistic, *avant-garde*, bohemian experiences – meant if they wash out at the first contact with his despised youth? He wants to leave and finds he's afraid to. He gets involved in a group dance, the *hora*, and now he's really cracking . . .'

Henny heard someone enter the office. He looked up and grinned apologetically as the tall man placed hands on hips and said, 'What the hell, Henny! You said you'd cut this crap!'

'You still with me, Henny?' Marv Weister asked.

'Yeah. But I've got to sign off.'

The writer's voice grew tight, unhappy. 'Hell. Now I don't feel like doing anything but talking. Want to come over?'

'Got an assignment, Marv. So long.'

'Well, say, try and drop over tonight, okay?'

'Don't know. We'll see.' He hung up, ground out his cigarette in the ceramic ashtray and leaned back in the swivel chair. 'Morden,' he said officiously, 'I've sent for

33

you because the books don't balance. If you can't do your job more efficiently, it's back to the stockroom.'

Richard Morden didn't laugh. He glanced at the liquor closet and said, 'This is the last time, Henny! The goddam last time. And using my phone when you have your own. I told you – '

Henny came around the desk and flopped on the couch. He grinned but his lips were tight and he drained his glass with one gulp. 'Sorry, Richie. Just like the feel of this office. And what's a drink?'

Richard Morden seemed about to answer heatedly, but then he sighed and went behind his desk and sat down. He ran a big hand over his balding head. 'I know you have troubles, Henny, but do you have to make your calls from here and drink my liquor when I'm not around to enjoy it with you?'

Henny's lips lost their tightness. 'I'm sorry, massa. Bill me for the booze.'

Morden began shuffling through some papers. Henny stood up and walked to the door.

'You need a few dollars, Henny?'

Henny Girado turned. 'Yes, dad. About five grand.'

'Would two hundred against an eight-hundred-dollar job be okay?'

Henny's eyebrows climbed. 'We've got a decent pic story?'

Morden nodded. 'Got it late yesterday. You weren't around, but it's your meat. *Luau* at a Hawaiian-type restaurant for a restaurant-management association. The story'll appear in the association's magazine. Color job. About twelve pictures to run in order, from beginning of the affair to the end. You'll shoot about five rolls of thirty-five millimeter. And you'll be one of the guests, in a manner of speaking. They want you to sit at a table, or on the floor, or however the hell they work it. You'll do

34

your shooting from the viewpoint of a guest attending the *luau*. You can even bring a friend. It's in three weeks – a Monday night.'

'Hey, man, that like V-Day!'

Morden and Henny grinned at each other, and then the big, heavy-set man got his checkbook from a drawer and wrote quickly, almost diffidently. He tore the check loose and shoved it across the desk. Henny came over and took it. 'Now I'll drink champagne for a week,' Henny said, and winked.

'By the way,' Morden said, 'how's your sister getting along?'

'Crazy!' Henny said, ignoring the question and studying the check. 'You blew your lid, baby. This says four hundred.'

'So I take half your eight when it comes in. So what?'

'That's right. So what? So what's the time?' He glanced at his watch and turned, running for the door. 'I got a date to sing at Ebbets Field, massa.'

'Sing?'

'Yeah,' Henny called over his shoulder. 'The "What-a-Friend-We-Have-in-Jesus Mambo" and similar selections.' He turned right, toward the darkroom, where he stored his equipment in a huge locker. A moment later he passed Morden's door on the way to the staircase, gadget bag slung over his shoulder, two camera cases dangling on his chest from straps around his neck, a third camera case in his right hand, a pack of cigarettes in his left. 'Rock of ages,' he sang, 'rock, rock, rock.' And then, from the staircase, 'Hey, Parson, you gotta get with it, swing it, knock it around. Anyone dig Eli-Eli round hyar?'

Morden visualized Henny up on the platform of the big religious rally and burst into heavy laughter. 'Anyone dig Eli-Eli round hyar!' He picked up the phone and dialed his home. His wife answered, and he told her everything Henny had said, and they both laughed. Then he hung up. But he would call her at least five more times during the day, to share a story, triumph or disappointment with her.

Phyllis Morden spent most of her day in the neat Greenwich Village apartment, but she might just as well have come to the studio with Richie; he included her in everything. It had been that way for almost twenty years now, and there was no doubt in Richie's mind that it would remain that way until one of them died. (Though he couldn't really think of Phyll dying.)

Richie Morden had married Phyllis Crest in El Paso, Texas, when he was twenty-two and she seventeen. They'd come to New York four months later, and loved it, and stayed. Richie was now forty-one, Phyllis just a few weeks into thirty-seven, and during all those years Richie had supported her nicely – until six years ago as a free-lance photographer working out of someone else's studio. He'd never allowed her to take a job, even though they were childless, and shared almost everything with her.

The 'almost' was necessary because Richie had been hiding an important facet of his personality from his wife. But then again, he hid it from everyone, and on only two occasions had it ever been put into words. The first time he'd been ten years old, sobbing out his fear in the arms of an old woman he'd called Aunt Della. The second, and last, time was back in 1952, when he'd gone to a party on New York's East Side without Phyll, had several drinks, and paired off with a colored girl and said things to her as they sat loving it up in a corner.

But outside of that, he was among the happiest of men, recognizing his good fortune in wife and career and position. And this office was his pride and joy, a place that had more style and atmosphere than his apartment, a room he preferred to any other in the world. He loved to sit behind the desk and talk to people, not like a big shot but still with the awareness that this studio was his. (Also remembering it was his by grace of an unexpected inheritance – *very* unexpected because who would ever think old Aunt Della had *that* kind of money and would leave it to him!) He wasn't an egotistic or foolish man, so that was as far as his penchant for bossism went. Besides, he knew the photographers who paid him rentals for use of the studio and through-the-studio jobs wouldn't have accepted anything more, with the possible exception of Laird Drake. Richie made about as much as his two pedestrian photographers – Van Roberts and Laird Drake – which was under seventy-five hundred a year, after expenses and before taxes. But he didn't have to rush around nearly as much as they did; started working later and quit earlier; generally lived a more normal life. And that was due to his having had ten thousand dollars to invest in a studio of his own six years ago. Up until then, he'd been just another free-lancer, tearing around the city, shooting cheesecake for bread-and-butter, shooting other stuff when he could land it; dashing out of town for a picture story and sleeping in cheap hotels to keep his expenses down and missing Phyll during the long evenings. And even worse than missing Phyll, the moments when, alone and vulnerable, he heard talk or laughter on the streets, Negro talk or laughter.

He had gained in kindness and understanding for other people's weaknesses because of his own. He was good-natured, easy on people; especially easy on Henny Girado because he knew Henny was a sensitive photographer, a gifted man with a camera but burdened with obligations that drained him of his income and left him saddled with a multitude of debts and worries. And easy on Van

Roberts because Van was just an average photographer but a hell of a bright guy, a college grad with abilities that would have taken him far in any business concern, executive material with no specific training. And weren't thousands such men making careers on Madison Avenue and Fifth Avenue and wherever else big industry took the time to hammer raw brain power into leadership potential? But Van didn't have a ghost of a chance there because he was a Negro. And that was another thing. Morden felt he should have at least one Negro in the studio to show himself he wasn't, well, running away from anything. Or was *that* a way of running?

He heard a burst of rich laughter, and for a moment his fear rose up – except that it was more a memory of fear than fear itself, a touch of sadness at an old song dimly heard. Because the laughter belonged to someone he knew, someone he helped. And that changed things. Whenever you helped people, it changed things.

Van Roberts came into the office, still laughing. He was of medium height, slim, with a long, intelligent face, mobile lips and big black eyes. He'd been told he looked like a cross between Sammy Davis, Jr, and a satyr, but he was lighter-skinned than Davis and much too composed, inwardly as well as outwardly, emotionally and sexually, to be satyrlike. Van was extremely happy in his marriage to a girl he'd met at New York University nine years ago and adored his three-year-old son. He lived in a good, middle-class housing project in lower Harlem, about which he made many a bitter crack (alluding to the North's segregation policies), but which he nevertheless liked. He was also hard put to hide from Morden and his fellow photographers just how much he enjoyed his work, despite its financial limitations. Of course, there *were* occasional run-ins with bigots in the photographic field – mainly in advertising; the clients, not the agency people – but since he hadn't been able to land much ad work, he actually had to *remind* himself to be sensitive every so often.

Van was building himself up to a mild hurt that very moment, but Richie Morden had no way of knowing it. 'You seen the new tenants on the first floor?' Van asked.

Richie shook his head. 'I didn't even know the old ones had gone.'

'Sure. That insurance agency left last week. Bigger quarters, a salesman told me. But, man, you'll really get a kick out of the new outfit. Hair weavers, they told me. Wig makers. Boxes of hair being moved in, and about ten old ladies standing around and talking. When I came past their door one asked me what's upstairs. I told her a photography studio, and she said' (he pitched his voice to a high, shrill falsetto) '"Well, well. I haven't got one decent picture of my granddaughter, so maybe I'll bring her in. You think I'll get a discount, working in the same building?"'

Morden laughed and touched his balding pate. 'If she gives me a discount on a toupee, I'll give her a discount on pictures. But the granddaughter better be nubile and stacked.'

They both laughed, and Morden added, 'One thing's sure – they'll be an improvement over that pack of horny insurance salesmen who were always trying to walk in on a cheesecake job.'

Van Roberts turned to the door. 'I don't know about that. Those old ladies talk a little too straight. One asked me whether I was the porter or the janitor.'

Morden flushed.

Van Roberts kept his back turned, whipping himself up to his brief moment of hurt and anger. 'I told her, "Neither, madam. I'm the shoeshine boy." She looked me over and nodded approvingly and said, "My, my, you dress so neat."' He walked out.

Morden watched the empty doorway. A few seconds later Roberts reappeared, suffering because he feared he'd made his friend suffer. 'Richie, when I grow up, I'll stop trying to hurt my friends.' He grinned shamefacedly. 'What's that old song? "You always hurt the one you love."'

'Sorry, daddy, I'm already spoken for.'

'You been taking lessons from Henny?'

'That damned hip-talk's catching.'

Roberts left, laughing.

Richie Morden sighed and began opening his mail. What the hell, he couldn't change the world. He couldn't even change himself.

3

Henny Girado left Ebbets Field at ten after four. The religious rally would continue another two hours, but he'd completed his assignment, working hard and fast, switching from one to another of his three Nikons as the need for normal 50-millimeter lens gave way to shots calling for wide-angle 28 or telephoto 105. He also used the 250 in his gadget bag several times.

Once, while squatting at the bottom of the temporary stand set up near what used to be home plate, an usher had asked if he liked using Leicas. He'd replied that just because a camera was of the 'candid' 35-millimeter type and looked expensive, didn't mean it was German. Then he moved away. He was touchy, in a professional way, about his Japanese Nikons, considering them the equal of the Leicas and resenting the layman's knowledge of the German brand to the exclusion of all others.

He'd moved around a great deal while working but never allowed his equipment to remain where it might – even as a remote possibility – be touched or damaged. For a man who was extremely casual about most things, this was sharply indicative. Henny himself explained it as an adjunct to survival and added that anyone would be careful of cameras costing $365 each (professional discount), independent of lenses and the items in his gadget bag. His entire outfit (including cameras and equipment at home and in the locker at the studio) totaled close to three thousand dollars. Losing that (to the bank which had it listed as collateral on a loan, or in any other way), he'd explained to his friend Marv Weister, 'would be like losing my kidneys!'

But it was even more than financial survival. Henny Girado loved his cameras as some hunters love weapons, or sports car buffs love the small, finely tooled powerhouses, or (and this was probably the closest parallel) as good musicians love their instruments. And added to even that was something else – the feeling of an artist for the equipment that helps him create (though Henny refused to think of himself as an artist). When Marv Weister had asked him *why* he'd become a photographer instead of something else, Henny'd replied, 'I *couldn't* be anything else. I'm not literate enough to write, and I'm not talented in any other way. If I didn't take pictures, I'd be a clerk, a messenger boy, a truck driver, and I'd die, daddy. Really die. Because I'd find nothing there to live on. I've got to feel I'm *doing* something, *making* something – okay, *creating* something. I can do that as a photographer – no other way.' Marv had suggested that Henny had a definite talent, an artistic bent for viewing life through a camera, and Henny had grinned, pleased, but then shrugged uncomfortably and muttered, 'Maybe, but the way I see it, taking pictures is my only out. I'm either a photographer or I'm a bum. I'm either a photographer or it's like I'm under the sod, man.' Weister, who along with others felt Henny's photographs were superior to most in some undefinable manner, didn't press the point but went on thinking of his friend as an artist.

Henny cleaned his Nikons and his seldom used Rolleiflex several times a week, examined them carefully – for signs of wear, he told himself, but actually for the pure pleasure of doing so – and kept careful tabs on the contents of his gadget bag. This bag, necessary to all professional photographers, held a multitude of things, among which were fifteen to twenty rolls of film, a Norwood exposure meter, one or two cable releases, a small strobe unit (a battery-type mechanism which produced endless flashes of light without requiring changes of bulbs, and which had therefore replaced flashbulbs among professional photographers), an extra synchronization cord used between strobe and camera, a half-dozen filters (rarely used) and a package of lens tissues.

At various times, the gadget bag had held less professional items, such as pints of rye, sandwiches, bananas or pears (he disliked apples), bags of red-shell peanuts bought in the five-and-dime, novels and extra-thin prophylactic rubbers. But all nonessential articles, and especially perishables which might damage his equipment, were placed in a transparent plastic bag and shoved deep into a corner.

Henny loved his profession and its tools. He loved his work, but in many instances it didn't require his full attention and he was able to think of other things. As at the religious rally. He took seven rolls, or 252 shots, of the crowd of fifteen thousand and of the forty-some-odd Methodist dignitaries. While shooting, he'd listened to the speeches, the prayers, the reports on charities and missions doing needed, compassionate work all over the world. Unconsciously, he was waiting for something to grip him, as he had when he'd attended Mass with his Roman Catholic parents back in Denver; as he had when he'd shot High Holy Day services at Temple Emanu-El two years ago for a Jewish organizational magazine; as he would whenever people spoke of God and reached for Him with prayers.

As always, he found nothing. And, as always, he felt a vague disappointment, knowing that with a faith he could shift a great many worries onto the shoulders of an omniscient God. Maybe he could even find the courage

43

to cut down on sending so much cash to Denver. Religious people were always saying that God took care of His own – and wasn't Elsa one of His own? Sure, she spent a good third of her life praying and another third saying, 'It's God's will.' The last third was spent suffering the results of this 'will.'

But he couldn't get from under that easily. He didn't dig religion.

At a quarter to four he concluded his assignment by walking across an open stretch of ground between speakers' platform and old third-base box seats, opening the gate and climbing the ramp. As he passed between packed sections of men and women, most middle-aged or elderly, most wearing sober dress and in-church expressions, he took an occasional shot, concentrating on individuals rather than groups. But not until he was almost finished, not until he had passed into the sparsely populated area deep in the shadows of the upper stands, did he find a subject that gave him a real sense of excitement, fulfillment and creativity.

The girl was about twenty; the boy a few years older. They sat eight or ten seats off the aisle to Henny's right, in the last row, an elderly couple far to their right, three or four elderly ladies scattered in the row before them. They leaned into each other, both pairs of hands intertwined, ostensibly listening to the speaker-of-the-moment, obviously engrossed in each other.

Henny didn't know whether they were active Methodists or whether they'd come here to be together in an atmosphere of serene belief. But whatever their reasons, he felt sure they'd made the right choice . . . because there was more of God in their quiet love than in any of the speeches, evocations and prayers he'd heard.

He never doubted they were in love. No one looking at them with a probing, practiced, sensitive eye could doubt

44

it, and he looked at them exactly that way as he shot twice and wound for a third. It was in the four-hand clasp, in the heads and shoulders touching in the nondemanding, nonsexual happiness they were experiencing. He shot again, and then the boy glanced at him and said something to the girl and she glanced at him too. They drew apart swiftly, embarrassed, and put the in-church expressions on their faces.

Henny walked on, sorry he'd broken the spell. But then he realized they would move together again in a few minutes. Nothing could stop their moving together for long.

He laughed at himself, at his sweetness-and-light thoughts, and still felt the deep-down ache, and went to his car on the narrow side street. He drove to a bar on Flatbush Avenue, called home and asked how Syl was. 'Fine,' the housekeeper said. 'You got money, Henny? You got my pay? You said – '

'Yeah. I'll give it to you tonight. We're rolling.'

'Ah, so maybe you put some away until next time you're rolling?'

He winced. 'Sure, sure. See you tonight.'

'What time tonight?'

'Oh . . . eight, nine, ten.'

'That mean one, two, three in morning. You leave envelope on table for me, hear?'

'I hear, and I obey.'

'What?'

'I said yes. But I'll be home earlier than that.'

'You say that always, and always you don't come home till morning. Just so you remember that tomorrow my day off. Wednesday I'm off. Just so you remember.'

'Yeah. I remember.'

'It's good thing, too, Henny. Your little girl, she should

45

know father. Three years old, and she don't know father. So on Wednesday, she knows father.'

'Yeah,' he said, leaning back in the booth now, eyes closed. 'Yeah, you're right.'

'And you should go sleep early. You need more sleep.'

'Amen,' he muttered. 'Now for the flip side.'

'And you should go church and take Sylvia to church.'

'I've just come from church.'

'I don't think so.'

'Bye, Hilda.'

'My name is Greta. See? I been here three months and you don't talk to me enough to know name.'

'Bye, Greta.'

'Goodbye, Henny. You come home early.'

'Yeah.' He hung up and kept his eyes closed and sang softly, 'Goodbye, Hilda, goodbye. Your name is Greta, goodbye.' He shook his head and walked out of the phone booth and over to the bar. 'Martini,' he said. 'Double. And keep the olives in the jar.'

The bartender was a sharp-faced little man with bright little eyes. He'd been talking steadily down at the other end where four men in overalls were drinking beer. When he served Henny the big martini, he eyed the three cameras still slung around the photographer's neck and the gadget bag on the next stool (Henny refused to leave fifteen hundred dollars' worth of temptation in a car whose right vent could be forced by a child's pinkie) and leaned forward confidentially. 'You a photographer? You been taking pictures them holy joes over Ebbets Field? You ever take pictures them models, you know, like in the magazines? I got a cousin says they put Scotch tape under their knockers to make 'em stand up. You got any pictures them broads?'

Henny smiled vaguely and sipped his drink.

The bartender leered. 'Yeah, I'll bet.' He leaned forward even more and dropped his voice to a whisper. 'You guys always got hot pictures. Lemme see a few and the drink's on the house. Wad'ya say?'

Henny swallowed his drink quickly, put a dollar on the bar and rose.

'Hey, what about it?'

'I'm not a photographer,' Henny said. 'I'm a deaf mute.'

'What?'

Henny picked up his gadget bag.

'Wise guy,' the bartender said.

Henny walked towards the door.

'All you guys are dirty,' the bartender called after him. 'All you guys and your dirty dames . . .'

Henny grinned.

He reached his battered Chevy coupé and unloaded his equipment into the back. He got behind the wheel and kicked the starter, then cut the ignition. He didn't know where he was going. He hadn't really known where he was going since his wife, Doris, had died. He'd just found himself running, faster and faster, senselessly, hopelessly, until now he didn't dare stop and think what his life was and where it was leading and what it meant.

Because it was leading nowhere and meant nothing.

And once a man realized that, he either stopped dead or did something wild in an attempt to get out from under.

Henny had considered a few wild acts in the past few weeks. Henny had awakened several times from his few hours of sleep to catch himself planning robberies – big robberies that would get him eight or ten thousand and end the rat race. And last night, while printing up thirty cheesecake shots at one in the morning, he'd suddenly stopped and said aloud, 'If I were dead, it would be peaceful.'

He'd long since passed the daydream stage of entering contests and trying to get on quiz shows which required a degree of specialization and retention of fact that he didn't possess.

He lighted a cigarette and let the memories come, because it was time he stopped running and faced the facts and gathered his strength for more running.

Henny was thirty-five. Two days before his thirty-second birthday he'd driven his wife to a private hospital in Flushing, Queens, about a mile from their four-room co-op apartment. Doris was going to have a baby, and she was a week overdue, and he was worried about her extreme pallor and terrible pain. But after all, having a baby was a natural thing and they had a good general practitioner and all the crap about specialists was made for squares, people who didn't subtract the 50-per cent larceny in the hearts of men from the things they said and did. Henny had always refused to be taken in by the ad-men, and he figured that obstetricians were unnecessary for births. Normal births.

Except that four hours later he found out that Doris hadn't had a normal birth, and that she'd hemorrhaged, and that the general practitioner hadn't arrived on time, and that when he did arrive he didn't spot the nature of the complications – the serious nature of the internal bleeding.

It all added up to one thing – one terrible, incomprehensible thing.

Doris died. In an age where practically no one died in childbirth, Doris died. The baby, a seven-pound girl, lived.

The doctor told him and showed him, and Henny Girado went back to his four-room co-op apartment and had himself a bottle of rye and looked around and asked what the hell it all meant. He didn't understand it. Doris was twenty-six. You didn't die at twenty-six. It was impossible.

Later, he went downstairs and, half drunk, raced his car to the hospital and ran up the stairs to the delivery room and burst through the swinging doors and stopped dead. She was there, all right. Just as she'd been when the doctor had given in to his demands and shown him. She was still on the wheeled cot, and a male nurse was sitting on a chair in a corner. 'You got to remember your little girl,' the nurse said. 'You got to pull yourself together, for her sake.' But he didn't do anything as Henny walked up to the wheeled cot and pulled back the white sheet and looked at the pale, still face, the face known and loved for almost five years.

And then he realized he hadn't even said anything to the doctor. Just walked with him and listened to the incomprehensible medical terminology and nodded at the white-faced murmurings of sympathy. Just let him get away with murder!

'Where's that goddam doctor?' he asked.

The male nurse shifted weight. He was a big, heavy-set man. He seemed to prepare himself for something unpleasant. 'He's here, Mr Girado. He's very upset – '

'Upset,' Henny said. '*He's* upset.'

The male nurse sighed and stood up. 'You want to talk to him?'

'Yes,' Henny said and put the sheet back gently over Doris' face, and suddenly remembered the time he'd covered her head with a blanket at a beach party. Fire Island, about two weeks after he'd met her at a party there. She'd been a model for only five or six months and he'd never shot her and he'd asked if she'd ever done nudes, and she'd looked at him out of brown eyes in a small, pretty face and straightened her small, curved body and said, 'No, Henny, not yet. But, if you'd like to.' He'd shot her, and she'd been perfect, and then he'd taken her out to eat and they'd talked. She attended the New School at night, was only thirty-one credits away from her degree, was bright and appealing and down-to-earth. And hip. They talked alike and thought alike, and she went with him a year, and then they were married. And four years later she was dead.

Yes, he'd covered her face with the scroungy old Army blanket and she'd laughed and said, voice muffled, 'You'll never scare me this way, Henny. I like the dark.'

So she got the dark, forever.

And the doctor was upset.

The tears had pushed at Henny's eyes and he'd turned and said, 'C'mon. I want the doctor.'

The male nurse led him out of the delivery room and down a hall and around a turn and up to a closed wooden door with a sign reading 'Private.' He opened the door. There was a desk, and behind it the short man with the round face and thick glasses and tired mouth. 'Mr Girado wants to see you, Doctor Hilbrand,' the male nurse said.

'Of course,' the doctor said, and Henny realized he was just sitting there, alone, hands on the desk, palms up. Henny looked at those pudgy hands, and the doctor withdrew them quickly, and Henny understood the man's suffering.

He had nothing to say to the doctor. Doris had needed a specialist, and he, Henny, had played it cool and given her a GP, and so it was no one's fault but his own.

'What can I tell you?' the doctor asked, voice thick and weak. 'It's the first time I ever lost a patient in childbirth. The first time. But what good is that to you? What can I say? I didn't recognize . . . But even if I had – '

Henny interrupted. 'About my daughter, Doctor.'

50

The man had looked grateful. 'Anything I can do to help.'

'I want to take her home. What do I do to take care of her?'

The doctor had asked him to sit down. The male nurse had left, nodding briefly at Henny. Henny and the doctor had discussed possibilities, and Henny had stuck to his plan of keeping the child with him. The doctor had explained about nurses and housekeepers, and Henny had refused to think of the added expenses. Eighty or ninety or a hundred dollars for a woman to take care of little Sylvia (Doris had chosen the name months before – Sylvia for a girl, Kevin for a boy), and more, and more, and more for food and other things.

Yeah, other things. Like his sister and her two kids in Denver.

While Doris had worked, he'd hardly felt the twenty, thirty bucks a week he sent to Denver to help out his sister, Elsa, who waited on tables at various beaneries while Mom watched over the two kids. With Henny's help, Elsa made ends meet.

But nine months later, pressed hard by housekeeper and sister and his own inability to pinch pennies, everything went to hell. His mother. His tall, strong mother.

He hated himself sometimes for wishing she were dead.

Anyway, he'd found himself racing, racing nowhere. Two years and four months of racing nowhere. A man forgot to be grateful that the war was over and he was out in one piece, something Henny had never thought he'd forget. A man forgot that life was sweet pot – people rather nice and jazz the greatest and food a never-ending excitement and books always waiting for the slow, quiet evenings. There were no more slow, quiet evenings. There weren't even any fast, noisy evenings – not in the old way; not with pleasure a real thing and women tremendously exciting. There was just an occasional need and an occasional relief and an occasional few seconds of forgetfulness. Like the times with Eugenia. And with others.

There were plenty of women available. For men like Henny, there'd been plenty available since apes began walking upright. And, no getting away from it, shooting cheesecake made it easier.

But when it stopped being fun, when it became mixed up with other time-and-thought killers – like movies – it couldn't mean much.

Movies. He'd always liked a good movie, but now he went five and six times a week – between assignments, late at night if he could find a Times Square spot showing something he hadn't seen or something he could bear to see again. Movies which he often dozed through; but they were a substitute for going home and cheaper than hitting a bar and easier than reading books.

Not that he'd stopped reading entirely. But it was getting to be more and more of an effort to use his mind in any way, because that made him think, and thinking made him consider Doris' death and Mom and his present situation; and that was far too painful.

Hell, man, you had to side-step the punches or you'd go down!

And yet, sitting in his car outside the Brooklyn bar, he understood for a second that he was going down anyway, and that he had to find something, something to make it all worth while.

He lost the thought quickly, deliberately, and checked his watch and wondered what to do. He had the cheese-cake to print, but he could do that tonight. He had the rally pictures to develop and print, but that could also be done tonight, with everyone out of the way, with a bottle of Bols at his side.

A movie?

He pulled away from the curb and kept his eyes peeled for a theater marquee, and at the same time hated the thought of yet another movie. But what else was there?

He saw the theater and pulled the Chevy to the curb. A big-time Western and a small-time mystery. 'Yahoo,' he muttered. He opened the door, then suddenly slammed it shut again and pounded his fist into the seat. No, damn it! He'd had it with movies!

'Easy, buddy,' he said aloud, as he had so many times during the war when his mind had rebelled against fear, against constrained panic. 'Easy, buddy-boy.'

He'd go to the studio and work.

4

Lester Bogen hadn't developed or printed anything in ten years, except for kicks, but he always gave detailed instructions on how hard his film should be pushed – how much contrast brought out – and exactly what sort of prints should be made. He was particular, and specific, about grain, gradation, and other fine points which could spell the difference between the merely good and the superior. It didn't make any difference that today's shots were cheesecake, and that his only reason for taking them was to get Eugenia Randolph. They were on film, and so deserved proper handling.

Victor Bloom, the small, thin, elderly darkroom regular (there was another darkroom man, Ernie Radish, but he did it part time, his regular job being assistant to Les Bogen on all non-cheesecake shootings) liked working for Bogen. There was never any doubt as to what Morden's senior photographer wanted, nor as to when he would pay. Vic also liked Henny, respecting his art, but there was no work there. Henny already owed him a hundred dollars.

Les Bogen was just leaving the darkroom as Laird Drake was entering. They bumped into each other. 'Oh,' the huge blond man said and made nervous gestures with his meat-hook hands, 'I didn't know you were here, Les. Warning light was off. I wouldn't have disturbed you.'

'Darkroom's open to everyone,' Bogen interrupted brusquely. Laird Drake was the one man at Morden he couldn't stomach; it was Drake's contemptuous approach to everyone who couldn't help him, and his fawning over those who could.

'Say, Les,' Laird said, following Bogen into the hall with the stooping, shuffling gait he affected with an important *short* man. (Another thing Les hated, because he recalled several times when Laird had puffed his massive, fleshy frame to its full size while talking to Henny and Van.) 'Say, I've been trying to whip up a story on American Revolutionary War battle sites, color, for the *Post.* You know – our great heritage and stuff like that. Who do you think I should contact? I want an editor who'll listen, and I'd like to use your name.' He smiled in what was supposed to be a disarming manner, but Les Bogen felt his intelligence insulted by such obvious toadying.

'Old hat,' he said shortly. 'As I've told you before, in order to sell a top market a piece of photography you've got to come up with a fresh subject and then dig around to see where and how it should be shot. Do this and you won't need any special contacts.' He walked away.

Drake followed, reducing the length of his enormous stride to stay off Bogen's heels. He was about six feet four and weighed close to two-fifty. He was a big, heavy, flabby man whose face had a pink-white cast which – when he was relaxed – made him seem even younger than his twenty-seven years. However, he was not often relaxed. Life for Laird Drake was a constant struggle to come within hailing distance of his erudite and successful older brother, Jamie, also a photographer but in the effete women's high-fashion line. Laird admired, hated and feared Jamie: admired him for his success, hated him for the same reasons and feared him for being bisexual . . . because he too felt tugged in that direction. His experiences with women had been disappointing – awkward, fumbling experiences that had left him red-faced with embarrassment. But the embarrassment always turned into a slow, festering anger, as though it had been the woman's fault Laird failed to rise to the occasion. And now he tended to view women with fear and suspicion, ready to laugh at him and make him feel small. He felt more comfortable with men, and sometimes, alone, he had found his sexual fantasies of success with women turning into fantasies of being in bed with a man. He would come awake sweating then, unable to push the lingering wonder from his mind. What would a man's body feel like? How would he feel, with a man's strong hands on him? Eventually he would force the thoughts back into the deepest recesses of his mind and be able to go on pretending he was a normal, red-blooded American male. His dream was to make it big in free-lance photography, like Lester Bogen; to make money and reputation and have so many women that the thought of anything else would never enter his mind. But he was, at best, a mediocre photographer and a very poor lover, and the only reason he was able to earn his seventy-five hundred a year was his fantastic industry, an industry motivated by fear.

Laird Drake was afraid of almost everything and everyone and contemptuous of anything and anyone he didn't fear. 'Yeah, sure,' he whined, still following Bogen, 'but you know what they say, Les. It's not *what* you know but *who* you know.'

Bogen stopped and turned. He looked up at the huge man and said quietly, 'If you feel that way, get out of photography. I don't pretend to be a dedicated artist, but I've learned one thing. You've got to like what you're doing, believe in it and work at it. I'll admit you work hard enough, on the surface, but are you getting at anything, proving anything, saying anything with your pictures?'

Drake laughed uncomfortably. 'Sure, Les. I've got my ideas.'

'All right. What are they?'

'Hell, it'd take me years to spit them all out. Like my American heritage – '

'That's not an idea; it's an institution. An idea is what Henny had when he went searching for children's homes – what they used to call orphanages – and photographed laughter, happiness, and yet refused to shut his lens to the loneliness of ten kids sharing a single nurse or attendant in place of mother and father. He did this because it was important to him; because it explains why he's holding on to his own kid. And then he located a wolf hunt, not in the wilds of Siberia or Alaska, but in Minnesota.'

'I'd rather you listed your own ideas, Les,' Drake said. 'After all, how can you use a man like Girado as an example when he's always borrowing film and cigarettes and money?'

'From *you?*' Bogen asked.

'Well, no, because I wouldn't lend him a dime. I know I'd never get it back.'

'When did he ask you?' Bogen insisted.

'Hell, don't give *me* the third-degree,' Drake muttered, attempting to dilute resentment with humor.

Bogen stalked away.

'Hey, Les, what brought all this on? I was only . . .'

Bogen stopped, annoyed with himself, and offered a quick apology. 'Sorry, Laird. I've got a lot on my mind.'

'Oh, she'll come through,' Laird said, and laughed, hoping the total effect was one of easy camaraderie.

Bogen nodded and felt a rare twinge of shame. That a man of Drake's caliber should have the opportunity to remark upon his personal life.

But then he shrugged and went to the first of two

57

small offices and sat down at his desk. He took out his appointment book and examined it, setting up the next ten days' work in his mind. After a while, he put the book away and checked his watch. Four-thirty. Sandy usually returned from classes at Columbia well after five. Commuting from Peekskill to Manhattan on the Central's limited schedule didn't allow her much leeway.

However, she occasionally drove to Harmon, the upper Westchester rail center, and could then catch late trains going and early trains returning; or she took her car all the way into the city. Also, she might have had a short day or cut a few classes.

He wanted to talk to her: chat a while and make plans for their having dinner together this evening at a good local restaurant. They often ate at the Bird & Bottle on Route 9, an exquisite place dating back to Revolutionary days. She would tell him about her friends, and her studies, and discuss the plays and movies she'd seen and the books she'd read. He would listen, enjoying every word, and then tell her about an interesting assignment (never dealing with undressed models), any interesting people he'd met, and usually present her with a book he'd picked up, or a record for her jazz and classical music collection, or a corsage, or an amusing Studio greeting card that had struck his eye.

He would relax completely, as he could with no one else in all the world. He would enjoy himself immensely, as he could with no one else in all the world. He would feel love and devotion, and experience a belief in life's inherent purpose and continuity, as he could with no one else in all the world.

Because Sandy was, in essence, all his world.

Just thinking of her, his face and eyes brightened.

He dialed the long-distance operator, gave his home number, listened to the phone ring at the other end.

When Louise answered, some of the expectant brightness left him. 'It's Les,' he said. 'Sandy around?'

'No,' she said. She didn't offer any further information. She was speaking to someone she vaguely disliked.

'She call?'

'No.'

'Did she drive to Harmon?'

'She took her car.' And then irritation entered her voice. 'I'm late as it is for my club meeting. You know Tuesday's my day for the Afternoon Garden Club. Must I stay here answering questions for the next hour?'

Since he himself had brought her to this state of vague dislike – made a stranger of her, deliberately, maneuvering her apart from him over a number of years so that he would feel no block existed to his satisfying his need for many women – he didn't react to her irritability.

'Leave a message in her room before you go, Louise. Ask her to call me as soon as she gets in. I'll be at the studio until six.'

'And after that?' There was open suggestion, suspicion, accusation in her voice, and now he *did* react. He had never allowed any suggestion of this sort to pass unchallenged. It was part of his constant campaign to keep himself spotless in *Sandy's* eyes.

'And after that I'll either come home or have dinner with a friend.'

'A friend,' she said, and laughed. 'Is that what they call them nowadays?'

'You're not making sense,' he said calmly, assuredly. Louise had never been able to confirm whatever suspicions she might have had – *must* have had, in view of their absolute lack of conjugality. Louise had never had a single concrete example of his being unfaithful. Louise lived her entire life in Peekskill, among the clubwomen scattered throughout the area. She had her meetings and her charity work and her visits to the veterans' mental hospital and other activities that he still wasn't sure about. She went to Manhattan only with a club group, to see matinees of comedies and musicals. She was always with friends – women friends. She actually detested men and had felt that way even when she'd married him. He'd known it, sensed that she wanted marriage only as a shield against the world, and he'd jumped at the chance to use *her* as a shield against involvement with women – emotional involvement.

But all this had been on a plane of thought not conscious enough to be used to direct their lives from the first day of their marriage. Neither of them, twenty years ago, would admit certain truths to themselves; and so they'd played at love and marriage, and had a child. That had shocked Les Bogen into an acceptance of his own personality; made him understand he had to have more than the then rare fling with a model. He had begun to use Louise's lack of sexuality as a springboard for arguments – cold, quiet, yet relentless arguments. He had always allowed her an avenue of escape – withdrawal to friends and outside interests. Eventually, she too had given in to her basic nature, dropping all pretense of wanting to live with her husband connubially. And while she was fond of the tiny girl with blond hair and pale brown eyes, she was only too glad to withdraw there too. When Les showed a surprising attachment to Sandy – surprising not only to Louise but to Les himself – she gave him full authority in the child's upbringing. After two years, they could afford a combination maid and nurse, and that made Louise even less important a figure in Sandy's life; and whatever diminished the mother's role increased the father's. Les Bogen and his daughter became more and more important to each other.

'I think you know what I mean, Les,' Louise Bogen

said, but now she showed her uncertainty in a weak laugh. 'Not that I'd condemn you – '

'I'm terribly sorry,' he interrupted, 'to ruin what is probably your first attempt at being broad-minded, but I wouldn't dream of having girl friends – for *Sandy's* sake.' (Which was the absolute truth, since Les Bogen never considered his women as friends, merely as foodstuff, staples to feed his huge appetite.)

'All right,' she snapped. 'I have to go now.'

'Don't forget the message.'

'Why don't you let her alone, Les? Why don't you let her get interested in a boy?'

The sudden switch caught him by surprise, and he was immediately enraged. But he controlled himself and laughed and said, 'You're absolutely insane. I've never stopped – '

'Yes, you have.' (He heard the excitement, the satisfaction in her voice. She knew she'd upset him, knew she'd reached some deep, vital spot.) 'By being so much more father to her than the normal – '

'Leave the message,' he said, raging coldly. 'Goodbye.'

'But you'll lose her *someday*,' Louise said quickly. 'And what'll happen to you then? You'll be all alone. You won't have friends, as I have. You won't have anything.'

He tried to answer, and for the first time that he could remember could find no answer.

She laughed. 'Any day now, Les, that boy will come into her life. Any day now.'

'I hope so,' he said and knew it was a lie, which made him rage even more. 'I want her to be happy.'

She laughed again and hung up.

He held the phone in a sweaty fist, staring straight ahead at the wall. Slowly, he drove the rage from his mind. But fear remained – fear that had entered as soon as Louise mentioned 'that boy' coming into Sandy's life.

He refused to accept his fear. He was upset, that's all; upset by Louise's stupidity. Of course he wanted Sandy to marry and have a normal life.

But she was only nineteen, and she'd found no boy interesting enough to date more than three or four times, not to say compelling enough to *love*. She would go on this way for many years yet. She would get her BA and go for her Masters, and then – if he could make her see what a triumph it would be – take her PhD in anthropology, her major. And all that time he, her father, would share two, three evenings a week with her, would share occasional weekends with her, would help her in every way he could.

Later, she would marry. Certainly. But that was a long way off. Years off. She was still very much a child. She was still his baby. She would marry only when she was fully matured – twenty-seven, twenty-eight, perhaps thirty or more.

He thought that over and put it to himself at its worst. 'Say she marries at twenty-four or -five. That's still five or six years. And the chances are she'll stay in the New York area, and I'll still see her.'

The phone clicked in his ear, and Marie's voice said, 'Mr Bogen? Are you on the line, Mr Bogen?'

He was startled and as a result directed his anger toward her. 'What is this? Can't I make a call without your cutting in? Get off the line!'

'But there was no connection,' Marie said, shocked.

'Get off the line!'

She got off the line. He hung up, immediately sorry he'd spoken that way to her. It was Louise's fault for upsetting him – Louise, who had never been able to upset him before.

Louise was an imbecile!

Then he thought of something else. Marie might have checked his line because of an incoming call. Sandy, perhaps.

He flashed the receptionist. She answered, voice shaky. He decided against apologizing. 'Did I get a call, Marie?'

'Yes.'

'Well, who was it?'

'A woman. She didn't leave her name.'

He was no longer interested.

'She asked if you were in, and I said you were, and then she said she was sorry but something just happened and she had to hang up and she'd call back later.'

He shrugged. 'Thank you.'

Marie didn't answer; she merely clicked off. Les sighed.

The phone rang. He picked it up. 'Les?' the throaty, almost deep voice said.

Les Bogen smiled and leaned back in his chair. 'Hi, Sandy. Mother give you my message?'

'No. I'm not home. I'm still at school. I brought my car to the city.'

'Fine. Then we can have dinner at the Chambord and drive home together. I came in by train because today's strictly a studio day.'

She seemed to hesitate a moment before answering. 'I'll pick you up in, say, half an hour to forty-five minutes. Okay?'

Some of his happiness evaporated. He'd always met her at whatever restaurant they were using or else picked her up at school. She knew the studio was forbidden ground.

'All right,' he said. 'Drive carefully. It's almost five and the streets will be jammed.'

'Wonderful, Daddy! Bye!' She hung up, as if afraid he'd change his mind.

63

He smiled slightly, knowing how disappointed she'd be when he met her downstairs and got right in the car. She expected to come up and be introduced to everyone.

Then he stopped smiling. Maybe it was time he moved on to another studio, one where he wasn't known. Or, better still, found a place of his own.

After a few moments' thought he got soap, towel and electric razor from his desk and headed for the washroom. He'd freshen up, then visit a florist and buy a corsage for Sandy. He'd left home before she had this morning (wanting to conduct some business with his photographic supplier and also to pay a call on an ad agency before his noon shooting appointment with Eugenia), so he didn't know what she was wearing. But she liked roses – small, red, budding roses – and they went with just about everything. Maybe he could also pick up another gift – a neat pair of earrings, perhaps. It was a special occasion. He was going to Pennsylvania tomorrow for three or four days – a country fair that *Holiday* wanted covered. He'd miss her.

At five-thirty, Henny Girado pulled into the narrow parking lot across the street from the studio. Jess, the colored attendant, gave him the high sign, so Henny walked over to the wooden shack. 'Hi, Jess. I know – I owe you some loot. Can it wait till next week?'

The tall, husky Negro shook his head. 'The boss-man said twenty on the books is twenty too much. It's cough up or blow, Henny.'

Henny thought a moment.

Jess said, 'You'll have to walk too far if you use the place on Sixtieth. And they don't give weekly rates worth a damn. And I'd miss the hell outa you.'

Henny grinned and got his wallet. He riffled through a sheaf of bills and extracted a twenty. 'Hey.' Jess said, 'that don't look like no beans-for-Christmastime to me, daddy.'

'What you saw was a mirage, man. Like the old lady's lovers – long gone. I don't own it. I don't even have the right to look at it.'

Jess took the twenty. 'You got a tough finance company?'

'The toughest.' Henny waved his arm to include the city, the country, the world. 'The biggest. They own me, Jess. It's like Lincoln forgot Girado.' He started for the street, then stopped. 'How'd your momma go for the Bessie Smith records?'

'Hey, man, I forgot! The greatest! She was *sooo* good to Poppa for diggin' 'em up. You wanna sell them sides?'

Henny shook his head.

'Five bucks for two records. How's that?'

'Not *those* records, man. They haven't cut any in thirty years.'

Jess had to take care of another customer, and Henny walked away.

He was at the curb, waiting for the rush-hour traffic thronging Fifty-second to halt for the corner light, when he saw Les Bogen getting into a Hillman Minx convertible on the other side of the street, in front of the studio. The driver was a girl, a dark blonde. Henny waved, but Les was busy talking and didn't see him.

Henny wondered whether it was his imagination or whether Les actually looked different. He seemed animated, happy, excited in a way Henny had never thought he could be. The blonde must be something special.

But with Les Bogen that was an impossibility.

Then the girl turned her head, spotting a gap in the stream of cars, and pulled the convertible away from the curb. In a moment they'd made it to the corner, and around it just as the traffic light changed. But not before

65

Henny had seen the blonde's face: a young face, a rather pretty face. But more than that, a familiar face – except that he couldn't recall who she was.

He shrugged and crossed to the studio. He had work to do. He had big worries on his mind. He couldn't be bothered with Les Bogen's women.

And yet, hours later, working in the darkroom after everyone else had left, he still remembered that young, pretty face and wondered where he'd seen it before.

5

Marie Riposta felt that this had been absolutely her worst day since she'd started working at Morden Photos. First, Henny Girado had been so mean in the morning. Then there'd been that model – Eugenia Randolph. Seeing her made Marie feel sick, though she didn't know why. (Shameless thing! Locked in the studio with Lester Bogen for two hours. Had they . . . been doing anything wrong in there?) And at one o'clock Stella Lago had joined Marie and her friends for lunch in the Automat and kidded with some guys at a nearby table, and the guys had kidded back, but only with the chesty redhead. And then Stella had the gall to start that business again about being introduced to the photographers. Fat chance! What would they want with a switchboard operator? And later, at around four-thirty, Laird Drake, who never spoke to her except to say he was going out on an important job and to please list his calls carefully, and who generally tried to act like a big shot, came down from the third floor and said he'd been expecting a call from the *Saturday Evening Post*. Since this was like the other things he said, and they were never true, she merely nodded. But this time he didn't check his actual shooting assignments – cheesecake and small story jobs for low-paying men's magazines – and rush out. This time he got white in the face and said he was *sure* the call had come and she must've goofed and he was sick of having his affairs mishandled and on and on, almost shouting. And he stood right over her, puffing himself way up, until she'd had enough and jumped to her feet and said she was going to Mr Morden and tell him she wouldn't stand for such treatment. Then he'd stepped back and become smaller and mumbled something about it-must've-been-a-mistake. So she sat down again, shrugging it off, because he wasn't much, no matter how hard he tried to be important, and she even felt sorry for him sometimes – he was always pushing so hard, trying to make people like him, or respect him, or something. But that wasn't the end of her day. About ten minutes later, she got a call for Les Bogen. Since the other two free lines were already in use, she knew he *couldn't* be using his phone; yet it was off the hook. Tears had come to her eyes for the second time in eight hours. Because this wasn't like him at all. He was a gentleman, no matter what the others said about him and his women. He was a kind, soft-spoken man, and his shouting at her . . . well, it really put the topping on this miserable day. And he never even apologized.

She could take Drake, and she was (subconsciously) used to the feelings aroused by pretty models and her flirty friend, Stella, but when two nice guys like Henny Girado and Lester Bogen jumped on her, both in the same day, it was too darn much!

She went home at six, and the Utica Avenue Express seemed dirtier, smellier and more crowded than usual. And then, when she came out of the station, it began to rain, and before she'd walked the three blocks home it was pouring, a real summer storm with thunder and lightning. She was soaked by the time she ran into the hallway of the four-family house. And as soon as she opened the door to their ground-floor-rear, five-room flat, Momma began giving her the business. 'Hey, you betta brush your hair and make yourself look nice, Marie. You gotta surprise tonight. Frankie called and said he's bringing home a friend from the shop – a friend for you.

Real nice Italian boy, he said. Gotta good future 'cause he's the best body-and-fender man they got. Makes almost a hundred a week and goes to school some nights. Studyin' for TV technician. You betta take a shower.'

And at the table in the dining alcove, John and Angie two of her three brothers, were already arguing with her father about the fights.

'You take Giambra,' John said, leaning forward, his thick, dark, handsome face intense. 'When he got his guinea up, he could take any shine in the world.'

Angie, the youngest at twenty-three, said, 'Naw! He ain't no Jake LaMotta. And even the Bull couldn't take Sugar Ray.'

'LaMotta fight Robinson when he too old,' Poppa boomed. 'You take Rocky Marciano.'

'Now there was a slugger,' John said. 'What about him, Angie?'

Angie shrugged his heavy shoulders. All the boys looked like Poppa – medium height, dark and husky. Marie looked more like her mother, except that her mother wasn't thin, nor as sharp-featured as her daughter. (The mother claimed Marie looked like an older sister still living in Sicily – 'She gotta thin figure and thin face. She nice but never marry.')

'Aah,' Angie said. 'Marciano was okay, sluggin' with a pack of punks and played-out old-timers. But how long d'you think he'd've lasted with a young Joe Louis or Dempsey?'

'Whatsa matter with you?' Poppa suddenly bellowed. 'You ashamed maybe of being Italiano? You lika be black man instead? Alla time you make like Italian boxers nothing!'

'What'ya yelling at!' Angie yelled. 'Do I hafta make myself lie, twist the truth, just because you want Italians to be the best in everything? Do I hafta – '

69

'You hafta keep your mouth shut!' Poppa shouted, pushing his heavy body out of the chair and rattling the settings on the table in the process.

Momma had turned from Marie to see what was going on. Marie suddenly shouted, 'Loud mouths! That's all you are, a pack of loud mouths! I can't stand hearing you fighting about the same stupid things every night!'

'Hey,' John said, smiling. 'Take it easy, Marie.'

Marie whirled on her mother. 'So Frankie's bringing a friend home tonight. And I'll bet the friend'll sit around and talk about the fights and take sides with either Poppa or Angie and we'll have a real ball.'

'Ball?' Momma said.

'Oh, let me alone!' Marie wailed, and ran through the living room and dining room, past the kitchen and down the foyer to her bedroom. Just before she slammed her door, she heard John say, 'You know what that girl needs, eh, Poppa?' and Poppa say, 'In Italia, we have her married five years, all arranged. Nice girl no hafta look like movie star.'

She threw herself on her bed but didn't cry. She lay there, wondering how she could change her life so that there'd be some pleasure in it.

For a wild moment she actually considered offering herself to Henny Girado: 'If you'd like me for a night or two, Henny . . .' But then she jumped off the bed and shook her head and whispered, 'I didn't mean it. I'll tell Father Russo about the evil thought. I'll never think things like that again!'

Marie Riposta began laying out her new print dress and suède high heels. She'd look nice tonight. Maybe *this* boy wouldn't be like the others her brothers had brought home for her. Maybe he'd know other things besides the fights and baseball and his job at the body-repair shop.

70

Maybe he'd look different too – slim and boyish. Maybe he'd be something like Henny Girado.

She went to the bathroom and got in the shower. For a while she washed briskly, but then her eyes closed and her breath quickened and her hands moved slowly, soaping her small breasts. Her nipples hardened, and she gasped, feeling excitement and guilt. The guilt went away as her hands continued their circular movements, kneading her breasts, agitating the sensitive nipples with soapy caresses. Her eyes glazed, and closed, and the hands touching her became Henny Girado's. *His* palms stroked her, *his* fingers closed and squeezed, eliciting a low moan from deep inside her. Then it was his mouth on her nipples, teasing gently, then harder. She felt a fire mounting in her belly, and one hand crept down over her smooth stomach, reaching between her legs. Her knees bent and she leaned back against the cold tile wall. It did nothing to diminish the fire inside her as Henny explored the lips of her vagina. They were in the shower together, and she couldn't stop him, even though she tried. 'No, Henny, darling.' But the finger – *his* finger – went on touching her, locating the delicate nub of her clitoris, stroking. She shuddered, her head lolling, her lips slack, her eyes tight shut. And Henny spread her legs wide and rammed himself into her. Marie groaned and went down on her knees, head arching back as she fondled her breasts with one hand and the other moved rhythmically inside her. The fire rose as she imagined his body pressed hard against her. His mouth was on her breast, his hands on her buttocks. He was inside her, deep there, lifting her up towards climax.

It came in a surging flood of pent-up frustration. Marie cried out, her body trembling, her head rolling on her neck. 'Henny! Henny, darling.' She took her hand from her vagina and reached for the shower tap as the guilt came back in great rolling waves.

When she came out to dry herself, she was near tears. God, what would happen to her! Would she go to Hell?

She had to tell Father Russo. And yet she knew she wouldn't. She'd tried, the first time she'd masturbated, and that was almost a year ago. 'I had bad thoughts, Father' was all she could say. She'd told him that a number of times, and he'd counseled her to do something constructive when the 'bad thoughts' came – like read her rosary, or think of a dear departed, or go out for a brisk walk. He'd also asked if she'd been reading any of those 'cheap books and magazines' sold in the candy stores.

What did she need with cheap books and magazines when her mind turned out violent love scenes every time she was alone, every time she stepped into the shower or lay down in bed?

Standing in the steamy bathroom, wrapped in the big, thick towel, she shivered. Oh, Lord, she was damned!

Then the feeling of terror slipped away, and she dried herself. But as she dressed, she murmured, 'Hail, Mary, full of grace . . .'

The boy Frankie brought home was short and heavy and balding. He thought Angie was wrong. 'Ain't no shine alive can take a paisano when the 'Talian boy gets mad. 'Talian boys gotta get *mad.*'

'That's a good point, Ant'ny,' Poppa said. 'A good point.' He grinned at Marie, who was trying to eat the manicotti Momma had made special for company. 'You gotta smart boy here, Marie. You better take him someplace and make sure he don' get away.'

The rain had stopped, so they went for a walk. Anthony held her hand and talked about TV-repairman classes. He was very respectful, but he didn't ask her for a date when he said good night outside her house. She was just as glad. This was one of the few boys she would have rejected.

When she came inside, her parents and brothers were watching the Late Show. 'So?' Momma asked.

'Thanks for nothing, Frankie,' Marie said, and her voice carried cool conviction.

Frankie shrugged. 'Maybe you're too particular.'

Marie colored and began to answer, but Momma said, 'She's right. He was too short, too fat. Marie can get better.'

Angie turned from the TV screen and smiled at her. 'Hey, *pizzarina*, why don't you try dating non-Italian boys? Bet you'd like them better.'

Poppa slapped himself on the forehead and said, voice thick with shock, 'What's wrong with this stupid? He tells his own sister – '

Marie laughed, and nodded, and said, 'Okay. So *you* bring me a date, Angie. You never have, you know.'

Angie shook his head. 'Not me, honey. Not me. You can get your own.'

Marie's mother saw that her husband was about to take up the cudgels with Angie, so she interrupted swiftly. 'Let's watch the movie and no talk.'

Poppa shrugged, muttered to himself, and subsided.

Marie wanted to watch the movie, too, when she saw it had Clark Gable, but she went to her room anyway. She was afraid she'd get into an argument if she sat with her family tonight.

She fell asleep quickly and dreamed she was being photographed in the nude, and there were men all around her, touching.

Henny Girado worked until eight P.M. before deciding it was time for dinner. He walked downstairs and was surprised to see that it was pouring. Time, life and weather seemed to stand still when one was in the darkroom.

He'd intended to walk to a French restaurant on Fifty-sixth but instead ran across the street, ducking his head into the downpour, and kept running until he reached the Chinese restaurant near the corner. He had barbecued spareribs, fried rice and a pot of tea. He took his time eating, smoked a leisurely cigarette afterward, and didn't get back to the studio until nine.

He went to Richie Morden's office, put on the light, said, 'Forgive a poor sinner, massa,' and had a stiff Bols, without vermouth. He sat drinking it in Richie's chair behind Richie's desk and then picked up Richie's phone. He wanted to call someone who'd give him pleasure, someone who'd give his life direction and purpose. But there was no such person.

Strangely, he thought of the young blonde who'd driven Les Bogen away from the studio late this afternoon. Her face. Her familiar face.

He shrugged. Maybe Les would give him her number after finishing with her. That shouldn't take long; two or three weeks was average for the great Bogen.

He shrugged again. She'd be just another chick. He'd use her and forget her.

He began to put the phone back on the cradle but knew he had to call Denver sooner or later. Might as well be sooner, now that he had some dough.

He got the long-distance operator and gave her all the pertinent information and took a long sip of his gin. A few minutes later, he said, 'Elsa? This is Henny. How's it going?'

'Fine,' the woman's voice answered. 'And what about you, Henny?'

'Great. How're the kids?'

'Reggie's got a cold. Clara's just fine; she's asleep.

74

Reggie's pulling my arm, dying to say hello, but not at these rates.'

'Yeah. I'm a little short, Elsa. I'll try to send something soon.'

'You've done too much already, Henny. I don't want – '

'Sure, sure. You'll print your own in the basement. You'll feed the kids on home-grown spinach. Now listen, I expect a good-sized check the week after next. I'll be able to send three, four hundred in, say, ten days. Will that be okay?'

There was silence. Then, 'Of course.'

But he knew it wasn't okay. 'You having trouble getting credit?'

'Well, it's been four weeks since . . . not that I have any right to expect . . . but I'm about three hundred dollars . . .' There was a choking sound, and the mouthpiece was covered.

Henny Girado passed his hands over his wide gray eyes. The Grayson Collection Agency and their client, the Charleston-Hedges Laboratories, would have to wait, as usual. Everyone to whom he owed money would have to wait, as usual. He was glad he'd at least made the monthly payment on his bank loan when he'd cashed Richie's check. 'Listen, sis, I'll try to send a few hundred out tonight.'

'Yes,' the choked voice said. 'But where'll it end, Henny? Mort's got three more years before he's eligible for parole. And who knows if he'll come back to me even then. And it's like a lousy soap opera, with me and the kids, and Mom laying there having to be taken care of like an infant, and you with a kid of your own.'

'We'll do great,' Henny said, mouth twisting in fear or anger or despair. (Somehow this day of all days had been terribly long, terribly black.) 'You've said it a dozen

75

times yourself — a few thousand and you can open a luncheonette or something and live upstairs and take care of Mom and the kids and make out nicely. We'll get the few thousand. A fat assignment or two and I'll mail you a big check and you'll be on your own, doing great.'

'How many years we been saying that now, Henny? How many lousy long years and me with a thug for a husband serving time and you breaking your back in New York?'

'Well, what do you want me to do?' he suddenly shouted, face white. 'You want me to tell you I'm not going to send another dime and to put the kids in foster homes and Mom into some charity ward where she can go nuts before she dies?'

There was the choking, crying sound again.

'I'd love to!' he shouted. 'I'd give anything to cut out! I want some sleep, dammit! I want to be able to answer the phone without a gut-ache! I want to be able to see and speak to people, all the people I know, without being kicked in the ass for owing them money! I want *out!*' Then he shook his head and breathed heavily and said, 'Hey, listen, Elsa, you got me saying stupid things, things I don't mean. It's a grind, but it'll come to an end.'

'Yes,' she said faintly. 'We haven't talked like this for a long time, Henny.'

'Yeah, at least a month.' He made himself laugh.

She answered the laugh, but he could see her sitting at the edge of the bed in the room with his mother, who was completely paralyzed by a stroke, and the eight-year-old girl standing near her, and the four-year-old girl sleeping on the cot in the kitchen, and the other two cots set up in the living room of the three-room apartment. He could see her face, never really pretty and now lined by worry and grief. A face that looked fifty and was over forty. A face that her convict husband would never come

76

back to and that would never attract another provider; and so her brother, her only hope, would go on squirming for a few hundred here and a few hundred there until the mother died and Elsa's kids grew up a little. Five years, maybe? Probably closer to eight or ten. And wasn't it a great thing to wish your own mother dead? Wasn't it!

'Tune in for the next installment of Elsa's Other Brother Henny,' he said, and shook his head at what screwy, corny tricks life could play, and really laughed. 'Will Elsa get the check on time? Will Henny make the payments on the diaper bill? Can these two Girados find happiness over the telephone?'

'You nut,' the voice in Denver said. 'I'd give anything to see you, Henny. Anything.'

'Well, maybe I'll get an assignment on the Coast this summer and stop over in Denver a few days. If so, you'll be baking lasagna for brother nut.'

'You bet, Henny. The best you ever tasted, next to Mom's.'

They were both silent a moment; then he said, 'I'll have to say goodbye, Elsa. Our three minutes must be up.'

'Already? Oh well, goodbye, Henny. Bless you. I'll pray for you.'

'So long, Elsa.'

'You pray too, Henny. Ask the Lord Jesus for help.'

'Yeah. It'd take a miracle at that.'

'Please don't mock, Henny. *Please*.'

His voice softened. 'I'm not mocking, Elsa. Not mocking you. Just myself. So long.' He hung up, finished his drink and started for the door. Then he returned to the desk and got long distance back on the wire. He explained that the call was to be charged to Henny Girado's phone, not Richie Morden's.

At his own desk, he examined a checkbook and chewed

on his lip. Eleven dollars and forty cents was the grand total in the account. But he'd be able to deposit enough to cover a check sent to Elsa before it came to the bank for clearance. However, that wasn't the problem. She needed money fast, and with her credit being almost as bad as his own, no one would be likely to cash a big personal check for her.

He went downstairs. The rain was slacking off. He hugged the building side and walked two blocks to a drugstore that sold money orders. He counted out two hundred, hesitated, then decided he couldn't risk losing his current housekeeper by being late with her salary; she was better than most of the others. He put the rest of the money back into his wallet, wrote a note to Elsa on a slip of paper, and put note and money order into an air-mail envelope. He mailed it at the corner and returned to the studio. That should get her out of the hole, and he'd try to send another hundred, hundred and fifty, within the next week or so.

Back in the darkroom, he examined the negatives of Eugenia and decided against printing them tonight. He'd do that tomorrow.

From a metal cabinet, he removed ten 35-millimeter contact sheets, each sheet containing ten or twelve shots he'd taken in a drug plant. He leaned against a side counter and went through the hundred-some-odd photographs and picked out three he considered good additions to his portfolio. 'Pretty-pretty,' he murmured as he set up the enlarger. All three had the same subject – a huge, smooth, gleaming aluminum blending tank, standing high off the floor on concrete legs. They were perfect black and whites, with the tank precisely centered, its tubes and coils rising above and out of sight, and two men, both dressed in white smocks, both serious-faced, almost stark, standing off to the north, looking up at it. In the first shot, all that could be seen of the men were their silhouettes. In the second, they were in the foreground, and in the third (his favorite), they were blurred images. In all three shots, they seemed to be worshipping the tank in some ultra-modern manner.

He took his time with the enlargements. He worked carefully, bringing out every bit of contrast, every shade of meaning. He didn't finish until eleven-fifteen. And then, suddenly, he was exhausted.

But he couldn't face the prospect of home and bed. He had to see someone, ball it up a little. He had to kick the blues; kick them hard.

He decided to drive over to Marv Weister's. Then he'd get on the phone and call some chicks.

He just hoped Marv hadn't had a fix tonight.

6

Richie Morden was in bed before ten that night, which was unusual for him. He and Phyllis generally caught a play or late movie uptown and then had a bite at a luncheonette; or watched TV until one A.M. and had their snack in the kitchen of their large three-room apartment; or read (historical novels for Phyllis; biography, first-person true-adventure and an occasional serious novel for Richie) until the wee hours. They enjoyed things too much to end the day early; they stretched it out as long as their eyes, minds and bodies would carry them. But tonight, on the way home, Richie had stopped in at a Fourth Avenue bar for a glass of cold stout – his major weakness, since he was trying to watch his weight – and had seen something that, along with Van Roberts' display of sensitivity, brought the old thoughts, the old fears, back into focus.

The Minor Key Bar was aptly named. Small, softly lighted, extremely quiet, with a constant background of good music piped in from a hidden phonograph, it was a spot Richie had patronized once or twice a week for the past six years. In all that time, he had never witnessed a disagreement or even heard anyone raise his voice.

Tonight the pattern was broken. Just as he was finishing his Guinness, tilting back his head to get that last frothy swallow of dark brew, the bartender, standing nearby, muttered an obscenity. Richie was surprised; more than surprised – shocked. The bartender was squat, aging, white of hair and kind of face and soft of voice. He had never said anything like that before, that Richie had heard.

Looking around, Richie understood. A tall, well-dressed man and tall, pretty woman had just entered and were taking stools one removed from his, on the left. They were Negroes, the first Richie had seen in this bar. They settled themselves and began chatting in low tones, waiting to be served.

They kept waiting. The bartender ignored them, moving to people on either side of their slightly left-of-center position at the bar, mixing two Manhattans, drawing a draught beer, and finally turning his back and fiddling with some bottles.

The Negro couple continued to wait patiently, but they were no longer chatting. The woman had lighted a cigarette and was examining her fingernails. Richie, watching from the corner of his eye, saw that her hands were trembling. The man was looking at the bartender, trying to catch his eye in the wall-length mirror.

A couple at the far end – on the last two stools near the street door – got up to leave. The bartender turned and said, 'Come again.' The couple replied and walked out into the street. The bartender resumed whatever he was doing with the bottles. The Negro man said, 'Two martinis, please,' voice soft and even.

'Okay,' the bartender said but didn't move from his bottles.

Richie wanted to leave. The situation was becoming unbearable. He told himself he understood the bartender's position: he had to maintain the status-quo patronage of his bar; otherwise, he might lose customers. At the same time, he began hating the man.

A lone man entered the bar and took the last stool near the door. 'Screwdriver, Fred.'

The bartender smiled, nodded, and reached for a

bottle of Wolfschmidt's. The Negro man said, voice still emotionless, 'I believe we were here first, bartender. Two martinis, remember?'

'Yeah,' the bartender intoned but went right ahead and mixed the screwdriver. Deliberately, he walked past the colored couple and set the glass before the new customer. The new customer paid with a bill. The bartender walked past the colored couple, then returned with change and set it down on the bar before the new customer. He leaned forward on his elbows and began to chat.

The colored woman murmured something to her escort and began to rise. The man put his hand on her arm and replied in the same soft, even voice he'd used throughout, 'But we haven't had our drink, dear.' The bartender kept chatting with the new customer.

'Are you going to serve us, bartender?' the colored man asked.

The bartender said, 'Sure.' He didn't move.

By now, every customer in the place must have been aware of the situation. A few looked annoyed – though at whom, Richie couldn't tell – but most didn't seem to give a damn.

Richie didn't plan it, yet he heard himself call, 'Another Guinness, Fred.'

The bartender came past the colored couple, once again his smiling, affable self. 'Large one, this time?'

'Small,' Richie said. 'And *after* you serve these people.' He motioned at the colored couple and cleared his throat convulsively. 'There are laws, you know.' He was angry at himself for the tremor in his voice. 'This is New York, you know.' He had to clamp his mouth shut to prevent himself from going on, from shouting.

The bartender hesitated, his plan of inaction broken. If this long-time customer made a scene, continuing to ignore the colored couple might do more harm than good. And there *were* laws. If a white customer backed up a colored customer's complaint, the State Commission Against Discrimination might be able to close the Minor Key.

His decision made, the bartender mixed the martinis. When he served the colored couple, he kept his eyes away from them. 'Thank you,' the man said, and for the first time his voice showed his hurt and anger.

The bartender served Richie the small Guinness, a bland expression on his kindly face, and ambled away to fill another order. Richie sipped, though his throat was almost closed by nervousness.

The colored couple finished their drinks and prepared to leave. The bartender left a customer in mid-order to hurry to their positions. He picked up their glasses and, right before their eyes, dropped them on the bar. The fragile stemware smashed. The bartender said, 'Oops.' He took a rag and brushed the pieces into a can and placed the can beneath the bar. He returned to his customer.

The colored man smiled a terrible smile and looked at Richie. 'An old trick,' he said, voice not quite so even. 'It intimates that we've contaminated the glasses. It tells us not to come back. But I think I will come back every so often, just to make him happy.'

'If you do,' Richie muttered, pale with shame and rage, 'you won't see me here.' He felt the need to say something more, to apologize for the bartender, and for everyone else in the room. But he gulped his stout and said nothing.

The woman tugged the man's arm, and they walked out. Through the glass door, Richie saw her put both hands over her face. The man said something, and she dropped her hands and seemed to straighten. They walked from sight.

Richie felt drained of strength and slightly ill, as if he'd taken part in a physically violent situation. The bartender hurried up, all bows and scrapes and soft vocal nuances. 'I'm sure sorry if that business upset you, sir. But I don't own the place and my orders are to discourage Negroes from drinking here. And it's not that the owner doesn't like colored people either. Neither of us got prejudices. It's the customers.'

'*I'm* a customer,' Richie said, unable to look at the man and yet feeling his rage drain away at the apologetic, almost logical explanation.

'Sure, but you're only *one*. You noticed no one else interfered.'

Richie nodded, raised his glass and reached for a pretzel. But the bartender didn't accept the dismissal; he was determined to state his case. 'If we allowed Negroes in here, it wouldn't be long before we'd have no white customers at all.'

'I don't believe a nice couple like that would chase anyone away.'

'Okay. But how many nice couples like that are there? Listen, when I saw how he acted, I felt terrible. I mean, he was as nice as you or me. But if you make any of them welcome, *all* kinds start coming around.'

'That holds true for whites as well as –'

'Be honest,' the bartender interrupted earnestly. 'You get ten Negroes in here and more than half will be the wrong kind. They'll get drunk and fight and this place won't be any better than a Harlem gin mill. Think you'll want to come here then?'

Richie had lots of answers. He could have pointed out that the Minor Key was located in a solidly white neighborhood and there was just no reason for droves of Negroes to descend on it. He could have pointed out that the atmosphere was such as to draw people who liked a very quiet, low-keyed spot, and that since it drew whites of that inclination, there was no reason to doubt that it would draw Negroes of the same inclination. He could have remarked that the cruelty shown in 'discouraging' colored customers was enough, in itself, to change the atmosphere and discourage many white customers as well.

He could have given at least a dozen good answers, but he was suddenly very tired. He said, 'Let's drop the whole thing.'

The bartender shrugged and moved away.

Richie left his glass of stout unfinished. When he got home, Phyll had pot roast and stewed carrots. He ate well and wanted to tell her what had happened, but he hesitated. Anything else, certainly. But this touched upon his own . . . problem.

Finally, as they were having cigarettes with second cups of coffee, and he was feeling that absolutely nothing could dim the pleasure of their relationship, he began talking about it. She listened, nodding, agreeing with his sympathy for the colored couple, his anger at the bartender, his despair at the social setup that led to such scenes. But when he finished, she said, 'It *is* a shame, dear, a *nice* couple like that. But the bartender *did* have a point. I'm not a real reb, but I certainly wouldn't want to go to a place that catered to colored.'

He didn't know what to say, so he nodded.

'You know *me*, dear. I was brought up in a good El Paso family and they didn't have to teach me that white and colored don't mix; it was, well, almost in the blood. But when we came to New York, I got over that and even grew to respect some Negroes – Van Roberts, for example. I've only met him half a dozen times, but he's a fine man, I know.'

85

'Yes,' he said quickly. 'A very fine man, Phyll. And most Negroes of his social level –'

'But there aren't many Negroes of his social level, are there?' she said, and smiled, and went on without waiting for an answer. 'As I was saying, I feel I'm a lot more liberal – inside, I mean; the way I really feel, I mean – than most native New Yorkers. But sometimes I get to feeling uncomfortable.' She smiled again, rather shamedly. 'One afternoon I took a bus uptown and there were three Negro men and one white boy and myself. That's all. It stayed that way for only a few blocks; then other passengers got on. But during those few blocks, I felt . . . afraid, Richie. I felt the Negroes were staring at me, wanting to *do* things.'

He nodded vaguely.

She laughed. 'Silly, isn't it? But if I had to sit here, alone with a Negro man, I'd be afraid again.'

'And if *I* were part Negro?' he heard himself ask. 'If you found out I was, say, a quadroon, would you be afraid to sit here with me?'

She laughed again.

He forced a grin. 'Well, would you?'

She shrugged. 'I've lived with you twenty years, Richie. How could I be afraid?'

He nodded, and promised himself never to say things like that again, and got up to help her remove the dishes. She didn't rise with him. She remained seated, and a thoughtful expression came over her soft, fair, pretty face.

'But I might feel disgusted, Richie. I don't think I'd mind sitting with you, but sleeping with you . . .' She laughed and stood up and began gathering dishes. 'You and your suppositions. You'll suppose us into a divorce before you're through.'

He busied himself helping her, laughing and talking

and acting as if everything were fine. But he was sick and wanted to lie down.

He did just that at a quarter to ten, leaving her at the TV set with the explanation that he had a splitting headache – which was the truth. A moment later she followed him to the bathroom to make sure that he took an Anacin, and then into the bedroom, where she asked, 'Would you like me to keep you company, Richie?'

'No, honey. I'm going to get some sleep. You wanted to see that TV show at ten. Go on or you'll miss the beginning.'

She kissed him and left, closing the door softly behind her.

He rolled over on his side, shutting his mind to every thought but one: He would wake up the next morning without a worry in the world. Which was almost the truth.

Marvin Weister was the writer who had done the text for Les Bogen's book, *The City Is a Woman*, and during the course of his research into Bogen's work had met Henny Girado. The two men, so different in so many ways, had become friends. Weister was two years older than Henny, a bachelor (if so virile a term can be used for so fractured a personality), and had written and published a great deal of fiction, but because most of it was bread-and-butter pulp and the rest for the intelligentsia, with attendant lack of public acceptance, he lived from hand to mouth. (This prevented him from lending Henny money and thereby saved their friendship.) His apartment reflected his financial condition; it was a shabby two-rooms-plus-kitchenette on West Ninety-third Street. The block was about fifty per cent Puerto Rican, twenty per cent Negro and the rest white. The thin, sickly looking (and sick in actuality, much of the time) author of over three hundred pulp short stories and four novels (none of which quite made its advance, and only one of which was reprinted as a paperback) had no prejudices when it came to race and color, but he did have fears. There had been an outbreak of muggings with the advent of warm weather, and Weister refused either to enter or leave his place after dark, unless accompanied by at least one male friend. It had complicated what was, to him, an already overcomplicated existence. It had also increased his need for the support of heroin, a drug he had so far managed to live with on a near-normal basis.

Weister had averaged one fix a week since the previous summer, at which time he had made the jump from alcohol and marijuana. Now, however, using his fear of violence as an excuse, he had begun upping his quota, taking an occasional extra fix. This, he was quite aware, might presage the beginning of the end for him, but in the small, deadly, personal battles he fought daily, he found that surcease from fear and doubt overrode any long-range perspective. And so he was drifting toward final addiction. And so he was drifting toward final elimination of self in a social sense, which was what he had been doing all his life.

But there was a more immediate problem which the extra fixes had created: a money problem. He had a singularly humane pusher – a Bronx candystore proprietor who charged only ten dollars a shot and had never tried to up the ante. Ten dollars a week was quite a load for Marv Weister to carry, since he barely made enough for food (especially since the pulps had virtually died), rent and cigarettes. Twenty a week loomed ahead as a problem equal to the national debt. It terrified him, and that in itself made the second shot all the more necessary.

And looming above fear of violence, fear of financial complications and fear of fear was fear of facing the typewriter without a crutch. Marv Weister could find only one reason for living – writing. And he couldn't write 'cold', had to approach each story with burning zeal. That in itself damned him. He had been working on a new novel for almost five months – which multiplied his damnation in fantastic geometric proportions.

He was sitting at the old Royal in a corner of his bedroom when Henny rang the downstairs bell. He leaped from his chair, rushed to the tiny living room whose double window faced Ninety-third Street, stuck his head out and looked down three stories to the dark street. Henny waved up at him.

Weister shook his head, said, 'I was working. Wait a minute. It's late. I should . . .'

Henny recognized the panicked inability to make a decision. 'Okay. Keep working. I'll see you around.'

'No. Wait.' He wanted to say he'd come down and they'd take a short walk. That way, Henny wouldn't be able to hook him for the evening. That way, he could return to the typewriter in half an hour.

But did he want to return to the typewriter?

Then he glanced across the street. Some Puerto Rican boys were sitting on a stoop, partly illuminated by light from a nearby window. They looked like members of a gang. They looked dangerous.

But he'd passed those same boys a number of times and they'd never said a word to him. Of course, it had been during the day, or early in the evening and now it was almost midnight.

'Have you any cigarettes?' he asked.

Henny said, 'Sure. Full pack. But I don't want to interrupt you.'

'Listen. Get a few packs. I know your full packs. Three butts and we're out. Get a few – ' He interrupted himself, said, 'Wait,' and ran to the door. He pressed the release buzzer, kept it pressed for quite a while. Then he sighed, as if he'd solved a major problem, went to a battered red armchair and fell into it. He ran long, thin fingers through thinning black hair in a brief combing, neatening process; but with baggy suntan trousers and faded polo shirt hanging on his bony frame, the total effect was not one of neatness. He sat quietly and heard footsteps pounding up. Henny always charged a flight of stairs, two at a time, fast. Where the hell did he think he was going?

The doorbell rang. Weister got up and moved slowly across the floor and stopped. 'Who is it?'

'Brigitte Bardot,' Henny's voice said, in a hammy French accent. 'I did so enjoy your last book, monsieur, and I want to repay you for the pleasure you gave me. May I come in for a moment, hah?'

Weister released the snap lock, drew a heavy hand bolt and opened the door. Henny walked in. 'I'll only stay a minute, Marv.'

'No,' Marv Weister said dully. 'I wasn't really working. I wouldn't have answered the bell if I was. I was just sitting. Come. See the master's creation.' He led Henny to the bedroom and pointed at a sheet of paper on the table and a sheet in the typewriter. 'One page, and one paragraph. Full day's results. And I've been at it six, seven, eight hours. Christ! Christ! Why the hell don't I get a job?'

Henny liked the writer, but he had no answers for him. From the beginning of their friendship, he'd recognized a brink-of-disaster personality, and he hoped that Weister would either withdraw from the brink in time or at least remain on the edge for the duration of his life. He picked up the sheet lying on the table, but Weister snatched it from his hand.

'No, Henny. I never . . . you know I never allow . . . it's shit anyway.' He clutched the piece of paper, as if about to destroy it, then put it back on the table. 'I'll get a fresh start tomorrow, early in the morning.' And then he laughed wildly and touched his lips with his fingers and said, 'Do you know how long I've been saying things like that? Since I was seventeen. And I never get a fresh start, and I never get up before noon, and I never write more than a lousy few pages a day. Why, *why* don't I get a job?'

Henny sighed. 'Because there isn't a job you could hold, Marv. Because writing's all you know, and the way you go at it doesn't allow for adjustment to job conditions.'

Weister reacted according to pattern. He smiled, revealing small, white, childlike teeth. 'Correct. I have no choice. I can only write, this way.' He turned and strolled to the living room and sank into his red chair. 'Let's have a smoke. You got any money?'

Henny gave him a cigarette, then stretched out on a shabby black-and-red-checkered couch across the room from the red chair. 'I got, but it's all spoken for. Who needs money anyway? All I need's my little green book.'

Weister grinned. 'Bless you, Father Girado, for the solace you give poor psychotics. Get on that phone, man, and find us some quail.'

'You sure you don't want to call a girl of your own?'

Weister laughed. 'I don't have any girl of my own, and you know it.'

Henny sucked his teeth. 'True, but I keep hoping you'll go out and find one, just for kicks.'

'Stop hoping. If you didn't pimp for me, I'd forget what it was like.'

Henny sat up. 'Who did your pimping before you met me?'

Weister snapped his fingers. 'That's the first new topic of conversation we've had in two years! A *mitzvah*, man!

91

Something about me you don't know. And one of these days I might discover there's something about *you* that *I* don't know. No one pimped for me before you. I used to pick up the scroungiest broads in creation, because they were the only ones who'd give me a tumble. I had fifty-year-old waitresses, and even they rejected my advances more often than not. I also had a steady for almost three years. She loved me.' He grinned, but sadly. 'She was young, and nice looking, but screwy as they come. She used to sing Swedish folk songs while we were in bed. You ever hear a Swedish folk song, man? *Crazy!* But I didn't really care for her. It was my Jew-boy prejudices. I have them, you know. I couldn't take her seriously. Unless a girl's name is Cohen, I can't take her seriously.'

'I get it,' Henny said, recognizing the outpouring of words as the beginning of Weister's ball. 'I'll work the phone, but keep talking.' (As if anyone could stop the cadaverous writer now!)

'How can you get it, being a *Talyena?* Anyway, she had the greatest body, and the worst mind. I mean the sickest mind, man. If you think *Finnegans Wake* is rich in confusion, you'd have to hear Sidney talk. Yeah, she called herself Sidney. The only other Sidney I ever knew was the toughest kid in PS Fifty-two. But, like *Finnegans Wake*, she was not only rich in confusion but rich in ideas and ideology and poetic imagery and pure didactic detail and also a genius at erotic improvisation.'

Henny made a few calls but kept listening. It was Marv Weister's compulsive, creative talking that made him so interesting. Weister could talk about almost anything, for hours, and even if the subject wasn't worth a damn, his verbal embellishments were always a joy. At least to Henny.

'Hey,' Henny interrupted, hanging up the phone for

the third time, 'we're having trouble, Marv. My latest sure-things are all tied up, or all knocked out.'

'What about the one who was here a few months ago – weird name but terrific woman? You know, she brought a dark little girl for me named Francie something-or-other.'

'Eugenia Randolph?'

'That's the one. I wouldn't mind seeing Francie again. Have you tried Eugenia?'

'No. I don't like to make a habit of any one chick. Besides, she just joined Les Bogen's stable.'

'Aha. And you feel morally and ethically restrained.'

Henny laughed. 'With *Les Bogen?*'

'Then why'd you mention it?'

Henny shrugged. 'You got me, daddy. Must be a holdover from dealing with one-woman men.' He remembered Les driving off with the lovely blonde and the way he'd looked at her, and tried briefly to pin down that familiar face. 'Well, if nothing else is available.' He picked up the phone and dialed swiftly. After a dozen or more rings, Eugenia answered. Music, talk and laughter sounded in the background as she said, 'Who goes there?'

'Hi, Irish.'

'Master Henny. *How*d'ya'do? You owe me money. Do I get paid this week?'

'Come on over to Marv Weister's pad and we'll discuss it. Bring a friend for Marv; maybe Francie what's-her-name.'

'You're trying to say you love me again. Sweet, sweet feller.'

'I'm merely offering myself as a chaser after the raw booze you had from twelve to two.'

'Raw booze hell. That was private stock.'

'Then it's time you *had* some raw booze. Get in a cab. I'll pay the boy.'

'You got martinis?'

'Sure.' He covered the mouthpiece. 'Marv, you got any liquor?'

'A fifth of gin and some rye.'

'Well,' Eugenia said, 'I'm having a little gathering here.'

'You with anyone?'

'Your boy Laird Drake brought up a Chinese dinner and lots of Scotch, and I called half a dozen friends, and your boy Laird ran down and got more food and liquor, and he hasn't even held my hand, so I guess I'm with him.'

'Kiss him goodbye and he'll never forget the thrill. Don't forget to bring a friend.'

'I'm not sure I can ditch him.'

'I'll be waiting. And if you have any vermouth, bring it along. We're a little short. And some butts. And don't ever call Laird Drake my boy. It's like he barks and I meow. See you in fifteen minutes.'

'Henny, I can't promise.'

'You got any of that *wild* caviar spread you had last time? Bring it along, huh?' He hung up.

'Will she come?' Weister asked.

'Maybe,' Henny said.

About half an hour later the downstairs bell rang and Henny got off the couch. 'Go change the linen, man.'

'Linen?' Weister asked, wide-eyed. 'What's that?'

Henny grinned. When footsteps reached the landing, he opened the door; and his grin weakened. In the hall were Eugenia Randolph, the dark little girl named Francie and Laird Drake. Drake was puffed up pugnaciously. Eugenia said, 'Hey, man, Sir Drake kindly drove us down so there'd be no cab tab. He also brought along his liquor. We'll continue the party here, he says. He wants to discuss literature with Mr Weister, he says. *Oy vay.*'

94

Henny stepped aside. 'Keep smiling. Remember that the species that adjusts survives.'

Weister said, 'Not unless it gets the chance to procreate.'

Francie said, 'Let's go look at your typewriter, Mr Weister.'

'Call me Roger,' Marv Weister said.

'Why, Marv?'

'My uncle's name was Roger, and he had eleven children.'

Francie laughed, and they walked into the bedroom and shut the door.

Laird Drake said, 'I wanted to talk to him.'

Henny said, 'You can talk to me, Laird.'

Laird Drake looked him up and down. 'What about? A quick loan?' He laughed and turned to Eugenia. 'Why don't we find a nice restaurant?'

Eugenia entered the apartment. 'Why don't you stop kicking things around and relax?'

Laird Drake's lips parted, but he was too shocked to answer. Eugenia had obviously hidden her claws from him until now.

Eugenia said, 'Come on in, Laird. Henny doesn't bite.'

Henny said, 'Why, you *know* I do, Irish. You even complained about it one time.'

Eugenia threw off her raincoat, put her hands on her hips and looked around. She wore a black skirt, white shirtwaist and spike heels. Her hair fell long and very blond. Her figure curved in spectacular fashion. She was a lot of woman, and Henny admired her as always. But tonight he was somehow tired, somehow disenchanted with things – even spectacular things like Eugenia. And as soon as he recognized this disenchantment, he fought it, knowing he had to fight it whenever it showed up, knowing if he ever allowed it to gain hold, he would stop

95

getting up in the mornings, would sink into apathy and defeat.

He said, 'We see and we applaud, Miss Latin Quarter. You may sit down.'

Laird Drake came inside and put a large, brown-paper bag on the red armchair. 'Liquor,' he muttered.

'Thanks,' Henny said, not blaming Drake for being irritated, and determined to make the situation comfortable now that Drake was part of the group. 'I'll mix some drinks.' He smiled. 'It's about time we office mates became acquainted.'

Laird puffed himself up again as Henny walked over. 'Where's *your* date?'

Henny widened his smile. 'I stopped dating when I was twenty, Laird.'

'Don't get wise with me,' Laird Drake said sharply. 'I'll break you in half with one hand tied behind my back!'

Henny's smile died. Drake had been with Morden Photos eight months, but this was the first time Henny'd had the misfortune to be thrown together with him in a small social group. At the studio, and studio parties, and the magazine brawls attended by many photographers, they'd never exchanged more than a word or two. Henny said, 'I've had a long day,' and then quickly, placatingly, 'What's the beef?'

'I was with Eugenia and you call up and tell her to come over and she tries to ditch me, that's what!' Drake bellowed.

'Why don't you take it up with Eugenia?' Henny asked, and cursed himself for creating the entire distasteful, unnecessary, sophomoric bit.

'Because where I come from we take it up with the man!'

96

The bedroom door opened. Weister and Francie looked out. Weister said, 'What's all the shouting?'

'Stay out of it!' Drake shouted.

'Keep it down,' Henny said, and now his lips were bloodless.

Drake stepped forward, puffing himself up so that he towered half a foot over Henny, and clenched his big, white hands into big, white fists.

Henny turned and walked away.

Drake laughed. 'Is that the kind of man you want, Eugenia?'

'Gee, dad,' she replied, 'these TV Westerns get lousier every day.'

'Yeah,' Drake said, not sure whom she was criticizing.

But she cleared that up immediately. 'I knew you were square, Laird, but I didn't know you were stupid. Buying me a bowl of rice and a pot of Scotch doesn't pin us for the apple-knocking festival. We dig a different beat.'

He blinked, looked as if he were about to cry, and then flushed angrily. 'You bet! I never could get along with sluts! I can make them pose for dirty cheesecake, but when it comes to making them act like ladies – '

'Have you ever considered a monkey gland?' Eugenia asked, smiling engagingly. 'It might solve your problem.'

He rushed forward, bent low and slapped her face. Her head rocked sideways and she cried out, more startled than hurt, 'Henny!'

Henny was standing in the kitchen archway. He was very pale and he said, 'I've always hated violence, Laird.'

Before Laird could figure that out, Henny disappeared. Laird straightened and stood still, shocked at himself for having struck a woman, uncertain as to what he should do now. But since Eugenia was merely staring at him, and Marv Weister and his girl were doing nothing, and Henny had left the room, he felt he would get away with the taboo act. Besides, he'd already convinced himself the people here were outside the pale, undeserving of normal gentlemanly behavior. 'Quite a crew,' he said, deepening his voice. 'Sluts and cowards.' He felt no fear, and that meant he was on top of the situation. He glanced at Marv Weister, who backed up a step. He grinned and began to feel a little uncomfortable. Time to go. Something might happen.

Something did happen. Henny came out of the kitchenette carrying two knives, one considerably longer than the other.

'I won't risk being mauled by a coward,' he said. 'I'll play it safe. Here, you take the big one.'

Laird said, 'Now who's being stupid, Eugenia?' But his voice shook.

Eugenia merely watched, certain it was some kind of a gag.

Laird laughed shakily and took the knife Henny extended. Marv Weister said, 'Henny, wait,' but Henny had already lunged forward, face stiff, rigid, intent. His friends had never seen him look like that, and it frightened them. Eugenia screamed softly, covering her mouth with both hands. Weister stumbled farther back into the bedroom, drawing the trembling Francie with him.

Henny didn't care about his friends. Henny didn't care about anything. Henny was no longer side-stepping the punches. He moved so quickly that Laird Drake barely had time to blink his eyes before he was overpowered.

Henny's left hand grasped Laird's right wrist and immobilized the long knife. At the same time he brought his own knife flashing upward, stopping just short of the juncture of Laird's chin and neck.

For an instant the two men stood frozen, one much taller and heavier than the other. In the next instant the larger man seemed to shrink, became soft and weak, stood revealed as a terrified child. He dropped his knife and croaked, 'For the love of God, don't!'

Henny stepped back quickly. 'I wouldn't have.' He cleared his throat and made a vague gesture with his left hand. His right, still holding the knife, hung limply at his side.

Laird Drake mistook Henny's embarrassment for a return of fear and jumped on it as a way of saving face. 'If you ever work up the guts to fight fair – '

Henny interrupted sharply. 'You mean, if I ever decide to give you the advantage in height, weight and undissipated youth. No, Laird. But choose any damned weapon you want, any place.' His face was tightening again, growing strange again. 'Right now. Any weapon at all. How about cars? What could be more equal than that? We'll head for each other down a strip of road.'

Laird realized he'd made a mistake. He saw that Henny had been pushed past a certain point, a certain very dangerous point. Yet the need to save face was as strong as his fear. 'You're insane,' he whispered, loud enough for Eugenia to hear.

Henny blinked his eyes and suddenly nodded. He took a deep breath and grinned crookedly and said, 'Marv, you've got a working knowledge of abnormal psychology. What would you say I've been trying to do?'

'Get killed,' Weister murmured, still far back in the bedroom. 'Let your family collect on your ten-grand insurance.'

'You really believe that?' Henny asked.

'No. Is everything okay now?'

'Sure,' Henny said. 'Laird's going to join us in a drink. Then he'll take Eugenia home, or wherever – '

'The hell I will,' Laird said, only an instant before Eugenia said, 'The hell he will!'

Laird's voice was thick, his eyes watery; he wanted

99

desperately to be with his brother and tell him how things were always fouling up when he tried to act like a man – both with women and with other men. He wanted to ask his brother to help, to teach him to be soft and cool and near-feminine; how to withdraw from the terrifying rat race of competing with men for women. He turned to leave, then remembered his liquor and snatched it up from the red armchair. He wanted to run but instead stamped heavily to the door.

Henny was feeling ashamed and guilt-stricken. 'I was wrong, Laird.'

'Balls,' Eugenia said, smiling fondly at him.

'Exactly,' Francie said.

Marv Weister whispered, 'Let him go, Henny!'

Laird Drake had to find some sort of parting shot. 'Degenerates,' he said, and slammed the door behind him. On the way down the stairs, he couldn't hold back the tears. He wept silently, a big, blond man who looked as if he could succeed at just about anything; a big, blond man who'd failed at just about everything. When he reached the lobby, he got himself under control and dried his eyes.

On the street, he almost collided with a wiry little Puerto Rican. 'Watch where you're going!' Laird snapped. The little man stopped and put his hands on his hips. 'Eh? You say something?' Laird hurried on, afraid all over again. Those little greasers pulled knives.

He got in his Dodge convertible and drove uptown, wanting a cigarette. But he'd given them up six months ago. Cancer. He wasn't going to endanger his health for anything. He may have flunked out of pre-med in Washington Square College, but he knew enough to read behind the medical reports.

Henny Girado smoked a lot. Laird hoped the bastard got it, right in the lungs!

He suddenly decided he was going to resume his boxing course at the gym on Fifty-third Street. He'd had only two lessons, but the instructor insisted he had the makings of a 'real heavyweight slugger.' He would put himself into top shape, and one day he'd get his chance at Henny Girado.

He ignored the fact that he didn't need further training to handle Henny with his fists; it was handling Henny when Henny refused to give away odds in height and weight that was Laird's problem. It was handling Henny when Henny insisted on evening things with some sort of weapon. It was handling Henny when he didn't have the courage to handle anyone, if that anyone was determined enough to really fight back. Laird needed instruction in the development of courage or the elimination of tension.

He reached home at one A.M. Home was a spacious, gracious, four-room apartment in a finely maintained prewar house one block from the East River. His mother was reading *Vogue* in the tastefully furnished Louis XIV living room. She wore a flowered silk wrapper; her hair was in curlers, partially hidden under a plaid scarf; she was using her pince-nez. A tall, slim, somber-faced woman with very small, very bright blue eyes, she made an attractive picture – at least to Laird, and especially tonight, when he needed her strength.

'You're pale, Laird,' she said, voice high and firm. 'I wish you'd get out of that cheap studio and accept the help your brother is willing to give.'

'Was Jamie here tonight?' Laird asked.

His mother, extremely proud of a tenuous lineage with Mary, Queen of Scots, had named her two sons in what she considered the very best Scottish tradition. Her husband, a successful doctor of Swedish descent, had given in graciously, but his name was never Drake. After his death, twelve years ago, Arlene Swanson had moved from Reading, Pennsylvania, to New York City, changed her name to Mary Drake, and her sons had followed suit with their last names. But lately Mary Drake had lost a great deal of interest in her Scottish ancestry. Her doctor had told her she had 'borderline' kidneys and must be extremely careful of her diet. She was concentrating on staying alive and would probably have changed her name to Salk if she'd thought it would help her receive better care from the medical profession.

'He was. He waited for you from nine until eleven. Then he said he had to get to bed.'

Yes, but with whom? Laird thought. *Male, female or neuter?*

'He repeated that he has an opening in his place and can break you in. He said that the high-fashion photography line was consistently profitable. He said you'd make twenty thousand a year within three years.'

'Did he say how I'd have to – ' Laird exploded, and cut himself short.

His mother surprised him. 'I believe you might be happier even in that,' she murmured, raised her pince-nez and turned back to her paper.

A second later Laird had convinced himself he'd misinterpreted her. How could a woman like Mother know about things like that? And if she did know, how could she be so casual about it, especially when it involved her own sons!

No, he'd been mistaken.

But if he hadn't, what did she mean he 'might be happier even in that'? She couldn't be commenting on his manhood, or lack of it. She couldn't know he had doubts.

Impossible. He was imagining things.

They had a cup of tea together, and she read him a witty item concerning French spas and said, 'Oh, the income he left me is adequate, but I do so miss those trips to France and Italy every summer.'

'He' was Father. He was never mentioned by name. Laird could barely remember what he had looked like. Even when he'd been alive, he hadn't been very important in the family. He'd always been busy with his practice.

Mother was talking about the funny people on the first floor. 'Hungarians or Rumanians or something.' She imitated their halting, accented speech, and soon Laird was laughing so hard tears came to his eyes.

When the door closed behind Laird Drake in Marv Weister's apartment, Henny stood looking down at the knife the big man had dropped. 'I need a drink,' he said. 'Or maybe a psychiatrist.'

'I'll get the drink,' Marv Weister said, emerging from the bedroom. He refused to think of his actions in connection with the moment of violence. He was an observer of events, not a lowly participant.

'And you can lie on the couch and tell us your troubles,' Eugenia said. 'Shall I get up?'

'You kidding?' Henny said, his grin returning.

'Why man,' she wailed, 'this has been such a square evening, I don't know what to do any more.'

'You know what to do.'

'And she do it good,' Francie sang.

'Which reminds me,' Henny said, and raised his voice. 'Marv, put some records on that Vitaphone of yours.'

A few moments later music was playing, liquor was poured, Francie and Marv had returned to the bedroom to discuss literature.

Henny put out the lights and motioned Eugenia to her feet. They danced a while and then stopped dancing. They kept moving to the music and went slowly into an embrace and kissed. They returned to the couch, and

103

Eugenia said softly, seriously, 'If you weren't so broke, Henny, I'd try to make it with you for keeps. We could both do worse.'

'*You* couldn't do worse, Irish.'

'That's a sneaky way out.'

He grinned and nodded. 'Yeah.' He kissed her, caressed her.

Some moments later he said, 'Let's see what the Johns paid for at the Latin Quarter. Let's have the routine.'

'You going *voyeur*, Henny?'

He shrugged.

She said, 'Okay,' and stood up and stripped quickly, dropping her clothes to the floor, retaining only her high-heeled shoes. She swayed to the music a moment, getting the beat, recalling a particular routine, and began to dance. It was a dance from a choreographer's fantasies, a routine with a single aim – the arousal of the audience. At first, she barely moved, her high heels motionless on the threadbare carpet as her hips began a languorous undulation in time to the slow beat. Her arms were by her sides, but slowly, in sequence with the music, they rose, stroking her thighs and hips, moving up to cup her breasts. She lifted them, her whole body moving now, pushing them together, her thumbs caressing the nipples so that they erected. Henny stared, fascinated. Eugenia licked her lips suggestively, staring back from under hooded lids. She took her hands away from her superb bosom and raised them above her head. She turned until her back faced Henny and he was watching her enticing bottom jiggle to the sound of the Vitaphone. She ran her hands down her sides, watching Henny over her shoulder, her face partially hidden behind a curtain of blonde hair. When she turned towards him again her hands covered the honey-colored thicket between her legs. She moved her feet apart, her head arching back as she swayed.

Henny's eyes roved over her magnificent body as his breath quickened and he felt his need of her mounting. She leant back from the waist, her hips thrusting forward, and as the music reached its climax her hands parted, moving to her hips.

Henny sighed. 'Oh, baby.' He stared at the moist red lips exposed by her wanton posture. The music crescendoed and died away. Eugenia ceased her seductive undulations and came towards him. Henny reached for her, wanting her.

But never before had he needed stimulation with anyone as beautiful as Eugenia Randolph. And even as he drew her down on the couch, he knew he was with the wrong woman.

They were *all* the wrong woman.

The right woman was buried in a Long Island cemetery.

7

It was two-thirty Wednesday morning when Henny escorted Eugenia and Francie from Marv Weister's apartment and put them in a cab. Then he got in his Chevy and headed for the Queens Midtown Tunnel. The air was clear and mild; the streets just about deserted. There were isolated pedestrians, a few couples standing out in front of night spots waiting for transportation, all-night-eatery help grabbing breaths of grease-free air at alley entrances to kitchens, an alcoholic draped over a brownstone's stoop, cops patrolling their beats. There were occasional automobiles – mainly cabs – and several patrol cars.

Henny rolled down his windows and absorbed the feel of the city, never really quiet, never really asleep in the way that other towns sleep. It was as if something huge and restive had dropped to its knees and bowed its head. But one knew it was still quite conscious. The city, the million-tongued chatterer, mumbled softly.

Henny usually enjoyed these late hours. He'd experienced many of them since Doris had died. He felt more awake then than during the daylight hours. He was, in the words of a disk jockey, one of the Night People.

But tonight he was old and tired: old with the suspicion that nothing really good would happen to him in the years ahead; tired with the bone-deep tiredness of a man who has gone through the motions of love, the futile motions of irreplaceable love.

He thought of the Bessie Smith records he'd loaned Jess. Bessie Smith had captured that bone-deep despair, at the same time retaining her shouting vigor. Like Henny Girado, he thought. The body goes strong, but the spirit sinks, sinks . . .

He was suddenly frightened. He tried to think of his little girl, but it did no good.

He began to sing, imitating Bessie:

> Once you had it all, daddy,
> Now it's gone.

He grinned crookedly and sang another Bessie Smith favorite:

> There's no sweet talk when you're stoney broke.

He put on the radio and fiddled with the dial and settled for a jockey who featured commercial tunes. He didn't really hear them anyway. He just drove and watched the city slip by and refused to think of tomorrow.

But when he woke up early that morning, he had to think. It was seven-thirty Wednesday, and if he slept any longer the housekeeper would leave and he would have to spend the whole day taking care of Syl. And somehow he couldn't stand still for that. He had to move. He had to keep moving. He had to work off the deep, deep blues.

> Once you had it all, daddy,
> Now it's gone.

He got into shirt and pants and padded in stockinged feet to the kitchen. The housekeeper was there. Syl wasn't, and he heard her playing in her room. He spoke quickly, barely looking at the woman, not wanting to see her and hear her and get involved with this apartment, this home he and Doris had loved, a place he couldn't tolerate today.

'I've got to go out,' he said.

'My day off,' she began, but he cut her short.

'I'll pay twenty dollars. To you, or to someone from your agency. Get me someone, huh? It's important.'

'You should spend time with your little girl, Henny. You should let her know you love her.'

'Yeah. But not today.' He turned and moved toward the bathroom. 'I'm going to wash. Get me someone, please.' He didn't wait for further arguments. He had to run and keep running. This was blue, blue Wednesday.

When he was washed and dressed, he re-entered the kitchen. Syl was at the table, and she said, 'Daddy! I wanna ride a pony. Take me.'

'Some other time,' he muttered, and stepped forward and kissed her cheek and stepped away. He didn't really look at her. He couldn't. He spoke to the housekeeper. 'You got someone to come over?'

'I stay myself,' she said. And then, whispering, 'Look at your baby, Henny. Look at her. She going to cry!'

He said, 'I'll buy you a present, Syl. I'll . . .' But there was no time for more. He didn't want time for more. He paid the housekeeper her salary, plus twenty dollars, and left.

He had breakfast in a luncheonette near the studio. When he finished, he walked around the block. It was a quarter to nine, and people were hurrying to their jobs, and he wondered how many were happy.

Once you had it all, daddy,
Now it's gone.

As he came around the corner and approached the studio, he found himself hurrying with the rest of the

108

crowd. He had to move fast. He had to get busy. He had to dig up an assignment. Of the four hundred dollars Richie had given him, he had only thirty-one left. And he still had to send Elsa another hundred, hundred and fifty. And she actually needed another two, three hundred to get in the clear. And he hadn't paid a dime to the Grayson Collection Agency, or any of his many creditors who hadn't hired collection agencies, yet. And next week was the rent on the apartment – one hundred fifty-six dollars. And the housekeeper's eighty-buck tab came week after week. And he needed money for the studio rent – a hundred twenty a month, due in ten days. And the bank would come up again in four weeks – forty bucks. And all the friends – or ex-friends.

He hurried. He hurried and sweated and wondered why the hell it all seemed to be closing in on him. He'd been more or less surviving, borrowing a buck here, paying a buck there, taking the dunnings with a little cold sweat, so why was it beginning to close in on him *now?*

He was running by the time he reached the door to the narrow, three-story building. He went up the stairs, two at a time, and almost knocked down a slender, elderly woman on the first-floor landing.

'Oh!' she said, and staggered.

He grabbed her arm. 'I'm sorry.'

She straightened her black-frame glasses and nodded. 'Nobody killed, thank God.' She looked at him. 'You shouldn't rush so. It's bad for the heart. My husband, God rest his soul, used to say whenever he saw anyone rushing. "Hey, mister, going to a funeral?"' She laughed, her shoulders shaking, barely making a sound. 'Poor Morris. He took it easy all his life, and still he died of a heart attack.' She looked at Henny again. 'If you knew my Morris, you'd laugh too. He always liked a joke, even

109

if it was on him. And he was so sure he'd outlive the world.'

Henny grinned and felt himself relaxing. The woman turned, about to open the door newly stenciled, GERNSTEIN & SON, HAIR GOODS. Henny suddenly wanted to prolong this conversation. Mom had spoken with an Italian inflection, and this was Jewish, he guessed; but the same cheerful acceptance of life, and death, was there.

'My name's Henny Girado,' he said quickly. 'I'm with the studio upstairs.'

She faced him again, her hand falling from the knob. 'Oh. The photographers. I met a man who said he was your shoeshine boy. But I don't think so.'

'Shoeshine boy?'

'A colored man. I think I was foolish. I think I insulted him.'

'He told you he was a shoeshine boy?'

She nodded. 'I think I should apologize to him. I asked if he was the porter or the janitor.'

Henny sighed. 'Van Roberts. He's a photographer.'

'Yes. I thought so later. I'm a stupid old woman. I'm not used to colored people smarter than me.'

Henny said, 'You'll have to come upstairs someday, with your co-workers, and look around and meet everyone. Then you and Van can become friends.'

She smiled, her teeth gray and obviously false. But her smile was still innocent, childlike, pure. 'I'd like to, Mister Girado.'

'Henny.'

'Ah. Henny. And I'm Mrs Gretz.' She hesitated. 'Eva Gretz.'

Henny put out his hand, and she placed hers in it. Then she said what he'd been hoping she'd say: 'Won't you come inside and look around *our* place? The boss,

110

Mr Gernstein, doesn't get in until nine-fifteen, nine-thirty. The son even later. And it's only the son who acts like a boss.' She made a face. 'Ah, so maybe he's got a bad life at home, or he wanted to be a violinist or something.'

Henny grinned.

She opened the door, and they entered what had been five separate offices and a storage room when the insurance company had been there. Now it was one huge room, with a tiny cubicle of a glass-walled office at the far end. Spaced around the huge room were ten or twelve wooden tables, a little longer than ordinary kitchen size, with two chairs at most and four at a few.

Six or seven women were already present, all elderly, and one table had its full complement of two. They sat facing each other, both working at the same job in the same manner.

'Weavers,' Eva Gretz said. 'Like me. See? It's easy, but it hurts the fingers.' She held out a hand, and he saw the grooved, worn, calloused fingers. 'Still, it's a living. Where else could an old lady make sixty, sixty-five dollars a week and not have to fight with young girls for the job? The young girls don't learn this job. A few, maybe, but the old ladies got the experience.' She led him over to the occupied table and nodded at the two women and said to Henny, 'You watch. Maybe you'll become a weaver too.' She laughed, and the two elderly women laughed, and Henny grinned.

'I'm going to the washroom to change,' Eva Gretz said. 'You look around, Henny.'

Henny stayed where he was. The two weavers were working on separate, identical looms which resembled nothing so much as detached banjo or violin strings. There were three of these strings on each loom, set one above the other, strung between foot-long poles. The

111

poles were about four feet apart and screwed into special vises which were clamped to the table's edge, one on each side of the weaver. To the weaver's left, the pole had a nail driven into it, and the three, black-thread 'strings' were tied to this nail. To the weaver's right, the pole had holes drilled through it, and into three of these holes were set long pegs around which were wound more than a normal spool of the strong, thick, black thread – for future weavings, obviously. The threads therefore started from the pegs as a banjo's strings might, separated by about an inch of space, and grew closer and closer together until they met at the nail.

In front of the weaver and slightly to her right was a thick bundle of hair pinned to the table by a removable metal rectangle of spikes set in a thick metal top – something like ten or twelve steel combs welded together and shoved teeth-down over the bundle of hair. The weaver reached for the hair, pinched off a small amount between thumb and forefinger and drew it from the bundle with a quick, jerking motion. The comb-toothed affair gave her a fifteen- or sixteen-inch tail of straight hair to work with. She then swung to the right – the end of the loom which had space between the black threads. Quickly, expertly, intricately, her hands flew through the taut threads, weaving one end of the thin tail of hair onto them. Then, with a thin, squealing sound (which was lessened by frequent applications of vaseline to the thread), she drew the hair to the left, and it was dangling next to the previously woven tail. As the line of tails grew longer – grew closer to the right – the weaver loosened her pegs, allowing the loom flexibility, allowing the line of tails to reach almost to the pegs without snapping the thread. The total effect, after the thread was cut a few inches from the pegs and tied together to prevent the tails from slipping off, was of a thin curtain

112

of shimmering hair, yellow blond in both cases under Henny's examination.

Then Eva Gretz was standing beside him, dressed in a faded blue cotton housedress. 'This hair,' she said, 'it sticks to everything, no matter what you do to clean it off, and it comes off on everything at home – the furniture, the food, everything. So we keep our work dresses here and change into them in the washroom. You like our business?'

Henny nodded. 'Interesting. What do you call the finished lines of hair?'

'Ah, you mean the switches.'

'And what happens to the switches when they're complete?'

She walked to a cardboard carton lying against the wall under a window, stooped and held up a completed curtain of hair. 'A switch. Then it goes to the wheels.' She moved to another table, where instead of two looms were four small black 'wheels' – short, thick metal spokes emanating from a removable hub. She sat down, grasped a spoke, gave it a turn. The rimless 'wheel' spun until the spokes seemed to blend into a solid mass. She pointed to the back of the 'wheel.' 'We tie one end of the switch here. Not me, because I'm a weaver. Then we turn the wheel so and twist the hair in and out, and soon you have a beautiful chignon to make your wife's hair look thicker, or to make some actress have pigtails, or to hide some older woman's bald spots.'

'Do you make toupees?'

'Wigs for men?' She shook her head. 'And we don't make them for ladies either. We just make the switches and the chignons. But the boss sends lots of switches to customers, and what they do with them I don't know. I think *they* must be the wig-makers.'

'So this could be called a raw-hair factory?'

113

'It's not even hair,' she said, and laughed at his surprised expression. 'It's made by some chemistry, some Du Pont. Who knows. But it's not real hair.' She walked to a loom table near the hall door, sat down and reached underneath to one of the ubiquitous cardboard cartons. She drew out a thick bundle of unwoven black hair tied with a rubberband. 'Feel it,' she said.

He felt it. 'Hair,' he said. 'Thick, soft hair.'

'Ah, you don't know hair. You didn't work with it all your life. In the old days we used to get *real* hair, lots from China, some from Europe, and some from right here in the States. The women would sell their hair. Sure, people were poor and they needed money and the women sold their long, beautiful hair. They didn't wear it like boys then. They wore it down to here.' She slapped her waist. 'Or they wore it tied in a big bun, and when they let it out – ' she slapped her waist again – 'down to here! Now even an old lady like me has a boy's haircut.' (Her hair was a very full bob, coming to just below the ears. The color was almost solid gray, with just a hint of what once must have been a startling red.)

'Thanks for the tour,' he said.

'So maybe someday you'll snap my picture,' she said, and took the bundle of hair from him. She placed it on the table, put a spike-toothed affair over it, began stringing her loom. 'It's late, and the old lady has to earn her bread and butter.'

Henny looked around and saw that the tables were filling with women. 'Do you think anyone would mind if I came back with a camera and stayed out of the way and took a few shots?'

'Who should mind?' she said, and smiled up at him. 'Just so long as I get my picture.'

He nodded and walked toward the door.

A woman sitting at the table behind Mrs Gretz's must

114

have been listening to their conversation, because she called out, 'Eva, tell him about Arnold. The Stinker might bother him.'

Henny stopped. 'The son?' he asked.

Eva Gretz nodded, beginning to weave. 'We call him the Stinker. Even if he uses perfume, he still smells bad, inside.'

The woman at the table behind and other women now working at other tables laughed. Henny grinned and went out the door.

He reached the second-floor landing and went to Marie's desk. 'I got a call yesterday, doll. I couldn't answer it. Any message?'

She checked her notebook. 'Yes. Please call Mr Carl Stevens at Treakle's Everything-Photographic.'

'Yeah,' he said flatly, and went back to the stairs and up to the third floor. He didn't have what Carl Stevens wanted – money.

But maybe he'd come up with some if the hair-goods place worked into a picture story. Maybe a big market like *Look*.

He stopped the daydream short. Daydreams were dangerous. He'd learned that lesson thoroughly in the last three years. Daydreams softened you up so that you couldn't take the next stiff hook to the guts, the next call from a Carl Stevens.

He slung his gadget bag over his shoulder, a camera around his neck, and went back down to the first floor.

When he opened the door to Gernstein & Son, he stopped short, swinging his head to encompass everything, absorbing the sight and sound and smell of the place. And he caught fire. Intellect and emotion melded in that delicate, subconscious combination that is necessary to any work of art. Though he would have winced at the thought, he became a camera, a living lens, and

115

swallowed his subject matter – which was a room full of elderly women, some thirty of them, and an elderly man just sitting down behind a metal desk in a tiny office.

The women were weaving in uneven rhythm, some finishing the swing of torso to the left, others starting the weaving process by leaning to the right, still others in mid-swing. The motion took on a oneness in Henny's eyes, a unity of visual symbolism – reapers in a field of hair; oarsmen on a sea of hair; people struggling, but beautifully, to maintain themselves. *Old* reapers, *old* oarsmen, *old* people struggling to maintain themselves in a basically young world.

His Nikon was out of its case a moment after he shut the door behind him. Sticking close to the wall, he moved slowly around the room, shooting quickly, almost frantically. His breath came fast, and he perspired, and then he was twisting to face the wall and changing film, and twisting again to shoot.

God, they were tremendous, these women! Their faces, so intent, or empty, or peaceful, or packed with emotion. Their work was automatic, and in their faces Henny, and his camera, read their long eventful lives. For, by the foreign languages and accented English he heard, he knew that these were women who had lived in another world as children, or maidens. These were women whose worn faces, swinging, creaking bodies and calloused, surprisingly quick hands were the products of a world infinitely foreign to modern-day America. These were women who had always worked and would always work, in a way that the readers of *Redbook*, or *Ladies' Home Journal*, or any big, middle-class American magazine could never parallel in their own lives. And so there might be a valid lesson here for American women, and subsequently a valid sale. But Henny couldn't give more

116

than a split second to the thought of market and viewer; he was too far gone in his work, his art.

Four rolls of black-and-white 35 millimeter gone, and he reloaded and stepped away from the wall and moved between the tables as quietly, as unobtrusively as possible, kneeling every so often to flash his gaze, his camera gaze, into the face of a subject, to get behind a three-string loom or a blur-spoked 'wheel' and shoot, quickly, the heart of a human being and the intricate simplicity of her work.

Five rolls gone, and his shirt perspiration-soaked under his corduroy jacket, and the excitement still high, and his mind stating briefly, astutely, 'Another three, four rolls, at least. Shoot fast, fast, fast – before too many of them stop working to watch, or work with the knowledge that they're subjects and not people, or someone breaks the spell.'

He reloaded and was at Eva's table. She looked up at him and smiled, and he snatched that gray-toothed false-toothed, warm and childlike smile. She said, 'So when do I get a picture for myself?' and he caught that blur-lipped speech with his eye and even as his eye caught it his finger opened the shutter and it was his to work with later in the quiet of the darkroom, his to bring forth as the true image of an attractive human being.

Seven rolls gone and he needed more – two or three more because this was a wonderful subject and he wanted close to four hundred shots to work with, to edit, to mold into a document of eight or ten great shots.

He turned his eye and his camera to the glass office, and the old man was looking at him. He shot him, and the old man began to rise, and he shot him again and then moved quickly and faced a window full of sunlight and shot a woman standing and stretching against it, her measurements abysmal by the lexicon of the cheesecake

117

connoisseur, her reality and sympathy and humanity incredible by the lexicon of the seeker after truth.

Henny Girado was happy. He worked and sweated and exulted and was happy. God, he wanted to *swallow* this room, this visual feast!

'You must be from upstairs,' the soft uncertain voice said at his shoulder. He wanted to ignore it, to go on until there was nothing here that wasn't on his film. But the realities of his craft took precedence over the drive of his art, and he lowered his camera and composed his mind and turned, smiling, nodding. 'Yes. Morden Photos. I thought I'd take some shots of your place and present you with a few nice prints later on.' He lighted a cigarette, offering the pack to the old man, who refused them. He inhaled, and exhaled words with his smoke, casual words: 'I might be able to sell them to a magazine, your company would be identified by name and address, and the publicity . . .'

'I'm Mr Gernstein,' the stocky, bald-headed man said, and put out a pudgy hand. 'Louis Gernstein. I own this place – me and my son.'

Henny shook the hand and smiled and dragged on his cigarette. 'Mind if I continue, Mr Gernstein? I haven't much time.'

'Sure. Go ahead. I'll just watch.'

Henny figured the cream was just about gone from this setup, but he dropped the cigarette and stepped on it and raised his camera. He'd taken seven more shots and was beginning to warm to the angle of shooting only hands in this final series when a strident, unpleasant voice said, 'What d'you think *you're* doing?'

Henny turned and saw the youngish man – twenty-five, he guessed – about two inches shorter than him and a little heavier and already half bald. His face was wide and his eyes deep, and those eyes were jumpy, betrayed a pervasive irritability, a blanketing unhappiness.

'I told him he could take the pictures, Arnold,' Louis Gernstein said, coming forward. 'He's our neighbor from upstairs.'

The unhappy young man looked at his father and said, 'Sure, and then he sticks you with a set of lousy pictures you don't want.'

Henny said, 'I'm going to use them myself – or try to use them – in a magazine story.'

'*That's* a magazine story,' the young man said, and swaggered to the office. At the door, he stopped, turned, called out, 'All right, girls, don't let the hair turn gray waiting for weaving!'

The father smiled apologetically at Henny. 'Maybe you'd better come back tomorrow morning.'

'Thanks, Mr Gernstein, but I was finished anyway.' He walked toward the hall door, slowing as he reached Eva's table.

She looked up at him and nodded sadly. 'The Stinker,' she murmured. 'Didn't I tell you? He don't know how to live, poor fool.'

'Exactly,' Henny said, wanting to stop but afraid of drawing the Stinker's attention to her. He adjusted his camera to explain his slow shuffle. 'I'll have your pictures ready in a few days. We'll make you the new pin-up sensation.'

'Yeah, sure,' she said. 'The pin-up of the Golden Age Center.' Her tablemate choked back laughter, and a woman at a 'wheel' table to the left also laughed and repeated Eva's statement to her three companions. The entire table laughed, and in a moment half the room was laughing.

'Hey!' the Stinker called from the office. 'What's this, girls – a night club or something? Let's get to work!'

Henny stepped into the hallway. The Stinker would kill himself trying to crush that crew. It was like trying to swim *up* Niagara Falls. Not a chance, man, not a chance!

He intended to go straight to the darkroom and work on the shots, but when he reached the second-floor landing, he saw a girl talking to Marie and heard Marie saying, 'I'm sorry. You *can't* go in. Only photographers and models are allowed in the studio. Besides, there's work going on.'

Ordinarily, Henny wouldn't have interfered. Marie was right – strangers, no matter how attractive weren't allowed to watch shootings. But this was different. The girl wasn't really a stranger. Her face had been puzzling Henny with its vague familiarity since yesterday afternoon. She was the blonde who had driven Les Bogen away in a Hillman Minx convertible; the blonde who had seemed to fascinate the experienced lecher as no woman had before, so far as Henny knew.

He hesitated a moment, almost reluctant to approach her, to expose himself to what he sensed – in one of those strange, prognostical flashes people call hunches – would be a terribly important meeting. Then he kicked the feeling and came toward them, saying, 'Hold it, Marie. She's a friend of Les Bogen's.'

8

The blonde turned to look at Henny as he approached, and again he was struck by the feeling he'd seen her before, or perhaps someone who looked very much like her.

'Les Bogen's friend?' Marie said, and fresh irritation sharpened her words as she saw, or sensed, Henny's interest in this girl. 'Why didn't she say so? All she said was that she wanted to do modeling and could she watch a photographer work.'

'Have we met?' the girl asked Henny. Her voice was distinctive – deep and throaty. Her delivery was also distinctive – slow, hesitant.

'I don't think so,' Henny said, looking her over. 'My name's Henny Girado.'

She smiled. 'Oh yes. Les talked about you quite a bit. Could you help me? I'd like to see the studio.'

'Hasn't Les shown you around?' Henny muttered, still busy looking her over, absorbing her freshness, her remarkable freshness. She was eighteen or nineteen, he guessed; about five-three, with sweet legs and narrow waist and good breasts. Her dress was a modified shirt-waist, light green, neither bargain basement nor Bergdorf Goodman. She had dark-blond hair, clean and shiny, worn boy-style. Her hairline was a half-moon, leaving not too much forehead, and her eyes were medium sized, light brown, rather narrow. Her nose was thin on top, wider at the base; not large and not small.

He decided it was a good nose. He decided everything about her was good. But her mouth was something special: very wide, with very good teeth behind it. Very mobile. Very, very kissable.

'Mr Morden doesn't like people standing around the reception desk,' Marie said sharply, rather hopelessly. She turned away from them, away from Henny's eyes looking at this girl, this *stranger*, with such personal intensity, such hunger.

The blonde's eyes dropped as Henny continued to stare. 'This is my first visit here.' She paused. 'If we haven't met how do you know Les and I – ' She raised her eyes again and made a little gesture with her hand, as if to bring Henny back to normal social behavior.

Henny grinned. 'Sorry.' He answered her question. 'Saw you driving away from the studio yesterday afternoon in a little convertible.'

'Oh.' She smiled. (As if relieved, Henny thought.) 'Well, since Les isn't here, will *you* take me inside?'

'Sure.' He moved past her to the studio door, opened it and held it as she walked past him.

Marie made a sharp sound of disapproval. Understanding, Henny turned his head, winked at her, murmured, 'Now, now, we must treat the great Bogen's fans with respect, mustn't we, Marie?'

Remembering the talk about Bogen, Marie tried to feel contempt for the blonde. But remembering Henny's obvious interest, she couldn't.

And neither could Henny, as he closed the door to the studio and watched the blonde walk to the old black-leather couch.

This chick didn't fit the mold. This chick seemed too unaffected, physically as well as mentally.

But then he laughed at himself. Les Bogen wasn't one to carry on platonic relationships.

He joined the blonde on the couch, dumped gadget bag and camera, and slid over close to her. 'That's Van

Roberts shooting the mulatto girl for *Tan* and *Jet*. Les tell you about him?'

She nodded, eyes fixed on the shooting area. Van was using a Rollei and color film. His model was a tall, fleshy, light-skinned, extremely pretty girl named Loretta Clark who'd appeared in many Negro magazines recently because of the combination of her looks and a very saucy, jutting rear end which she manipulated to fullest advantage. Loretta wore heels and pink-net tights. The tights left nothing to the imagination, but Van was shooting so that the laws against pornography would be circumvented.

The colored photographer finished a roll, turned to reload and winked at Henny. 'Loretta was just telling me she'd like to change her luck and date an ofay for a change. You free tonight, Henny?'

The model giggled. 'Van! I'm never gonna tell you anything again! And I didn't say *change my luck!*'

Henny stood up and bowed low. 'Loretta you name the time and pad.'

Loretta giggled again and shook her head. 'If I do take that plunge, I'll do it only once. And if I do it only once, I want the name, the champ, the big man in the field.'

Henny glanced at the blonde, but she was merely watching, listening. She didn't seem to know who Loretta was talking about.

Les must have dug this one out of a finishing school!

Van said, 'You'll have to stand in line, honey. Mr Bogen's willing, all right – no silly ole prejudices *there* – but he's handling two, three a week.'

The blonde had stiffened. Van went on, kidding the voluptuous model as he finished loading his camera. The blonde became progressively more pale.

'Hey,' Henny said, mouth suddenly dry, heart pounding

– for no damn reason at all, he told himself. 'I hear you might take off for Puerto Rico, Van. What's the score?'

Van Roberts stopped speaking of a book he thought Les Bogen should write, titled *What Kinsey Didn't Know*, and gave Henny a puzzled look. 'Hell, man, you know about that local Mardi gras. I told you myself only the other day.'

'Yeah, but I want to know exactly when and where and so on,' Henny replied, floundering in his sympathetic reaction for the blonde, who was still sitting stiff and pale.

And then she said, voice a little deeper than before, 'Bogen's the real thing when it comes to Romeos, isn't he, Van?'

The photographer was ready to go with his next roll. He nodded, directed Loretta into a hands-on-knees, head-turned-to-look-over-shoulder, derrière-into-camera shot, and said, 'Hold that sensitive pose, momma.' He snapped her again, and again, then placed her in a new pose, using a chair and a mop, and answered the blonde. 'The real thing, all right. Don't you know our great Mr Bogen, or are you a man in disguise?'

Henny said quietly, 'She dates him, Van.'

Van shot again, nodded, sighed, said, *'Oy vay.'* He turned, rubbing his chin. 'And you asked *me.*' He shrugged. 'Lady, Les Bogen never hid his history before, so I refuse to feel crushed.'

The blonde laughed, but it didn't fool Henny. 'Just a gag, Van.'

'Hah!' Van said, and smiled, obviously relieved. 'That's a short-lived gag when the subject's the big man.' He began shooting again.

Henny leaned back, looking at the shooting area but not seeing it. He was trying to figure out this girl; and he was waiting for her next move.

124

Richie Morden came in. 'Morning, all.' He walked to the couch, nodded at Henny and looked at the blonde. Henny said, 'Richie, this is – ' he turned to the blonde, realizing he didn't know her name – 'the mystery woman,' he said, grinning, hoping she'd smile the way she had before at Marie's desk.

She smiled, but it wasn't much more than a muscular display. 'Norma,' she murmured.

'Norma,' Henny said. 'She's a friend of Les's. Dropped around, but Les was out.'

'Les is in Reading, Pennsylvania,' Van said. 'He'll be shooting out there until Sunday or Monday, depending on the weather. Didn't he tell you, Norma?'

She hesitated, then nodded. 'I came up to look around on my own.'

'Norma wants to model,' Henny said. And to the blonde, 'Richie owns the place.'

The blonde stood up. 'I have to go now.' She didn't look at anyone.

Richie flicked his eyes over her. 'I know, honey. We're very dull compared to Monsieur Le Bogen.'

Van laughed, and the blonde showed her teeth. Richie was smiling at his own joke, but when he looked at the blonde his smile died and he murmured, 'Ooops. Did I say something wrong?' And then, before she could answer, 'It was never wrong before.'

The blonde's voice was tight. 'You must all be very confused people. You say what you claim you've always said about Les Bogen and then you apologize for it.' She walked to the door.

'Leave your address and phone number with the receptionist,' Richie Morden called, glancing at Henny and raising his shoulders. 'I'm sure we can throw some work your way, Norma.'

She stopped but didn't turn. 'Thank you. I . . . Good-bye.' She walked out.

Henny wanted to go after her, but he was too confused by the whole bit to know what to say, or to want to say anything.

At the same time his mind went back to a phone call he'd made four or five months ago, and he began considering one possible explanation for Norma's face seeming familiar to him. Except that if he was right, her name wouldn't be Norma.

'That wasn't a happy girl,' Loretta said, pulling in her valuable can. 'What gives, daddy?'

Van Roberts turned to Henny and Richie. 'Yeah, what gives?'

Richie said, 'It's obvious, isn't it? She's got a case on Les Bogen.'

Henny muttered, 'All together, men.'

'Oy vay,' the three photographers said. They looked at one another, and then Richie and Van laughed.

Henny grabbed his equipment and walked out before they could see *he* wasn't laughing. He stopped at the desk and asked Marie whether the blonde had left her name and number.

'No,' Marie said coldly. 'Anyway, if she's Les Bogen's girl friend . . .'

Henny sighed. 'You're beginning to drag a little. Remember what I told you about the receptionist we had to ship back to Staten Island? Brooklyn's even closer.' He went to the staircase and up to the third floor.

Marie handled a call for Richie Morden, switching it to the studio. A delivery came in and she signed for it and put it aside for Les Bogen. Then she called her friend Roberta to set the time for their lunch date. Roberta would call June and Carrie. Marie hoped that Stella Lago wouldn't come along, today of all days. She said so to

Roberta. Roberta said, 'You sound nervous, Marie. Tough morning?'

Marie made sure she was alone and dropped her voice to a whisper. 'I don't know how I could've been so wrong about a guy, but that Henny Girado – remember the one I always said was nice? – well, he's turning out to be a real *bum!*'

She had to cut the conversation short because another delivery boy arrived, and then Richie Morden came out of the studio and gave her a list of supplies to order for Van Roberts and himself.

But later, combing her dark hair in the washroom, she thought of Henny and of how he was always being called by people asking for money, and of how a few had even come up to the studio, and her mouth twisted. The longings she'd had for him, the completely thwarted longings, helped the first buds of hatred and contempt take shape. Even if he was a photographer and she only the receptionist, she still did better than him financially, in the long run. Maybe Mr Morden would get tired of Henny one of these days. Maybe the people to whom Henny owed money would make trouble, real trouble. Maybe then Mr Smart Guy Girado would see who got tossed out of Morden Photos!

Leaving the washroom, she almost bumped into Henny, who was on his way to the darkroom. He grinned and said, 'Hey, don't ever take me serious, like when I bite your head off.' He continued on his way.

But this time, despite her natural inclination to do so, she didn't melt and reinstate him as her dream man. This time she brought back all the bitterness she'd felt when he'd . . . *ogled* the blonde. This time she made herself see him as a sinner, an evil man, a leering lecher with designs on anything in skirts. Anything except *her* – which was the thought she tried to block and couldn't block,

127

the thought which made her hatred and contempt grow stronger.

'We'll see,' she muttered as she stalked toward the Automat. 'We'll see who gets shipped to Brooklyn. We'll see.'

She had no plan. She didn't actually believe what she was thinking. But it made her feel good. And if anyone ever asked her advice about Mr Girado – *well!*

After Henny left the studio, Richie Morden and Van Roberts discussed the blond visitor, Norma. Van found it hard to believe that Les hadn't wised her up thoroughly before moving in. 'He operates only one way, Richie. He lets them know everything, if they don't already, and proceeds to capitalize on it. Also, he couldn't hide his love-life even if he wanted to. There are just too many past and present members of the club around. No, I figure that girl Norma isn't on his string. Maybe she just *knows* him.'

Loretta said, 'But that girl got *sick*, Van! I saw her face. She got sick when you was talking about Bogen. She couldn't just *know* him. She's carrying something big for him.'

'Put that in the past tense,' Richie said, turning to the door. 'If she did have any ideas of deep and tender emotions, she was shocked out of them by learning the truth. Any girl would be. It's Les's major protection. The very size of his rep with women is enough to make any one woman despair of a regular boy-girl relationship.'

Morden went out to the receptionist, gave her an order list and then proceeded up the stairs to his office. As soon as he approached his desk, he saw the empty low-ball glass. He flushed and saw the two butts in the ashtray. Even before examining them, he knew what they

128

were – Camels, Henny's brand; and Henny was the only photographer in the studio who didn't smoke filter tips.

He sniffed the glass. Bols, of course. Henny had impeccable taste in other people's liquor.

'Damn it!' he said aloud. 'I told him only yesterday!' He was heading for the door, angry enough to find Henny and tell him to pack his equipment and get out, but then he stopped and took himself in hand. No. He couldn't toss the poor bastard into the street. Who else would take him in? Besides, what did it amount to? A few cents' worth of gin every so often, a messy ashtray. What the hell.

But even as he returned to his desk and sat down, it rankled him. He liked Henny Girado a little less than he had yesterday; and yesterday he'd liked him a little less than the day before.

Laird Drake came to the studio at twelve-fifteen. He wanted to ask Marie whether Henny was around, but the receptionist had already left for lunch. Laird went to the studio door, put his hand on the knob, and hesitated. He dreaded the thought of meeting Henny. The humiliation he'd suffered last night was still too fresh in his mind. And yet he couldn't slink around.

He steeled himself and opened the door. Van Roberts looked up from his Rollei. 'Hi.'

'Hi,' Laird replied, relieved that Henny wasn't there.

'You want to do some work?' Van asked. He didn't know this relative newcomer too well; he wasn't sure whether the man would speak out if he needed the studio. 'I've been here almost three hours. I'm actually finished, but Loretta's letting me shoot some extra stuff to peddle around – '

'No, that's all right,' Laird interrupted. There was none of his usual, compulsive competitiveness present, as there

129

would have been had he been talking to any other photographer of Van's financial level, a level about equal to his own. Any *white* photographer, that is, because Laird Drake had an inherent belief in the inferiority of Negroes. No need to prove himself with *them*.

Not that he ever put this belief into words. It was just a *feeling* he had – probably the only one which gave him a degree of security and pleasure.

He nodded, began to close the door, then stopped. 'By the way, who's upstairs?'

Van Roberts had returned to his shooting. 'Got me,' he muttered, and said, 'Loretta, hold that scarf higher, higher. Yeah.'

'Is Henny up there?' Laird asked somewhat impatiently. The man might give his question a little attention!

'Think so,' Van muttered. 'Now drop it, honey.'

'Well, *thanks*,' Laird said haughtily.

Van looked up surprised. 'He was here some time ago, but he left and I'm not sure if he went up or – '

'All right,' Laird said, and shut the door.

'You know what, man?' Loretta said to Van.

Van was staring at the closed door. 'Yeah. But let's not jump to conclusions.'

Laird went up to the office he shared with Henny Girado. Quickly, he stuffed film and an assignment book into his gadget bag and headed for the darkroom where he'd stored his two Leicas in the metal cabinet. He passed the closed door to Richie's office and then was at the darkroom door, also closed. The red warning light above the frame was on, but he didn't allow himself to hesitate this time. He knocked.

'Hold it a second,' Henny's voice said.

Laird fought the urge to leave. He had an assignment:

the rehearsal of a new musical comedy featuring near-nude chorus girls. He had to get his Leicas.

'Okay,' Henny called.

Laird went in, opening and shutting the door quickly. Henny looked up from the fixer tray. He blinked and said, 'Hi, Laird. Crazy business last night, huh?'

Laird nodded, went to the cabinet, got his Leicas and turned to leave.

'Still sore?' Henny asked placatingly.

Laird went out without answering.

Henny shrugged and returned to his film. So far, it looked as if he'd done well in the hair-goods place.

A few minutes later he walked away from the trays and over to a chair against the wall near the steel cabinet. He sat down and lighted a cigarette and tried to dream up a market for the hair-goods pics; and found himself thinking of the blonde who'd called herself Norma. He didn't want to think of her, and yet he was resigned to doing so. First of all, he liked her. No getting away from it, she really sent him. And then there was his suspicion as to who she actually was.

Henny Girado had called Les Bogen's home about five months ago, against Bogen's express wishes that no one ever call his home. But he'd needed a quick hundred, desperately, and Bogen was the only hope he'd had, and so he'd called. (He got Bogen's unlisted number by walking into Richie's office and searching his desk until he found the book of 'staff' addresses and telephone numbers.) A woman had answered. He'd asked for Les, and she'd said her father was on his way into his studio in the city. Would her mother do? He'd said no thanks, it was all right and hung up. He'd remembered her voice: deep and throaty. And her delivery had been slow, almost hesitant.

Henny stood up and blew smoke toward the dim green

light and told himself he wasn't at all sure Norma was actually Les Bogen's daughter. How could he be sure when Lester kept his family completely divorced from his business; when no one in the field had ever visited Lester's home or met his wife and daughter? Outside of Richie Morden, the probability was that no one had even spoken to them on the phone.

But there was the way she'd paled when Van had kidded about Les's reputation as a lover. There was the deep shock, the deep hurt.

He winced, remembering it, and at the same time felt a touch of exultation. If she wasn't one of Les Bogen's vaginal army . . .

He laughed at himself, ground out his cigarette and got back to work. If she wasn't a member of the Bogen fan club, she was a member of the Bogen family. That made her as accessible as the Dalai Lama.

He continued working. But he didn't feel like working. He'd worked too much in the past three years. He wanted to play – really play, as he had with Doris. He wanted a woman, the right woman.

He thought of the little blonde and said aloud, 'Man, talk about your forbidden fruits!' and thought of the blonde some more. 'Sick, man, sick,' he muttered, chiding himself, warning himself.

He ate at one-thirty and thought of the blonde while sitting at the crowded, noisy counter in the crowded, noisy luncheonette. He returned to the darkroom at two-ten and thought of her while examining his negatives. Vic Bloom, the darkroom man, came in at three to do some work for Richie Morden and Laird Drake, and Henny talked to him while setting up some previously developed negatives for printing. And *still* he thought of her.

He left the studio at four-thirty and went to the Paris

theater and saw a Fernandel picture. Fernandel usually made him forget most things. Fernandel was a bust today.

Henny had dinner in an inexpensive but good French restaurant on Forty-ninth. When he finished the split of *vin ordinaire*, it was eight o'clock and quite dark outside. He began to feel panicky. He couldn't stop thinking of the girl. And he had to stop thinking of her. There were a million 'don'ts' in the way, and not a single 'do' to help him along.

He went to another movie – an English comedy. He didn't laugh. He got out at eleven-fifteen and went into a nearby bar and had four martinis. He talked to a middle-aged redhead with a nice face and a very nice body, and she seemed anxious to show him her 'cute little apartment,' and he just couldn't make himself go with her.

He began the drive home at one A.M. He felt he was coming apart at the seams. He *knew* he was when he couldn't kick an eighteen-year-old chick from his thoughts.

He sang, 'Once you had it all, daddy' at least five times and couldn't get a single laugh out of it. He put on the radio, twisted the dial, and cursed bitterly when all he could find was popular ballads and chattering disk jockeys – no jazz and no classical.

'Goddam city of morons,' he said. 'Goddam world of morons.'

Finally he said, 'Okay. So think of her, you square. Think of her!'

He dropped all his mental defenses and thought of her. He thought of taking her in his arms and kissing her and telling her he was a tired, lonely, frightened man. He thought of how her body would feel held tight against his, and how her mouth would taste. She hadn't looked more than about twenty, and he imagined her breasts would be pert and firm. He thought about touching them,

133

kissing them. He thought about her nude, waiting for him, and how it would feel to make love to her. But mostly he thought of how she'd stroke his head, his face, and soothe him, and give him her love, and make the world purposeful.

He laughed. 'And then we'll marry and live happily ever after.' He laughed again, and again, listening to the sound of it in the car. Then he stopped laughing and merely drove. His face, illuminated dimly by the dashboard lights and occasionally by street lamps, looked very much as it had the day they'd buried Doris.

Book Two

9

It was a rough week for Henny Girado. But then again, it was a rough *life* for Henny Girado, and he was used to it. He worked Saturday and Sunday, shooting a New Jersey dude ranch for Viewcitement Corporation, the cheapest magazine outfit in New York. That meant he would make under a hundred dollars after expenses, and due to his current frame of mind he didn't even have the solace of a night with some would-be model. Monday morning, he went to the studio before eight to get his hair-goods pictures in shape for Dennis Parish, the agent. He had a half-dozen black-and-whites that were really satisfying.

He hadn't seen Les Bogen since last Tuesday, and he didn't want to see him. He felt sorry for him, and he hated him – both for the same reason. That reason was still only a possibility, but one that had grown progressively stronger in Henny's mind – Les Bogen's daughter, Sandra Leslie Bogen. Henny knew her name because Les had purchased a piece of fine Oshkosh luggage two years ago and brought it to the studio and showed it to the then-secretary, Audrey Masters. Henny had happened along and asked what the initials S. L. B. stood for, and Les, preoccupied, had answered quickly, without thinking, and then pursed his lips and murmured, 'Why don't you go play some old Wayne King records?' Since Henny knew Les's wife's name was Louise (had it been Richie who'd told him that?), it stood to reason that Sandra was the daughter.

Henny worked in the darkroom until ten-fifteen, undisturbed by even his own thoughts. He'd managed to push the blonde from his mind by accepting the probability that he would never see or speak to her again. And even if he did, she wouldn't be likely to consider him an eligible male – not if she was Les Bogen's daughter.

With *that* young chick, he held nothing but deuces.

At ten-thirty, he was sitting at his desk examining the contacts he'd made of the hair-goods pictures when he heard someone enter the adjoining office. He leaned back in his chair and looked through the connecting door. 'Hi, Les.'

Les Bogen nodded and stepped out of sight. Henny put down the contact sheets, lighted a cigarette and waited. Les Bogen reappeared, coming through the door. He seemed to be his usual, urbane, composed self, but there was no way of reading those ancient eyes.

'How've you been, big man?' Henny murmured.

Les dragged Laird Drake's chair away from the door wall and placed it alongside Henny's desk. He sat down, ran a pinkie over his mustache, said, 'As always, Henny. As always.' But in the next instant he showed Henny he was lying. 'Richie told me you were present when a young blonde came to the studio and introduced herself as a friend of mine – Norma. Remember her?'

Henny nodded and called himself a jerk for the sick feeling, the vicarious feeling of despair. It was Les Bogen's life and Les Bogen's daughter. Henny Girado had troubles of his own.

'Yeah,' he said. 'Nice. She didn't stay long.' He picked up his contact sheets, hoping Les would let it go at that. He just wasn't up to playing games.

'The way Richie tells it, she became rather disturbed when certain humorous allusions were made as to my many friends.'

Henny shrugged, eyes on the contacts. He knew what Les was after – assurance that Henny Girado had no idea as to the blonde's actual identity. With Richie and Van obviously in the dark, he was the only one left.

'You were sitting right beside her, Henny. Would you say she was disturbed?'

'I guess so,' Henny muttered, flipping to another contact. 'I didn't really notice, Les. Loretta Clark was on the shooting stage and that rear of hers always gets me.'

'I share your interest in Miss Clark. In fact, I intend to investigate further someday.'

Henny looked up at that point and met Les Bogen's ancient eyes. They were narrow now, probing now. Henny answered in the way best calculated to reassure Bogen; the way Bogen had indicated with his remark about Loretta. 'And I share your interest in Norma. Just let me know . . .' He couldn't finish. Les Bogen hadn't flushed, or paled, or even blinked his eyes, but he had laughed. And Les Bogen rarely laughed, and *never* at crude remarks. It was the tip-off to his anger, his pain, and his relief at what he thought was Henny's ignorance of the truth.

When Henny stopped in mid-sentence, Les Bogen's relief gave way to renewed concern. 'Let you know what, Henny?'

Henny suddenly had enough. 'I've got an important call to make, Les. Excuse me, will you?'

'Certainly.' Bogen stood up and walked toward his own office, but he paused in the doorway. Henny quickly picked up the phone and asked for an outside line. 'Close the door, will you, Les? I wouldn't want to corrupt your morals.'

Bogen smiled thinly and complied. Henny waited a moment, then hung up. He smoked his cigarette and thought of Les Bogen and thought of the blonde.

Trouble. Pain. Why the hell did life have to get so complicated? Why the hell couldn't people just go along, quietly, having a few laughs and a few kicks? Why was there always a hangover after the ball?

The phone rang. He looked at it, afraid to answer, afraid not to answer. It might be the collection agency or another creditor. It might also be one of the several small magazine outfits that used him for quick assignments such as Viewcitement Corporation.

He didn't have any assignments lined up until the Hawaiian *luau* bit next week, and half the pay-off on *that* was down the drain. A man had to expect dead periods between assignments, but if he could just get a little ahead this month.

He answered on the fourth ring and recognized the voice immediately despite its quality of brittle nervousness.

'Mr Girado?'

'Yes.'

'This is Norma. I wonder if you're free for lunch today?'

'Why?'

'I beg your pardon?'

'Why do you want to have lunch with me?'

She didn't answer for a moment; then, 'Does a girl have to give reasons in a case like this?'

'Definitely, in a case like this.'

Another pause. 'My name isn't Norma, Mr Girado.'

'My name is Henny, Miss Bogen.'

'How did you know?'

'I recognized something of Les in your face, I guess.'

'No one else did.'

'Maybe no one else looked at you the way I did.'

Some of the brittleness left her voice. 'Oh? And how *did* you look at me?'

'A girl usually notices things like that.'

'I'm afraid I wasn't thinking of things like that.'

140

'You were thinking of your father.'

'Yes.'

'And you still are.'

'Well, not entirely.' She stopped and laughed unconvincingly.

'*I'm* not interested in your father, Miss Bogen. At least not in the way you want me to be. I won't spend a lunch giving details.'

'Details,' she intoned.

He said nothing.

She said nothing.

The silence dragged out to a full minute.

'Well, it was nice talking to you, Miss Bogen. If you'd like to speak to your father, he's at his desk in the next office. At least he was there a few minutes ago. But you'll have to call him direct. I won't go in and say, "Sandra's on the line, Les." Because he doesn't know I know who you are. And there's no reason to let him know. It'll only make him more unhappy.'

'Why should he be unhappy?' she said coldly. 'He still has his women, hasn't he?'

'Yes. But has he still got you?'

'That's none of your business!'

'Exactly. Goodbye. Nice meeting you.' He wanted to hang up, cut out on this lousy situation, this senseless conversation. But he also wanted to keep listening to her husky, throaty voice. 'Maybe you'll accept your father as he is in a few weeks. Maybe you'll forget about . . . the details. Maybe then if you want to have lunch, we'll make it.'

'Have you got a reputation similar to Daddy's?'

'Goodbye,' he said again, and this time he did hang up.

He put the contacts in the drawer and ground out his

cigarette butt and stood up. The phone rang. He sat down again.

'Mr Girado?'

'How nice to speak to you, Miss Bogen. It's been all of ten seconds, hasn't it? Have you decided you'd like to join my stable?'

'I'm sorry about that,' Sandra Bogen said. 'Really sorry. I've been somewhat upset the last few days. Please take me to lunch.'

'On what basis?'

'I don't know,' she said, voice thickening. 'But please take me to lunch. I just want to talk to someone who knows Les – Les as he really is. I just want to – ' She stopped.

Henny sighed and used his left hand to get another cigarette. 'Did you give him a rough time, Sandra?'

'My friends call me Sandy.'

'I'd like to be a friend.' And he meant it. He meant it much more than he wanted to. 'Sandy.'

'Yes. I gave him a rough time. But I didn't come right out with it.' She made an impatient sound. 'We'll talk at lunch.'

'I'm dating you, then?' Henny said.

'Call it what you like.'

The twisted grin came to his lips. 'Again, Sandy, I have to refuse your kind offer.' Before she could say anything, he added, 'And for a very simple reason – I like you too damn much. As the boys in Denver used to say, you're my type. So it can't be a business luncheon, or a business-mixed-slightly-with-pleasure luncheon. All pleasure, doll.'

'Well, isn't that the most ridiculous – ' The line clicked in his ear.

He winced and put the handset back in the cradle. But he wasn't quite as unhappy as he'd been before. He'd

142

made his point, and it was an important point; and he remembered the hunch he'd had on first meeting Sandra Bogen at Marie's desk.

Richie Morden had a two-thirty appointment with Keith Enders of the Losch-Roem-Enders Advertising Agency on Sixty-fourth near Third. It was an important appointment because he hoped to convince Enders that Morden Photos could handle a 'busy' account like Chelsea Tobacco. Chelsea Tobacco was an old English outfit that had recently decided to move in on the US quality pipe and cigar market. They used a lot of small, spot ads in newspapers and magazines – photographs of men's faces smiling because of the pipe or cigar stuck in their mouths, with a small, complete figure of a woman somewhere in the upper right- or left-hand portion of the ad. The woman was about to succumb to the aroma of Chelsea Tobacco, or Sheverton Gold-Leaf, Chelsea's forty-cent cigar. Until now, the agency had been spreading the account all over New York, using six or seven studios. But Richie had been cultivating the younger member of the firm and felt it was time to make his bid for the entire Chelsea setup. That's why he'd worn his best lightweight suit. That's why he left his office at one-thirty for the hotel barbershop on Forty-ninth.

The colored boy came up to his chair as Richie told the barber to make it a very light trim. 'Shine?' the boy asked.

Richie looked at him. He was about sixteen or seventeen, light-skinned, with good features and a sober expression. He didn't grin or put on what Richie thought of as the darky act in any other way. He merely waited.

'Yes,' Richie said. 'Thank you.'

The boy blinked at him before kneeling to the footrest

143

with his equipment box. That 'thank you,' Richie realized, had been slightly out of order.

'How about a nice sun-lamp treatment?' Abe, the head barber, murmured as he set about trimming Richie's thinning hair.

'No,' Richie said. And then, 'How come you always ask me that, Abe, when I've never said yes once in all the years I've been coming here?'

'Never said yes once?' Abe murmured, nonplussed. 'Well, I guess I never noticed, Mr Morden. I ask all my customers. They like that tanned look.'

'I'm tan enough,' Richie said, tone of voice indicating he didn't want further conversation. At a buck fifty a trim, plus two bits tip, he had the right to a little quiet.

After a while he examined his face in the wall-length mirror. His skin wasn't really dark. Not unusually so. Not at all indicative of anything but white blood – or white genes, since there was no difference in blood. Anyway, he didn't care for tanned skin, had never been a sun-worshiper.

He closed his eyes, annoyed by the resurgence of what wasn't even a true problem. That business in the Minor Key Bar last Tuesday had set it off, and he'd made it worse by asking Phyll those stupid questions about how she would feel if he turned out to be part Negro.

Once again, as he had so many times in the past, he asked himself why, why the hell it should torture him all through his life when he wasn't a bigot, had never been a bigot even back home in Texas.

Not that it had tortured him *recently*. Most of it had ended six years ago when he inherited almost thirteen thousand dollars from the wonderful old lady he'd called Aunt Della, who wasn't really his aunt but just a lonely old woman who'd lived next door to him in El Paso and who shared his secret fear, shared it as perhaps no one

144

else ever could. 'Stop your worryin', son,' she'd said, way back then. 'Even if you are part nigra, you think it's gonna kill you? You think it's gonna make you lose your home and nice stepfolks and all? Boy, no one'll ever know, because you yourself don't know. And even if you did, you'd keep your mouth shut, and things would go on.'

He'd refused to accept her comfort, appalled at having blurted out his terrible fear, saying, 'How can *you* know?' She'd smiled gap-toothed and leaned forward and said, 'Boy, I'm an octaroon – I'm one eighth nigra. Leastways, that's as close as I can figger it. Mebbe I'm one sixth, or even one fifth. Now don't you try telling anyone because I'll say you're crazy and no one'll believe you anyway. But that's how I know. Because I *am* what you're just afraid of being. That's how, boy.' From then on they'd been like mother and son, and she'd eased his burdens and given him comfort and he'd believed her, believed her . . . until years later when he wondered, as he did now, whether she hadn't said it just to ease him, just to draw him closer.

He opened his eyes and again looked at himself in the barbershop mirror, at his face and his balding head over which Abe hovered with scissors and clippers. He *wasn't* colored, had no reason to think he was colored. (Usually, he would also tell himself, And even if I were, it would be one tenth or one eighth or one fifth or something like that, and what earthly difference could it make *now* in my life, in my marriage? But this time he didn't go on to that last, rather comforting stage of reasoning. Tuesday night he'd received an answer from his love, his wife, his wonderful Phyll. Tuesday night he'd learned she would probably feel 'disgusted' sleeping with him.)

He continued to examine his reflection in the big mirror and asked himself why he was so disturbed by what Phyll

145

had said Tuesday night. He had anticipated, or should have anticipated, her reply to his hypothetical question. After all, Phyll had been born and bred in Texas, the same as he, and she had never been a rebel against established society – her very acceptance of life, her very normalcy, was what made her the comfortable, comforting, solid, enjoyable creature she was, so why expect her to say she could live with a man once she learned he was part Negro? And since she would *never* learn that about him – because as Aunt Della had said, he himself had no way of learning it – why give a damn one way or the other?

But he did give a damn, a hell of a big damn, and he couldn't help it. Once again, as he had so many, many times before, he thought back as far as he could, searching the old, rehashed, blurred memories for some clue as to his antecedents.

The very earliest memory he had was of running to a woman known as Maw Collins. She was a cook at the orphanage near El Paso, and she always had a hug and a kiss for him. Maw Collins was an elderly Negress. He had survived the sterile orphanage existence as well as he had mainly because of her hugs and kisses. He had lived on her love, and when she died, he had thought he too would die. That was some years later – exactly how many he wasn't sure – but he remembered she had given him a birthday cake only a month before her heart attack. His seventh birthday. After that, he suddenly became aware of the fact that there were other children in the world besides those who lived in orphanages. He also became aware, probably through conversations with older orphans who had seen more of the outside world than he had, that non-orphanage children had mothers and fathers and homes and lived together in a wonderful unit called 'family.'

'Sweet Lord Jesus,' he had prayed, 'give me a family.'

He had stopped praying after what he'd termed 'a long time' because nothing had happened – a long time, by his seven-year-old standards, being three or four weeks. He had, instead, begun questioning members of the orphanage staff. 'Where'd I come from, Miss Geely? Did I have folks, Mr Ammerson? How'd I get here, huh?'

The staff members had been reluctant to answer, but once they saw he *had* to know, they told him.

He'd been abandoned at the age of two or three days in the balcony of an El Paso movie house, and the method of his abandonment indicated that his parents had been determined no one should ever know who they were. That in itself suggested to Richie that they'd committed a terrible crime by having him, and what greater crime was there than someone with Negro blood, and someone without, mating? Forcing a side door, they (or he, or she) had gained entrance to the movie house early one Sunday morning in April and deposited him on the balcony seat. (The orphanage used that date – the twelfth – as his birthday.) He had slept quietly, dressed in his diaper, white undershirt and thin blue blanket – all labels removed – until about ten minutes before the first feature went on. Then he had cried, and a cleaning man had found him. The cleaning man, a young Negro (his life, Richie reasoned, was constantly involved with Negroes), called the manager, who in turn called the police. And then to the orphanage.

So there he was. No one had said he was part Negro. The orphanage was for whites only. But, because he'd had a head of black, curly hair, and a dark complexion, and dark eyes, he'd run into taunts at those times when children seek out their fellows' weak points so as to be able to tease, ridicule and attack them. Instead of hearing 'Cock-eyed, cock-eyed,' or 'Skin-and-bones skinny,' or

'Fatty, fatty, two-by-four, can't get through the kitchen door,' or 'Big-nose Jew-baby,' he heard, 'Black, black, hide-in-a-sack, Nigra.'

While at the orphanage this taunt merely bothered him, as the other taunts bothered other children. But then he was visited by Mr and Mrs Lloyd Morden, and they asked his name, and he gave the one given him at the orphanage: 'Richard Wilson.' They talked with him, and he liked them both; and when they left Mr Ammerson said, 'Richie, behave yourself when Mr and Mrs Morden are around. They're very interested in you.'

Mr and Mrs Morden had no children. They came back three more times, and then he was asked if he would like to go home with them – to live.

On the quiet, middle-class street in El Paso, he found the love he'd lost when Maw Collins had died not quite a year before. Except that now he had *more* love – a real mother and father, a real family.

At the age of eight, Richie Wilson became Richie Morden and began a full, rich, happy life. No resentments for him that he was adopted; he knew just how lucky he was. No doubts for him that his parents' love was real; he grew complete on it.

But the dark touch of rot on the otherwise whole personality came into being. It was born during the times he heard his adoptive parents speak disparagingly of 'Nigras.' It was fed on the memory voices of his fellow orphans chanting, 'Black, black, hide-in-a-sack, Nigra.' It was strengthened by his biological parents' method of abandoning him, and his being found by a Negro, and his having been loved (and loving in return) the Negro cook. And more than all of that, it was his young brain, building on air, imagining a kinship with every colored child on the street, with every colored man or woman, with all the supposed weaknesses of the Negro race.

The touch of rot grew, but only slightly. And then he became friends with the old woman who lived alone next door in the neat little red-brick cottage, and whom he called Aunt Della, and who drew out of him his until then unvoiced fear and told him she was part Negro and that his fear was foolish. She insisted she'd had all-white babies, but he'd heard stories of supposedly white women having black babies from supposedly white husbands and it terrified him, became part of his unconscious, so that when he met Phyllis Crest, at a church picnic (they were both Baptist; both passive rather than active in their belief), he immediately began preparing her for his 'theory' on marriage. It all boiled down to *no children*, though it was embroidered with a great deal of talk about 'enjoying one's life to the fullest in a great metropolitan area, like New York.' Luckily for Richie, Phyllis Crest had no burning desire to be a mother. Her own mother's health had been destroyed by bearing seven children, two of whom had died. The mother now suffered from a multitude of painful and embarrassing ailments, and Phyllis preferred avoiding these to raising a family. She and Richie got along beautifully and were married eight months later. Twenty-two-year-old Richie had a good camera, a number of camera-club prizes, and an offer of a job in a New York studio through a friend of his father's. Four months after his marriage, he took his seventeen-year-old bride to Manhattan, and there they'd remained, except for a few trips back home during the first nine years. For the past eleven and a half years, they hadn't left New York City, except for brief auto trips to New England and Canada. They loved Manhattan and no longer had any desire to see Texas. They were happy. And the surprise legacy from Richie's old neighbor, Aunt Della, had given them the studio, which made their happiness complete.

Complete, Richie told himself, looking down as the colored boy finished his shoes and stepped aside. Complete happiness.

He thought then of the weird party he'd gone to without Phyll – about nine or ten months before Aunt Della had given him the added security of his own studio – where he'd spent the entire evening with a colored girl and said things.

'That's nice, eh, Mr Morden?' Abe asked, holding up the hand mirror behind Richie's head.

'Yes,' Richie said, and pushed away the disturbing thoughts with a grin and a quip. 'But you took too much off the top, Abe – I can see scalp.'

Abe returned the grin and patted his own bald head. 'Ah, Mr Morden, if I could figure out a way to put hair on bare scalp I'd not only make a fortune but I'd get myself one of your models.'

Richie paid him and tipped him, then gave the colored boy forty cents – ten cents more than usual – and left. He hailed a cab and sank back in the seat and looked out the window as they turned uptown. What the hell, he had the world by the short hairs! He had everything a man could ask for!

Everything.

10

As far as Lester Bogen was concerned, the very worst had happened: Sandra had found out about his other life.

And yet, as soon as he learned this, he realized he'd been prepared for it in some subtle, subconscious manner. Without ever admitting it to himself, he'd understood that a secret such as his couldn't be kept forever.

The point now was to make her see that he wasn't a monster, but merely a man who'd dallied a little. Besides, she couldn't know the *extent* of his dalliance, couldn't have learned how great a lecher he was, couldn't even suspect that except for her his very life was composed of moving from one female to another.

He knew, more or less, what Richie and Van had said in front of her, and he knew that because of her reaction she'd get no more information out of them. As for Henny, well, he trusted Henny's judgement in such matters.

Les Bogen had first learned something was wrong when he returned home Sunday night from his four-day Pennsylvania shooting assignment. He'd driven his powerful Studebaker Golden Hawk into the garage, parking it between Sandy's Hillman and Louise's Buick hard-top, and begun to close the center panel of the three-section door. Then he'd seen something glow off the driveway to his left, and stopped. It was too early in the season for fireflies, and this had been more like a cigarette glow than anything else. He watched, and the glow came again, and he called, 'Sandy?'

For a moment there'd been no answer. Then: 'Yes.'

He stepped out of the garage and walked toward what

151

was still just a point of light. 'Enjoying the night air, dear?'

'Yes.'

He could see her now; she was standing under the big red maple which was some fifteen feet off the driveway, just before the first of three gentle terraces which rose to heavy woodland behind the house.

'A little late, though, isn't it?' he said, coming up close to her, leaning forward for the kiss he expected. She merely stood there, face hidden in the shadows, but he could see that it was turned downward, that her head was down and that it didn't rise to greet him.

At that moment he knew something was wrong. And outside of a sudden death in the family – and she wasn't reacting properly for that – there was only one other thing that could make her act this way. But he hoped he was wrong and went along slowly. He took her arm, found her hand, squeezed it and kissed her cheek. 'Missed you very much, Sandy.'

'Really?' she murmured. 'That's odd.'

He was sure then and suddenly frightened. 'What's wrong?' he asked.

'Wrong? Nothing, Les. Because I smoke a cigarette outdoors at one A.M., does it mean something's wrong?'

'I thought . . .' he began, and then stopped. Maybe he'd better let it go for tonight. Maybe he was jumping to conclusions.

'It's only that I love you, Sandy,' he murmured, but he took his hand from hers and moved away. 'Please remember that.'

'Of course,' she said, and her voice, so tight, so unhappy, chilled him. 'I'm broad-minded, Les.' She laughed briefly. '*Broad*-minded. That's quite apropos, isn't it?'

152

He had to stop and face her then. 'Exactly what do you mean?'

'Don't you know?'

'I asked you a question, Sandra. Answer me.'

She laughed again, and it was worse than her voice. 'Nothing. I'll be in a little later.' She walked off into the darkness.

He could have called her back. He could have insisted on obedience to his request for an answer. But what good would that have done? He didn't want her obedience; he wanted her love.

What he needed was time – time to find out exactly what she'd learned; time to plan a way of explaining himself; time to heal whatever breach had opened between them. He never doubted it could be done. He *couldn't* doubt. It was as if he were to doubt that he would live through the night.

Louise was already in bed, and so he went right to his room without having to speak to her. (These separate rooms would be one of his excuses to Sandy, and everything else would follow in adult and reasonable fashion.) He didn't come out when he heard Sandy moving along the corridor. He lay in bed, smoking a tasteless cigarette, wishing it were morning so he could go to the studio and find out if she'd been there.

As anxious as he was to leave, he stayed in his room Monday morning until he heard Sandy pull her Hillman out of the garage. She would either drive all the way to the city or park at the railroad station in Peekskill, catching the seven-sixteen commuter train. The train would allow her to reach Columbia University with enough time for breakfast before her first class. The car was used only when she was going somewhere afterward or had overslept and missed her train.

Les washed, dressed and went down to the kitchen.

153

Louise was, of course, still sleeping and wouldn't get up until nine-thirty or ten. Elsie, the combination maid-cook, was sitting at the table sipping coffee and reading a digest-sized magazine. She was a small, thin woman in her mid-sixties who lived only five minutes drive from the Bogen home and therefore slept out, arriving at six-thirty each morning in her ancient Dodge sedan and leaving after dinner each evening at about seven-thirty. If the family wasn't around for dinner – as it generally wasn't – she left something on the stove or in the refrigerator. Though she'd been with the Bogens almost twelve years, Elsie Dudonic was as far from the stereotyped version of a family retainer as one could get. She never spoke of her private life to any member of the family, nor seemed to pay the slightest attention to what went on around her unless it concerned the preparation and serving of food or the cleaning of the house. Now she looked up and said, 'Morning. Want breakfast or just coffee?'

Les shook his head, went to the refrigerator and poured some juice for himself. He gulped it and moved toward the door which led to the playroom, which in turn led to the garage. Elsie said, 'Sandy's sick, maybe?'

Les stopped. Elsie's commenting upon a member of the family was enough, in itself, to shock him. 'Why?' he asked.

'Don't know. Just looked pale and red-eyed and . . . different. Never saw her look like that. Been acting funny last few days, and now, this morning. She sick?'

'She went to school, didn't she?'

'Yes. Guess she's all right then. Wouldn't you say?'

He turned to face the old woman. She dropped her eyes and sipped her coffee and said, 'None of my business, Mr Bogen, but I never seen her so nervous before, so unhappy. You find out what's wrong. Looks like boy trouble to me – *bad* boy trouble.'

154

He said, 'Don't be foolish.'

She shrugged and sipped again and turned a page of her magazine. He left, his stomach upset.

He drove much too quickly, using the Hawk's power to break speed limits all the way in to Manhattan. Then there was the usual stop-and-go on the West Side Highway, and on the trip cross-town. Before he put his car in the parking lot, it was nine-thirty.

Twenty minutes later he'd finished talking to Van Roberts. He knew that Sandra had been here and given a phony name, and that she'd learned her father had the reputation of a successful lover. He also knew neither Van nor Richie suspected who she really was.

Richie came in. Les spoke to him and confirmed what he'd gathered from Van.

Later Les went up to the third floor and spoke to Henny. That interview was less satisfying than the first two. He wasn't sure, but he had the feeling Henny didn't accept 'Norma' at face value.

Still, that wasn't too important. What *was* important was assessing what had happened to Sandy. The way he saw it, she had heard a few semihumorous remarks about Lester Bogen's successes with women and known in an instant what his life had been like all these years – or *part* of what his life had been like. She'd also known why he and Louise had no life together; or perhaps (and this was what he had to make her believe) she'd felt that he was the way he was *because* he had no life with her mother. But no matter what her immediate reaction, she'd turned on him, as indicated by her coldness last night, her distress this morning (witnessed by Elsie), not understanding what his lechery was, not being able to see that it was totally amoral, totally without emotional meaning.

She was wild about pistachio nuts. He was wild about

155

women. Their appetites were similar, both being devoid of elements of good and evil.

But she would never see it that way.

He went home early that night. Louise said Sandy had called. She was going out on a date and wouldn't be home until very late. Then Louise asked if anything was wrong with Sandy.

'What makes you think that?'

'I don't know,' she murmured. 'She sounded so strange on the phone. In fact, she's acted strangely all week.'

He made an impatient gesture and went to bed.

Sandy came in at two-thirty, but he'd been waiting up and called softly to her. 'I'm dead tired,' she said, and her voice was thick – with alcohol, he guessed. 'Let's chat some other time.' She went to her room and locked the door.

She slept late Tuesday morning and Les had to leave without seeing her because her door was still locked. And when he called Louise at three that afternoon, Elsie answered to say that Louise had gone to a Presbyterian church bazaar and wouldn't be home until nine or ten that night. Yes, Sandra had called. Yes, she'd be home in time for dinner – early, in fact. She was using her car and would be in at five, five-thirty.

Les told Elsie to forget dinner and go home.

'What?'

'Do as I say. I'm taking her out tonight.'

'Well, if you're sure.'

'I'm sure.'

'She all right?' the old woman asked.

'I liked you better before you became interested in the family,' he said sharply.

'Everyone's gettin' nervous around here. I'll hafta start puttin' vitamin B in the puddin'.'

Despite his anxiety, Les had to smile. He hung up,

went down to the parking lot, got his Hawk and headed home.

At five-twenty, sitting in the living room and reading the *Times*, Les heard a car entering the garage. He put the paper down and rubbed his hands together nervously. But when Sandy came up from the playroom, he was seated at the dining-room table mixing two rye highballs. 'In here, honey,' he called.

There was a moment without answer, without sound of movement, and he stopped mixing ice, Angostura, liquor and ginger ale to listen to it. Then he said, 'Everyone's unfaithful, Sandy. Everyone, *to* everyone. I know.' He spoke as if she were sitting across the table from him instead of being in the next room, separated from his sight by a wall, hearing his voice because of the doorway in that wall. 'Everyone except me.' He waited for a laugh, or some other sound of derision. There was nothing. 'I'm the one faithful man I know. I'm totally faithful, to you. The day I first held you, as an infant, in my arms, I knew I'd finally found someone I'd die for. I'd never die for my country, Sandy. At the first threat, prisoner Bogen would hand over the secret defenses and consign the fort to the conqueror's sword – if you were safely out of it. But if you were in it, I'd suffer anything, everything.'

He paused again, and she came to the doorway and looked at him. Her face was tired, her eyes were blank. She'd never looked at him that way before, and his voice rose desperately. 'I'd try to kill anyone who menaced you, Sandy. I'd give my life to save yours, if it were a matter of choice. I've thought it through many times and wondered at being able to feel that way.

'I'm like everyone else, Sandy, except with you. With you I'm better than everyone else.'

She came to the table, sat down and looked at the two glasses. 'Is one of those for me?'

He nodded and finished mixing the drink and gave it to her. He mixed one for himself and raised the glass. She was looking down at the table. He said, 'To a mature and understanding view of one's parents.'

She looked up. 'I doubt if the psychologists would approve of *such* understanding, Daddy.'

At last, he thought. *At last she's beginning to talk*.

'If they don't, they should,' he said. 'Every man I know, married or single, has occasional experiences with women.'

'*Every* man?'

'Yes,' he said, and wondered if he was right. It had never mattered to him what other men did, and it didn't really matter now, but he wondered.

'You once told me Van Roberts was happily married.'

'Him too,' he said, and made himself sound sure. 'Men talk, and I know.'

'Henny Girado, before his wife died?'

He smiled. 'Henny? If you knew him, you wouldn't have to ask.' He smiled again, making it just a little superior. 'And Morden and Drake and anyone else I've ever worked with. And the butcher in the shopping center and the druggist in town and every damn one of us, except for the incompetents and the fanatics.'

She drank in silence, and he joined her. She put down her glass and stood up. 'Then I've been a baby, haven't I?'

He shrugged slightly, deprecatingly.

'I guess the French are right, aren't they?'

'In their acceptance of humanity's foibles, certainly. In their politics, no.' He grinned, but she refused to recognize his joke.

'And you practice this . . . worldliness continuously?'

158

'Hold it,' he said, laughing. 'I merely admitted – was forced to admit – that I've had a few experiences.'

'From what I heard . . .' She shook her head and turned away. 'This is idiotic. I don't know what we're talking about.'

'Then sit down, honey, and finish your drink,' he said anxiously. 'Later we'll drive to the Bird and Bottle for dinner.'

'No, I don't feel like a drink, and I'm too tired for dinner out.'

He was suddenly without words, full of fear. He couldn't get to her.

She turned again, face still tired. 'But I'm glad we had this talk.'

He smiled weakly. 'You used to say that as a little girl, when I explained things to you. You said it when I showed you how to plant a rosebush, and when I stopped you from killing a praying mantis, and other times.'

'Yes. Because I'd learned something. And I've learned something now. Whatever foolish ideas I had about maintaining a degree of purity – '

'Stop it!' he shouted. 'God damn it, that's entirely different!' And as soon as his voice died away he knew he'd made a terrible mistake. He'd contradicted himself.

She was smiling. 'Here's to a mature understanding of one's children.' And then she was gone, running up the stairs to her room.

He didn't follow. He finished his drink, and hers, and went down to the garage. He drove to Oregon Road and a gas station just outside town. He told the attendant to fill 'er up, and walked over to the glass-walled telephone booth. He dialed the operator, asked for a number in Manhattan, and listened to the phone ring ten times at the other end. He got the operator again and gave another number, and Eugenia Randolph answered. 'Hello,' he said.

'Hello, big man.'

'How about dinner and a quiet talk?'

She laughed. 'I'm too beat for one of your quiet talks, big man. Me for the sack early tonight. I've got a nine A.M. appointment at Crescent Studios tomorrow.'

'Another time, perhaps. Goodbye, dear.'

'Gee, it's pitiful to hear your disappointed wails, daddy. You oughta learn to control yourself.'

'I'm *very* disappointed, Eugenia. Want to change your mind?'

She hesitated.

He checked his watch. 'It's six-thirty. I can be at your place by seven-forty-five.'

'I shouldn't, Les. I want to be asleep by ten. I've promised myself nine, ten hours of sleep for weeks.'

He knew she'd say yes in a minute, but he didn't want any brief, rushed evenings. Besides, someone new might provide the extra thrill he needed tonight. 'You're quite right,' he said, his mind made up. 'You have to be fresh and at your best for a shooting. I'll speak to you in a few days. Goodbye.' Before she could answer, he hung up.

Calls from Peekskill to Manhattan were forty cents for three minutes, evening rates. He was out of change, so he left the booth and returned to his sleek, gold-and-white sports car. The attendant said, 'Check your oil and water, sir?' Les said no, paid the two-eighty tab with a five and asked for plenty of coin. When the man returned with his change, Les moved his car to a spot near the phone, re-entered the booth and found the slip of paper in his wallet. The number on it belonged to a model he was going to shoot Friday at six-thirty.

It was rushing the game a bit to try her before her first clothes-off job, but she'd seemed a particularly good

160

prospect and he didn't think there'd be any need for a slow build-up. He'd met her at a party given by Magazine Associated Corporation, a small but highly successful outfit that turned out a dozen picture quarterlies, two fact-detective bimonthlies and a flashy monthly imitation of *Reader's Digest*. Her name was Lois Montana, and she was a very big girl with red hair, heavy breasts, wide hips and long, long legs. She'd recognized his name and ignored the difference in their sizes (in high heels she was three inches taller than he) and said, 'Ah'd sure be grateful if you could throw a little work mah way, daddy. Ah got some TV spots comin' up real soon, but ah need steak money.' He'd made their appointment for the evening so she'd know the score. However, he intended to try and sell her pictures to a high-paying outfit since she had some reputation on Broadway as a sex-machine ingenue and had been written up by Earl Wilson a few times.

She answered the phone on the second ring. 'Hello, Miss Montana,' he said. 'This is Lester Bogen.'

'Mr Bogen! Why, isn't this a coincidence! Ah was just sittin' here all alone, thinkin' about the nice man ah met at that magazine place party, when the phone rings and there he is! Can I do anythin' for you?' This last was said with the sly innuendo expected of sex-machine ingenues. 'Ah mean, can I be of *service?*'

He thought, with amusement, that he should be insulted: neon signs and loud-speakers for Les Bogen.

'Yes, there is something you can do for me, Miss Montana. I'll be in your section of the city in about an hour and a half, and I'm wondering if you'll have dinner with me. That'll be about eight o'clock.'

'Ah generally eat earlier,' she muttered; and he had a sudden vision of the big girl clutching her stomach as her

161

time for dinner passed and the hunger pains came. He grinned in the booth.

'I'll speed,' he said. 'Seven-thirty?'

'Well, d'you like Mexican food?'

'Whatever you like, I like, barring fried grasshoppers.'

She giggled. 'How sweet! Mexican food's a favorite of mahn. Ah just love the tacos and enchiladas and frijoles and that wonderful beer – Carta Blanca. There's a place only ten minutes away so we won't have to waste time.' She giggled again.

'I can taste it now,' he murmured.

She was still giggling when he hung up.

He arrived a little after seven-thirty to find her waiting in a figure-hugging green knit dress that set off her red hair and accentuated her lush curves. Les complimented her on the outfit and she clutched his arm, murmuring thanks into his ear as her big breasts pressed hard against his bicep. They ate swiftly, and mostly in silence – Lois, Les noticed, had an appetite to match her size – and drank five Carta Blancas between them. By nine they were in her apartment.

Lois offered him a drink and Les accepted a martini. They sat around for a while drinking and talking about their forthcoming photographic session. There was no doubt in Les's mind that Lois Montana was ready to jump into bed with him, but they played out a conventional game, making small talk until mention of the session gave Les the opportunity to compliment her on her body.

'It looks wonderful in that dress,' he smiled. 'I'm sure it would look even better without it.'

'Ah could give you a preview,' she replied, smiling archly.

Les nodded, and she rose to her feet, reaching behind

162

her for the zipper of the green dress. It slithered to her feet and she kicked it away. Underneath she wore a lacey black brassiere and matching panties over a black garter belt. She had the pale, creamy skin of a natural red head, and her body was every bit as good as Les had anticipated. He set his drink down as she unsnapped the brassiere, freeing her large breasts. They were paler than the rest of her body, the nipples dark brown and swollen, rising from the lighter circles of the aureoles. Les felt himself responding as she slid her panties down her long legs and pirouetted before him.

'You like what you see, Les?' she asked him huskily.

'I like it a lot,' he replied.

'Ah'm glad,' Lois smiled. 'Ah want to show you how glad.'

She went down on her knees before him, reaching out to slip his coat from his shoulders. Les let her undress him, moving only enough to help her tug his clothing loose. Naked, his reaction was obvious.

'Ah declare,' Lois murmured. 'That looks good enough to eat.'

Les smiled as she bent forwards, her mane of red hair tumbling over his thighs and stomach. He felt her lips close on him, then the caress of her tongue. She slid her mouth the full length of his shaft several times, then began to move her lips over the head. At first she moved slowly, but as he groaned and stiffened, she began to move her lips faster. Les felt the familiar promise of release mounting, and looked down at the red head bobbing between his thighs. Through the curtain of hair he could see his penis sliding in and out of her mouth, the shaft glistening with her saliva. Lois's eyes were closed, and she was moaning as she sucked him towards climax. The image did it for Les. He exploded into her willing mouth, bucking on the couch as she drank the full pouring of his orgasm.

When he was spent, she raised her head and licked her lips, smiling at him.

'Was that good, Daddy?' she asked throatily.

'That was very good, my dear,' Les replied.

'Then why don't ah mix us a couple more drinks.' Lois rose to her feet in a fluid motion. 'And we can take them in the bedroom while we think about what to do next.'

'I already have some ideas,' smiled Les, rising.

At eleven-thirty, with her big white body pulsating beneath his, encircled by her arms and legs, stoking her passion with the practice born of countless such encounters, he paused and tried to find a reason for what he was doing; tried to find a feeling of shame and repentance within himself.

He found no reason but that of pleasure.

He found no feeling but that of delight.

'Daddy,' she mumbled thickly, 'you've tortured your momma long enough!'

He put his lips to hers, and the delight welled up until it was all the purpose a man could seek in life, and he brought her back to pulsation, to near fulfillment. And he paused again.

'Daddy.'

He was in serious trouble with Sandy.

If a man found evil in the sex act, if he felt dirtied and shamed and repentant, he could make a wife or child forgive him. The man who suffered inside for what he considered his sins was sooner or later forgiven. But the man who felt only delight, only physical fulfillment, could never weep away the hurt and accusation in the eyes of his family. Clean and composed, he was called lecher, degenerate and sinner. True to himself, he was labeled

164

betrayer. It was one of the contradictions of Christian society.

'Daddy, please.'

He began moving again. He looked at her and spoke to her and delighted in her. 'You're wonderful,' he whispered, and his voice began to shake. 'You're so much woman. You're lovely, perfect. Goddess, long limbed and full breasted. Goddess of love, I love you.'

He meant every word of it, and she understood him. He meant it every time he said it, and he said it to all who were alive to his effort, emotionally free to participate with him. So very many. And every time there was a difference, a delightful difference which made *that* woman the goddess of love whom he loved. Whoever had coined the all-cats-are-gray-in-the-dark phrase was either inexperienced or lacking in true desire. *No* woman was like another.

He told her that, and more. He didn't stifle his ecstasy but let it find expression in deep-throated words, words of love. When he felt himself slipping, he exercised control, waiting for her, wanting to give as much as he was taking. And only when her nails tickled his shoulders in restrained indication of near explosion did he throw away his control.

He left at twelve-thirty. She begged him to stay the night but he shook his head. 'I can't, dear. I didn't make the proper arrangements. Next time, perhaps.'

He entered his home at two-ten Wednesday morning. All the lights were out, but as he passed Sandy's closed door he heard a small sound. He paused, and listened, and heard the sound again. Laughter, or, rather, a brittle imitation of laughter.

He tried the door, and it opened. 'You awake?' he whispered.

'Yes,' she said, voice clear, free of sleep. 'Have fun?'

165

'In a way. I was disturbed, so I drove to the city and took in a movie.'

'I see.'

'You don't see at all,' he said. 'But you will. Just remember how much you mean to me, how much we mean to each other. Just understand that one thing has nothing to do with the other.'

'I'll try,' she said, but there was no understanding in her voice.

'Don't you believe me?' he asked, and moved toward the white blur that was her head resting on its pillow. 'Don't you know that I've always told you the truth?'

'That's very funny.'

'Always told you the truth when it came to *our* relationship,' he finished.

She rolled over, putting her back to him. 'Please, Daddy, we'll talk again, some other time.'

'I think we should talk now,' he said, sitting down at the edge of her bed. 'Your mother and I – '

'Some other time,' she interrupted, voice going shrill. 'Please. I want to . . . *to stop despising you!*'

His heart jumped sickeningly. Quickly, he stood up and left the room. When he slipped into bed, he closed his eyes and whispered, 'Dear God of creation, God who made beauty as well as ugliness, birth as well as death, reason as well as blind obedience to society . . .' But then, trying to go on and define a god who would consider morality stupid and sensuality desirable, he foundered, and lost the feeling for prayer, and realized that prayer was ridiculous for him since he had no god.

11

On Tuesday, Henny gave his hair-goods pictures to Dennis Parish, and the studio salesman shrugged. 'Very fine, very sensitive, but for who?' He re-examined the prints and shook his beautifully tonsured head. Parish was about the same size and basic build as Les Bogen, but he'd added fifty extra pounds to that basic build and looked positively cherubic, what with his pale blond hair and pink-white cheeks and small, moist-lipped mouth. 'It's ashcan. Great, but ashcan. I'll try it around.'

Henny knew the agent well enough to recognize a compliment.

They talked a while. Then Henny took a duplicate set of prints down to Gernstein & Son on the first floor. As he walked toward the tiny glass-enclosed office, he passed Eva Gretz's table. The slim, sprightly widow smiled at him in mid-weave and murmured, 'You got my pin-ups?'

'Three beauties, Eva. But first I'll give Mr Gernstein his.'

'The old man's out today,' Eva murmured. 'The Stinker's in there. But since you're giving him something for nothing, he'll act like a *mensch*.'

Henny grinned and went on to the office.

The Stinker, Arnold Gernstein, sat behind one of three desks in the crowded little office. He looked up, his half-bald head gleaming with perspiration, his deep-set eyes unhappy, his young face drawing down toward the tight mouth, which was drawing down toward the narrow chin. 'I told you,' he said, 'I won't buy any lousy pictures from you or anyone else.'

Henny opened the envelope, removed the three prints of Eva and put the envelope with its fourteen remaining prints on Arnold Gernstein's desk. He ignored the man's statement. 'Here're the pictures I promised your father. No charge. I hope to get them published soon. The publicity shouldn't do you any harm. Tell your father that, huh?' and he walked to the door.

'Well, say, that's okay.'

Henny nodded and opened the door.

'Thanks.'

Henny nodded again.

'You know how it is,' the younger Gernstein said. 'Everyone's got a gimmick. Everyone's out to stick you. You gotta watch 'em all the time.'

Henny nodded a third time and left. As he walked to Eva Gretz's table, he found himself pitying the Stinker. With a philosophy like that, even the best of circumstances wouldn't save life from becoming a nasty business. Laird Drake seemed to live by the same lousy credo.

He gave Eva Gretz her three prints. She examined them and refused to hand them over to her tablemate until she'd gone over them twice more, and then looked up at Henny and said, '*Zehr goot!* Very good, Henny. You are – ' she paused, searching for words – 'you are more than a man who takes pictures of weddings and babies and families. Much more.'

Henny's sense of satisfaction was vast.

The tablemate – a small, stout woman with glasses and a soft face – said, 'But why didn't you look at the camera and smile, Eva? Here I can't even see your face, and in this one your hands are moving, and even the one where you look up you're not smiling clear.'

Eva Gretz reclaimed the photographs and smiled at Henny. 'What can you expect from a *Galitziana?* I will always keep these . . . photographs.' She pronounced the

168

word with difficulty and with obvious intent to distinguish them from the ordinary 'pictures' of ordinary photographers. 'I have never known before what I look like, what I *really* look like.'

Henny touched her rough-skinned hand and left. In the hall he paused a moment, digesting the sense of accomplishment. During that moment he felt very lucky to be Henny Girado.

But the moment passed, and he went up to the third floor to ask Richie if there was any prospect of a job. Richie shook his head and then said, 'I give you more than your share, Henny. I wish you'd remember that when . . .' He shrugged. 'Ah, to hell with it.'

Since Richie seemed nervous and unhappy, Henny didn't risk asking him what he meant. Instead, he grinned and said, 'I'm with you, daddy, whatever the beef,' and left quickly. But as soon as he turned down the hall, out of sight, his grin disappeared. It was piling up against him. It was getting to be a drag. He felt as if he didn't have a friend left in the world.

He went to his office. Van Roberts was in the adjoining office, and they exchanged 'Hi's' through the open door. Then Henny closed the door, without offering his usual quipped explanation, and dialed Marv Weister's number. The writer answered on the sixth ring, and his frustration was immediately evident. 'Who is it?'

'Henny. And I need your miserable company, genius, so don't brush me off.'

'I was working.'

'Fuck your work,' Henny said.

'What?'

'You heard me, man. I'm your friend. I provide you with tail and companionship at all hours of the day and night. Now comes the pay-off. Now I need someone to talk to, to be with. And I'm honoring you. The fact that

169

you're the only friend I have . . .' He stopped then, unable to carry on with any degree of humor.

'Of course, Henny,' Marv Weister said, and now Henny heard more than frustration in the high-pitched voice. 'Only, I'm not up to par. I'm . . . a little on the ragged side.'

'That's par for you, daddy.'

'No, I mean – '

'You had a jolt?'

'Late last night, or early this morning. I'm fighting the bogymen now.'

'I'll buy you lunch,' Henny said. 'So I'll owe one million and five bucks instead of a mere million.'

'Breakfast for me,' Weister said.

'Okay then? Fifteen minutes?'

'Sure, buddy.'

Henny relaxed his grip on the phone. 'Thanks.'

'For what?' Weister muttered, voice sick and embarrassed.

'For not being a creditor. For not beginning to dislike and despise me.'

Weister said nothing.

Henny said, 'I'm in love. I'm in love with an eighteen or nineteen-year-old chick. I've been with her less than an hour and I'm in love and I'm nuts. Where do you buy that goddam horse?'

'I wouldn't tell you,' Weister said, 'even if you were serious.'

'You *forget* with it, don't you? Christ, I want to forget so goddam many things!'

'You remember later. And you're sick later.'

'Yeah. Just kidding. But there must be something.'

'C'mon over,' Weister said. 'I'm gonna puke now.' He hung up.

Henny went down to the parking lot. Jess, the colored

170

attendant, called to him as he walked to his car. 'I put the records on your back seat, man. Thanks again.'

Henny waved and got into the battered Chevy and pulled out onto the street.

They sat in the little restaurant, at a back table, and all around them businessmen talked over drinks and food; and they said nothing and toyed with their forks and ate nothing. They'd had four martinis apiece.

'You ready to tell me about that chick?' Weister asked, pushing his plate away. His face was sickly white, his eyes heavily ringed; he looked smaller and thinner than ever.

'I'm sorry I even mentioned it. It's nothing. It's silly crap. I need money, not eighteen-year-old chicks.'

'No, Henny.'

Henny looked at him. 'Tell me, master,' he muttered, but there was no derision in the statement.

'You need that chick.'

Henny waited.

'You need someone to love. More than anything else, Henny.'

At a nearby table a man laughed long and hard. 'So the poor jerk lost out on eight thousand.'

Henny shut his ears to everything but the sick, weak voice across the table.

'You're dead, Henny. You're no Les Bogen. You're dead without someone to love. And your kid . . .'

Henny shook his head. 'Forget her.'

'You're trying to, Henny. It's no good. She's going to suffer.' He paused. 'My father forgot me. *Voilà* – the result.' He grinned. It was a terrible thing to see, and Henny dropped his eyes.

'I'm a Bronx boy,' Weister said. 'Bet you never knew my father had thirty grand a year out of his little East

171

Side dress house. Bet you didn't know he had one beaut of a complex. He was sure he was sterile, and he was just as sure that I wasn't really his kid. My mother died when I was eight, and off I went on the grand tour. School in Switzerland, et cetera.'

Henny said, 'You kid me not?'

Weister grinned, more naturally this time. 'Hard to believe, huh? And at thirteen, Lawrence Terril's New Hampshire school for boys. Don't worry, I attended morning prayers like a good Episcopalian.'

'Christ,' Henny muttered.

'Don't take the Lord's name in vain,' Weister intoned. 'I didn't. I knew what I was, all right, but I also knew my father wanted me to be something entirely different from him. He was making me into the perfect *goy*. That way, he thought, he could look at me when I was an adult and say, "See? The bitch lied. He was never mine." Then he could give me a few bucks and tell me to go to hell.'

'But you – '

'Of course. I'm now the perfect expatriate Jew. Not expatriate Episcopalian, mind you. Jew. Always the Jew.' He lighted a cigarette and looked around the room. '"The Alien Corn."'

'Maugham's story?'

'Thank you for being semiliterate.'

'You're welcome.'

'Anyway, I'm the alien corn. My old man dropped dead when I was sixteen, and I left the good prep school where I was dying day by day, and I went to live with an aunt. In one month I'd absorbed the Bronx the way I'd never been able to absorb Switzerland and New Hampshire in eight years. In one month I knew what my background was and immediately rejected it.'

'Your father must have left money.'

'Six hundred bucks – all mine.'

172

'I don't get it.'

Weister shrugged. 'He wanted to be the richest eunuch in the world. He played the stock market. Even Merrill Lynch couldn't control that frantic personality. My father was lucky to have the six hundred.'

'Okay. So you were free. Why the steady blues?'

'Free? With that crazy mess of memories? With no mother and a father who couldn't put enough miles between us? You know better than that.' He looked at his cigarette. 'I put it all in my first novel. It got terrific reviews, but no one wanted to read it. It was straight down, man, all the way. It was – as the *Saturday Review* said – a *Pilgrim's Progress* in reverse. It was deadly.'

Henny muttered, 'I should read it, Marv.'

'Well, why don't you?'

Henny shrugged.

Weister said, 'You've never read anything of mine but some pulp stories.'

'I will, Marv. I'm so screwed up right now – '

'You won't,' Weister interrupted. 'And I understand.'

'I'm glad one of us understands. I keep meaning to read your novels.'

Marv Weister smiled. 'You're my friend, Henny. You're afraid of not liking my work. And you know I couldn't take that, because my work is the whole bit with me.'

'Let's get out of here,' Henny said, and caught the waiter's eye.

In Marv Weister's apartment, drinking gin and vermouth in uncertain proportions, Henny said, words beginning to thicken slightly, 'So, it's good for me to love an eighteen-year-old chick, huh, genius?'

Weister said, 'It's good for you to love anyone, Henny, because that's what you lack. You haven't allowed yourself to love.'

'Too far out for me, man. Put it into specifics.'

'You're all alone. No man can be all alone and survive.'

'I beg to point out that you, my esteemed friend – '

'I'm not surviving, Henny.' He smiled thinly. 'Even with your inestimable procuring services. I'm afraid of everything and everyone.'

'The hell you are.'

Weister shrugged. 'Okay. So I won't make you uncomfortable.'

'No, Marv. It's not that. It's just that you underrate yourself.'

'What do you know about it?' Weister muttered. 'I'm so damned afraid that I pray to die in my sleep. I'm so damned afraid – ' He stopped. 'But it's Syl we were talking about.'

'No, daddy. It was the eighteen-year-old chick.'

'It was Syl.'

Henny got up and poured himself more gin and did the same for Marv.

'You never look at your kid, do you?' Weister asked.

'Listen, I don't want to talk about that. I came here because – ' He stopped and looked at his glass. 'Okay. I never look at my kid. That's the way I'll put it for you, a writer, a guy who has to have everything either black or white. But the truth is that I *do* look at her, once in a while. And I *do* talk to her, and I *do* love her.'

'Once in a while.'

'Yes.'

'And she's three now?'

Henny sat down on the couch again, looking at Weister, who sat in his red armchair. 'Yes.'

'And you think she's going to be okay because you've got a housekeeper – lots of housekeepers?'

'She'll be all right. Soon as I get some dough I'll spend more time with her.'

'You're full of crap.'

Henny flushed.

'If you wave your fist at me,' Weister said quickly, 'I'll fall apart and say whatever you want me to say and then you'll be alone again, listening to yourself, your own thoughts, your own lying thoughts.'

'I can't stay home with her,' Henny said, his voice choked. 'I just can't. She makes me jumpy.'

'You poor romantic bastard.'

Henny's flush deepened.

Weister said, 'Go on, get mad. Go on. You're hip and all the rest of it, so how can you be romantic? Besides, you consider the very word an insult, don't you?'

Henny gulped his drink and said, 'You're an ugly little prick.'

Weister bowed his head. 'Thank you, sir. I've touched that great hip soul. You want to hear more?'

'Why should I? Why should I believe your goddam guesses?'

Weister's head moved to the side, a slight, inquisitive, strangely appealing gesture. He was stretched out in his chair, his legs straight out before him, his arms – even the one holding the drink – limp and motionless, nothing moving but his lips and eyes. It was as if he'd divorced himself from his body and thereby gained superiority.

Nirvana, Henny thought. The brain afloat in a sea of pure thought. 'Move your legs,' he said.

Weister looked down at himself, and suddenly his eyes blinked. He was atune to Henny now, so very much atune that he understood the thought behind the photographer's statement. 'I can't,' Weister said. 'They're dead. I'm dead. All but my head. I'm just a head.'

'Cut it out,' Henny said, and burst into laughter, and Weister joined him. But Weister refused to move his

175

body. And after the laughter was done, Henny said, 'All right. Why am I a poor romantic bastard?'

'Doris,' Marv said.

'Too obvious.'

'You're not immune to the obvious, buddy.'

Henny poured another drink for himself, corked the bottle and tossed it to Weister. The writer moved his left hand and caught it.

'You're alive after all,' Henny said.

'No, Henny. I haven't the courage to love, so I'm dying. And you, you're yellow too.'

Henny waited.

'You're afraid of Syl because she reminds you of Doris. At the same time, you're holding on to Doris because you – '

'Because I loved her,' Henny said defiantly, and then muttered, 'Now you bust the bubble, daddy.'

Weister waved his hand. 'So you loved her. She's dead three years.'

'I'm a romantic bastard,' Henny said, nodding. 'That's what you meant?'

'Now I bust the bubble. You're even more romantic than that. Sure, you loved her, and her memory is part of it, but only a very small part of it. You're healthy enough to shake a dead lover.'

Henny's eyes blinked. 'Okay.'

'But you're fond of that most romantic of all neuroses – death-guilt.'

Henny drank. 'Throw the bottle back,' he said.

Weister threw it and Henny had to lunge to the right and make a circus catch. 'I never could play ball worth a damn,' Weister said. 'No dad to teach me.'

'Wonder how Yogi Berra made it.'

'Yeah.'

'So why,' Henny asked, pouring a drink, 'am I here

176

now? To tell you I've fallen for a chick. So whose bubble is busted now?'

'Ah,' Weister said, leaning forward and waving his glass and spilling some of his drink. 'Ah, that's the whole goddam point.'

'Tell me, daddy. Tell me.'

'No, Henny. *You* tell me. What sort of impossible situation did you find, or create, to make falling in love safe? Is she dying of cancer? Is she married and in love with her husband? Is she a syphilitic whore whom you could never bring to Syl?'

'You're hip, daddy,' Henny said, surprised at being convinced.

'Yes?'

'She's Les Bogen's daughter.'

Weister stared at him, and slowly a grin began to push its way onto his thin, pasty face. And as his smile grew, so did a corresponding one on Henny's face. And then they were both rolling around and clutching at their stomachs and laughing, laughing.

They didn't talk much after that. They stopped drinking and the edge went off their rapport and Weister brought out something he'd never shown Henny before – his scrapbook of reviews, Henny read them and looked up. 'You're a regular Shakespeare,' he said in dialect.

'What else?' Weister replied.

'So why don't they sell?'

'Maybe I'm not the stallion type,' Weister replied.

Henny grinned.

Weister said, 'One thing more. You going to try and see that girl?'

'No.'

'But if she tries to see you?'

'She won't. Why should she?'

'To talk about Les. To pump you.'

'She's already tried that. I said no.'

'She called you?'

Henny told him about it.

'I see. And what if she calls again and says she'll see you on *your* terms?'

'Why should she?'

'Why did you fall for her?'

'You just told me. She's safe, out of reach.' He paused. 'I don't buy that, Marv – not entirely.'

'It's not true, Henny – not entirely. Nothing's ever entirely true. But let's accept it, as we did before, for the sake of a beautiful theory. Let's say it *was* true, initially. Of course, what happens from here on is straight boy-girl stuff.'

'Nothing'll happen,' Henny muttered.

'But you hope something does?'

Henny sighed.

'Okay, so what's to prevent her from wanting to see you for the same reason you – initially, okay? – wanted to see her? You're forbidden fruit, Henny. You're part of her father's hidden life.'

Henny stood up. 'I'm a very simple man,' he said. 'I'm beat by all this thinking and talking.'

Marv Weister smiled, but it was weak and pensive. 'You have to go now?'

Henny nodded.

'Okay. So long.'

'So long.' Henny opened the door. 'You're really quite a brain.'

'Yeah, but what sort of *man* am I?'

Henny grinned, as if it were a joke, and left. On the way back to the studio, he thought of tomorrow – Wednesday – and spending the day with Syl. He'd do it. He'd show her a good time.

But by the time he reached his desk, he'd convinced

himself that he had to be around the studio in case an assignment developed. And Sandra Bogen might call.

He laughed aloud. Van Roberts in the next office, called, 'Sounds like a good punch line, Henny.'

'The best, Van. The best.'

He called the housekeeper away and asked if she'd stay with Syl for twenty bucks. She said no, definitely, she had to visit her uncle. He asked if she'd get a replacement. She sighed and said, 'Your little girl, Henny. Your poor little girl.'

'Listen, I don't want lectures!' He stopped himself, muttered, '*Will* you get someone for me?'

She said, 'I stay myself. But this is last time!'

He went to the darkroom and watched Vic Bloom work on a series Laird Drake had taken at a Broadway girlie musical. The stuff was prosaic, even for a girlie musical. 'Stick around,' Vic said. 'Next comes the big man's Pennsylvania-fair stuff. Most of it was color, but I'm handling five rolls of thirty-five-millimeter black-and-white. He's always got something good.'

Henny said he was hungry, and left. He went to a movie. He got out at seven and had a sandwich and a beer, and went to another movie. He returned to the studio at eleven, letting himself in with his key, and checked Marie's notebook. One call – Carl Stevens of Treakles Everything-Photographic. The message was: 'Have Mr Girado call me – PLEASE.' The 'please' was underlined three times.

Henny shut the book, lighted a cigarette and wondered if he should work up more samples for his portfolio; maybe enlarge a few of the hair-goods pics and put them on fine paper.

It made sense. A good portfolio could get him more work.

He remembered his movie equipment stuck in a closet

179

at home – camera, projector, cutter-splicer – the works. How long had it been since he'd used them, dreaming, dreaming?

Years. Since Doris died. And even before it hadn't been anything *but* a dream. Sure, everyone had a big ambition.

What was it Eva Gretz had said about the boss's son – 'Maybe he wanted to play the violin.'

With Henny Girado, it was wanting to make honest motion pictures, his own motion pictures, on the order of *The Little Fugitive*, a superior piece of cinema turned out by Morris Engel and Ruth Orkin on practically no budget at all.

He wondered if the gag films he'd made with Doris and ex-friend Mal Corwin – one hundred fifteen bucks owed for over two years had queered *that* friendship – were still around the house.

But what difference did it make? He wouldn't bother with them anyway. No sense in it. He'd never play the violin.

He walked slowly down the steps to the street and stood smoking his cigarette for a moment or two; then he reluctantly entered his car and drove home.

Marv Weister was sitting at his typewriter. It was one-fifteen Wednesday morning, he'd written four pages, and he hated every single word.

He shoved back the chair and got up and went to his bed, unmade for three days now. He looked at it with distaste and lay down.

For a while he merely stared at the ceiling; then he rolled over, grabbed the bedding and bunched it in his small, bony fists.

He remembered telling Henny about needing someone to love. He told himself the same thing. But he wasn't strong enough to love. Loving entailed living, and he couldn't live. Loving entailed getting off your ass and going out and projecting yourself – as he had with Henny – and then projecting differently to a girl's family and maintaining a degree of normalcy day in and day out so she wouldn't be frightened away.

'Christ, Christ, I can't do that. I could never do it before, and I'm so far from what I was before. Christ, Christ.'

He realized what he was saying and remembered morning prayers at Lawrence Terril's School for Boys, and sat up. He looked around quickly, as if afraid someone was there to see him. He got off the bed and went to the living room and shut off the light and returned to the bedroom and shut off the light there too, and knelt in the darkness beside the bed. 'Dear Lord, help me. I'm so afraid. You're the strongest God in the world.' But he remembered that Mohammedans outnumbered Christians, and he also remembered his Aunt Rose and her pungent opinion of *goyem*, and he was ashamed. He got up and put on the light. He went to the living room and put on the light there too. He looked at the phone. All he had to do was pick it up and dial the number and say, 'Please call my cousin Alfred.' The voice would ask, 'Alfred who?' and he would give the name Mr Elders had given him at the last fix. Masters or Hooper or Pratt or whatever the pusher happened to choose. Then there'd be a pause, and the voice would say, 'Who is this?' And he would give his name and make an appointment and go to the Bronx candy-store not too far from where his Aunt Rose had lived, when she'd lived. And there would be the back room and the bent spoon and the little stove and the needle and the quick injection. Then home by subway, and before he'd reach home the subway would

181

hold no terrors for him. Nothing would hold terrors for him. He'd be free, and happy.

Why had he lied to Henny? Why hadn't he told him the truth, told him of the marvelous release heroin offered?

He shook his head then, turning from the phone. No, it wasn't release. It was surcease, a putting off of the inevitable, a momentary pushing away of the fear and pain and loneliness. And then these terrors returned, stronger, much stronger.

He wanted a cigarette. He checked the apartment and found his pack, and it was crumpled, empty.

He cursed Henny for having smoked them. He went to the window and looked down and saw no one in the street and was still afraid to go out alone. He told himself he was a fool. He was Marvin Weister, who'd drawn rave notices from every major newspaper in the United States on his first and third books. Even the second, considered the least important, hadn't been treated harshly – and *it* was the one that was reprinted. Marvin Weister, whose third book had been published only sixteen months ago. Marvin Weister, who was writing another.

'But am I?' he said, and the panic was high in his throat. 'Am I?'

He forgot the cigarettes. He went back to the typewriter and sat down and read his four pages. He took a pencil and began crossing out and writing in. He made a small, raging sound and put a fresh sheet in the typewriter.

At four A.M., he completed his final version of the four pages. He still wasn't completely satisfied, but they'd have to do.

He went to the kitchenette and had a glass of milk and went to the bathroom and then to the bedroom. He lay down in his underwear, too tired to get his pajamas from the closet. Besides, they weren't clean.

182

He asked himself why he couldn't write the way he talked. Look how he'd talked to Henny! He'd had the man pegged perfectly and worked his words around him until the problem, the personality, lay clearly exposed.

But on paper . . .

He worked well when he'd had a jolt.

No, he always threw the stuff away or had to revise it heavily.

But while high, the words seemed to flow and the exultation was strong and he believed in himself and his work.

God, he wanted a jolt!

Next week. One a week. Or maybe, just maybe, he'd take another shot this week. He'd done it a few times in the past. It didn't mean anything. He could handle it.

Maybe he'd call the candystore tomorrow.

No, he'd wait. It could destroy him.

He was almost asleep when he asked himself the dangerous question. *So what?*

12

On Wednesday morning, Henny was in the darkroom at eight-thirty, working with the enlarger to get two good blowups of his best hair-goods pictures for use in his portfolio. It was almost ten before he was satisfied. He went to the office. Laird Drake was there, sitting at his desk and writing. Henny said, 'Hi.'

Drake looked up, folded a sheet of paper and placed it in his pocket.

'I'm going down for a cup of coffee, Laird. Join me?'

Drake shook his head.

'I think we should get together, daddy.'

Laird stood up. 'What for? We have nothing to discuss.' He began putting things into his gadget bag; then he paused. 'Unless you've decided to meet me man to man, without knives?'

'I said I was sorry. I said it twice. I'm saying it again. Now act like a man.'

'It's you who should act like a man. And when you do . . .' Drake clenched his big fists at his sides. Henny stared at him, a flush moving into his cheeks. Drake took his bag and left.

Henny spoke to the empty desk. 'Don't try it. Please don't try it. I'm even happier now than the night – ' He cut the violent thoughts short and left the office. Halfway down the stairs, he heard the faint ring of a phone. It could be his, Drake's or one in the adjoining office. But he wanted that cup of coffee.

When he reached the street, he felt the first sick twinges of a headache.

What was it he'd read in some psychiatrist's book? Headaches are the results of repressed rage or fear.

He changed his mind about going to the luncheonette. He'd have coffee, but there'd be a stiff shot of rum in it.

He went to the Clover, a little bar on Seventh Avenue. It was almost empty, and he took a stool as far away from the other two customers as he could get. The bartender said hi, and Henny ordered black coffee and rum. He lighted a cigarette, and his drink came, and he raised the cup and sipped. It was steaming hot, and he gulped as much as he could without scalding his mouth.

He finished, ordered a second, and relaxed a bit. There was a TV set over the street end of the bar, and he turned and watched it. He finished his second drink, ordered a third, and spent a long, long time finishing that. At eleven-thirty, he had a sandwich and a fourth rum royal and smoked two more cigarettes.

It was twelve-thirty when he returned to the studio. He went to Marie's desk and asked the receptionist if there'd been any calls for him. 'Three,' she said, not looking at him. 'A woman. The same one each time.' Her voice was very cool.

'What about the message?'

'No message.'

He grunted, trying to stop the sudden excitement. 'You don't love me any more, huh, doll?'

She looked at him. 'I'm busy, Mr Girado.'

He shrugged and walked toward the studio.

'Mr Bogen is shooting.'

'And he's got a reserve on. I know.' He reached the door and knocked.

'Come ahead,' Bogen's voice said.

Henny walked in. Bogen was shooting his department-store account – the stage held a table, chairs, one male and one female model dressed in robe and negligee

185

respectively. 'Yes?' Bogen said, straightening from his Rollei and looking at Henny.

'You saving dough, Les?' Henny asked, seeing that the assistant Bogen used on all jobs but cheesecake was absent.

'Ernie's lining up some props for another job,' Bogen replied. 'Is that all I can do for you.'

Henny nodded at the models, who were relaxing now that Bogen was off-camera. He walked up close to Bogen and murmured, 'If you need help, I can use twenty bucks.' He grinned, but he was dead serious.

Bogen shook his head. 'No, thanks.'

Henny lowered his voice even more. 'Then how about twenty until next week?'

Bogen sighed.

Henny grinned again, painfully. 'I haven't had an assignment in a week.'

Bogen took out his wallet and gave him two tens. 'How much does that make, not counting the film?'

'I've got it all down in a notebook in my desk, Les. About two hundred, more or less.'

'Think I'll ever see it again?'

Henny's shoulders slumped. 'Okay. You've kicked me. Can I leave now?'

Bogen turned away, face paling. 'Don't ask me again, Henny. It irritates me.'

Henny walked around him, faced him, said, 'I wouldn't want to irritate the big man.' He shoved the two bills deep into Bogen's breast pocket and left the studio.

'I told you not to bother him,' Marie said smugly, reading the distress on Henny's face.

Henny stopped. 'Get off my back,' he said, but he was speaking to everyone, not just Marie Riposta.

She shrugged, and smiled coldly, and turned her head, dismissing him.

He went upstairs. He called four magazine outfits, asking for work. He got nothing. He called a fifth, and Elroy Frankle, photo editor for Viewcitement Corporation, said, 'We're going on inventory for a while, Henny. Summer's coming, you know.'

Henny hung up and checked his telephone book and then slapped it shut. Yes, summer was coming, and things were slowing down, and he couldn't take any slowdowns, any loss in income. He had bills.

The phone rang. He picked it up. 'Henny Girado?' the voice asked.

Henny took a deep breath and forgot money or the lack of it. He glanced at the door connecting the two offices, to make sure it was shut. It was. 'Hi, Sandy.'

'Hi. You're a hard man to get hold of. I called three times.'

'You must want me bad.'

She laughed. 'I'm not sure of that, yet.'

'Well, let's get down to business. I'm still not interested in a talky luncheon. Does that end our relationship?'

'No.' She paused. 'What were you doing when I called? I mean before.'

'I was sitting in a bar watching TV. Did you ever watch daytime television?'

'I don't think so.'

'It's bad, daytime television. It's even worse than nighttime television. It's like you're someplace where everyone talks *down* at you, showing they think you're an imbecile. It's deadly.'

'Oh,' she said.

He sighed. 'Haven't I given you enough time, Sandy? Haven't you worked out the words yet?'

'The words?'

'Whatever you're going to say that'll bring us together.' His voice grew quiet and intense. 'I want that. I want that very much. Do I have to go on about television, and books and movies, while you work out the formula?'

'I'd like you to come to my home tonight. About seven-thirty or eight.'

'Your home? I, ah, don't think your father would approve. He must think of me as at least as old as himself – probably ten or twelve years older.'

'And almost as lecherous.'

'It was a mistake,' he said. 'Sorry. Forget that stuff about wanting us to get together. I didn't give the odds enough thought. I can't make it with you on any reasonable basis.'

'Who needs a reasonable basis? Play it cool and get what you can.'

'Goodbye,' he said, voice dull. 'I can do that with half a dozen chicks who live less than half an hour from here.'

'Wait,' she said. 'I *do* want to see you, Henny. And neither of my parents will be home.'

He still wanted to call it off. He still felt it was a mistake. Les had come clearly into the picture, and that made a difficult situation impossible. But her voice had been so right on that last statement – soft and throaty – and he could visualize the lovely face. He said, 'I haven't got the address.'

She gave it to him, and explicit directions. Now he wanted to go on talking to her, but she said she was in school and had a class and goodbye. And he was holding a dead phone. He hung up and was surprised to find he was sweating. Life was full of surprises, not all this good. Or *was* this good?

He went to the washroom and examined himself in the mirror. He looked okay. A little dark stubble of beard, maybe, and the green corduroy trousers a little baggy, but that's the way he always looked. Rinsing his face would fix everything. Sure, he never changed for chicks. It spoiled them.

But he knew he would go home, shower and shave. He would wear his tan flannel slacks, white shirt and tie, and good hound's-tooth jacket.

'Like the senior prom, man,' he muttered, returning to his office. It didn't curb the rising tide of excitement.

His phone was ringing. 'Bring daddy a job and the day'll be perfect.' He lifted the handset and said hello.

'Henny? Mal Corwin. How's the boy?'

Henny sighed inwardly, silently. Corwin had been a close friend until about a year after Doris had died. Now he was a creditor.

'Pretty good, Mal. Say, I've been meaning to get a few bucks over your way, but things've been rough.'

'That's what I called about, Henny. It's been nine months since I last mentioned that hundred fifteen. But now I need it, kid. How about settling up? Don't you think the tab's due?'

'It's way overdue, Mal,' Henny said, and had to clear his throat. 'I know it and you know it, but at the moment . . .'

'C'mon now, Henny! Almost two years! And I need that dough!'

'I'll try next month, Mal.'

'Okay. No more stalling, huh? Next month for sure?'

'Yes,' Henny said, and wondered if he'd be able to do it, and wanted to shout and rage and stomp someone, anyone.

But when he said goodbye and lighted a cigarette, most of the violent feeling went away. He reminded himself that he'd have to endure similar dunnings for a long, long time, perhaps the rest of his life. If he let it get him, he was finished. And he didn't want to be finished, not with the lovely blonde waiting up in Peekskill.

Sandy.

He didn't use her second name, even in his thoughts. Just Sandy. Sandy and Henny. The two of them, isolated from the rest of the world.

He refused to laugh at himself.

He went to Richie Morden's office. The owner-photographer was getting ready to leave on an assignment of his own. 'Listen, Richie, can you advance me another couple hundred on that *luau* job? Things are tight.'

Morden said, 'Okay, okay,' voice sharp and angry.

Henny stared at him, and when he spoke his own voice held anger even though it was soft, almost a whisper. 'What's eating you, Richie? I haven't been any more trouble than usual.'

Richie Morden immediately recognized the truth of that statement, but it only served to make his irritation rise. However, he mastered emotion and acted on reason. He nodded, said, 'I can go another two hundred, Henny. I guess I could even go the remaining four hundred and pocket your check when it comes in.'

'Two hundred would be fine, Richie.'

Morden wrote a check. Henny took it and turned to the door and then said, 'I've been operating with you this way for some years now, Richie. I *have to*, what with my stinking finances. But you've never lost a dime on me, and you're one of the few people I don't owe – '

'I'm sorry I jumped you, Henny,' Morden interrupted, and his irritation was still there, and he fought it. 'We'll continue as usual, of course.'

Henny went to the door, saying he just had time to make the bank. He was relieved but didn't want Richie to see it.

After cashing the check, he drove home. The housekeeper and Syl weren't around; they were probably out for a walk. He washed, dressed and left. He'd pay the

190

woman her salary and extra twenty tomorrow. It was nice to have two hundred bucks in your wallet, even for only a few hours, and even if it didn't really belong to you. And he especially wanted to feel solvent tonight.

He decided to kill a few hours in a movie.

Richie Morden got his gear and left the office a few minutes after Henny. He thought of the job he was going to do – an Italian street party in upper Manhattan, the section called Italian Harlem. Colored people had begun moving into the area, and this had caused friction between groups of young people, and part of his assignment was to show that the friction was minor.

But a street party wasn't indicative of day-to-day living. A street party didn't change the fact that whites looked down on Negroes, and Negroes resented whites, and they feared and hated each other.

He got in his car and put on the radio, and when that didn't help, thought of Van Roberts. Van hated no one; no one hated Van.

That didn't help either.

The whole world seemed fraught with racial hate for a moment, and anyone belonging to *both* camps seemed doomed. And there was Phyll, his wife, who would feel 'disgusted' if he were part Negro.

Why had he ever brought up the subject with her? Why couldn't he have left her opinions an unknown factor?

But, at the same time, he began to understand that some sort of probing, some sort of discussion, had been inevitable. A man had to know what his beloved thought of him, *of what he was*.

Except that he himself didn't know what he was!

He relaxed a bit. But he also realized that he'd been giving more thought to his 'problem' in the last week

191

than he had in all the years of his marriage. It worried him. It could lead to trouble.

It was three-thirty. Marie Riposta leaned back in her chair and dabbed at her face with a handkerchief. Warm. Soon it would be summer and everyone would start going to the beach. She didn't like the beach. She felt better fully dressed.

A call came in for Laird Drake, and she switched it upstairs because he'd walked up a few minutes ago. Victor Bloom was also upstairs, and Les Bogen was back working in the studio after a late lunch break with his two models.

She was wondering whether she should send out for a Coke, or maybe a milk shake because that was fattening and she wanted a few more pounds, when her friend Stella Lago appeared on the second-floor landing and moved toward her. Marie's stomach tightened.

'Hi,' Stella said brightly. 'I played sick so I could drop over and see your place. I've been dying to, Marie. Hope you don't mind.'

'Me mind? Why should I?' But she did. She minded terribly. The nerve, the fantastic nerve of the girl, coming up like this! After all!

Marie composed her thoughts. She wanted Stella out of here before the voluptuous redhead could meet any of the men. She didn't ask herself why; she merely acted on it.

'Listen, Stella, it's against Mr Morden's rules for strangers to be in the studio. I can't show you around at all. I'm sorry, but it could mean my job. You understand.'

'Not even a *peek?*' Stella asked, face falling. 'Just a quickie?'

Marie got up. 'No. Honest, I'm sorry, but you'll have to go. I'll walk you down.'

Les Bogen came out of the studio. 'Did my assistant call?' he asked Marie, and the next second his eyes were moving over Stella. He liked what he saw. The redhead was tall, full-bodied, high-breasted and saucy. And she smiled at him.

Marie said stiffly, 'No. Mr Radish didn't call, Mr Bogen.'

Stella said, ostensibly to Marie, 'Are you sure I can't watch a photographer working? I'd give anything for just a quick peek.' She looked at Les and giggled. '*Almost* anything.'

Marie smiled unconvincingly and began to move Stella toward the landing. Les Bogen said, 'Are you interested in modeling, Miss – '

'Lago,' the redhead said. 'Stella Lago.' She smiled happily, knowing what was going to happen. 'I'm *very* interested. Of course, I have no experience, but I could learn.'

'Really, Stella,' Marie said, 'Mr Bogen is busy.' But she too knew what was going to happen.

Les Bogen said, 'That's all right, Marie. Come in, Miss Lago.'

Stella said, 'Thank you,' and smiled at Marie and walked through the door Bogen held open for her. The door closed, and Marie was standing alone. She returned to her desk and told herself it made no difference to *her* if Stella wanted to act like a slut!

But she was raging and didn't know why. And even if she had known why, she would never have admitted it to herself – not *jealousy!*

At five, Stella came out, with Les Bogen and the two models. The models said goodbye and left together. Les and Stella stood near the studio door, talking softly, and Stella laughed a lot. They ignored Marie. Then Les patted the redhead's arm, and Marie heard him say, '. . . across

193

the street. Five minutes, dear.' He went back into the studio.

Stella came over to Marie, her face shining. 'Gee, he's the nicest guy. Real cool!'

'He's married,' Marie said.

'Yeah, he told me,' Stella said, and smiled again. 'But we're only going to have dinner, so what's wrong with that?' She didn't wait for an answer. 'So long, Marie. See you.' She ran to the steps and out of sight.

Marie hated her.

And when Les Bogen walked by her desk a few minutes later, giving her a preoccupied nod, Marie made a momentous decision. She was going to find a quiet, high-class restaurant-bar, and go inside and sit at a table and look around. *And meet someone!* Yes, she'd get picked up! She'd find a handsome guy and show Stella, show Les Bogen, show her brothers and parents – show them all.

At six o'clock, quitting time, she no longer felt quite as hurt and angry, but there was still the desperate need to prove something to herself. These girls – the models and Stella and lots of others – promised a man more than a *date* by the way they acted, the way they talked and laughed and looked. That gave them an edge, because a man had more to gain and naturally . . .

But would a man move toward *her* even if she put herself in a place – like a bar – where just being there promised more than a date?

She had to know.

She went to the washroom and applied make-up – more lipstick than usual, a little line of eyebrow pencil around her eyes, an extra touch of perfume behind her ears. Her dress was all right – not what she would have chosen for the occasion but good enough – a pink-and-brown cotton print, in at the waist and out in the shirt and skirt. She finished primping and looked in the mirror.

She was dark and slim (not thin, she told herself). She was . . . attractive.

She called home from her desk, told her mother she was going to a movie with friends and not to worry if she came home late. Her mother asked, 'What friends, Marie?'

'You don't know them, Momma.' Her mother said, 'I don' like the idea. I think you should come home. Your poppa get mad.'

Marie was suddenly enraged. 'I'll do what I want! I'll go where I want, with whoever I like, and no one'll stop me. Not you, not Poppa, not Frankie, John or Angie! I'm not gonna sit home so you can have an old-maid daughter to yak at.'

'Marie!'

'Just let me alone! Just let me live my own life!' She felt close to tears and hung up. She didn't want to cry. It would make her eyes red, streak her cheeks. She was going to that nice place off Fifth Avenue, and she had to look her best.

The 'nice place' was a hotel bar several blocks uptown from Rockefeller Center, just east of Fifth. Marie had passed it several times, when meeting her friend Roberta, who worked a block farther east. She'd glanced through the dark-glass door and had seen a small bar and well-dressed men and, on the west side of the narrow room, eight or ten tables at which women, alone or with men, sat eating and drinking. There was an air of quiet respectability about it, and for Marie, who had never been in a bar with a man – not counting the pizza joints in Brooklyn – it seemed much safer than any of the other places she passed on the streets of Manhattan. She went there now.

She didn't enter right away. Her courage failed her, and she walked completely around the block. Back on Fifth, she almost headed for the subway; but then she thought of Stella with her bright red mouth, a mouth so quick to laugh, so quick to say flippant things to men. She also thought of going home, of sitting at the table with Momma and Poppa and her brothers, of the drab talk of boxing and baseball, and then the television, of the way they talked about *her* – 'Maybe you're no Gina Lollobrigida, but why don't you go out with that nice Anthony Macri on Church Avenue?' They thought she was ugly! They thought that unless *they* got her a guy, she'd become an old maid.

All right! She'd show them!

She came around the corner and walked up to the glass door and opened it. She stepped inside and was met by low talk, laughter and music. Her heart pounded sickeningly, and she wanted to be home with her family, wanted to admit she was no Stella, wanted to accept her defeated status.

At that moment she remembered the shower and the . . . evil thoughts.

It gave her the added touch of desperation she needed. It carried her down the narrow, dimly lighted room, with bar on her right and tables on her left. The tables were set close to one another, all against a wall-length, pink-leatherette bench. Simple dark-wood chairs with pink-leatherette seats faced this bench on the opposite side of each table.

Then she was slipping between two tables, sitting down on the bench, ordering a martini, because that's what most of the photographers drank at studio parties. The waiter asked, 'Anything to eat, *madame?*' She shook her head. 'Not right now.' He went to the bar. She opened her purse and put her hand inside and merely touched things. She was afraid to look around. She wanted something to do.

She wanted to go home.

But she reminded herself of the shower; and her next thought was clear, concise, sustaining. If she was going to sin, let it be with a living man.

She snapped her purse shut as the waiter placed her drink on the table. 'A package of cigarettes,' she said, and was pleased at the way her voice sounded – calm, cool, assured.

'The brand, *madame?*' the waiter asked.

She liked him. He was small and nondescript and aging. He had a French accent and seemed to bow a little as he spoke. 'Kent,' she said, because her brother Angie smoked Kents. She didn't smoke – not really. She'd puffed an occasional cigarette, especially on dates, when she'd felt she had to find something to do. She felt that way now, more than ever before.

She picked up her drink but quickly set it down again because it was filled to the very top and her hand trembled and she was afraid of spilling it. She wanted to look around but didn't dare to. She stared at her drink and felt tension rising, and wanted to pray for strength, and decided that praying in a bar was out of the question. She leaned back, trying to look relaxed but still didn't raise her eyes.

The waiter returned and placed the cigarettes on the table. She looked up and smiled. 'Thank you.' The waiter nodded and hurried to another customer. Now she could swing her eyes after him and thereby bring herself to look at the men along the bar and eventually at whoever occupied the table to her left. After that, she could look at the table on her right.

She did none of these things. As if every pair of eyes in the room were forcing hers down, she looked at her drink. A tiny trickle of cold perspiration began to run down her sides. She felt as if she were about to snap in two, she was that tight.

197

The cigarettes.

She reached for the pack. It was the flip-top type, and she opened it quickly. She drew out a cigarette, put it between her lips, lighted it after striking the match four times. She puffed, and smoke drifted from her mouth, and she followed it with her eyes. She looked at the bar. Men sat with their backs or sides to her. Two faced each other, chatting, and one of these two glanced at her casually. She dropped her eyes. She couldn't force them up again.

After a while she reached for the drink. Her hand still shook, but she wanted the alcohol badly now and didn't put the stemmed glass down even when liquid spilled over her fingers. She got it to her lips and gulped.

She'd never drunk much: a glass of wine every so often when Poppa insisted she try some with her dinner, or a Pink Lady which she'd ordered on several of her rare dates, and nursed throughout the evening. Yet she barely tasted the martini, felt no sting in her taste buds because of her extreme nervousness.

She finished the drink and set down the glass and put out her cigarette stub. She lighted a second cigarette, on the first strike of the match this time, and began to feel better.

The gin-wine mixture affected her quickly. She moved her legs so she could cross them under the tiny table, and puffed her cigarette, and followed the smoke with her eyes. She looked at the bar. She looked at the men. The two who'd been chatting were gone. A man and woman, also chatting, were in their places.

Along with her relief, she felt disappointment. That young one with the tweed jacket had glanced at her. Maybe he'd have done something –

She saw her waiter and nodded at him. He came to the table. 'Another martini,' she said, and was shocked at the trouble she had with her tongue. It was getting thick, and on just one drink.

But the waiter merely nodded and hurried to the bar. Marie decided she would nurse this second drink. The worst thing she could do was get drunk.

She looked at the bar a third time – men, one couple, two well-dressed women sitting together at the far left end. No one looked at her.

She was alone. Here, as everywhere else, she was alone. Nothing was going to happen.

That thought frightened her even more than coming into the bar had. She turned her head and looked at the table on her right. A middle-aged couple was eating a dinner which completely covered their little table. They ate seriously, silently. They looked very married.

She began to feel foolish, and that was even worse than feeling afraid. She laughed at herself bitterly for believing that exciting things ever happened in bars – at least to girls like her.

And she turned to her left, no longer hoping and therefore no longer fearing. The man was dressed in a beautifully cut brown suit. He had graying hair and a large, clean, fair-skinned face. His eyes were grayish blue. They were looking at her. He said, 'Did your young man stand you up?'

She nodded, said, 'I'm just as glad,' and smiled. And wondered at herself, marveled at what she was doing. He wasn't what she wanted. He looked forty or more – but a *young* forty or more, she decided an instant later when he smiled, teeth white and even, a deep line creasing his right cheek. Then his smile went away and he said, 'I'm also glad. It gives me the opportunity of speaking to a lovely young lady.'

She turned away. The waiter was standing before her,

placing her martini on the table. He looked at the man. 'Anything for you, Mr Erlich?'

'No, Steve. My double Scotch is good for a least half an hour.'

The waiter left.

'Steve,' Marie said. 'I thought his name would be Pierre or something.'

Mr Erlich laughed. 'The accent's real, all right. His name is Steven Chartraine. Not *all* Frenchmen are named Pierre.'

'Thank you for the lecture,' she said coolly. He was almost old and she didn't fear him and she spoke the way her feelings, and the liquor, told her to speak.

'Oh, I didn't mean . . .'

She smiled at him, dispensing forgiveness, and he said, 'May I join you?'

She hesitated.

He said quickly, 'I would *so* enjoy speaking to you.'

She shrugged and raised her martini and sipped. He stood up and she saw that he was quite tall – about five feet ten or eleven. And well built – solid without being heavy. He squeezed between their tables, carrying his drink, and sat down in the chair across from her. He said, 'Thank you. My name is Larry Erlich. I live only eight or ten blocks from here, a nice apartment on the East Side of town.' He smiled again, and again she watched the pleasant crease form in his right cheek. 'But it's lonely, living alone.'

Normally, Marie would have reacted tartly against the possibility that he was about to make some sort of proposition. This time, she was in a bar, and talking to a strange man and not at all worried about what the strange man would think of her. She said, 'You don't know how lucky you are. There are times I'd give ten years of my life to live alone.'

'Ah? You live with your family?'

She raised her cocktail. 'To my family.' She drank, and felt her head spinning, and laughed. 'My refined, quiet family.'

Larry Erlich drank with her. 'I see. Well, it certainly wouldn't be difficult for a young and pretty woman to get her own place.'

'Money, dear Larry,' she said, and was amazed at her smooth voice and easy words. And then accepted herself and ceased being amazed. 'The right apartment costs far more than the average working girl can earn. And I am very average.'

'Not so,' he murmured, and his hand was covering hers, touching with understanding and sympathy for a moment. Then it was gone. 'You are very definitely not average. You are here, speaking to me, and criticizing your background, your home. The average working girl – if there is such a person – would never dream of doing such a thing.'

She thought a moment, then said. 'You're right.'

He raised his glass. 'May we drink to my being right a second time?'

Only after she'd taken a sip of her martini did she understand what he'd said. 'A *second* time?'

He wet his lips. 'Yes. I believe you're going to accept my invitation.'

She let her eyebrows climb. The liquor filled her brain and body and she felt very much in control of the situation. 'Let's hear it,' she said.

'There's a fine off-Broadway drama I've been wanting to see, but I hate to see anything alone.' He glanced at his wristwatch. A very expensive-looking watch, Marie thought, and then, looking him over, realized that everything about him was expensive. 'It's not quite seven,' he said. 'We could have a bite of dinner and be at the

201

theater by curtain time – eight-thirty. Later, if you're so inclined, we can eat again.'

She leaned back and cocked her head on the side and smiled.

'You look very lovely that way,' he murmured.

She believed him. She *felt* lovely. She laughed throatily, liking the sound because it was new to her. She laughed again, letting herself go, and he smiled and said, 'Tell me what is funny so I may join you.'

'I thought you were going to ask me to come to your apartment.'

'Are you disappointed?'

For a moment she thought she was losing control of the situation. His eyes had grown so shiny, his voice so eager. She was sure she'd seen his hand tremble before steadying itself on his glass. 'No,' she said. 'Relieved.'

'Ah,' he said, and it was as if he were shrinking away from her.

She gave him no help. She lighted a third cigarette and finished her martini and looked around the room.

'I don't even know your name,' he finally said.

'Marie.'

'Just Marie?'

She nodded. 'I'm hungry, Larry. You seem to know this place. Order something good, please?'

'Then you're going to the theater with me?'

'Yes.' She rose, and he jumped to his feet and moved the table aside so she could get to the aisle with ease. 'Pardon me,' she said, remembering that it was nicer than excuse me. She walked toward the illuminated sign in the rear of the bar. She walked with the knowledge that his eyes were on her; with the feeling that other eyes might also be on her. She felt the liquor, but it merely served to make her walk as she'd always wanted to walk – that and the eyes on her. She let her hips roll smoothly, kept her head up and back, her breasts out. Yes, she was slim, even thin, but her body was young and healthy. Let him look. Let him hunger. *She wanted to be hungered after!*

When she returned to the table, Steve, the waiter, was already serving honeydew melon.

The meal was wonderful – a spicy stew and salad and dessert. They had a bottle of red wine with it, but Marie became less affected by alcohol because of the food. Still, her gaiety, her grasp of the situation, remained, even increased, as they left the bar. It was raining as they went by taxi to a small theater within sight of New York University. The play was exciting; something without traditional beginning or end; something about a man who both loved and hated his mother. Marie would never have thought anyone could make two full hours of drama out of *that;* especially since it had little she could later tell her friends when they asked her what the story, the plot, had been. But then again, she wasn't thinking of her friends. She was thinking of what would happen when the play was over.

As soon as they left the theater, she checked her watch. 'It's eleven-thirty, Larry. Tomorrow's a work day for me.'

'It is for me, too,' he said, holding her arm and looking into her face. 'But I would gladly go without sleep if we could – '

'We can't,' she said, but softly, smiling. The rain had stopped; everything smelled cool and clean. 'Please take me home.'

'Just a mouthful of food?' he pleaded.

'One dinner an evening is enough for a girl.'

'With your figure,' he murmured, hand tightening on her arm, 'what cause for concern?'

They were looking at each other, and she was so

relaxed, so very pleased with the evening, even though he wasn't young, even though she was sure she could never think of him as a boy friend. The term itself seemed ridiculous when applied to Larry Erlich, to this man with short-cropped graying hair, still thick though; to this stranger with deep-set eyes, warm and understanding eyes. 'Some men find me a little too lean,' she said, and smiled, waiting.

'They are either in need of glasses or are fools!'

She was surprised at the anger in his voice.

'Thank you,' she said. 'Now, please call a cab.'

He called a cab. They got inside, and as she settled herself her dress hiked above her knees, and she saw how his eyes flashed and how his mouth grew tight, hungering. And she was glad.

She gave the driver her street but not her number. Larry Erlich leaned back, nodding sadly to himself. 'I see,' he intoned.

She moved close to him, took his hand, settled her head against his shoulder. 'My second name is Riposta,' she murmured. 'The phone is in my father's name – John.' Then she called to the driver, giving him her address.

Larry Erlich took out a small notebook and a pen and wrote swiftly.

'The little black book,' she murmured happily. 'I go down in good company, I hope?'

He smiled. 'The very best. But you outrank them all.'

'I don't believe that,' she said, settling herself once again against his shoulder.

His arm went around her; his hand took her hand; he whispered, 'Believe, Marie, believe. Your youth – your slim and lovely youth – makes the others seem corrupted, dying things. Believe.' His face came around and close, and his lips touched her forehead and nose and then – so softly, so naturally that she had to help him – her mouth. He kissed her, and while she was helping him her lips parted and she was no longer in control of the situation.

The instincts – the implanted fears and training of all her previous life – came alive then, insisting that she push him away. And she began to. But even before *he* could react to her tightening body, her tightening lips, *she* did. She felt the old Marie returning: the tense, perspiring, unhappy Marie; the unkissed, unloved Marie; the girl of rigid inferiority. And she put her lips to his ear and whispered, 'No, Larry! I'm burning, burning.'

Everything she did with this man was right. Her choice of words was perfect. He resumed kissing her, and when the old Marie made her tighten every so often, he remembered what she'd said and thought of her body as burning, burning, and her rigidity as a last-ditch defense.

She opened her eyes once and saw that they were crossing the Manhattan Bridge. She closed them again, and his hand on her arm moved under her arm and she knew what he was going to do and she tightened for the last time. For when his hand cupped her breast, two fingers spreading and then closing, scissor-wise, over the nipple, she wanted him, and in wanting him she became what she'd been playing at.

They ignored the cabby. They kissed violently, and his other hand stroked her slim thighs through the light cotton fabric. And then his fingers pressed down, through dress and underpants to touch her secret body, to bring such burning hunger that she would never again be satisfied with a daydream.

A moment later he stopped, drawing back and whispering, 'My God, I can't stand – ' He shook his head and turned away and held only her hand, and then pressed her hand to him, to *his* hunger and *his* burning. 'My God,' he choked. 'Can't we go back to the city? Someplace?'

205

She removed her hand gently, wanting to continue touching him but realizing now what he meant: that there was no more after this but the final act.

They sat apart. She looked at the cabby, and he seemed unaware of them, and yet she knew he couldn't have been unaware of them before. And still she felt no shame. She opened her purse and applied lipstick, turning her head and her mirror to catch light from the streets. She took out a cigarette and said, 'May I have a light, Larry?'

He turned to her, and she smiled. He answered her smile, but very weakly. He used a lighter, and she puffed smoke and enjoyed it. He took a cigar from his pocket. 'I need it,' he said. 'I know it offends most women, but I need it. May I?'

'Of course,' she said, surprised that he'd denied himself all through the evening. And it was his obvious pleasure at drawing in the smoke that made her suddenly, and for the first time, believe that he truly considered her something special. For a man to want a woman was one thing. For him to stop smoking for almost five hours because of her was another.

They said good night in the cab, very quickly, right in front of her home. He didn't get out with her, but when she was on the street and he'd closed the door, he said softly, 'Marie, give me your hand.'

She was already beginning to react to the proximity of her family, to the now overpowering reminders of the everyday Marie Riposta, but she wanted the evening to end right. She controlled the impulse to glance over her shoulder at the windows behind her, and at the cab driver. She put her hand through the cab's open rear window. Larry Erlich took it, and kissed the back, and then turned it over slowly, and pressed his lips to the palm. 'I will call you,' he murmured.

'Good night,' she said, and went up the stoop and into the hallway.

She heard the cab drive away, went to her apartment, and opened the door softly. All the lights were out, and she tiptoed toward her room. As she passed her parents' door, her mother whispered, 'Marie? You all right?'

'Yes,' she said, not wanting to smash the wonderful evening completely by discussing it with her mother.

'What time is it?'

'Late, Momma. Good night.' And she went on to her room.

She half expected her mother to follow her and ask questions, but it didn't happen.

It was one-thirty when she finally got into bed. She'd showered and brushed her hair and dressed in a very thin, black lace nightgown her brother Angie had given her on her eighteenth birthday. It was the first time she'd worn it, and looking at herself in the bathroom mirror she'd felt lovely and wished that Larry Erlich could see her.

In bed, she remembered the ecstasy of the cab ride, of the feel of his hands on her body – all new to her. And the way he'd placed her hand on him, on his pulsing maleness.

He hadn't been old then. He'd been a man: and what difference did a few years make?

But he had gray hair. And he lived alone. And who knew what would happen if they were in his apartment and she didn't want to let him. She could imagine it, and as she did a dull fire built unnoticed in her body. There would be drinks – martinis – the gin-wine mix designed to weaken her defenses. But she was not sure she was capable of summoning any defenses, not after the way she had felt when he had touched her. And he *would* touch her, and not through the material of her panties

207

and skirt. He would undress her, gently and expertly. Then he would undress himself, and as Marie pictured him naked, the raw maleness of him, her hands crept to her breasts, touching and stroking, arousing memories of Larry's hands. He would touch her there, and *there*, and she would want him and try to stop him, but the martinis would lull her, and Larry's touches would arouse her, and she would pull him to her, and he would love her.

Marie wailed as the image exploded into orgasm and she felt herself wet on her hand.

God, she'd taken some awful chances tonight!

But, she reminded herself, she'd *wanted* to take chances.

Crazy! Just plain crazy! Why, she might have been raped and become pregnant or diseased!

She fell asleep, pleased with her daring, more pleased that she'd escaped unharmed. She dreamed of Larry Erlich; of his face and his kisses and his maleness. And there was no thought of rape or disease.

In the morning she dressed and had toast and coffee and answered her mother's questions with monosyllabic lies. 'Movies . . . No . . . Yeah . . . So-so picture . . . Goulash . . . nothing to drink – just Coke . . . Cab from the station . . .'

She walked to the Utica Avenue subway station. She had only the slightest of headaches, but remembering the photographers talking of hangovers, she bought a Bromo anyway. She just made a train that was about to pull out, and it was jammed. Standing in the middle of the car, she hiccuped slightly, and a tall guy with long sideburns, standing close by, looked at her and turned away and stared at a plump, pretty blonde wearing a tight pink sweater. The blonde, seated with another girl, gave him a quick, flirty glance, and giggled to her friend and glanced at him again. He grinned and stared even harder.

Marie turned her back on them. No one looked at her, and she stifled another hiccup and began to feel tight and sweaty and unhappy. After a while, she got out of the car and walked down the platform, not even checking to see what station it was. Two more trains came and left before she felt ready to continue. When the third train arrived, she waited until several men and an elderly woman had pushed through the doors of the car nearest her; then she entered. She tried to walk as she had last night – head up and back, breasts out, hips rolling smoothly. But she felt foolish, felt tired and skinny and ugly, and stopped near the center poles, shoulders slumping. There was no Larry Erlich watching her, hungering for her.

He'd been an old guy, and out for only one thing and she must've been crazy! If he ever called, which she doubted, he'd get a quick please-don't-bother-me-again!

She got off the train and walked toward the studio. A priest came hurrying past her, eyes fixed on the pavement.

Yes, she'd have to tell Father Russo about it.

13

Henny Girado left his home at six Wednesday evening. Before he'd reached the Hawthorne Circle at the end of the Saw Mill River Parkway, rain began to fall. By the time he reached Route 202, his exit off the Taconic Parkway, it was coming down in blinding sheets. Lightning cut through the overcast, which, along with the seven o'clock dusk, made night complete and headlights necessary. 'Crazy!' he muttered, but he was enjoying the storm. A fresh smell came in through the open vents: a smell of green things expanding under the deluge; a smell that somehow made him want to hear good jazz. He fiddled with the radio, but several New York stations had faded out, and those he could get had ballads and rock-'n-roll. 'We're way out, man,' he muttered, and reached to shut it off. Just then a Red Norvo disk went on. He grinned and lighted a cigarette and listened. 'Like Lourdes, daddy. A freakin' miracle.'

When he swung off the Bear Mountain Expressway at Division Street, he examined the slip of paper on which he'd written Sandra Bogen's instructions, then turned left, drove slowly along the two-lane road until he reached the big convalescent home, and turned left again. The road became black-top, narrowed considerably and climbed steeply. He passed a few houses, widely interspaced, and entered a section of thick forest. A few minutes later there were more houses, their lights dimly seen through the pounding rain. The road kept climbing, and turned, and suddenly leveled off. He was now driving along the top of what he figured must be Gallows Hill, and when a flash of lightning ripped through the sky, he was able to see a deep valley off to his right. It was impressive, and he remembered reading that Jackie Gleason had a home somewhere in the area.

'Gleason and Bogen,' he muttered, 'sitting atop their mountains, counting money and women.'

He slowed to a crawl when he passed the abandoned red barn Sandy had mentioned, and saw the pebbled driveway and rural mailbox about twenty feet ahead, on the left. His headlights illuminated the reflecting letters atop the mailbox: BOGEN.

He made the turn, shifted into second for the steep climb, swung left with the driveway, and was suddenly before a huge garage with three separate doors. All three were up, and he could see inside. The interior had no partitions, and there was a Hillman Minx convertible parked on the right, leaving enough room for two full-sized cars. He pulled inside, using the center slot, and cut ignition and lights. He got out, keeping in mind the position of a door almost in line with his left fender. But he didn't have to make it through the darkness. The door opened and Sandra Bogen, in a figure-hugging black dress, was silhouetted against a lighted playroom.

'Real dramatic, doll. Thunder and lightning and rain, and then the door opens and the lovely lady says . . .' He paused.

'Come into my parlor.'

'You muffed it,' he said, coming forward. 'It's more effective if you play it down. You should've said, "Good evening," very quietly.' He climbed two concrete steps, and she moved aside to let him pass and closed the door. He turned to her. 'Or maybe, "Welcome," in a sad, sad voice. Because this might be a sad, sad occasion if Poppa Bogen walks in.'

'Do you always talk so much?'

'Almost always. But maybe a little more when I'm scared to hell.'

'Are you scared now?'

He ran his eyes over her and nodded. 'I know I should get out of here, and I also know I want to stay more than anything in the world. And I always end up by doing what I want.'

'*Everything* you want?'

'Yes,' he said, and looked her over again. She was as he remembered her, not more than five feet three – a beautiful little chick; a sweet little dark-blonde with a face that was far from perfect, feature by feature, but which reached out to him as no face had in three long years. And just as at their first meeting, he was most captivated by her mouth – very wide, very firm, very mobile, very, very kissable.

He said, 'Nice dress. Nicer than the one you wore at the studio.'

She looked down at herself. 'My best. Something I didn't think I'd ever wear for a house date. Especially with an experienced old widower.' She stopped. 'I'm sorry. My father told me so much . . .'

He smiled. 'I don't feel seventeen years older than you.'

'How old are you?'

'Thirty-five, going on and on and on.'

'You're only *sixteen* years older than me. I'm nineteen, going on twenty.'

'Hey! Crazy! What a load off my mind!'

She laughed. 'You're a character.'

'You're not hip,' he said.

'Maybe.' She turned quickly. 'Let's go upstairs. I want to show you the house.'

His smile dimmed. 'This would do me fine, Sandy.' He

looked around. 'Nice portable bar and couch and chairs and record player. Fine.'

'Are you afraid to enter Les Bogen's home?'

He winced. 'I was wrong. You're hip, all right.'

'I want you to come into the house. *My* house, Henny.'

It was her saying his name that did it. The discomfort went off by itself someplace and died. He followed her, admiring the sleeveless black sheath dress, so very simple and yet so beautifully made. He reached out and grasped her bare arm, high. She faltered; stopped. 'Yes?' she said, and the natural huskiness of her voice was increased.

'I want to look at you again,' he said. 'I want to say something to you. We're going upstairs to see your home, and we've met only twice, counting now, and we don't know each other. I feel we should know each other. I feel we should walk into your home old friends.'

She turned to him, smiling, and seemed about to say something funny. But then she met his eyes, and his crooked grin. 'I know I did the calling,' she said, 'and the inviting. And I know, more or less, what I want of you; what I want of all companionable and attractive men – pleasurable company. But what is it you want of me, Henny?'

'Not what I've wanted of every girl I've dated since my wife died – if you can call such an advanced form of early-to-bed, dating. Not anything that makes sense, Sandy.'

She laughed briefly. 'Oho, love at first sight.'

'Something like that,' he said quickly, as if to head off more brief laughter. He gestured with his left hand, his free hand. 'Maybe it's square to blurt it out like this, but the whole bit is square – my being here, my wanting – '

'Your wanting what?' she asked.

He tugged her arm, and she came forward. He put

213

both arms around her and drew her tight against him and looked down at her.

'Your wanting what?' she murmured.

He kissed her, doing it very slowly, wanting to savor what might well be both first and last kiss. Because all it would take would be a burst of laughter on her part – laughter at the 'character' who talked 'love at first sight'. He brought his mouth down on those wide lips, and they were soft and warm and alive. They quivered, and he tasted them, and they were the best – not like movies, man, but like living; like living right up at the peak.

He drew back then, before it could grip him further. 'Maybe I knew someone like you, back when I was a kid. Maybe you touch something in my subconscious, or unconscious, or whatever is out of my control. Maybe I don't really want you but my maternal grandmother. There's got to be a reason.' He paused then, remembering what Marv Weister had said, and then dismissed Weister's reasoning. There was an intangible here, a lovely intangible that transcended literary psychology. 'There's got to be a reason,' he went on, 'or else I'd be back in Manhattan, screwing some girl, any girl, who wouldn't mean more to me than I'd mean to her.' He paused again, this time to see the effect his words would have on her; because she was, after all, a stranger, and maybe she would smash the picture her face presented by a reaction he wouldn't be able to stomach.

She said, 'Stop talking.'

He stopped talking. Their lips came together, and opened, and their kiss deepened, became intimate. He heard the little sound she made deep in her throat, and answered it, and began caressing her body gently, gently.

After a while he drew back and said, 'It was a long trip. Can we sit on the couch?'

She hesitated a split second before nodding, and he wondered at that.

But then they were moving to the couch. He sat down first and looked at her. He swallowed and dropped his eyes and told himself to hold tight, buddy, hold tight. He didn't want to feel so strongly. Christ, he didn't want to go so fast, so far – so far back into life, real life. He couldn't follow through the way such feelings required.

But she kept standing there, and he finally looked up and saw she'd changed somehow. He didn't like the change.

'What's wrong?' he asked.

She shook her head. 'I want to go upstairs.'

He rose quickly. 'Yeah. I'm sorry.'

'Don't be sorry, Henny.' For a moment she seemed about to come to him in the way her kisses had promised she would, but then she turned and went to a short flight of stairs.

He knew he was being stupid, unreasonable, but he felt that it was wrong for her to turn away like this.

He reminded himself that she was, after all, a complete stranger, and very young, so how could he expect her to start jiving just because he made pretty speeches?

And yet, he couldn't shake the feeling that he'd been very close to her, and that everything he'd expected was normal, natural for their relationship, and that she'd done something *unnatural* by walking toward the staircase.

'I could use a drink,' he said as he followed her up the stairs, into a large, modern kitchen. 'And some music. You got anything live?'

'I've got Bach, Stravinsky, Scarlatti and lesser greats.'

'They'll do.'

'I've also got Goodman, Cozy Cole, Turk Murphy, Dizzy Gillespie, Charlie Parker and many, many others.

215

Especially Charlie Parker. I've got one record of Parker and Gillespie that's the very end.'

'They made a stack that are all the very end.'

'No. This one is the best. You'll see.'

'What's it called?'

'It's a long-play with several numbers. But the takes and retakes of "An Oscar for Treadwell" are perfection.'

He looked at her and again felt he'd judged her correctly when drawing her to the couch, and again couldn't understand her moving away. 'I've heard it,' he murmured, and reached for her. She let him take her back in his arms and kiss her, but this time she was merely a spectator. He let go. 'I'd like to hear it again,' he said.

'First the grand tour.'

She showed him the house. It was a nice house, a big house, but still only a house. Henny dug people and food and music and books and photography. 'Nice pad,' he said.

They were on the second floor of the big side-to-side split level, in the foyer leading to the bedrooms, and she said, 'I'm glad you think so highly of it.'

He laughed. 'It's like the Taj Mahal with flush toilets, doll.'

'That's better,' she said. 'That's the kind of compliment a girl likes to hear.'

'Now let's go dig the music. And don't forget the liquor.'

It wasn't quite nine as they sat listening to the Gillespie-Parker record, sipping mild rye highballs, munching on popcorn. They were on a long, wide couch, facing a picture window which overlooked the valley. It was still raining but no longer storming.

'If it stops,' Henny said, shoulder pressing hers, 'I'd like to see the estate.'

'Estate. Four acres and woodchucks.'

'Crazy.'

'But it'll smell nice after the rain.'

He put his face to her neck. 'Couldn't smell nicer than here.'

She said nothing. He drew away and drained his glass and lighted a cigarette. He listened to the music but somehow couldn't enjoy it. He'd started out squaring with her, and it had worked, and then nothing had worked. He felt that instead of the peal of contemptuous laughter, she'd given him a slow double-take and decided he was nuts. And even though it had taken him about an hour to feel this, it hurt as much as if it had come in one agonizing second.

He stood up. 'Thanks for the ball. Drop around the studio some time. I'll buy you a wild Italian lunch at a place down the street.'

'But it's only nine. If you're worried about Lester . . .'

'Yeah. Let's say I'm worried about Lester.'

'He won't be home until after eleven. He said he had work to do.'

'He's shooting tonight?'

She shrugged. 'He *said* he had work to do. You want to comment?'

He shook his head, and looked at her, and felt a terrible sadness, a terrible sense of loss, because he was losing himself, Henny Girado, the man who'd almost returned to life. 'Goodbye, Sandy.'

'But why?'

'I don't know,' he said, suddenly tired of words. 'The whole thing's bugged.'

'How? We're here, and we like each other, and we're going to walk around the grounds. The rain's just about finished.'

'If I stay, I want plenty,' he said harshly. 'Not polite

conversation. Not hand-holding.' He paused. 'This is a switch. I'm here because I felt I had to be here, with you. I didn't think I'd try for a thing. But now, there's been a change, and you're acting wrong.'

It would've been so easy for her to jump on that, to ask what the hell he expected out of an hour-long relationship. But she was too hip, too honest. 'All right. Let's finish the record and I'll show you around outside. And then . . .'

He sat down again. He leaned back and closed his eyes and let the Bird fill him. He absorbed the music, the creative drive it held, and tried not to think of anything else. But the woman whose arm brushed his was too important to shut out, even for the few minutes of musical genius. The woman beside him was a question, and he wondered how she would pan out as an answer.

He also wondered if she guessed how important the outcome was to him, if she could possibly know that he'd been outside life for years and that she could draw him back into it.

They walked through the garage into the damp darkness. 'A flashlight spoils things,' she said, and they left the driveway and climbed a wet-grass terrace and a hill behind the house. They walked, she leading him by the hand, and a few drops of thin rain still fell, and the delicate freshness of vegetable life made breathing a conscious pleasure. Patches of clear sky began to show, and she said, almost to herself, 'I'll always thank him for giving me this. Mother didn't want to come at first, and I might have been born and raised in the city if part of him hadn't needed this – the nights after rain; and the days of hot sun or glittering snow; the ground without pavement. That's what he gave me, and himself. I've had it all my life, all the long hours of childhood and the shorter hours of adult days. He had it one or two days a week, and evenings, and occasional week-long vacations. We shared it during those times. It's been wonderful. Have you ever had it?'

He realized she hadn't used his name in a long time now not since they'd left the playroom. He said, 'I had a little of it as a kid, and I have it now when I shoot outdoor stuff. I like it. It isn't a necessity with me, but if I was married and could work it out, I think I'd want it. My little girl would love it.'

She didn't ask about Syl.

They kept walking, and she pointed out trees and bushes and flower beds and a stream. Then they reached a high point and turned to look out over the house and into the valley. The sky was opening up in larger patches of stars, and they could see completely across to a line of hills on the opposite ridge. 'Isn't it lovely?' she asked.

'You addressing me, ma'am?'

She looked at him. 'Since you're hip, and everything you say means something, *that* must mean something.'

'Don't you like my name?'

'I think your name is darling.'

'It struck me you haven't used it since we became friends downstairs.'

'Oh?' She shrugged. 'I didn't notice.'

She led him back to the house. They sat on the living-room couch with fresh drinks. The hi-fi played softly and she told him about her sociology courses at Columbia and asked how far he'd gone in school.

'Graduated High.'

'And then?'

'The Air Force; almost four years.'

'And then?'

'Cameras and New York.'

'You don't believe in higher education?'

'Yes, I do. I just haven't had time for it.'

She was quiet a while. 'My father said you're one of the best-educated men he's ever known. He said you read constantly.'

'Used to, honey. If you want to like me, it's going to have to be without cap and gown, symbolic as well as actual.'

She finished her drink and checked her watch; then she stood up and went to the wall switch. She turned off the lights in the living room, except for a soft lamp beside the couch, and took the glasses and popcorn back to the kitchen, and shut off the light there. She returned to the couch and carefully sat down in his lap and kissed him.

He didn't understand it, but he wanted to recapture the wonderful rapport they'd had in the playroom. He was puzzled by her body movements, suddenly so salacious, and couldn't shake the feeling that she was further away from him than ever. But then she took both his hands, placed one on her breast and the other on her thigh, and murmured, 'Sweetie.'

She still didn't use his name.

He had a hunch about that but was so anxious to find her that he pushed away the hunch (and the knowledge that he'd never find her *this* way) and went along.

Besides, she set him afire as no woman had since Doris. He forgot his doubts and concentrated on what she seemed to be offering. He kissed her, and after a moment's hesitation, she kissed him back. Her mouth was as exciting as before, even better this time, because her tongue met his and began to probe. His hand tightened involuntarily on her breast, squeezing the yielding flesh through the material of her dress and brassiere. Through the roaring of the blood in his ears he heard her moan, and realized that he was stroking her thigh. She had her arms around his neck and shoulder, pressing her body hard against him. It was a wonderful body to have

220

pressed against him, better somehow than anyone else's. She wriggled a little, seeking even closer contact, and the movement of her bottom on his lap sent a burning, demanding surge through him. With another girl – Eugenia, or another of his dates – he would have had no hesitation. He wanted her as much as he had wanted Doris, which meant more than anyone else in his life, but he felt curiously uncertain. Sandy appeared to be responding, seemed to want him with the same firey urgency. But it wasn't quite right.

The way Henny was feeling, the niggling doubt was easy to push away.

He went on kissing her, caressing her breast. His other hand slid down the silky material of her dress until he encountered the slightly rougher texture of her nylon stocking. The skirt was ridden up over her knees, and he eased his hand beneath the hem, almost expecting her to stop him. She didn't. Instead, she wriggled again, her bottom grinding against his erection so that he sucked in his breath as the ecstatic shock ran through him. When she stopped moving her skirt was looser, and Henny ran his hand gently over the long, smooth firmness of her thigh. The transition of sensation, from the texture of the nylon to the warm softness of her flesh, sent a shock through both of them. Sandy moaned without taking her lips from his, and reached down to tug the skirt of her dress up around her hips. Henny stroked her thigh, then traced the line of her suspender until his fingertips touched the edge of her panties. Sandy said, 'Darling.' And this time it sounded like she meant it.

Henny drew his fingers slowly over the sheer material. He could feel her pubic hair, and then the soft touch of her inner thigh. He slid his hand between her legs. Sandy moaned again, and let him move her legs apart. He touched her womanhood through her panties. The material was damp. He moved his fingers back to her inner thigh and inserted them under the elastic. Sandy moved her thighs farther apart, pressing harder against him. Henny felt the lips of her vagina warm and wet to his gentle touch, inviting him to continue. He slid his forefinger between the lips, seeking the button of her clitoris. He found it, and she gasped as he began to rub it, her body trembling.

The doubts he had felt earlier were forgotten as he concentrated on bringing her to climax. His own excitement was mounting to an almost unbearable pitch, making it easy to forget the hunch.

Everything became clear a few minutes later. There was a choking, angry, grieving sound, and Sandy slid off his lap, and he turned his head to see Les standing in the kitchen doorway looking at them. Henny turned to Sandy, and she was only now pushing her dress down over her thighs, and she still had a wet-lipped, sexful cast to her face and an abandoned position of the body – much more abandoned than the situation called for. She looked . . . triumphant. She was gloating over Les's embarrassment and anguish.

But even as Henny stared at her, her eyes left Les and came to him, and something that wasn't triumph or gloating flashed across her face. 'Henny,' she whispered, and for a second she seemed frightened.

'I'm hip,' he said calmly, and stood up. 'Glad to be of service.'

'Henny.'

She was using his name now, using it the way he'd wanted her to.

But wasn't that a laugh?

Still, instinct told him she had drawn close to him again in that all-important way.

He told himself he'd better get a new set of instincts;

the old ones didn't work too well with this little chick. Not that he'd ever have occasion to use them on her again.

Les had disappeared from the kitchen doorway. The last thing Henny wanted to do was find him, yet he knew he had to. He liked Les, despite the money bit earlier that day. He didn't expect Les to like him after this, at least for a while, but he had to speak to him.

'Les,' he called.

'Down here,' the voice answered, and it seemed as calm, as studiedly controlled, as ever. 'In the playroom.'

Henny hesitated. 'That where you keep the shotgun?'

There was no laughter, no sound of any kind.

The lamp in the living room went out, throwing the whole ground floor into darkness. Henny glanced back at the couch. He couldn't see Sandra Bogen too well in the dim light coming through the picture window, but she seemed to be sitting with hands over face.

He found himself wanting to go back there and comfort her. But he laughed it off.

He grinned his crooked grin and went to the kitchen. He opened the door to the playroom and announced his coming: 'Man, it's like Daniel walking into the lion's den, only this here Daniel's got no Helper upstairs.'

14

Lester Bogen knew dozens of men but had no close friends. The nature of his life – its consistent duplicity – precluded real friendship. Besides, he didn't miss friends because he had no time for them. There was Sandy, and there were women, and there was work. Life was full enough.

However, he often thought that if he had to pick a friend, a confidant, it would be Henny Girado. Despite the difference in their ages, and the irritations brought about by Henny's borrowing without being able to repay, Les felt an affinity for Henny; liked and admired him; even envied him at times. He wasn't sure what there was to envy in the tall, dark, stooped widower with the overwhelming financial burdens and the harried, crooked grin, but he suspected it was a basic honesty – honesty with self that led, quite naturally, to humor and courage and clarity of thought. Henny might be pushed into the ground, but he would never be defeated in the way a Laird Drake was, would never lie to himself and others the way most harried people did. Henny, Les Bogen felt, had too clear a picture of life to attempt anything so wasteful and futile as self-seducing fantasies – the big-shot stories of a Laird Drake, or the defeat-of-death sex affairs of a Lester Bogen.

Les would occasionally tell himself that he was obsessed with the fear of dying, and that his need for many women stemmed from the fact that only in the carnal act did he completely forget death. But this was merely giving himself a psychological basis, an explanation for something which – especially when he *wasn't* with a woman and was feeling somewhat low – required self-explanation. Most of the time – as when he'd paused for thought with Lois Montana Monday night – he found pleasure itself the only explanation.

Waiting in the playroom for Henny Girado, Les was feeling very low. This served to make him remember his own supposed weaknesses and Henny Girado's supposed strong points.

Les Bogen occasionally suffered the pangs of inadequacy with a woman. This was confined to fearing rejection, even though rejection was extremely rare since he picked his subjects carefully, and his reputation was enough to weed out most nonplayers. But when the exception occurred – as it necessarily had to when a man approached as many women as Bogen did – it cut deeply. It was then he envied Henny Girado for another quality: supreme confidence. Henny feared no rejection because he never accepted rejection. Henny either made out or it was a funny bit. The concept of rejection never entered into it.

Les had seen Henny, at studio parties, take off with a gorgeous model after an approach that consisted of a few hip cracks, a whispered suggestion and a crooked, appealing grin. At other times, the very same approach resulted in the girl's laughing and shaking her head and laughing some more as Henny kept talking. Then Henny would amble away, laughing at the laughter he'd created, and try someone else. If there were enough unattached females, he was bound to put one to bed that same night. And if he didn't, he would sit around, drinking everyone's liquor and putting records on the phonograph and making people laugh. When Henny balled, as he put it, he made everything fit the mold of balling – of having fun. No matter what happened, he fed on it as pleasure.

It was a quality so few possessed, a quality so few had the *ability* to possess. And his current state of financial frustration, which cut down on his natural ebullience, didn't change Les Bogen's opinion, or admiration.

But admirable or not, Henny was something apart from Les Bogen's family, from Les Bogen's daughter. The studio was in another world, and Henny went with the studio, and Les had never even considered Henny and Sandy in the same thought. Of course, Sandy had her boy friends and occasionally dated one for several months – but this was still vastly different from having a man from another world (the world Les Bogen had to keep apart from Sandy because of his own role in it) show up at the house, show up with his arms around Sandy!

It shocked Les Bogen as even Sandy's visit to the studio hadn't. It hurt him on several levels instead of the single level of Sandy's coldness. It also frightened him because it opened a door he had previously refused to consider in existence.

If Sandy dated someone from Morden Photos, she would be in a position to learn the full story of her father's outside life. (*Marriage* with anyone from the studio was a horror not even admissible as vague supposition.) And that was one thing Les Bogen would fight to prevent; one possibility which could make him a desperate, vicious opponent, even if the man involved was someone he liked.

A frightened Les Bogen was a dangerous Les Bogen. And it was Henny Girado who had frightened him.

Les was sitting on the couch when Henny came down to the playroom. 'Mix yourself a drink,' he said quietly, indicating the beer-keg portable bar near the staircase.

Henny nodded, poured three or four ounces of Johnny

226

Walker into a low-ball glass, turned to Les. 'Here's to Sandra,' he said.

Bogen's eyes blinked, but he raised his glass and drank. Then he said, 'I'll keep it simple, Henny. You're thirty-five to Sandy's nineteen. You have a child and debts and obligations that make marriage impossible – at least to a young college girl. That's if marriage were even the vaguest possibility in your mind, which I doubt.'

'You don't mean that, dad,' Henny murmured, and sipped his Scotch. 'You know it would have to be a very definite possibility in my mind – perhaps subconscious, but there – or I'd never have come near her. Everything else I need, I've got, or have you forgotten this is old quick-as-a-bunny Girado?' He grinned, and received no response, and began to laugh a little. The situation was so uncomfortable, it was growing funny – like a funeral, man. 'Anyway, this was a first date, and it doesn't rate deep analysis.'

'Your being here rates *very* deep analysis.'

'No, dad.' Henny's smile was gone. 'Sandy's putting me on that couch when she knew you'd walk in is what rates the analysis. She used me – someone from your own studio; someone who knew your background – for a bit of sweet revenge.' He drank the rest of his Scotch, set the glass on the barrel, lighted a cigarette. 'She stabbed you, Les. And I'm not a boy friend, only a knife.'

Les Bogen nodded. 'All right. But promise me you won't see her again.'

'Really, Cunnel Bogen, suh!'

'I mean it, Henny.'

'Let's put it this way, dad. I'll promise no such thing because it's too big a boffo, too *East Lynne* for my jaded taste. But since Sandy's had her use out of me, I doubt if I'll be around.'

'That's not good enough, Henny.'

'As the mermaid said to the passionate sailor, "Sorry, but it'll have to do."'

Bogen looked at his glass, and drank, and murmured, 'I think Richie would be forced to put you out of the studio if I insisted he make a choice between us. With your present credit rating, you'd have trouble relocating.'

Henny laughed briefly and came to the couch and sat down, close to Bogen. 'That might very well finish me, Les. I might have to try collecting double indemnity on my ten-grand insurance policy.'

'Funny boy.'

Henny Girado's face went gray. 'Yeah. Keep 'em laughing, even when they're cutting your throat. Someday I might get tired of laughing.' But then he shrugged and grinned. 'I think I'd've preferred the shotgun.'

Bogen kept his eyes down. 'The solution is simple, Henny. Just give me your word you'll never see Sandy again.'

Henny stood up. 'I'll never see Sandy again because she'll never care to use me again. However, if she really – ' He stopped. 'You want to know how we got together?'

'I'm not in the least interested,' Bogen said, still examining his glass.

'I thought of her from the day she came up to case the studio. I was hooked by something.'

'I said I wasn't interested.' And now his voice was cold. 'You haven't given me your promise, Henny.'

'Good night, dad.'

'All right,' Bogen said, and lifted his eyes. 'As long as you don't see her, we'll consider the matter closed.'

'Ah, released from the indignity of a loyalty oath.'

Bogen watched him. 'You probably hate me now, and that's a good thing, because it'll help you remember that everyone with the name Bogen is off-limits.'

Henny turned, walked toward the garage door, then stopped and turned again. 'Dad, I was hurt pretty bad tonight. The way I figure it, I've got to multiply that hurt a few times and add some unhappy thoughts about what Sandy might learn about me that I wouldn't want her to learn, and I'd have your particular misery. You can't hate a man for that. But I've got to give you Doctor Girado's advice for lovelorn fathers: Tell her the whole damned truth and let her get sick about it. Don't try to explain. Don't squirm out from under. She's close to the age when she'll be pulling away from Daddy's loving arms anyway, so it won't be too – '

'Good night, Henny.'

'Give her time and she'll be ready to remember the good things, Les. It's the only way. You of all people should know how useless those keep-off-the-daughter signs are.'

Les Bogen shook his glass and hummed softly, as if Henny were no longer present.

'Use your *experience*, Les.'

Bogen got up, still humming, and went to the portable bar to freshen his drink.

Henny said, 'Yeah, well, I hate to cut you short, Les, but I've got to go. I can't stand around listening to all this chitchat. You oughta remember that loquacity is a virtue only in politicians and pollybirds.'

Bogen's lips twitched.

Henny went out the door, into the garage.

Bogen sipped his drink and then heard Sandy moving around upstairs. He put down the glass and ran a pinkie over his pencil-line mustache. He had to go up there and say something, do something to bring her to her senses.

But what?

He finished his drink and decided to have another and give the situation further thought. But Sandy came down at that moment, and the words jumped out of him. 'Sandy, baby, we can't go on this way.'

She was looking at the door to the garage.

'You heard talk up at the studio, but you have to understand that talk in my business is notoriously risqué, and you're exaggerating its importance anyway.' He floundered, and she didn't help him out. In fact, she hadn't even looked at him; she was still staring at the door to the garage.

He tried again. 'You must know there's been very little affection between your mother and myself for many, many years. A man considers himself free, single in a moral sense when such a situation – '

'I didn't hear his car drive off,' she interrupted. 'Did you?'

'His car?' Les muttered, still trying to formulate explanations.

'Yes. Henny must be out there, waiting for something.' She took a step toward the door.

'I'm speaking to you!' Les Bogen shouted. 'I'm saying things, important things, perhaps the most important things I've ever said, and you've got your mind on that – ' He rushed forward and grabbed her arms and shook her violently. 'You've known him a few hours! A few lousy hours against all the years you've had with me!' As quickly as it had come, his rage was gone. 'Christ, I'm sorry, baby.'

She looked down at his hands on her arms, and he let her go. She said, 'Don't ever do that again. You haven't the right to.' She walked toward the garage. 'I'm going to tell him I'm sorry.'

But before she could reach the door, a car started up, backed swiftly down the driveway to the spur and roared off. She ran forward and opened the door in time to see the Chevy's taillights disappearing.

'I'll call him,' she said.

'He'll humiliate you,' Les Bogen answered desperately.

'Perhaps, but I'll call him anyway.'

Bogen made himself laugh. 'You sound as if that screwball had some special charm. You sound as if he might compete with the college grads, the young doctors and lawyers and engineers who date you. Haven't I told you he's over thirty-five, has a child, supports a sister and her two children and a paralyzed mother? Don't you know he's completely insolvent and runs around – '

'You've forgotten something, Daddy.'

He said nothing, waiting for her to reject his attempt to devalue Henny, an attempt he'd known was ugly and stupid and doomed to failure from the start.

'You've forgotten the psychology texts,' she said. 'Or, as Carl Sandburg put it, "*Why* did the children put beans in their ears when the one thing we told the children they *must not* do was put beans in their ears?"' She shook her head sadly, mockingly. 'You're telling me I must not put beans in my ears.'

He was about to comment on the aptness of the Sandburg quotation; about to say that the total effect of a Henny Girado on a normal girl would be very much like her trying to live with beans in her ears, but he heard the heavy roar of Louise's Buick, and Sandy turned and went upstairs. He poured a fresh drink and gulped it as Louise came in from the garage. She was tall, blond, still young and untouched by menopause at forty-one, with what most men would consider a good figure. But her face was empty, vacuous, cold – at least in Lester's opinion.

'Hello,' she said in her high-pitched voice. 'Have a nice evening? I had the most interesting time of my life.' (She said this at least once a week.) 'We had a guest lecturer at the club who gave a complete breakdown of soil types in the Upper Westchester area. Acid conditions prevail, he said. And then we had dinner and cocktails and a group discussion.' She finally noticed that his face was pale and set. 'Oh. You've been talking to Sandy?'

'Who said anything about talking to Sandy?'

'Well, you look so upset, and she's been acting strangely, and I have the feeling – '

'Your imagination was always inclined to the melodramatic.'

'I can see that acid conditions prevail here, too.'

He stared at her.

She giggled shrilly. 'I think that was quite good.'

'Will you shut up?' he whispered. 'Will you?'

She paled a moment but then smiled thinly. 'I do believe she's finally making her break. She's pulling away from you, isn't she, Les? And you can't take it, can you? You're afraid.'

For a moment he felt he would strike her, his fear and rage were so great. She read it on his face and went swiftly to the stairs and left the playroom.

Les Bogen didn't know what to do. He couldn't think of life without Sandy's love. He felt sure he could still recapture it, if only she stayed away from the studio; stayed away from Henny Girado.

He slammed his glass down on the barrel bar. Damn Henny for daring to come here! Damn him for wanting Sandy! *Damn him!*

He felt his face twisting and realized he was beginning to hate Henny Girado. It shocked him.

Henny Girado didn't go home. He drove to a roadhouse near the highway and took a seat at the bar, away from several other customers, and nursed five bottles of beer for almost two hours. In addition to everything else, he was angry with himself. He kept remembering how he'd sat in his car in the big garage, waiting for Sandra Bogen

232

to show up and make some sort of apology. After all the straight talk he'd given Bogen, and himself, he'd obeyed the crazy hunch and sat there and almost prayed for her to come. Ten or fifteen minutes, but it had seemed like half a year.

After leaving the tavern, he drove to Manhattan and the studio. Not that he had anything specific to do. He could work on his portfolio, certainly, but he could do that any time. It was just that – as had become increasingly evident lately – he was unable to face his apartment and his bed.

It was one-thirty Thursday morning when he parked the Chevy in front of the studio building. He unlocked the front door with his key and went up the steps to the night light on the first floor. He continued on to the second floor and threw the hall switch that lighted the third-floor landing. He went up to the third floor, opened the door, and felt along the right wall for the set of three switches that would illuminate the interior hallway. Just as he found them, a phone rang.

It was so unexpected, and so loud in the stillness, that his body jerked. He got the lights on, strode to Richie Morden's office and picked up the phone. 'Hello?' he said, wondering who the hell it could be.

'Is that you, Henny?' the voice asked, sounding surprised.

His mouth was suddenly dry and the palms of his hands wet. 'Yes.'

'This is Sandra Bogen.'

'Yes.'

'Well.' She laughed nervously. 'I never thought you'd be there at this hour.' She laughed again and lowered her voice to a whisper. 'I called twice before – at twelve and again at about one. I have a phone in my room, near my bed, and I couldn't sleep, and I wanted to talk to you, so

I tried the studio. But I didn't really expect . . .' She paused, and when he said nothing, continued. 'I couldn't call your apartment because I'd wake your little girl, so I just . . . you know.'

He couldn't let her stumble on that way. He was beginning to feel happy, beginning to come alive again, and he wanted to hear what he'd waited to hear in the garage up at Peekskill. 'Anything I can do for you?' he asked quietly.

'Yes,' she whispered.

'Then speak up, doll.'

'I can't. My father might hear.'

'I didn't mean that. I meant – spill it.'

'Yes, well.' She paused again and then spoke very quickly. 'I'm sorry. You know what for. I want you to say you forgive me.'

'I forgive you. Is that all?'

'No. I want you to say you'll see me again.'

He stood in the dark office and grinned. The grin wasn't crooked, wasn't funny or sad, wasn't anything but an expression of delight. 'Your father forbade me, in very forbading terms.'

'We'll forget my father,' she said, and her voice climbed to normal speaking strength. 'You'll help me forget my father.'

'Check.'

'You mean you'll see me?'

'Call me noble.'

She laughed. 'Henny, thank you.'

'Glad to be of service.'

'You know what I mean. It was such a dirty trick.'

'Agreed.' He kept grinning, and rubbed his head with his left hand, and said, 'I'm so damned noble, I can't wait to start being *actively* forgiving.'

234

'Tomorrow's Thursday,' she murmured, thinking aloud.

'Today,' he corrected.

'Yes. And I've got classes until three-thirty. Any time after that, Henny. Anyplace you say.'

He made a quick decision. She was something special; he would do something special. 'Lucky chick,' he said. 'I'm going to be home with Syl tomorrow. You can grab a cab to Queens and visit the Girados in their palatial pad. Get a pencil and I'll give you the address.'

'I'll drive my own car, and I've got the address. The Queens phone book makes such interesting reading. Not much plot – '

'Please,' he said.

'Forgive me. It's my youth, and my present state of nervousness.'

'I'll bet you could use my soothing presence.'

'Ummm.' Her voice deepened. 'Henny, I'm going to cut my classes tomorrow. I'm going to have breakfast with you.'

'I'd love it. But I don't want – '

'Just this once. Besides, I've been so confused this last week that I've done nothing but stare at the classroom walls. And I don't think I'm going to continue at Columbia anyway. I want to work. And while I love living in the country, it's time I got a place of my own and – '

'Save something for tomorrow. I want to look at you when you talk. I want to read those brown eyes. Then maybe I can help you decide whether what you're planning is right for you.'

'Yes. But I hate to say goodbye.'

And then another voice sounded in the background, and Sandy's voice grew brittle. 'I'm on the phone, Les.'

The background voice spoke again.

Sandy said, 'Good night, Henny,' very clearly.

He said, 'That's tellin' him. Now I can start wearing sidearms to the studio.'

Her voice dropped to a murmur. 'Want me to tell him you brushed me off?'

'No. I'm an old Air Force man. I like sidearms. See you at breakfast. Nine, nine-thirty, ten?'

'Nine, Henny. And think of me tonight.'

The background voice, Les Bogen's voice, was going full blast as Sandy hung up. It made Henny's grin grow crooked, regain its usual element of sadness; but a second later he picked up the phone and dialed. When the housekeeper finally answered in a sleepy, irritable voice, he said, 'This is Henny. Sorry to wake you, but I've got some good news and want you to be able to set your clock, or whatever it is you do on your days off.'

'Today, Wednesday, my day off,' she muttered, and cleared her throat. 'I stay home for you again, Henny, but what you – '

'I know you stayed home for me, honey. And I appreciate it. But *tomorrow* you're getting your day off. Tomorrow I'm staying home with Syl.'

'Oh, well, sure. Then I don't charge you for day off. But you bring my pay, Henny.'

'It's in my pocket,' he said. 'Good night.' He hung up and went into the hallway and shut the lights and went down the stairs and out into the street to his car. He didn't bother with the radio. He made his own music.

236

15

At eight the next morning, having had five hours of sleep, Henny was awakened by his housekeeper, Greta Borenson, who tapped at his door, peeked inside, then entered when she saw he was under the covers and stirring. 'You get too little sleep again last night,' she said, shaking her long, naturally somber face. She was a widow of fifty-two, tall and solidly fleshed. And solidly opinionated. She lectured Henny whenever she got the chance but was really very fond of him.

Fond of him or not, she didn't believe she'd stay with him long. In fact, she was already looking for a position with more future. (No housekeeper lasted long with Henny, though all seven had liked him. It was his late hours, his tendency to forget their days off occasionally, his poor financial status, which became evident when household money ran out and their salaries were a week overdue.)

'Okay, Hannah,' he mumbled, clinging to the euphoria of sleep. Waking up meant facing problems, big problems, and hell, man, who looked forward to that?

But suddenly, as Hannah was testily stating her name was Greta, he remembered Sandra Bogen. He sat up. 'Christmas Eve. Santy Claus's coming down the chiminy, Gramma, and my presents are piled up under the tree. O come, all ye faithful.'

Greta Borenson backed up a step. 'My pay,' she said, faltering. 'You got my pay?'

'Why, sure. Didn't I tell you this was Christmas Eve? Santy Claus wouldn't forget you, Hannah.' He started coming out of bed, in his shorts, and she gasped and fled to the door. '*Greta!*' she said as she ran outside. 'If you don't remember, I quit!'

'Greta,' he called. 'Greta, Greta, Greta, Greta.'

'All right!' she shouted through the closed door. 'I don't quit!'

He took his shabby, muddy-brown flannel robe from the closet and got his wallet from the top of the dresser. Doris' face with the sweet, solemn smile looked out at him from the wood frame. He looked back at it and felt a strange little twinge and said, 'Well, baby, I didn't think it would happen.' He shook his head, feeling unsure, afraid, adrift.

He left the big bedroom and walked a few steps and looked through the open door into the smaller bedroom where Syl slept in a gray walnut bed he'd bought her a year ago. Greta (he would remember the name, now that the threat of quitting had been introduced) slept on the wide, comfortable cot against the window wall.

The room was empty, and he heard Syl's high, sweet voice in the kitchen. He walked another few steps and was entering the living room. Off the living room to his right was the narrow kitchen which had just enough space for a small table set against the wall and three chairs placed at its available sides. Syl sat facing the doorway, a glass of milk clutched in her little hands, the remains of a soft-boiled egg in a cup before her. She was big-eyed, round-faced, dark the way Doris had been, pretty the way Doris had been. But she had Henny's funny grin, and when she saw him she gave him that grin, and he suddenly couldn't understand why he hadn't looked at her more often. God, she was so *cute* she made his chest ache!

'Daddy's here,' she piped, and looked at Greta, who sat watching her.

Greta turned her head and smiled at Henny. 'You see how happy you make her, just being here? You should make her happy *more*, Henny.'

'You're right.' He went to his daughter and kissed her cheek and inhaled the fragrance of her hair. She was wearing a pink party dress Henny'd never seen before, and shiny red buckle-on shoes. 'Hey, you really dolled her up, Greta. How'd you know we were having company?'

Greta rose, shrugging. 'I want her to be nice for *you*. I want you to look at her, think of her. You need woman, Henny.'

'Why, Greta. If you only knew.'

She flushed. 'Yah. I know you with those girls who take pictures. I mean you need woman for Sylvia. I mean woman to marry.'

'Models marry,' he said, grinning at his daughter, who was following the conversation with glances of her big black eyes.

'Yah? Then marry one.'

'I did,' he murmured. 'Syl's mother.' He made a what-the-hell gesture with his hand, and felt the wallet in it, and took out the two hundred Richie had advanced him yesterday. He counted out eighty dollars and put it in Greta's hand. She recounted it slowly, laboriously, moving her lips. Then she nodded and put the money in her big black handbag.

'Now I need money for house. Only three dollars in drawer.'

'What?' Henny asked, and tried to sound suspicious. People said that all domestics cheated; that it was a tradition in their line. 'Are you sure?'

'You look,' she said, pointing at the utility-table drawer where they kept the household money in a small metal box.

'But where'd it go?' he mumbled, already thinking of

239

how little time he had to wash, shave and dress for Sandy.

Greta wasn't at all perturbed. 'Count bills,' she said. 'I get bills for everything – even one bottle aspirin. I get bills and I put bills in drawer. You check, and then you see.' She walked to the door, patting his arm gently as she passed. 'Anyone cheat man with troubles like you get big sin. Goodbye.' She went out.

As always, on being left alone with Sylvia, he had a moment in which he found himself without a thing to say. He looked at her, and she looked at him over the rim of the glass of milk, and then she said, 'Daddy, are you mad at me?'

'Mad at you? Of course not, honey.' He sat down at the table, in the seat Greta had vacated, reached out and touched her soft, smooth cheek. 'What makes you think I am?'

'Your face was mad.' She stuck out her lower lip and bulged her eyes and said, 'Grrr! Big bad wolf goes grrr!'

He laughed. 'That's just the way I look.'

She stared at him. 'Why don't you come home like Lucy's daddy?'

Even as he tried to think of an answer, he was wondering how children managed to say exactly what the cornball sob sisters insisted they said. 'Who's Lucy?' he said, stalling for time.

It got him off the hook completely. Lucy was a girl who lived 'downstairs in a big 'partment and she's my friend. I skip with her. She has a doll with wet diapers. Pretty Doll, that's her name. She has more dolls. I hold her hand when we skip.' And on and on, and he was fascinated. It seemed only a few days ago that she couldn't put two words together, or at least form an intelligible sentence.

Greta was right. Everyone who spouted square corn

was right, lately. It hardly paid to be hip when you couldn't laugh at anything any more. He needed a woman – a woman for Syl. The kid wouldn't forget her questions so easily in a few months, or a year – her questions as to why he didn't come home 'like Lucy's daddy.' And soon there'd be questions about why she had a series of 'Mommies' instead of a steady one like Lucy and all the other kids. And then the scars might begin to form – the mental scars Marv Weister had warned about.

He told her he was going to wash and not to spill her milk. He went into the bathroom and left the door open so he could hear if anything happened. As he shaved, he thought of Sandy, and Syl; and then reminded himself that he was married to his financial obligations, his debts, his big, heavy millstones.

With lather on his face, he went to the living room, put some records on the Emerson combination TV-radio-phonograph he and Doris had received as a wedding gift from Doris' folks, and returned to the bathroom, after glancing into the kitchen to see that Syl was still playing with her milk. The music cheered him – Peggy Lee with her educated, sophisticated voice; Charlie Parker when he had his big band (mediocre stuff mostly, but the few minutes that the Bird sang alone made the records worth while); some jazz concert sides; and Sinatra's 'Swingin' Affair.' And long before they were finished, Henny was dressed.

At five to nine, he was sitting in the living room, assuring Syl that he would take her out since it was a mild, sunny day, checking his watch every ten seconds and beginning to wonder if Sandy would really come.

At nine-twenty, he was holding Syl in his arms and jitterbugging to Peggy Lee and fighting the sinking sensation, the fear of having been robbed of Sandy, when the doorbell rang. He began to set Syl down, then

241

changed his mind and carried her to the door. When he opened it, Sandy was there. She looked at him and his daughter, and heard the music, and said, 'I'd like to join the party. May I?'

Syl said, 'Where's a party? I wanna go too.'

Henny said, 'Here's a party, now that Sandy's arrived. Look at Sandy, Syl. Look at the lovely lady.'

Syl didn't do much looking – she was anxious to get back to dancing in her father's arms – but Henny made up for her lack of interest. Sandy stepped past him into the living room and shut the door. She wore a pale-blue pull-over sweater, a darker blue cardigan over it (open all the way), a blue-gray plaid skirt and sensibly heeled black leather shoes. Her face was pink and glowing; it seemed lighted from within. Her hair was blonder, brighter in daylight, shiny-neat in its slicked-back boy's cut. She said, 'Syl, would you like to show me around your apartment? I'd especially like to see your room.'

Syl said, 'No. I wanna dance.'

Sandy said, 'Okay. I'll look around myself.'

Syl said, 'Don't touch my circus doll. Her hair falls off.'

Sandy said, 'Which one is that?'

Syl said, 'Lemme down, Daddy!' When Henny obeyed, she took the hand Sandy extended. 'I'll show you.'

Sandy winked at Henny and murmured, 'See, she's not as tough as she thinks she is.'

Henny grinned and sat down on the couch and watched them walk into Syl's room. His stomach rumbled emptily, and he thought of bacon and poached eggs and rich black coffee, prepared and served by Sandy. He could hardly wait.

Half an hour later he was sitting down to the meal he'd wanted, partially prepared and totally served by Sandy. He'd had to poach the eggs himself – a portion for each of them – and she'd watched closely as he'd broken four eggs into a dish and slid them, ever so gently, onto the steaming water in the top of the double boiler. 'I'll remember, for next time,' she'd murmured, smiling, yet obviously unhappy about not having been able to do it herself. 'I never cooked anything but the simplest – ' He'd stooped and kissed her on the lips, having seen that Syl was busy dragging a stool over to the window. Then he'd moved quickly to the table.

So there they were, at opposite ends of the table, with Syl now climbing onto the chair between them. They ate and drank and looked into each other's eyes and smiled and ate some more. Sandy had cream with her coffee, and Henny smoked a cigarette with his, and Syl said, 'Funny faces,' and broke into incredibly high-pitched giggles. 'Funny, funny, funny faces.' As she'd done before, she stuck out her lower lip and bulged her eyes, and then giggled some more.

Sandy hunched her shoulders and laughed, very much like a little girl herself. 'Is that the way we look, honey?'

Syl nodded vigorously. 'Funny, funny,funny faces!'

Henny gave his daughter a mock-hard stare and said, 'I think we'd better take you outside and lose you somewhere. Then Sandy and I can have a long chat.'

Syl turned quickly, eyes wide on his face. 'No,' she said, voice quavering. 'No, Daddy! I don't want to be lost somewhere! No!' And before he could formulate the words, or thoughts, to comfort her, she was crying.

Sandy was out of her chair and kneeling beside the little girl. 'Your daddy was only fooling, honey. It's a grownup joke. He didn't mean it.'

'Of course not,' Henny said, and now he was irritated that he'd frightened his child. (He wondered whether children with the security of a normal home life – normal

243

parents – frightened as easily.) 'Can't you tell when Daddy's joking?'

Syl continued to cry. Sandy looked at him and shook her head. 'Of course she can't tell when you're joking. She's three years old. Can't you remember when you were little?'

'Hell,' he said, getting up and stalking to the window and glaring out. 'No one remembers when they were little.'

'Well *I* do,' Sandy snapped. 'I remember how terribly frightened I'd get at the thought of losing my home and parents.'

'That's because you and Syl are contemporaries,' he replied, still glaring out the window. 'Me and Grandma Moses have more trouble remembering.'

Sandy laughed and said, 'Ooops. Here it comes. Our first big problem. How to adjust May and December.'

His irritation was gone in a flash, and he turned. Syl was drying her eyes and trying to extricate herself from Sandy's arms. 'Leggo, you,' she said. 'You're not my mommie.'

'True,' Sandy said, rising and looking at Henny. 'That'll take a little time.'

Henny said, 'Yeah,' and smiled, but the remark brought too many realities back to mind, and he didn't want realities now. 'Let's go to the park. There's a lake and we can sit around.'

'Yes, yes, yes!' Syl screamed. 'The park! The park!'

They used Sandy's convertible. Kissena Park wasn't very large, but neither was it as overcrowded as most New York parks. And on this weekday morning in May, it was almost empty. A few mothers pushed baby carriages and strollers around the paths, a few children under school age ran across the grass, several old men sat playing checkers and dominoes on benches under the

244

trees. The sun shone brightly, the air was warm, and Syl trotted along the path and then across the grass toward the lake. Henny watched her, amazed at how attractive a child she was, at how complex a being she was. Again he wondered how he could have ignored all that comprised this little girl. And yet he had, for three years and two months. 'I've never really seen her before,' he said to Sandy, and took her hand.

'I don't understand,' she said, voice soft as he squeezed her fingers.

'Neither do I. It's like she was just given to me, today, and I'm seeing her for the first time and I'm wondering how she developed, how she learned the words and the mannerisms she's got. They didn't come from me, that's for sure.'

'Why is it for sure?'

'Because if she'd learned from me, she'd have said, "Yes, Daddy, let's make the park. Yes, let's you and the chick and me hit the green and ball, Daddy, ball! It's like we were gophers, Daddy, so let's dig!"'

Sandy laughed, then stopped laughing and said, 'But you yourself haven't been talking that way today. You're different today, Henny.'

'Am I?' He nodded. 'Yeah, maybe I am. But then again, Marv Weister, a friend of mine, once pointed out that I'm two different people; sometimes I'm hip and sometimes I'm square. He said I straddle the fence – part daddy-o and part plain daddy.'

'I don't think that's it,' she said.

'No? How would you explain it?'

She shrugged. 'No one can be all hip or all square – no intelligent person, that is. What fits for a wild night with the music playing, the wine flowing and the sex glands operating doesn't fit at all for a bright afternoon in the park with a child – especially your own child.'

245

He nodded. 'Sounds right.' He squeezed her hand again. 'But the sex glands are operating more today than at any time since – ' He stopped.

'Since your wife died,' she said, and used her free hand to press his arm. 'That's what you wanted to say, wasn't it, Henny? Please tell me.'

'It was.' He looked at her and murmured, 'But I'm afraid. This doesn't add up too well. Now, in the park, and maybe later on in a restaurant and a movie and a car – sure, we'll sing together. But for the long haul.' He shook his head. 'We wouldn't stand a chance.'

'Why, Henny?' She didn't seem worried. 'My father isn't that much of a problem.'

'Not your father – me and my family. I'll spell it out for you, but later. Right now, let's find a nice spot behind a tree and live it up.' He saw that Syl was getting close to the lake. 'And let's catch that little square!'

They ran after Syl, and each grabbed a hand, and they led her off around the lake, talking to her and laughing at her remarks. They found a quiet spot between two trees, far enough from the water to give them peace of mind with Syl. It was also far enough away from any other person to give them a feeling of privacy. They sat down on the old blanket Henny had brought along. Syl ran over to one of the trees and began digging in the earth at its base with her hands. Henny and Sandy watched for a moment or two, then lay down. They turned toward each other; and Henny looked into the light-brown eyes. 'Hello, chick,' he murmured.

'Hello, stranger,' she replied.

'Yeah,' he said. 'That's the funny bit, isn't it?'

'Yes. We've known each other a total of three or four hours.'

'And I – ' He rolled away from her, onto his back, and

246

laughed deep in his throat. 'It's too much. It knocks me out. *Crazy!*'

'Now you're using the patois for a cover.'

He rolled onto his side again and looked at her. 'Dig that jumping to conclusions. Psychology One and Two, at least.'

'A little psychology,' she murmured, her face very close to his, her eyes locked with his. 'But I'm an anthropology bug myself. My major, you know.'

'I didn't know. I'm impressed.'

'No you're not,' she said, and wet her lips with a quick touch of her tongue. An insect buzzed nearby, and they both listened until the sound disappeared. 'I like it, but I don't need it. I'd like to be able to read all about it, on my own. I wasn't meant for college, Henny.'

'No?'

'No. I like books, but somehow the classroom atmosphere chills me. I guess I'm nonacademic.'

'Or lazy.'

'Are you sorry you didn't go to college, Henny?'

'Maybe. I have no way of knowing. But I don't think so. If and when I ever get out from under, I'll use my mind again. Reading. Thinking. Reasoning. Any way I want to. Anthropology, of the popular sort, was a great kick for me. But history was stronger.'

He pushed his head across the blanket and brushed her lips with his. They stayed that way a moment; then her hand went to the back of his head and pulled him closer and they kissed hard. His left arm went around her shoulder and his fingers touched her neck and her hair. They parted, and she murmured, 'Henny, Henny.' And then, quickly, avoiding for a moment the meaning behind what they were doing, the meaning that went beyond a nice day in the park and a male and a female, 'Where'd you get the name Henny?'

247

'Silly, huh?'

'No. It suits you perfectly. It's not stern or self-important. It's a little-boy name, and yet not all little boy. It can't be your real name.'

'It isn't. My real name's Henry. But no one's called me that since I was a year or two old. I was even registered in school as Henny Girado.'

'Can I have one more kiss?'

He took her in his arms, and this time their bodies also met, but briefly, because there were adult voices across the grass and Syl was calling out and, more than their exposed position and Syl's presence was their sudden hunger, almost painful in its intensity. They drew apart and sat up, as if by spoken agreement.

'A snake!' Syl screeched, holding up a worm. 'A snake, Sanny!'

'She called to *me*,' Sandy said, and got up and ran to the child. They discussed the exciting find for quite a while, and then Syl brought it over to show to Henny. 'I'm gonna keep it in a box and give it milk and it'll be my own snake.'

'You bet,' Henny said.

They had lunch in a little Chinese restaurant on Main Street. Henny gave Syl a taste of fried rice from the dinner-for-two he and Sandy ordered, but she spit it out and said, 'Yuchi!'

'I guess that means she doesn't like it,' Henny said.

The waiter, who was still standing by the table, waiting to see what the little girl would have, said, 'Got nice cheese sannich, milk, rice cookie.'

'Yuchi!' Syl said, and squirmed in the baby seat which had been placed on the booth's regular leather bench. She and Sandy sat beside each other, facing Henny.

'Got *all* cheese sannich,' the waiter said, still smiling.

Syl opened her left fist, revealing the battered remains

248

of the worm, still moving in the indestructible way of worm-kind. The waiter's smile weakened perceptibly, and he said, 'Yuchi.'

Syl looked at him in surprise; Sandy and Henny laughed.

Sandy ordered an American cheese sandwich, rice cookie and glass of milk for Syl. Before it arrived, she took the three-year-old to the ladies' room and managed to part her from the worm. Syl ate everything, including the rice cookie, and stared big-eyed at the waiter when he came past their table. She accepted the two leechi nuts he gave her on the way out.

They came back to the apartment at one-fifteen, and Henny rubbed his eyes and said, 'Time for Syl's nap.'

'Looks as if you're the one who needs a nap,' Sandy said.

'Yeah. Long nights the last few weeks.'

'Work?' And then she laughed quickly and said, 'Don't answer that.'

'It *was* work,' Henny said, 'even when it wasn't supposed to be. It'll always be work, from now on, unless you're the girl.'

'I'll put Syl in bed,' Sandy murmured, and they held hands a moment.

Syl, who was lugging a doll from her room, said, 'I'm not tired.'

Sandy firmly turned her around and led her back into the bedroom. Syl protested with, 'Now I won't kiss you.' Sandy undressed her, tucked her under a light blanket, and got her kiss anyhow. A few minutes later she tiptoed out and closed the door softly behind her.

'She wasn't tired,' she said, and smiled.

Henny was stretched out on the couch, eyes closed. He squinted at her, said, 'C'mere,' and pushed himself farther up against the back, making room for her alongside him.

249

She sat down, then lay down as his arms tugged her. He moved a little, and she moved a little, and suddenly they were kissing, bodies pressed tightly together. His hands moved over her, as they had in her home, but this time there was a difference in her response. She gave herself to the kiss, the embrace, naturally. And then she pulled her mouth from his and said, 'Henny, I'm going to shock you.'

'Talk, talk, talk,' he muttered, and kissed her again.

She pulled her mouth away again. 'Henny.'

'Didn't you accuse me of talkativeness last night? But it's women who do it up brown. All women love to talk. Even the one woman in the world; even Sandra Bogen.' (He was sorry he'd used her last name, because he suddenly thought of Les, and he didn't want to think of Les. There were lots of things he had to think of in relation to this girl – such as explaining his fantastically screwed-up financial situation – lots of things that would discourage her, and discourage him, and bring their lovely feeling to an end.) 'Why can't we forget talk?' He kissed her, and she let herself go, and for five minutes the feeling between them was pure delight. Then he began to lose himself and his hand went under her skirt.

She squirmed free and sat up. 'Henny.'

'It's okay,' he said thickly, and smiled. 'I don't care if we never do it. I don't care because you're the one girl I want all over, not just there.'

'I said I was going to shock you, Henny.'

'You're the mother of three.'

She smiled briefly. 'No. I'm a virgin.'

He laughed. 'Why, doll, that doesn't shock me. I'd hoped as much.'

'Isn't that sort of middle class for a hip character like you?'

He sat up and took her in his arms. 'Baby, with you

I'm very square indeed. With you, I hope for all the old virtues physically and the new emancipation mentally.'

'I want to go to bed with you, Henny.'

'Oh, boy. You bet. Yahoo.'

'Stop it!'

'Hey, don't get mad. All I'm trying to say – '

'You're saying that you've had plenty of sex, can gratify yourself a dozen times a week, and that I should play the role of Pure Thing in your life. Isn't *that* selfish?'

He paused, and then nodded slowly. 'Yes, Sandy. Selfish as hell. I *was* saying that, though I didn't know it. But I thought – ' He rubbed his face. 'I should've slept more this week. I need all my eight candles of mental light with you. But I thought that since it isn't just another ball, we should go slow.'

'Do you love me?'

She was looking right at him, and he couldn't get away from those eyes, and he couldn't put off saying the square words, the incriminating words, the words he'd thought he'd never say again – because, man, this love bit was a projection of an erection. And once you said that funny rhyme – projection of an erection – you were never the same with chicks, you always took 'em from the bottom up, you always knew the goal. If you considered marriage, you did so because a wife was a comfort, someone to cook and sew and all that jazz. But love? Why, daddy, you outgrew it like corduroy knickers.

Yet here it was, coming right at him again. What he felt for this lovely girl was what he'd felt for the woman he'd married, perhaps even more because of the three-year emotional drought. What he felt for this girl was another soap-opera bit, like supporting a child and sister and the sister's two children and a paralyzed mother.

'Yes,' he said. 'I love you, Sandy.' And his eyes dropped and he felt embarrassed; and an instant later he felt like crying. He fell forward, burying his face in her neck and shoulder, and mumbled, 'Don't laugh at me. Don't play tricks on me. I can't do a thing about it, but I love you. I can't make you an offer, but I love you. And you'll hurt me too much if . . .' He couldn't go on; he was prostrate before this girl, this child-woman. The years of struggle, of arid relationships despite the occasional laughs and pleasures, had left him terribly susceptible to his present feeling. He trembled against her and said, 'Don't use me ever again, Sandy. Don't ever work on Les through me.' He raised his head and looked at her. 'Are you sure you're not doing that now, maybe without knowing it?'

'I'm sure. And because I'm sure, I know I love you. You made my father less important, Henny. Up until last night he was the only man who really mattered, and I wanted to hurt him for . . . being that way with women. But now I don't care; or at least I don't care enough to let it dominate me. I've got someone more important than my father – a man of my own.' She cupped his face in her hands, murmuring, 'You, Henny darling. You, my tired old sugar-daddy.'

'Hey, not so old, and no sugar at all.'

'Will you make love to me?'

He flung himself back full length on the couch, hand rising dramatically to forehead. 'Demands, demands, *demands* on me, day and night. Will I never find rest? Oh, all right, if I must.'

She refused to lessen the emotion with humor; her face remained solemn as she rose and walked toward the foyer.

'Where're you going?' he asked, and knew, and remembered Doris' picture.

'I'll call you, Henny. Come in when I call you.'

He loved her, and he wanted her, but he would have

been so much happier if they'd stayed in here, on the couch. He'd had women visit him at the apartment Wednesday evenings, when the housekeeper was out and Syl asleep, but they'd never gone into the bedroom, Doris' bedroom. He was a square John that way.

And even with Sandy . . .

She called him. He got up and moved slowly to the closed door and paused, and then opened it. She was lying in bed, the covers up to her chin, her face pale,, her eyes glittering feverishly. But when he came to the bed and sat down at the edge and touched her head, her eyes lost their glitter, regained their softness. He stood up and began to undress; and saw her clothing draped neatly over the straight-backed chair. He also saw that Doris' picture was gone from the dresser, and this made his hands stop moving.

'I put it in a drawer, Henny. I did it for you. Was it wrong?'

He shook his head, easier in his mind now that he knew she understood his discomfort. And when he got into bed and drew her cool body against his own, the last vestige of discomfort, of fear, of doubt that this was a good thing, disappeared. She didn't have to dance for him, speak for him, use erotic skills. She merely had to be there, her eyes on his, until they fogged and rolled slightly and then closed as his lips descended on hers. He was gentle at first, but her arms went around him and began to stroke him, even as they pulled him hard against her, and the fire that she lit inside him drove his mouth harder against her soft and welcoming lips. He felt her breasts, naked against his chest, and the curve of her hip, the swell of her buttocks. Her pubic hair teased against his erect penis, and he had to fight an urge to take her then, urgently, satisfying the burning, overwhelming need in him.

He made himself take it slowly, wanting to, because he wanted her to enjoy it. He took his lips from her mouth and put them on her breasts. She responded eagerly, turning onto her back and arching, raising herself to meet his hungry mouth. Her nipples were hard beneath his tongue, and teeth, and lips, and she said his name as he sucked her, clutching his head, his neck, his shoulders. He put his hand between her legs, and her thighs parted avidly. She was wet. He took his mouth from her breasts and began to kiss her stomach, easing his lips down over her navel, her pubic hair. He kissed her thighs, and ran his mouth softly over the wetness of her vagina. Her buttocks tensed, and he looked up at her. She was watching him, her eyes dreamy, her lips slightly parted and glistening. She smiled and said, 'I want everything, Henny. Everything.'

As he brought his mouth down, her hips rose to meet him, and her hands came down on the back of his head, urging him on. He drifted his tongue between the lips of her vagina, tasting her as she moaned huskily. She tasted good, and he tongued her thirstily, feeling her writhe and press harder against his face. He found her clitoris and took it gently between his teeth. She cried out aloud then, and he began to lick the delicate nub. Sandy began to shudder, slowly, with an undulating, wave-like motion. Henny felt her juices slicken his face, and clutched her hips as he drove his tongue inside her, then over her clitoris again. Her shuddering quickened until she was trembling and gasping his name over and over. Then her buttocks lifted from the bed, and she let out a little scream as the orgasm took her. She rammed herself against his mouth, juices flooding over his tongue and lips. Abruptly, she stiffened, her spine arching as a long, slow sigh came from her open mouth. Henny raised his head as she fell languorously back on the bed. He wiped his lips with the back of his hand, and retraced his path up her body.

Her mouth was waiting for him, hungry. They kissed, and he rested his weight on his elbows, luxuriating in the wonderful feeling of her body beneath him. She reached up and put her hands on his face, drawing him gently away. 'I want you, Henny,' she murmured huskily. 'I want you so much, darling.'

Henny could feel her lips wet and waiting against the head of his penis. He moved his hips slowly forwards, and Sandy lifted slightly to meet him. Her eyes closed as he went inside her, and he began to kiss her lids, her cheeks, her neck. He was gentle, afraid of hurting her, inserting himself slowly until he felt the pressure of her hymen against his tip. Sandy moaned his name again, and held tight to his shoulders as she suddenly drove herself onto him. He broke the hymen, plunging deep inside her as she let out a shuddering cry and said, 'Darling Henny, I love you.'

After that, it was pure bliss. Henny drove rhythmically into her, and Sandy wrapped her legs about his waist, moving in time against him, so that she answered his quickening thrusts with a mounting urgency of her own. He kissed her neck; she dug her nails into his back. It heightened the ecstatic pleasure. Henny slowed as he felt himself approaching climax. He wanted it to be perfect, he wanted them to come together. He felt Sandy begin to shudder again, then the movements of her hips grew more urgent, more demanding. She plunged against him, taking him deep into her, and he became more rapid in his thrust as he felt her climax building. Her mouth found his, and their tongues met as the delicious agony of coming orgasm mounted to bursting point. Henny drove furiously into her, the blaze she had lit in him filling his loins, climbing the ramming column of his penis. Sandy screamed his name as her body stiffened, shuddering violently against him as he burst inside her.

'Sandy,' he gasped. 'I love you, Sandy.'

She was the right woman.

16

Lester Bogen had felt deep despair when he heard his daughter's voice at one-thirty Thursday morning and left his bed to enter her room and find her talking on the phone to Henny Girado. He'd repeated a few of the things he'd said earlier in the evening and known he was compounding his own defeat, and then had come to her bed and sat down. He'd tried for the closeness, the wonderful father-daughter rapport they'd had until a week ago, but she'd said, 'I'm tired, Father. I haven't your boundless energy.' He hadn't dared challenge that remark and walked to the door. Then she said something that showed even more clearly that he was losing her, for good. 'I'm sorry, Les. I have no right to keep harping on your way of life. I won't do it any more. I'm going to start concentrating on my own life – seriously, I mean. I think it's going to change very soon.'

He'd left quickly, not wanting to hear more. Henny Girado – that's what she meant. Henny Girado was going to change her life.

He really hated Henny now; and didn't he have good reason? Henny was almost twice Sandy's age, a widower with a child, with crushing family obligations and debts and a spotty personal life. (He saw nothing unusual in this last criticism, in his wanting a very proper man for his daughter.) But no matter how many times he repeated the litany of Henny's deficiencies, it wasn't the real reason for his growing hatred. In his heart, he didn't *blame* Henny for having misfortunes; he actually admired him for the way he bore up under them, as well as for his

257

'clean' manner with women. He hated Henny because he knew Sandy was interested in him. He hated Henny for intruding at a time he, Les, needed *all* of Sandy's emotional interest in order to bring about a healing of the breach between them. He hated Henny for reducing Sandy's role as Daughter and increasing it as Woman. He was sure she would have gone along merely dating boys, not getting seriously involved with them for many years. And he would have had those years as the most important person in her life.

He didn't know how he could stop Sandy from falling in love with Henny (and from what the widower had said, and the way he'd said it, he knew that Henny was already deeply interested in Sandy), but he did know he would do anything and everything possible. If he could reduce Henny's potential as an eligible male in any way, that way would be thoroughly tried.

Getting Henny thrown out of Morden Photos was one such way; it would make an already serious financial situation impossible. And hadn't he warned Henny about it only hours ago? Then, with Henny in real trouble, some sort of arrangement might be arrived at – some sort of financial agreement between them.

Les Bogen didn't like himself very much after coming to that decision, but a moment of thought helped him fall asleep. The thought centered around one fact – Sandy was a good half his pleasure in living. Rather than lose half his pleasure in living, he would break up a romance.

He came down to breakfast at eight-thirty the next morning, knowing that Sandy had already driven off in her Hillman. Elsie Dudonic asked him what he wanted, and he replied, 'Just coffee.'

'You and your daughter,' the elderly housekeeper said, pouring from the electric percolator. 'She had just juice. But she's lookin' better. Much better. Laughed and joked

258

and said she'd have a big breakfast in the city. Guess there was nothin' to worry about after all.'

It didn't make Les feel good. It made him even more anxious to get to the studio and begin his destruction of Henny Girado. He gulped his coffee and left.

Racing his Hawk toward the city, he organized his thoughts and set up a rough plan of operations. As in a job of reportage, one had to plan carefully or the job would be a failure.

He would try to get Henny thrown out of the studio. But it would be risky to barge in on Richie Morden and say, 'Either Henny goes or I go.' Morden might resent an ultimatum and jump the wrong way.

The ultimatum was part of it, certainly, but it should be bolstered by sound *reasons* for Henny's leaving. And it should be supported by at least one other person besides himself.

If Henny had irritated others at the studio, there might be a potential ally waiting to be tapped. Laird Drake acted as if he disliked Henny; and perhaps Henny owed money to Van Roberts, or even Richie. Then there were Marie Riposta, Dennis Parish, Victor Bloom, and his own assistant, Ernie Radish.

He would take it slow and easy. He would seek out each one, separately, sometime today, and carefully broach the question of Henny's being an undesirable co-worker. Several might pan out – especially Ernie Radish, who had failed to collect fifty dollars from Henny for almost a year now and who could be influenced even without that.

Les Bogen lighted a cigarette and inhaled deeply. It tasted good. The sun was bright; the weather was warm without being uncomfortably hot; it looked as if it would be a fine day.

An especially fine day if things worked out. And he

should know by late afternoon, perhaps before he shot his beer commercial.

Henny Girado and Sandra Bogen were sitting in Henny's living room, sipping Pepsi-Cola and ice in tall glasses and holding hands, when Syl came out of her room in panties and little undershirt, rubbing her dark eyes. 'I want soda too,' she said.

'You'll get milk,' Henny said.

'But I want – '

'A milkshake,' Sandy said. 'A real chocolate milkshake. Isn't that exciting?' She dropped her voice, muttering to Henny, 'If you don't have chocolate sirup or powder, I'm dead.'

'We have it.'

'Then on to the soda fountain!' Sandy sang, leaping to her feet and rushing to Syl and sweeping the child into the kitchen.

'What's a real milkshake?' Henny heard his daughter ask. Sandy chattered brightly about everyone's just *loving* real chocolate milkshakes and that they'd make it in the milk bottle since it was almost empty.

'But I like Pepsi,' Syl complained.

'Yuchi!' Sandy said. 'Wait'll you taste a real chocolate milkshake.'

Henny grinned. Sandy was almost too good to be true. It was as if she'd been with him and Syl for years. And being with them, they became a family.

But tonight she would return to Peekskill, and the family would fall apart. Greta would come in the next morning; Henny would take off for the studio, and that night would log late hours in the darkroom or a movie or a bar, and the next morning would rush back to Manhattan and do the same things again. He wouldn't see Syl for

260

days at a time, and soon the old protective lack of awareness that he had a child would be back in effect.

Of course, there was always next Wednesday, when the housekeeper would be off. And the Wednesday after that. And all the other Wednesdays after that. A man could live from Wednesday to Wednesday, if they were all like today.

They wouldn't all be like today. There'd be a few more, and then Sandy would want to know when they could really become a family, would want to know when he was going to marry her. Because this was a marrying affair. This was love that needed the day-by-day normalcy of Squaresville as well as the rare moments of hip passion. (For Sandy was hip in that all-important way; she'd been a virgin until an hour ago, and yet she'd known every movement to make him happy, had done every single thing he could have expected from a much more experienced woman.)

So now he had talking to do. Now he had to spell out for her the extent of his financial predicament.

'The soap opera,' he muttered, and lighted a cigarette and waited. 'The freakin' soap opera.'

They went for a walk, the three of them. It was five-thirty, and people hurried along the apartment-house-lined streets, and Syl sang in a thin little voice a song she'd heard on a children's TV show:

> I am a little girl, three years old,
> My mommy made me a petticoat, trimmed in gold,
> A dollar in my pocket, a penny in my hand,
> Am I not cute, the way I stand?

They listened, and she sang it four times.

Then Sandy spoke of how happy she felt and compared it to how she'd felt for the past week – since learning of

261

her father's other life. 'But I think I knew even *before* I came to the studio,' she said. 'At least I knew he was hiding something. The Tuesday before last, I phoned, hoping he'd be out and I could go up and look around and get the suspicion – well, maybe not suspicion, but it was a definite feeling that something was wrong – get that feeling out of my mind, disprove it. But he was at his desk and the receptionist said she'd get him in a minute. I said I had to go, and hung up. Later I called again, and he said I could come to the studio and I was so happy because I was sure it indicated my suspicions were silly. But when I drove up, he was waiting in the street and didn't let me visit the studio. That's when you saw us drive away. That's when I made up my mind to go up while he was out of town.' She hugged his arm. 'But I don't care any more, Henny. I don't care about any man but you. You've made me so happy.'

'Sandy, I've got to tell you why I can't play this for keeps, yet. Maybe never. *Probably* never, because I don't see myself climbing out for too many years.'

'Nothing can be *that* bad, darling.'

'Yes it can. You ask Syl to sing her song again, and I'll try to put the whole thing together in my mind. I haven't done that in quite a while, you know. I've avoided putting it together. I've avoided adding up all the red. It bugs me, but good. Now I'll do it. And later, when Syl's asleep, I'll spell it out for both of us.'

'All right,' she said, and smiled. 'But nothing you say is going to queer this, Henny. Nothing.'

At four that afternoon Les Bogen stood in Richie Morden's office. His voice was quiet, confident, as he said, 'That's the way it stands, Richie. The irritations have built up until they've created an impossible situation. He owes me money, and film, but even that isn't the whole story. He's, well, bad for the business reputation of the studio. And, as I said, I found out that he's made Marie quite unhappy on several occasions, and Laird Drake too. And my assistant, Ernie.'

'You're saying you want him *out*?'

'That's it, exactly.'

'It's a gag, isn't it?' Morden asked, tone of voice indicating he knew it couldn't be a gag. 'I figured you and Henny for friends – pretty close friends in a way. There must be more than money and film involved.'

'On my part, yes. But it's personal and I can't explain. As for Marie, Laird and Ernie – '

'To hell with Marie, Laird and Ernie,' Morden interrupted quietly. 'If *they* came in here and asked me to do a thing like this, I'd bounce them all. But you, Les.'

'Yes, me. And I'm afraid I have to carry it a step further, Richie. If Henny isn't told to leave, then *I'll* leave. I can no longer work in the same studio with him.'

Richie Morden leaned back in his chair, staring at Bogen. 'This is ugly talk, Les. This isn't like you at all. You know Henny's position. You know what'll happen to him if he can't work with friends, with people aware of and sympathetic to his particular problems. He'll go down the drain.' Morden leaned forward again. 'You wouldn't want to be responsible.'

Les Bogen had given this very angle quite a bit of thought during the afternoon and had come up with a perfect answer. He was going to *help* Henny Girado in his extremity. 'I'm going to discuss that with Henny,' he said. 'I'm going to make him an offer that can solve all his financial problems.'

Morden gave a short, harsh laugh. 'What the hell, Les!'

'I can't explain further,' Les Bogen said. 'Now, if you'd like to call Marie, Laird and Ernie into the office to support my statements?'

Richie Morden shook his head. 'As I said, they don't matter a damn. I just can't afford to lose my name photographer, Les. But I want you to know I don't like it, don't understand it, and resent it. Not that I haven't had my fill of Henny.' He shrugged, and sighed, and said, 'Okay. I'll give him the good news tomorrow. But I'm not going to rush him. I'm giving him a full month, Les.'

Bogen nodded. 'I understand.'

Morden dropped his eyes. 'I feel like a bastard.'

'Not you, Richie. Just me.'

Morden looked up. '*You* feel that way?'

'Of course,' Les Bogen said coolly. 'You don't think I enjoy doing a thing like this, do you? It's a necessity.'

'I still don't understand. And I still dread telling him.' He paused. 'Not that I haven't considered this very thing myself quite a few times. And to tell the truth, it's going to be a relief in some ways. *That's* why I feel like a bastard – because I'm glad in a way; because it'll be great not feeling sorry for him every day, not feeling guilty when I take a job for myself that he needs, not feeling angry when he drinks my liquor and uses my phone. But telling him, Les. That's the bitch!'

'Would you rather I told him?'

Morden nodded instantly. 'But will – '

'He won't be hurt, Richie. I meant what I said – I'm going to give him a chance to solve his financial problems once and for all.'

Richie Morden stood up and came around the desk and went to the liquor closet. He poured two Scotches – knowing Les Bogen's preference – gave one to Bogen and raised the other. 'To the right thing,' he muttered.

They drank, and Richie said, 'Do the right thing, Les. Hurting people is a sin.' He grinned a little, shamefacedly.

Les Bogen looked at him. 'You believe in God, Richie?'

'Of course. Doesn't everyone, one way or another?'

Bogen thought a moment. 'Perhaps, but that one-way-or-another covers too much ground.' He finished his Scotch and put the glass on the closet shelf and said, 'Haven't you ever hurt people, Richie?'

'I don't think so. Not deliberately.'

'Ah, those ground-covering words again. "Deliberately." When you lay a model, aren't you hurting your wife?'

'But I don't lay models,' Morden replied. 'I haven't had an outside piece since – ' He stopped then, remembering the party almost seven years ago, the party which Phyll hadn't attended and at which he'd met the lovely colored girl. 'Call me Stacey,' she'd replied when he'd asked her name. 'We'll never see each other again, so call me Stacey.'

'Since?' Les Bogen probed, smiling slightly, sure that Richie was hedging or lying outright.

'Since I'm married,' Richie said, and returned to his desk.

'I don't believe that,' Les said, still smiling. 'It wouldn't be normal, Richie.'

Richie Morden shrugged. 'Once,' he said, and then added, 'and that's the truth, Les, for what it's worth. My desires, drives, whatever they are, run in different directions.'

Les Bogen nodded, said, 'I'll handle that business with Henny,' and left. He still didn't believe Morden, and it made his day even better.

He walked toward his office. As he approached the door, he felt that his mustache should be long, with twirlable ends, and that he should be chuckling evilly.

The thought made him smile. 'Pay the mortgage or I

265

take the farm,' he muttered. And then, entering the office and approaching his desk, 'Give me the girl and I tear up the mortgage.'

What would Henny give to be free of debt? What would he give to remove his sister from his back? What would he give to face life afresh?

From what he'd managed to learn, Les Bogen figured it wouldn't take more than seven or eight thousand dollars to put Henny back on his feet and give his sister the small business – luncheonette as he remembered it – which would make her independent, allow her enough to support herself, her children and her invalid mother.

Say it was as high as *ten* thousand.

Ten thousand was more like a million to Henny Girado. Ten thousand was more like lifeblood than money to Henny Girado. But ten thousand wasn't too much to Les Bogen; it would still leave him with over forty thousand in various bank accounts as well as a forty-seven-thousand-dollar house, completely paid for. Six months of really heavy work, six months of taking on all the assignments offered him and digging up a few more on his own, would put that ten thousand back in the bank.

But ten thousand would mean new life to Henny. Ten thousand was a hell of a lot of money to him, especially for giving up a girl he'd known only a few hours!

Normally, approaching Henny and saying, 'Give up the girl and I tear up the mortgage,' would be unthinkable. Debts or not, Henny would laugh his head off. Henny would choke on the offer, desperate to take it or not, tears in his eyes or not.

But now, out of the studio, Henny would be more than desperate. He'd be in full panic.

And even if Henny were foolish enough to turn down an offer, other pressures could be brought to bear on him. Such as buying up all his debts and hiring a tough

266

agency and then forcing him to declare himself bankrupt, which would put him out of the photography business.

But no use pursuing *that* thought any further. It was unpleasant and might not be necessary.

Still, it was good to know that a man like Henny was vulnerable in so many ways.

Laird Drake opened the connecting door and came in from the office he shared with Henny. 'Did you speak to Richie?' he asked, and then smiled nervously, as if sure Les Bogen had been kidding him when he'd asked if Laird would be willing to back him up on a demand for Henny's departure.

'I did,' Les Bogen said, 'and it's all over. Henny is leaving us within a month.'

Laird Drake smiled – a triumphant, happy thing. And, unaccountably, Les Bogen hated him.

'Great!' Laird said. 'Just great! Now we won't have to put up with his damned – ' He waved his hand, unwilling to become specific because becoming specific entailed revealing the way Henny had humiliated him. 'Great!' he repeated.

Les Bogen stood up, checking his watch. 'I'm half an hour late for my beer account,' he said. He walked toward the door.

'Mind if I come along?' Laird Drake asked, beginning to follow him.

Les stopped and turned, eyebrows rising. 'Indeed I do.'

Drake laughed and waved his hand and said, 'Sure, Les. So long.'

As Les Bogen went down the stairs, he couldn't help wondering at his own approach to this affair. Had the man involved been Laird Drake (though he couldn't see Sandy spending five minutes with such a man!), Les would never have considered handing over ten dollars, not to say ten thousand, merely on Drake's word never to see Sandy again. But with Henny Girado, a man he now feared and hated, there wasn't the slightest doubt. Because his present fear and hatred were mixed with past liking and continuing respect. Henny Girado would stick by an agreement, if it was within the realm of possibility, as paying off his debts was not. Henny would neither see Sandy nor reveal his reason for not seeing her once he agreed to do so. Les Bogen felt he could trust Henny Girado with his life.

But in the next instant, thinking through the implications of such trust, he decided it wouldn't hurt to play safe. His lawyer could draw up a contractual agreement – a legal loan – which would place Henny squarely in his debt; in his debt and under his thumb! Sandy, of course, wouldn't be mentioned, but there were ways –

Marie Riposta looked at him as he went past her desk. She wet her lips, as if trying to ask him about Henny, but said nothing. Les came out of his thoughts and said, 'He's leaving, Marie.'

She paled. 'Gee, I didn't think Mr Morden would really . . .'

Feeling sorry for her, he said, 'I did it on my own, dear. I didn't bring you into it.'

Marie muttered, 'I'm glad,' but as soon as he entered the studio she ceased to believe him. She felt simply lousy. Gee, she hadn't wanted . . . But she *had* told Mr Bogen she agreed that Henny should be tossed out, what with his debts and dodging phone calls and giving the studio a bad name at some photography-supply houses. And why should she feel sorry? Henny had threatened to get *her* fired, hadn't he? He'd said it right out, twice, though maybe he hadn't meant it – not really.

The heck with him!

There was an outgoing call to handle and then an

incoming; and then she began thinking of Larry Erlich and hoping that he wouldn't call her at home. What if he *came over* and her family saw how old he was and asked how she'd met him? Boy, she'd catch it from Momma and Poppa!

But he wouldn't do that. He wouldn't even call, most likely.

She sighed and reminded herself she had to tell Father Russo all about it next week at confession. Or maybe she'd wait until the week after. No rush. She hadn't done anything *really* bad.

As Les Bogen entered the studio, Ernie Radish was directing two healthy-looking girls – one very blond, the other very brunette – to stand on either side of a tall, athletic-looking young man. All three models stood on a plywood imitation of a dock, with a Florida Keys backdrop. The girls wore halters, shorts and boating caps. The man wore slacks and a very tight polo shirt which emphasized his muscular arms and shoulders.

Ernie was short, plump, approaching fifty, and wore frameless glasses. He was saying, '. . . very, very, *very* happy smiles, girls, when Fred pours the beer. Remember, it tastes like mother's milk with alcohol. We'll need about thirty-five – ' He saw Bogen and nodded quickly. 'Ready to go, Les.'

'Good. I'll use the Graphic View for color; the Rollei for black and white.'

Ernie came up close, murmured, 'How'd it go?'

'Henny's leaving.'

The small man nodded. 'Guess it's for the best.'

Les knew he was unhappy about it. Les knew he'd hoped Richie would fight the move. But Ernie, unlike Van Roberts, Vic Bloom and Dennis Parish, had not been able to find the courage to go against Les Bogen's obvious wishes. Van Roberts had answered Les's initial question – 'Don't you think we'd be better off without Henny Girado?' – with a blunt, 'I think we'd be better off without questions like that, Les. Henny's my friend, as are you.' Vic Bloom – working on some of Les's stuff in the darkroom – had said he didn't understand the question and please not to enlighten him. Dennis Parish, reached by phone at his home, had said, 'I get it. But I like his stuff, Les. Count me out.'

Ernie Radish dropped his eyes from Les's, and Les, again feeling sorry, said, 'You didn't enter into it, Ernie.' He then turned and looked at the shooting stage. The brunette smiled and hipped around a little and said, 'I've heard a lot about you, Les.'

Les Bogen ran his eyes over her, noted the continuing movement of legs and hips as she gave him a subdued come-on, and said, 'By the way, if you kids are good, I might have some further work for you. Cheesecake, among other jobs.'

'I don't do cheesecake,' the blonde said. 'My father would murder me if he ever picked up a magazine and saw me that way.'

'I sure could use the extra money, Les,' the brunette said.

Les made a mental note to call her sometime soon; then he strode to the studio camera, peered through the ground-glass back, and inserted a holder. The brunette gave him a little more hip movement, stressing her availability. He said, 'We're not shooting motion pictures, dear.'

She stopped. He shot the pose, knew he wouldn't use it, walked to the stage as Ernie pulled the holder. He began setting up the scene the *right* way, the balanced and tasteful way. He moved the models around until they were edgy, told them a ribald joke and caught them just right. 'Again,' he said, as Ernie slammed a new holder into place and pulled the dark slide, then reinserted the exposure guard and pulled the holder. 'And again.' Another holder. Then he shifted the scene a bit.

Six shots on that scene, and Ernie rushed to cart away the old props and bring in new ones, all of which he'd picked up at the theatrical renting warehouse earlier in the day.

With his assistant handling changes of scenery and film, Les Bogen lost himself in his work. It didn't matter that he despised beer and disliked hard-sell ads; it was a job, and any job he did had to be right.

He worked three solid hours – until almost eight o'clock. At about five-thirty, Richie Morden came in and set up a window backdrop on the far right wall and shot a small ad assignment – a modified cheesecake job, blending pretty 'housewife' in diaphanous negligee with no-starch, no-iron curtains. He was done before six-thirty, shooting quickly with a Rollei, and left. Then Dennis Parish wandered in and stood around, trying to make small talk with Les. Receiving nothing but grunts in reply, he shrugged and wandered out again.

When Les Bogen finished, he said, 'Thank you,' to the models. The brunette tried to catch his eye, but he turned to Ernie. 'Get the film in the soup. I want prints tomorrow night. The Rollei stuff was shot at three-twenty. Give it nine minutes at sixty-eight degrees, please.' Then he walked out, feeling tired, drained of energy, yet also thoroughly satisfied. The ad would turn out well. He'd have at least twenty good prints for the agency's four-shot photographic comic strip. The job was done correctly. There was always a great deal of satisfaction in that, whether you were doing a socially significant piece of reportage on the UN or a stout-women's girdle ad. It was the act of shooting, the blending of eye with lens, the sense of rightness when subject matter was manipulated

271

over a series of ten or twelve or a hundred shots into that wonderful state of grace where balance, proportion and shading were pleasing to the eye – the critical, artistic, photographic eye.

It wasn't an easy thing to explain, even to many photographers. Henny Girado would understand. Henny felt the same way.

He was in the third-floor washroom, cleaning up for dinner, and he stopped drying his face and smiled at himself in the mirror. He felt rather monstrous.

He went to a good Italian restaurant a few doors from the studio, ordered a martini and examined the menu. He would forget the calories and have a big, leisurely dinner. And then call Henny Girado.

17

At seven o'clock Sandy and Henny had finished a sandwich dinner, and Syl had eaten cereal and mashed prunes
and begun falling asleep over her milk. At seven-twenty
Syl was in bed and Sandy was just sitting down beside
Henny on the couch. Outside, there was a rush of wind
and the damp smell of an approaching storm.

'The weather reports say it'll rain again tonight,' Sandy
said. 'It'll clear up tomorrow, and rain tomorrow night,
and clear up Saturday morning. Isn't that unusual,
Henny? Three nights of rain and three days of sun,
counting yesterday.'

'Crazy,' he muttered.

'Yeah, crazy!' She laughed and hugged his arm and put
her head on his shoulder. 'You're one of the Earth
people, Henny.'

'Me, a teen-ager?'

'Sure. Certainly not a dictator.'

'Dictator's an adult, huh?'

'Wouldn't you know, hipster?'

He shrugged. 'That's rock-'n-roll stuff. That's to
impress people. The kids want to be different.'

'And the things *you* say?'

He shrugged again. 'It comes easy. It comes from long
years of being with jazz buffs, and hip photographers,
and hip people in general. The musicians originated the
words, certainly, but it has little to do with musicians
now. It's representative of a *class* – Moon people, if you
want to differentiate. A small group, I guess.' He made

273

an impatient gesture. 'You've got me off the topic. I have to tell you – '

'Why you can never marry me.' She kissed his neck. *'That's* crazy, man. Real crazy.' She kissed his neck again.

He sighed. 'Maybe. But let me talk, huh?'

She moved away and put her hands in her lap and sat stiffly, at schoolgirl attention. 'Yessir, Mr Girado. When can I leave the room?'

It was his turn to refuse to mitigate a situation with humor. 'First of all, I gross a little under fifteen thousand a year.'

He talked, and she asked an occasional question, and the picture emerged. His expenses for home and studio accounted for about one hundred forty dollars, or half his weekly income. His expenses in Denver averaged another seventy, eighty dollars a week, leaving him with about seventy dollars. Taxes and personal expenses took all but ten or fifteen of that.

If he'd been able to come out ahead ten or fifteen dollars each week, it wouldn't have been too bad. However, he had a two-thousand-dollar loan in a bank on Fifth Avenue which required payments of forty dollars a month, if he wasn't to lose close to three thousand dollars worth of photographic equipment. Also, he owed various sums to five photographic-supply houses in town, ranging from three hundred to eight hundred dollars. And to top it all, he owed money to several dozen people from New York to Los Angeles – people he tried to pay every so often; people who'd dunned him in some cases and, failing to receive their money, had dropped him as a friend.

He couldn't be sure – there were so many small debts of fifty to seventy-five bucks – but he figured that he now owed a grand total of six thousand dollars and was dropping further behind at the rate of ten or fifteen dollars a week, no matter how hard he worked.

If he looked ahead (which he'd refused to do for almost a year before this), he could see a time when there'd be no new places from which to get film and other supplies, no new acquaintances from whom to borrow even a five spot, no bank willing to risk any sum on a man with his credit rating. And when that time came, he would be bankrupt, through as a photographer. And then what would happen to him, and to the people who depended on him? As he'd told Marv Weister, if he couldn't be a photographer, he was dead. He'd never survive as a clerk, a counterman, a salesman. He'd die, daddy. Literally!

He stopped talking sweat standing out on his face, and said, 'It scares hell out of me. That's why I never think of it. That's why I can't think of marriage.'

She took his hand. 'I didn't know it was this bad, Henny. I've never known anything about money troubles.' She paused. 'But it seems to me you *must* think of marriage.'

He grinned his funny, crooked grin. 'Sure, so there'll be someone to take care of Syl when I jump off the bridge.'

'So you can save whatever you're paying the housekeeper. How much is it?'

'Eighty a week.'

'See? It's so simple I can't understand why you didn't marry someone, *anyone*, before! Your wife stays home and takes care of Syl. Just by doing that, she's earning eighty dollars a week – the eighty you now pay a housekeeper. And while a wife shouldn't cost anything – I'm convinced she could actually *save* money on the household and certainly stop you from eating so many outside meals – we'll say she's extravagant and allow her twenty a week. Which still leaves sixty of your eighty. And say another twenty goes toward the red. That still leaves forty. Forty dollars a week to pay off the bank loans and other debts. Forty a week to re-establish your credit. In two years, you'll be able to face everyone with the knowledge that your debts are shrinking. In five or six years, no debts at all, to speak of.' She laughed. 'So where's the big problem?'

He stared at her. 'You make it sound good. Except, of course, there's the problem of finding a girl who's willing to start off minus six grand and plus a kid.'

'You've found her,' she said, and hugged his arm. 'I'm brazen, but who cares?'

'And there was also the problem of falling in love, which I couldn't, until now.'

'I thank you; my mother thanks you; my – ' She stopped.

'Yeah. Your father won't thank me.'

'He doesn't count. So we've decided that your only way out is to marry me. Correct?'

He hesitated; then nodded. Always before, marriage had been an impossibility – mainly because he couldn't imagine living with any one woman, any woman who wasn't Doris. Nor could he think of Syl calling any of the chicks he knew 'Mommy.' Nor, when he got around to it, could he imagine anyone's wanting to marry him if he spelled out his financial situation, which he would have to do. Eugenia, for example, had remarked only last week at Marv Weister's pad that she'd have liked to make it with him for keeps, 'if you weren't so broke.'

But Sandy had answers for everything, and she made sense.

Except that she was talking in what could be called the first flush of sexual experience. She still hadn't left him, hadn't sat down alone somewhere and thought out how

276

tight a squeeze her life would be with him, hadn't considered exactly what the deal entailed – becoming a housewife and staying in a Queens apartment with a three-year-old child (who wouldn't be nearly as much fun as she was now, once the novelty wore off), hadn't added up exactly what she would lose – the beautiful home in Peekskill and the luxuries and the pocket money and the complete lack of responsibility.

And there was Les. He would really have something to fight now. He would be in the right too, as far as any objective observer would be concerned.

Doubts would have to enter Sandy's mind, once she gave the matter solid thought.

He told her so. She said, 'Oh, I won't dispute that, Henny, but in the end, I assure you I'll – '

'Let's drop it for now. We've known each other only hours. It's ridiculous to talk of marriage. Let's go on for a while, and then we'll see.'

She nodded. 'Yes. I intended to do that anyway, to see how *you* would feel.'

'Then we won't mention marriage for a long time, huh?'

'At least a week,' she said, and laughed, and kissed him. He put his arms around her, and she put hers around him, and the kiss became a fierce, fervent, demanding thing.

He pulled away. 'No more, baby, please. Let's give it a cooling-off period.'

She stood up. 'Chicken.' She walked to the closet, slipped on her cardigan and went to the hall door. 'If I don't go quickly, I won't go at all. Good night, darling.'

'Good night, sweetheart.'

For the first time since he'd met her, she blushed. 'I'm so happy, Henny!' She left.

He smoked a cigarette and tried to think of reasons against the whole bit, but he was too happy.

He turned on the TV. The phone rang. He answered it, and the voice said, 'Henny? This is Carl Stevens from Treakle's Everything-Photographic. I tried to get you earlier in the week. Listen, the boss is on my neck about the money you owe us because I always handled your orders.'

'I'll try to get a few hundred over to you early next month, Carl. I'm a little short.'

'You've been saying that for six months! I did you a favor, Henny, filling that big order, and you promised payment three months ago – complete payment on the six hundred you owe. Now you give me a song and dance!'

Henny Girado didn't interrupt. He took the tongue-lashing in silence. He knew he deserved it, but that didn't stop him from turning pale. When Carl Stevens stopped speaking, Henny cleared his throat of thickness and said, 'I'm sorry, Carl. Sorry as hell. Try and be patient.'

'Damn it! If you don't pay off, I'll personally call every photographic-supply house in town – right down to the smallest – and let them know you're a fuckin' four-flusher!'

Henny took it again, white as a sheet this time, and finally said, 'I hope you won't do that, Carl. It'll finish me and end all chance of your being paid. I'll do my best to dig up a few hundred.'

There was a hissing sound, and a click.

Henny returned to the couch and smoked another cigarette. His hand trembled so badly that he dropped ashes all over his lap.

He went to the kitchen and took the bottle of rye from the top cabinet and had a shot. He poured another, mixed it with water and took it back to the living room.

He thought of Sandy and turned off the TV. He sat drinking, and finished the rye, and felt better. He got a book from the open case on the north wall – the wall opposite the picture window and the corner in which the combination Emerson stood. It was a Civil War job – *First Blood*, by Swanberg – something he'd bought over a year ago and never started.

He started it now and was soon engrossed in the ever-fascinating story of Fort Sumter.

But it was really Sandy – her willingness to be part of his screwed-up life – that eased the sickness inside him and calmed the trembling of his hands.

The phone rang again. He answered it without hesitation. 'This is Les Bogen, Henny. Sandy there?'

Henny was startled but recovered quickly. No use beating around the bush; the situation had to be out in the open anyway. 'No, Les. She left about half an hour ago.'

'I see. Spent the whole day with you?'

'Yes.'

'That makes it easier for me to say what I have to say.'

'Shoot, daddy.'

'I warned you what I'd do if you saw Sandy again.'

Henny's mouth went dry. 'So you did, but that doesn't mean Richie's about to listen.'

'He listened, Henny. You're out of the studio. You have a month to relocate.'

Henny Girado didn't want to believe it, but he did. 'I'll talk to Richie tomorrow,' he said, trying to keep his voice steady. 'And when you speak to Sandy, you'll understand.'

'I wouldn't understand, as you put it, if your name were Petrarch and hers Laura. And Richie won't go back on his decision. He knows I'm calling to tell you, Henny.'

The full implication of what Bogen had done to him

became immediately evident. 'You bastard,' Henny whispered. 'If I wasn't afraid of hurting her, I'd tell Sandy just how – ' But he didn't like the sound of that, and stopped, and repeated lamely, weakly, despairingly, 'You whoring bastard.'

'Now comes the good news,' Bogen said calmly.

'You're generously allowing me to keep one of my testicles.'

'I'm going to offer you enough money to pay off all your debts and buy your sister that small business you once mentioned.'

Henny said, 'What is this, Les? Why get me tossed out of the studio if you're going to give me eight or nine grand? Because that's how much it would take. Why try to ruin me one minute and then set me up so that *any* studio will do?'

'There are stipulations to the loan, Henny.'

'Don't say it, Les.'

'I'm going to, Henny. And if you have any regard at all for your family, you'll accept.'

'You crazy bastard. That's what comes of owning a television set. Those old movies . . .'

'I'll loan you eight or nine thousand – we'll figure out the exact amount needed – and we'll sign a contract.'

Henny laughed almost hysterically. 'I don't think it's legal, Les. I don't think you can draw up a contract which states that you give me eight grand, in return for which I never see Sandy again. I don't think you could haul me into court for breaking such a contract.' He laughed again, a long time.

Les Bogen waited patiently and then said, 'It'll have nothing to do with Sandy. It'll be an out-and-out loan, with no interest and no specified date by which payment must be made, which can be called up within, say, any three-month period. We can list your cameras and furnishings and car and clothing and the business we'll buy your sister as the collateral, since everything will be clear of debt by then. The rest will be a gentleman's agreement. You'll promise never to see Sandy again and I'll promise never to call up the loan. You'll keep your word and I'll keep mine. You'll trust me and I'll trust you.'

'Ah,' Henny murmured. 'Clever, daddy, clever. One false move and I'd be stripped of everything and left to starve.'

'But you won't make false moves, Henny, if you agree. I know that.'

Henny Girado didn't answer.

'Think how it would be to pay off all the people on your back, Henny. You'll be starting life fresh.'

'I started life fresh when Sandy came here today. I love her.'

'Don't make me hurt you even more, Henny.'

'More? Is there more you can do?' And he knew there was, and Les Bogen knew he knew there was.

'I won't go into details, Henny. I won't explain that I know all the photographic-supply houses, as do you, and that I can, for example, *warn* those you're still able to buy from on credit. And I might even create a league of your creditors and hire a tough collection agency and take you to court.'

'Thanks for omitting the details,' Henny intoned.

'Well, Henny?'

'You're nuts, Les. I'll go out and get myself another studio.'

'You're kidding yourself, Henny. And it isn't right to kid yourself when a child's welfare depends upon you. You wouldn't want to hurt your daughter, would you, Henny?'

Henny Girado squeezed the phone, and his face turned

281

white and he shouted, looking down into the mouthpiece, 'You sonovabitch! And how'd you like it if I hurt *your* daughter? You rotten bastard! How'd you like it if I knocked her up and kicked her out?' But it was Sandy he was talking about, and even the white-hot rage, the venomous hatred – both the results of panic – couldn't make him forget that.

Les Bogen understood. 'Go on,' he said quietly. 'You were speaking of my daughter.'

Henny took a deep breath and tried to steady his voice, but even so it trembled as he said, 'Les, please don't do this. It's stupid and cruel.' And that was all he said; that was all the pleading he did, because if Bogen were going to change his mind, it wouldn't take more, and if he were going to continue with his plans, kissing his feet wouldn't help.

'Tell you what,' Bogen said. 'Accept my offer and I'll throw in Morden Photos too. *I'll* leave instead of you.'

'You'll throw in Morden Photos too,' Henny said dully.

'I'm sure you'll do the right thing, the *only* thing, Henny.'

'The right thing, the *only* thing, is to rip you apart.'

Bogen chuckled. 'Forget that, Henny. Because of my size, and social habits, I decided very early in the game to be fully prepared to handle the occasional irate boy friend. Few turned up, and most were only cold glances and hot words, but two others . . .' He sighed. 'I spent almost as much as you owe learning the art of jujitsu. I received instruction six hours a week, every week for three years, from a Japanese expert. When I finished, he said I should be very careful never to lose my temper. I never do. But I still put in an hour of mock-combat with another, younger instructor every so often.'

'Then there's *nothing* I can do, except to tell you to take your offer and shove – '

'Think it over a few days,' Bogen interrupted imperturbably. 'I'm sure you'll see that I'm being very generous, when I really don't have to be. It's because I actually like you, Henny.'

'I can't even laugh, Les.'

'It's true.'

Henny Girado hung up. He went back to the couch and picked up *First Blood* and tried to read. He couldn't even see the print. He went to Syl's room and stood looking at the door, and then went into the master bedroom and lay down in the dark. There was still a trace of Sandy's delicate scent.

He returned to the living room, trying to think, trying to understand what was happening to him. Only two things were clear:

He loved Sandy and she had made life seem good again, hopeful again.

If he continued seeing Sandy, Les Bogen would calmly, competently destroy him.

He paced up and back, searching for a way out. He had to find another studio, and big-paying assignments, and fight Les Bogen.

A sob tore from his throat – a deep, harsh, violent sound which shocked him. And before he could get over the shock, he sobbed again. And then he was standing in the middle of the room, head up and arms at his sides and weeping, weeping for the first time since he'd been a child of seven or eight.

He finished in a few minutes, washed his face in the bathroom and had another drink from the bottle of rye. He put on the TV and sat looking at the screen and saw and heard nothing.

Quite suddenly he knew what he was going to do.

No use trying to break out of the vise. No use trying to

283

fight the mountainous debts. Les Bogen had made that impossible.

So tomorrow Henny would speak to Les. He would take Bogen's money and pay off the whole goddam world and put his sister on her own. He would stay on at Morden Photos and have a real ball. He'd give Syl the best of everything, maybe even a mommie, a nice one that she'd like. Sure, there were millions of chicks.

He went to bed. He tried hard not to visualize Sandy, but the ache grew and he sat up and told himself to stop singing sticky ballads. He'd made it with dunnings and loneliness, and he'd make it with memories of Sandy. 'Like it's Lawrence Welk, man,' he muttered. 'You learn to live in the same world with it.'

He lay down again and closed his eyes.

Book Three

18

Marie Riposta was uncomfortable. The temperature was above eighty and the reception room didn't have a single window and the high-powered fan did nothing but push the stale air around and around. And then there was her *inner* discomfort, based upon two separate incidents. The first, and weightier, was the gift she'd received from Larry Erlich last Friday, just two days after their date. She knew she had to return it, and yet here it was Wednesday and she still hadn't done so. All it required was contacting United Parcel and having them pick it up. But she just hadn't gotten around to it. And then there was the second incident, which took place on the same day she'd received the gift from Larry: Henny Girado had come to her desk and said, unsmilingly, 'I hope you and the others won't be too disappointed, but I'm not leaving the studio as rumored.' She'd actually felt relieved – of guilt – but his face, especially his eyes, had looked so terribly tired, and she'd blanched at the thought that he might know she'd backed Les Bogen.

But Bogen had assured her he hadn't used her name.

Anyway, Henny had spent some time with Morden and Bogen in Richie's office and then left. When she asked Mr Bogen what had happened, he smiled and said Henny was going to visit his family in Denver for a few days. He'd be back on Wednesday, which was today, which made the reception room even more uncomfortable!

And another thing which didn't add to her comfort was the way Laird Drake was acting. She'd heard him say something to Les Bogen about its 'not being cricket' to have Henny stay on after bringing everything into the open, and Bogen had been real short with him, saying, 'Sorry,' and walking away. Now Drake kept jumping on her about calls he expected from big magazines like *Life* and *Holiday*, and she knew darn well he'd never done business with them.

And Mr Morden himself wasn't exactly Laughing Boy lately.

The present from Larry Erlich was the big thing, of course. She'd come home from work last Friday, looking forward to a quiet weekend, with maybe a movie and lots of TV, yet at the same time feeling sad and thinking about that play she'd seen with Larry Erlich and wondering whether there were others like it – other worlds of thought which he could show her. Her mother met her at the door with 'Hey, you gotta big box from United Parcel, Marie. Came this afternoon. You buy anything at this expensive place?'

The 'expensive place' was indicated by the neat white label on the large cardboard carton – nearly three feet high and two feet square – standing in the living room. The print above her typed name and address read, 'Erlich's, Fifth Avenue – Fine Furnishings,' and the number placed it a block or two downtown from Central Park. Marie knew the area but only through window-shopping jaunts. The shops there were about the most expensive in the city.

She opened the box, managing to pocket the tiny envelope lying atop the white tissue paper, which in turn lay atop a mass of shredded celluloid packing, without her mother's noticing it. The gift was a lamp, one of the most beautiful Marie had ever seen. The base was white bone china with two large, intricate floral designs in red, pale yellow and delicate blue which wound from the bottom to the neck. The shade was silk Shantung, an off white, and extremely simple.

Marie's mother put her hands to her mouth and gasped, 'You spend your whole salary on this!'

Marie said something about being carried away at the time and added, 'I'll return it, Momma.' Then she walked to her room, stunned. The lamp was obviously worth well over a hundred dollars – maybe two hundred!

Sitting at the edge of her bed, she opened the envelope. Inside was a white card bearing the Erlich-Fifth-Avenue heading in tiny capitals, plus address and telephone number in minuscule italics. The rest of the card was covered by neat handwriting:

DEAR MARIE:
I want so much to see you again yet am strangely afraid of picking up the phone and calling. Therefore, this gift. If it pleases you, would you call me at my shop? I am there most weekdays. Or better still, why don't you come down in person? I would be so happy to show you around.

LARRY

She had torn up the envelope and begun tearing the card in two, but then she had stopped and put the card in her purse, telling herself that she would need the address when returning the lamp.

And now it was Wednesday, five days since she'd received the gift, and she still hadn't acted.

The phone rang, and she answered, and her friend Roberta said, 'Marie? How about lunch? June and Carrie say okay.'

Marie said, 'No, I have an appointment,' and didn't know why she'd said it since she had no appointment.

Roberta's voice grew excited and rather acidy. 'Yeah? You mean a *date* – with a feller?'

'I mean an appointment,' Marie said coolly, and was annoyed with herself, and was even more annoyed with Roberta for prying.

'Well, don't act as if we never *talked* before!' Roberta

snapped. 'I don't know what's got into you lately. You ducked out on lunch with us last Friday, and yesterday, and don't think we swallowed that I-gotta-eat-at-the-desk business! Maybe you'd rather eat with girls like *Stella!*'

'Take it easy,' Marie muttered, and then placated her friend with, 'I really have to stay at the desk, Roberta.'

'How come it never happened before, huh?'

Marie sighed. 'I can't explain now. I've got to answer another call. So long.' She hung up, feeling slightly guilty. The only bit of truth she'd given Roberta was the 'I can't explain now.' She certainly couldn't explain – now or ever. How did one tell a long-time friend that she, and two other long-time friends, had suddenly palled, had suddenly become distasteful? How did one put half thoughts and vague feelings into speech – thoughts and feelings that made one want to get away from friends and parents and everything!

'Hey, doll, laugh it up. Daddy's back and all's well that ends well and isn't this the livin' end?'

She looked up, and it was Henny Girado, and she was glad to see him.

'Yeah,' he said. 'You couldn't wait for me to come back. You and Les and Richie and Laird and maybe Van and the others. You all love me so much.'

He was grinning, but the terrible weariness was still in his eyes, and she saw he'd been drinking. She surprised herself by saying, 'I *do* love you, Henny, in my way. It's just that I'm . . . an awful baby.'

He stared at her, and his grin weakened. 'You're kidding.'

She read his vulnerability, his defeat, without understanding what she was reading, and stood up and came up to him and kissed him on the cheek. 'Welcome back, Henny,' she said, voice thickening momentarily with everything that had been happening to her. 'Welcome, daddy.'

He nodded, and it was as if he were giving her a little bow. He turned and went quickly to the landing. There he stopped. 'Les Bogen upstairs?'

'No, Henny. He won't be in until twelve or one. Don't you want to check your calls? You got quite a few.'

'I'll handle them all, soon. No more debts for daddy.'

'There was a girl,' Marie said, picking up her book and looking through the pages. 'Sandy. She called Friday and I told her you'd left town and wouldn't be back until today. She called this morning, early, and when I said you hadn't come in yet she said she'd call again.'

'Okay,' he said, and his voice was dull. 'Any jobs?'

'One. But it was a rush and I turned it over to Richie and he handled it through Van.'

Henny nodded and went upstairs. Later he went out and came back with a package that looked like a bottle.

Marie began thinking of the lamp and what she should do about it and found herself reaching for the phone. She would speak to Larry Erlich. She would tell him she was returning his gift. She'd ask him to please not bother her again.

He hadn't bothered her.

The thought was there before she could fight it, and she put down the phone, no longer knowing what she could say to him.

Laird Drake came out of the studio. 'I'm expecting a call from *Holiday*,' he said sharply. 'Please switch it to me the moment it comes in.'

'Yes,' she said. 'Don't I always switch your calls – anyone's calls – the moment they come in?'

'Don't be insolent!' He walked to the landing and felt her eyes on his back and whirled, as if to intimidate or startle her. 'Well?'

She smiled and shook her head and turned away. Poor sap!

Laird Drake wanted to say something, do something,

to put this . . . *wop* in her place! He wanted it with all his heart but couldn't think of a thing. He stomped upstairs, raging.

Marie shrugged. A few minutes later Drake came down again, fast, and kept going toward the street. She heard the door slam behind him. Then she gave Henny an outside line, took a few deliveries and saw Henny leave. He sure looked plastered!

Van Roberts came in with his wife, little boy and a voluptuous model named Yolanda Ferris who did cheesecake for the Negro mags. They all went into the studio, after Van introduced his family to Marie. Marie wondered how he could let his wife watch that sort of shooting.

Then Les Bogen came in and talked to her, and there were more calls and more deliveries. And then it was twelve and time for lunch. She freshened up in the washroom and went down to the street and walked to a luncheonette, and then passed it. She kept walking, toward Fifth, and realized she was thinking of Larry.

No! She wouldn't play around with an old man!

Of course not. She'd merely go to his shop and tell him she was returning his gift. She'd thank him. Nothing wrong in that. He'd understand from the way she would act – the *cold* way she would act. But she would also show him she appreciated the gesture.

She stopped, confused at what her purpose – her real purpose – would be in visiting him. She turned and retraced her steps to the luncheonette. She had egg salad on white and iced coffee. Then she went back to the studio.

God, it was hot for May! She'd take a shower when she got home. And she'd tell Momma to call the United Parcel service and return the lamp.

She typed three letters for Richie and handled the phone and accepted deliveries. The day dragged on. By four-thirty she had a splitting headache.

* * *

Les Bogen had experienced calmer periods in his life, but the week from Thursday to Wednesday was not without its satisfactions. At home Thursday night, he saw that Sandy was excited, elated about her relationship with Henny, and he carefully avoided giving her the opening to talk about it. In fact, he got out of her way entirely by pleading an upset stomach and going to bed. The next morning Louise surprised him by showing up for breakfast at eight o'clock, after Sandy had left for school. 'Your daughter has met a man,' she said.

'She meets many men,' he muttered, gulping his juice.

'I think this is the *important* one.'

He grunted and decided against eating breakfast at home.

'Not that she gave me any details. She just said she wanted me to know she'd begun seeing a photographer at your studio – Henny Girado – and that while there was nothing definite about it, she felt she would not be dating any other men. She said she'd tell me more in a few weeks, when they made some plans. Has she discussed it with you?'

'No. And don't worry about it. Girado's not the man for her.'

'Worry? I'm not worried. I'm very happy for her. And I don't think your opinion's going to stop them.'

'Girado himself will stop. He hasn't the slightest idea of settling down, so forget it.'

'How can you be so sure?'

He shrugged and left the house.

That evening he was home early, and Sandy was already sitting in the living room staring at an anthropology text without shifting her eyes or turning the pages. Elsie, the housekeeper, was moving around the dining-room table. She'd placed only two settings. 'Mother out?' Les asked Sandy from the kitchen doorway.

She looked up, eyes clouded, and nodded. 'Some sort of bazaar.'

Les turned to Elsie. 'What's for dinner?'

'Thought I'd broil some chops or steak and serve a salad.'

'Then you haven't actually prepared anything?'

'Just a salad.'

'It'll keep.' He turned to Sandy. 'How about dinner out?'

She looked up again and nodded. 'Yes. I want to talk to you, Daddy.'

'Fine. I'll just shower and change. Won't take me fifteen minutes.'

Half an hour later they were seated in an air-conditioned diner on Route 202, Sandy having vetoed any full-fledged meal. They ordered hamburgers, French fries and iced tea, and Les took out cigarettes and offered them to Sandy. She accepted, and he lighted both hers and his own, and said, 'Summer's early this year. We'll have to visit the country club next week.'

'Daddy, I'm in love with Henny Girado.'

He winced but only inwardly. He hadn't expected so precise a statement. 'I see,' he murmured. 'And he?'

She paused. 'He said he's in love with me.'

'Then there's nothing more to discuss.'

She looked at him in surprise.

'Well,' he said, 'I expressed my opinions last week. I'm not going to press the point.' When she said nothing, he added, 'But if it will help prepare you for the inevitable disappointment, I'll state that when Henny left for Denver, his plans included looking up several old flames.'

'That was before Thursday.'

'That was Friday morning, Sandy. A moment after he phoned to learn if he could catch a late-afternoon plane.'

'You can't expect him to show his hand in front of you – not after the way you ordered him to stay away.'

'I ordered him to stay away precisely because I wanted to avoid this situation. He thought you were as experienced, as hardened, as the women he's accustomed to and therefore felt safe. But you've probably shown him you're infatuated with him, and he's snapping the relationship short. Why do you think he suddenly decided to get out of town?'

She laughed, but her face was pale.

He squelched the sudden vicarious ache, the flash of sympathetic pain. She'd be over it in a week, and life would become right again for both of them.

He reached out and covered her hand. 'Baby, I know what I'm saying.'

She jerked her hand away. 'You can't!' Just then the waitress came with their order. As soon as the waitress was gone, she continued. 'You can't know that! He didn't *tell* you, did he?'

'Obviously not. But knowing Henny as I do . . .' He shrugged.

'You always *liked* Henny. From the way you used to talk, I knew he was the one man in the studio you admired. But because you have some silly idea that he'd be bad for me – '

'I know he won't marry you.'

She was frightened by the cool assurance in his voice. She began to say something, stopped, and then ground out her cigarette and reached for her hamburger.

'I'm sorry, Sandy. I'm merely preparing you.'

'Don't be an idiot! You can't know how close we were Thursday.'

'I can guess.' And then he was sorry.

She flushed. 'You *would* stress that.'

He recovered quickly. 'Yes, and so would Henny. He'll talk of love, and play at love, but he'll never marry you.'

She bit into her hamburger.

He sighed. 'I hope I'm wrong. If I am, I'll give you the

biggest dowry – ' He stopped then, not because of anything she did or said; she was eating, trying to ignore him. He stopped because the lie had become too vicious.

He ate. He finished everything. She left more than half her meal.

Saturday she moped around the house. He suggested they all go to the country club and try the swimming. Sandy refused. Louise said she'd like to, and he was stuck with his invitation. After two hours at the club, they returned. Sandy was in her room. Les tapped at the door and went inside and said, 'They've got a good show at the Hollowbrook Drive-In. How about it?'

She said no, she was going to do a little studying. Exams were coming up in two weeks.

Sunday she sunbathed in the back area, facing the terraces and the heavy thicket of woods which ran down on east and west sides almost to the house itself. He joined her, and they exchanged a few words about the weather's getting so warm so soon, and then they merely sat.

That night he mentioned the drive-in movie again, and she said no again. The next night he was waiting when she came home. Louise left for a club meeting at seven, and Elsie Dudonic left for home, and they sat at the dining-room table smoking cigarettes over coffee.

'At the risk of being repetitious,' he murmured, 'are you interested in a movie?'

She shook her head.

But at eight-thirty she appeared on the landing outside her room and looked down to where he sat in the living room. 'That movie invitation still open?' she asked, voice tense. 'I don't seem to be able to study.'

'Why don't you call one of your young men?'

'Let's not start that again. Please!'

He nodded and stood up. 'We can see both features.'

Tuesday she stayed late in the city, seeing a show with

296

a girl friend. Wednesday morning she was up at five-thirty, showering and breakfasting. She left at six-thirty, and he lay in bed, pitying her and congratulating himself. Today it would end.

Richie Morden was very pleased that Henny and Les had resolved their differences, and especially pleased with Les's statement that Henny would soon be free of the mass of debts that had plagued him, and his creditors, for years. They didn't offer details, and Richie understood that the deal between them was confidential. Normally, he would have been eaten up by curiosity, wondering at length exactly what had occurred between them to make Les first attack Henny and then help him. But Richie wasn't in a normal frame of mind. Richie was obsessed with his own particular *bête noir*.

Wednesday morning he was sitting in his office trying to work out some ad ideas for Keith Enders of the Losch-Roem-Enders Advertising Agency. Enders had practically promised him the entire Chelsea Tobacco account if he could come up with something really fresh to push their quality cigar and had done so in front of both his partners at the party last night.

But it was that very party, thrown by the ad agency for clients and associates, that made thinking in terms of business – thinking in terms of anything but his old fear – almost impossible.

He got up and went to the liquor closet and poured himself a stiff Scotch. It was only ten o'clock, and he never drank in the mornings, but he had to try something to shake the memories.

'I'm away for a few days and everything goes to hell.'

Richie looked up to see Henny standing in the doorway.

'Marie's turned human and you've turned alcoholic,' Henny said. 'Tell me all about it, daddy.' He came inside

297

and reached for a glass. 'And while you're confessing your lost weekends, pour me a double Bols.'

Richie smiled, glad to be taken away from his thoughts. 'Have a good trip, Henny?'

'A ball, massa. I ate home-cooked and wallowed in childhood sweethearts. *Crazy!*'

But Richie felt he'd never seen Henny look sadder, more tired, less like a man who'd had a good time. He poured the gin, and Henny tossed it down and turned to the door.

'Have a seat,' Richie said. 'Tell me all about it.'

'Important calls,' Henny muttered. 'Big deals. I'm a man of finance now. I'm fulfilling contracts and *ipso facto* clauses and all that sorta jazz. Gotta hop, daddy. Gotta fulfill and fulfill.'

Richie was alone again, and his thoughts were at him again.

That party last night. That lousy party last night. If he hadn't gone to that party, he wouldn't have seen the girl, and if he hadn't seen the girl, he wouldn't have remembered that other girl and that other party.

But he knew that was bad reasoning. Just because there'd been a colored girl at last night's party – he still wasn't sure whether she was a guest or a hired entertainer, since she stayed close to the piano and sang quite a bit – didn't mean he had to remember things from years back. Hell, he saw colored girls every day of his life.

But not socially. Not at parties where they were treated as guests – whatever their actual status. Not where they brushed past him and he smelled their perfume and heard their laughter and was forced to think of them as *women*.

Thinking of a Negress as a woman made him – yes, *forced* him to – remember the only time in his life he'd treated one as a woman. And that made him remember the sense of freedom, the wonderful end of tension. And that made him afraid.

Almost seven years ago. He was working out of a small downtown studio, renting space along with two other photographers, and he'd had a bad six-month period, earning just about enough to support Phyll and himself, never dreaming he would soon receive an inheritance that would make purchasing a big studio possible. So when one of his clients, the publisher of two cheap girlie magazines, invited him and his wife to a party, and Phyll was laid up with a stiff cold, he still felt he had to attend.

Driving to the East Side address, he'd wished the evening over and done with. Not only did he dislike going places without Phyll, but his host for the night was one of the few people he actively resented. Brian Stokes was an aging bachelor who talked too much about inequality in the South and did it too violently and too contemptuously. Richie was in constant contact with the type of individual categorized as 'liberal,' since they were quite prevalent in the photographic and publishing fields. He respected their views and felt that despite his background he was one of them. But Stokes was the kind of man Richie thought of as a *professional* liberal, one who used a militant professed belief in racial equality as his one topic of conversation, as his opening wedge with women, as his final argument in dealing with 'out-of-towners.' Stokes had a very limited personality and had latched on to the 'Negro problem' as a cover for all his inadequacies. At least that was the way Richie saw it.

But since Stokes did use colored models in his *Sepia-Goddess Digest*, a cheesecake annual featuring mulatto nudes, and always invited at least one colored person – nine times out of ten, female – to his frequent parties, he was reluctantly considered on the side of the angels by more valid friends of constitutionality.

The symbol of Stokes's liberalism this night was a girl of twenty, quite dark and quite pretty, with huge eyes and red lips and a watchful, pensive air. The watchful, pensive air was probably due, Richie thought on first seeing her, to the fact that she was very much alone in this room of whites, despite the fact that there were several men and women talking to her. And after being greeted by his host, tossing off one martini and sitting down in an armchair with a second, he was able to note that she was a stranger to everyone here but Stokes, since the introductions were flying thick and fast.

Richie spent an hour talking to some people he knew and then found himself being led to the colored girl, who still sat on the couch and who now had two soft-spoken young men to listen to. 'This is Richie Morden, honey,' Stokes said, and walked away. Richie nodded, and the two soft-spoken young men spoke about the NAACP and the need for supporting it, and the colored girl – whose name Richie had not caught – agreed with them and drank a highball and looked at the empty glass while the two soft-spoken young men made sense in discussing ways and means of leading the South to integration instead of dragging it there.

Richie stood around and listened and finished his third martini and watched a few couples dancing to radio music. When there was a lull in the conversation, he said, 'Would you like to dance?'

The colored girl nodded and excused herself. The two soft-spoken young men gave Richie an approving nod, as if he were earning a merit badge, as he fox-trotted away. It was the first time Richie had ever held a colored girl in his arms, and he suddenly realized it and felt himself trembling. She looked up at him and said, 'Are you all right?'

Because of the three martinis and the need to explain himself, he decided on the truth. 'I'm sorry. I never danced with a colored girl before, and I . . .' He didn't know where to go from there.

She said, 'Would you rather we sat down?'

'No, of course not! I just wanted to explain. I'm enjoying the dance.' He made a sound of exasperation and drew her closer and said, 'I'm so glad to finally be dancing with a colored girl.'

She blinked her eyes but still maintained her air of watchful pensiveness. 'Why?'

'Because I'm – ' He caught himself. He'd been about to tell her what he hadn't put into words since he'd poured out his fears to Aunt Della!

'Because you're from the South?' she prompted.

'Yes,' he said, glad of the way out. 'How did you know? I pride myself on my complete loss of Texas drawl.'

'Oh, it was just a guess. Southerners generally make more of this kind of thing than Easterners.'

'I don't know about that. The people here are making a good deal out of this sort of thing tonight, aren't they? I mean, all the *concentration* on you. I haven't seen another girl here get nearly as much attention as you. That's not very normal, is it?'

She nodded and looked up at him again, *directly* at him for the first time, and he was sure she hadn't looked directly at anyone else that night.

'What do you do?' he asked.

'Go to school. NYU. And model occasionally.'

'How did you meet Stokes?'

'He came up to a studio and I was being shot and he watched and talked to me and later got my number from the photographer. He invited me to this party.'

'And he patted your hand and spoke of universal equality and patted your hand again.'

'But not my ass,' she said. 'That's what you're getting at, isn't it?'

He laughed, startled. 'That's exactly what I'm getting at.'

'You don't like him?'

301

'No.'

'And your reasons?'

'I think he's a phony.'

'Many bigots justify disliking liberals by that remark. Better a phony liberal who hurts no one than an honest bigot who's quite capable of beating a Negro for daring to ride up front.'

'You're right. But I think he's a phony, and I'm not a bigot.'

'Prove you're not a bigot.'

'How?'

'That's the point. Prove Stokes is a phony.'

'I'm not good enough with words.'

'Yes. So I've got your word that you're a true-blue Southern liberal and Stokes is a dirty old New York phony.'

The music stopped, and the disk jockey launched into a commercial. Richie loosened his grip on the girl but didn't let go. 'That's not fair,' he murmured.

'Who cares?' she replied, also murmuring. She paused, then shrugged and said, 'The only thing I care about is being treated like a human being, and my best chance for that is with people of my own race, not in a room full of liberal whites, phony and otherwise.'

'Then why are you here?'

'Why are *you*, if you dislike Stokes?'

'I can't afford to risk offending clients.'

'And I can't afford to risk offending possible purchasers of my photographs.' But in the next breath she said, 'That's not quite true. I didn't have to come here. It was the first time I'd ever been invited to a white party – not counting school groups – and even though I agree about Stokes being a phony, I wanted to see what would happen.'

'What happened?'

'No one patted my ass.'

He laughed again, and the music started, and he pulled her tight against him, much tighter than before. They danced, and he began breathing quickly, and she cleared her throat and said, 'I'm flattered, Mr Morden. But come to think of it, bedtime integration was practiced even during the days of slavery, not to say in more recent times. And by the firmest of segregationists.'

He liked this girl, wanted to gain her full confidence, her full belief. He was also excited by her and, more than that, was at ease with her as he'd been with so few people in his life; as he'd been with Aunt Della.

'Let's sit down and have a drink,' he said.

'I think it's time you gave some other crusader a chance.'

'I'm going to tell you something. I'm going to prove myself.'

'You couldn't before.'

'I'm going to prove myself,' he repeated.

They found an armchair in a dim corner and she sat down. He turned to get the drinks, but she stopped him. 'You said you were going to prove yourself. I don't see how you or any other white man on God's earth can do that. I want you to do it now. And if you can't, I want another drink and another companion. Or maybe I'll allow all the crusaders to get down to honest lust by removing my inspiring presence.'

He stared at her and wet his lips and then bent over and put his mouth to her ear. He kissed her lobe, and she said, 'It feels good, but I'm waiting.'

'I'm part Negro,' he whispered, and as soon as he said it the wonderful sense of freedom swept over him, the marvelous relief from tension. He'd been carrying the fear, the *fact* as he felt it at that moment, for so many years, all alone, always bottled up inside, and now it was out. 'No one but myself knows it; I'm probably an octaroon.' He straightened and said, 'Now *you* know it. Can I bring the drinks?'

She nodded, staring at him. 'It's a cheap victory,' she murmured sadly. 'I'd hoped that somehow a white man could prove he really . . .' She shrugged. 'But no human being can prove he fully accepts another. There's really no way. It's a matter of trusting, of believing. And when one party is a minority-group member and the other his oppressor . . .' She suddenly laughed and crooked a finger at him. He bent low again, and she whispered, 'I'm going to forget what you said. I'm going to make believe you're a pure-white Southerner just crazy for me. I'm going to have a time, daddy.'

They both had a time.

The party thinned out, and Stokes locked himself in the bedroom with a tall blond playmate, and the two soft-spoken young men went behind the kitchenette drapes and spoke not at all. Richie and the girl shared the armchair and drank. After a while they saw they had the living room to themselves and went to the couch.

They had both had a little more to drink than they were used to, and Richie found it easy to lose his customary reserve. It didn't seem to matter that they were in the living room, and might be discovered at any time. Presumably the few other guests remaining were engaged in similar pursuits. It was, anyway, the last thing in Richie's mind as he put an arm around the girl's shoulders and drew her against him. She put her arms around his neck, and opened her mouth as he bent to kiss her.

She had a wild, exciting mouth. It was the first he had kissed since marrying Phyll, and it moved under his lips, her tongue meeting his. He put a hand on her breast, and the next thing he knew, she was busy with the fastenings of her red dress, sliding it clear of her shoulders, and then working it down over her hips until it lay discarded on the floor. Richie sucked in his breath as he stared at her. Her breasts were full, contained by a filmy pink brassiere, like two rose petals cupping dusky fruit. Her waist was slender, encircled by a garter belt of the same pink, the suspenders running down under the brief panties of a matching shade to pale stockings. Her hips flared seductively, and her legs were long and shapely. But it was her color that stoked the fire in Richie. It was the same deep chocolate as her face, paler, when she unsnapped her brassiere, on the bosom. Freed, her breasts fell slightly forwards, the skin stretching, accentuating the dark peaks of her nipples. Richie touched them, and they became erect under his hands. He groaned, and drew her down onto the couch beside him. He wanted desperately to take those nipples in his mouth, more to enter her, make love with her. He began to suck on the nipples, and they grew hard under his caresses. Her hands moved about his clothing, and without taking his mouth from her sweet-tasting breasts, he moved to help her strip off his coat and shirt and tie.

It was an agony that was wonderful in its anticipation as he took his lips from her breasts to remove his remaining garments. As he did so, the girl slipped out of her panties. When Richie turned towards her again, she was lying back on the couch, wearing only the garter belt and stockings. Her pubic hair was curly and jet black, but the skin of her hips and abdomen was paler than the rest of her body, a marginally lighter chocolate shade.

Richie bent to kiss her belly. Her skin was dry and warm, and faintly musky. He could smell her excitement, and it aroused him, so that he returned his attention to her lips, kissing her hard and long. She kissed him back, her long-fingered hands wandering over him, touching squeezing, teasing him to an incredible peak of excitement. He went to roll onto her, but she pushed him gently back, easing up from him until he was comfortably stretched on the couch. She slid one stockinged leg across his stomach until she straddled him, lifting on her knees as she reached down and began to rub the tip of his penis against the moist lips of her vagina. Richie put his hands on her breasts, rolling the hard nipples between forefinger and thumb. The girl let out a little moan and lowered herself onto him. Richie felt himself engulfed by her hot, wet vagina. It seemed to suck him in as she contracted her muscles, and he humped his hips, seeking to go as deep into her as he could. She put her hands on his chest, her breasts dangling close to his eager mouth, and began to move more urgently. Richie put his hands on her hips, his fingers curving over the soft flesh of her buttocks, and began to pump in response. She drove against him, her neck arching back as her climax approached. Richie felt the pressure building in his own loins, mounting and mounting, until his hips thrust upwards, lifting her to her own orgasm, as he spent himself inside her. She gave a shuddering cry, and dragged his face from her breasts, devouring his lips as she kissed him, and clutched him, and trembled in the ecstatic grip of climax.

Richie enjoyed himself immensely. But it was murmuring his secret into the ear of this girl as he made love to her that provided most of his pleasure.

When they got up, the girl touched his face with gentle fingers. 'You know what? I no longer believe you. I think I've been had.'

He began to protest, but she moved her fingers to his lips and said, 'It doesn't matter. I'm never going to see you again, so it doesn't matter.'

It was then he asked her name, and she said, 'Call me Stacey. We'll never see each other again so call me Stacey.'

He hadn't wanted to accept that. The wonderful sense of relief, of freedom from the bottled-up fears, was something he would certainly want to experience again. He decided he would convince her in the car.

He drove her to a narrow side street off Amsterdam Avenue in mid-Harlem. Since it was Saturday night, things were still very much alive. He looked about as he drove, and told himself he was insane to believe he belonged here, and never did try to convince Stacey they should meet again. In fact, he sweated for quite a while afterward, thinking they would run into each other or that she might tell someone who knew him what he'd told her.

But he never did see or hear of her again, and when he questioned Stokes six months later, the publisher remembered her only with difficulty, and then said, 'Dolores something-or-other. She's a college kid, really. I guess she's had it so far as cheesecake's concerned.'

He was relieved. And yet he never forgot how wonderful it had been to speak freely. And this frightened him. If he dwelled on the wonderful feeling too often, he would want to do it again. And if he did it again, his whole world might fall apart.

So he began blocking the memory of that evening from his mind and did quite a good job at it – until the business in the bar, and then the party last night.

He poured himself a second Scotch and was just raising it to his lips when Henny appeared in the doorway again. 'You must be tuned in to the stuff,' Richie said, smiling. 'Every time I reach for the bottle, you're here.'

'I'll laugh at your joke,' Henny said, blinking tired eyes, 'if you'll give me a double.'

'Bols?'

Henny shrugged, swayed slightly and said, 'I've been drinking so much of everything, daddy, it makes no difference any more. If you give me gin, I'll make martinis in the stomach. If you give me bourbon, Manhattans. Let's try Scotch.'

They drank, and Henny lighted a cigarette and turned to the door. 'What the hell,' he said thickly. 'I'm gonna pick up a fifth and really get happy.'

'What's wrong?' Richie asked.

'I'm rich,' Henny said. 'You know what the movies teach – you get rich, you get troubles. Money is the root of all evil. That's what's wrong.'

He left.

19

Henny bought a fifth of Bols gin from a retail shop on Seventh Avenue. The walk through the bright May streets did him no good whatsoever. He felt like divorcing himself completely from people, from the goddam world. But that was, of course, impossible. One went on. One had kicks and laughs. Especially when one was out of the red. And he'd soon be way out, man. Way, way out.

A few feet from the studio, he approached a little blonde and his eyes – blurring from alcohol and lack of sleep – told him she might be Sandy. He dropped his head as he went by.

Back in his office, he sat at his desk and put his hand on the phone. Sandy had left word for him to call her. But she'd be at school now. Anyway, he wouldn't call Sandy. Not part of the deal. She'd call him and he'd give her some hard, cool words, and she might call again and he'd give her the hard, cool words again, and she'd either stop calling or would keep on until she got the idea that he was cutting out – no more jam, momma, 'cause poppa figures you got marryin' ideas.

He opened the Bols, heard someone behind him and turned in his chair. Laird Drake was in the doorway glaring at him. Henny said, 'I get it. You hate your own guts. You can't admit it, so you pick on me.'

'You drunken swine,' Laird whispered.

'That's a good one, daddy. I'm sure you can sell it to J. Arthur Rank.'

'You yellow-belly tramp.'

Henny turned his back, waving his hand in dismissal. 'Go fight with the other kids in the schoolyard.' But then he heard Drake stepping forward, and he lunged to his feet and opened his top drawer and grabbed the long scissors and said, face pale, 'C'mon, you square bastard. Scissors at twenty paces. C'mon, I'm through playin' games.'

Drake had been poised, as if about to leap at Henny. His big body had the prerequisite tenseness, the combative angle, but then he twisted and ran from the office.

Henny blinked his eyes and shrugged. He sat down and poured Bols into a paper cup and drank. He poured again, raised the cup to his lips, and paused. 'Wait,' he said aloud. 'Anything you got to do before getting stoned?'

He thought, and shook his head, and said, 'No. Go ahead and get stoned.'

He drank the Bols, poured another, drank half of it and then said, 'Wait. Old Marv. Haven't talked to old Marv. Gotta tell him. No, can't tell anyone. Big secret. But gotta say hello to old Marv.' He lifted the phone and leaned forward and peered at the dial. It was getting hard to see.

He nodded wisely and finished his paper cup of gin. 'Clear the head,' he said, and grinned, and dialed.

Marv Weister sat before his typewriter. He'd been sitting there almost continually since Sunday night. He hadn't written more than two pages in all that time – nearly three days – but he didn't dare leave his chair, didn't dare leave the manuscript and the typewriter, didn't dare leave his purpose in life.

He'd had about four hours' sleep last night, and less Monday night, and none at all Sunday night. Sunday night he'd sat and trembled. Marv Weister had received a shock – traumatic in intensity, debilitating in character – Sunday afternoon.

Sunday morning he'd tried to work, and the words had

310

come slowly, even more slowly than usual. He'd felt sweaty, dirty, itchy, even though he'd showered the night before and again on rising that morning. He kept combing his hair, scratching his scalp with the comb. He kept wiping his face. He drank a small glass of orange juice and then had to fight nausea to keep it down.

He needed a fix.

But he fought the need. He'd visited the little Bronx candystore only three days ago – Thursday – and before that late Tuesday night, after the store had closed for its legitimate trade. That meant he'd had two injections of heroin within three days. That meant he was slipping into an abyss from which there'd be no return.

He'd called Morden Photos and learned that Henny was out of town and tried to think of someone else to call. God, he had to talk to someone, be with someone, forget the terrible need!

He would call Francie, the girl Henny had supplied for him. But when he got to the phone, he realized he didn't remember her last name, if he'd ever known it.

He had to call *someone!*

His publishers. He would talk to Oscar Enwright, the gentle, erudite editor who had handled his three published books. He'd tell him.

But *what* would he tell him? Certainly not about the heroin! One didn't tell one's publisher things like that!

And he couldn't tell him about the work in progress. He'd used up that topic months ago, when he'd first described the book to Enwright at a luncheon.

A woman. God, if he only had a woman! A woman would make him forget the terrible ache, the terrible desire.

Or liquor.

He ran to the living room and the nearly empty fifth of bourbon on the lamp table. Panting, as if he'd covered a mile instead of fifteen feet, he unscrewed the cap and put the bottle to his mouth and tilted back his head. He gagged, and held it down, and took another drink. He gagged again, and this time had to run to the bathroom. Liquor was no good. Women wouldn't be any good either. Neither would talking to his publishers or Henny or anyone else. Nothing would stop the agony; nothing but heroin. He'd read enough about addiction to know *that*.

After washing, he sat down at the typewriter. He read over what he'd written the day before, made a few penciled changes and put a sheet of paper into the roller. He stared at it, and his mind remained as blank as the clean white paper.

His scalp began itching. His neck and face and groin began itching.

At three P.M. he left the apartment and took the subway to East 180th Street. He walked six blocks to the candystore on the tenement-lined street and went inside. The fat old woman behind the counter looked up from her tabloid newspaper and recognized him. 'You want something?'

He came up close and, even though no one else was in the little store, whispered, 'My name is Dennison. My cousin Alfred said he'd meet me here. I spoke to him a few minutes ago on the phone.'

'All right,' the old woman said. 'I know you. All the time he's got to have the names and the Cousin Alfred and the rest of it. Password for today, and my head gets mixed up.' She shifted weight, leaning back against the wall. 'But if I ask him to buy me a stool, that's too much trouble.'

'Can I go in?' he asked, glancing at the door in the rear, next to a telephone booth. 'I'm in a hurry.'

'No. He's got another friend in there. It'll take a few minutes.'

'Oh.' He stood at the counter, and the old woman read

312

her paper, and the minutes crawled by, and he said, 'Listen, can't you tell him – '

'I can't tell him anything,' the woman snapped. 'If I could, I'd tell him to stop this rotten business.' She waved her hands. 'You look sick. Take a cold drink. Cherry, chocolate, maybe a Coke?'

He shook his head.

'Then plain Seltzer. Here, try some.'

He didn't want it, but she gave him the glass and he had nothing else to do and he couldn't stand there doing nothing. He sipped, and the cold liquid was good, and he drank half the glass.

And drinking that half glass of Seltzer helped save him from jail. The street door opened and a big man in a brown suit walked in and the woman said, 'What . . .' The big man didn't stop at the counter but went straight to the back door and tried the handle. 'Locked,' he said to a shorter man who came in behind him.

'Kick it down,' the shorter man said authoritatively.

The old woman put her hands to her mouth and moaned, 'Oh, oh, oh, oh.'

Marv didn't understand for a moment; but then three patrolmen came in and another two blocked the entrance outside. He gripped his glass of Seltzer and wanted to scream and said, 'Hey, what's going on here?'

The big plain-clothes man kicked the door, under the knob, times. The door flew open and caught on the thick inner chain. The plain-clothes man kicked again, and the chain tore from the door frame, and both plain-clothes men went into the back room. Marv realized they had guns in their hands and was shocked, and then asked himself why the hell he should be shocked. Mr Elders was a dope pusher and dope pushing was a criminal act and the police were apprehending a criminal. And he, Marv Weister, was also a criminal because he used narcotics and using narcotics was a serious crime.

313

He would die if he went to jail. It was bad enough living the way he lived, and being locked in a cage would finish him. Even for one night, it would finish him!

He fought down the screams and held his glass of Seltzer and watched. The small room with the cot and table and two-jet gas burner was empty. Mr Elders and his customer had gotten away. Thank God.

But then there was a noise out front, and he turned and saw Mr Elders and a short, dark boy being shoved toward the door by two patrolmen. Mr Elders and the boy came hurtling into the store, arms twisted up behind their backs, faces pale. Marv shrank back from the violence and said, 'Say, what *is* this?'

The big plain-clothes man looked at him. 'Roll up your sleeves.'

'What?' Marv asked, fighting to hold his voice steady.

The big plain-clothes man stepped up to him, and Marv smelled after-shave lotion and sweat. 'Roll up your sleeves, mister.'

Marv put down his glass of Seltzer and turned to the shorter officer. 'My name is Marvin Weister,' he said quietly, desperately. 'I used to live in this neighborhood with an aunt. I come by every so often for sentiment's sake. I dropped in here for a cold drink. I've engaged in no criminal activity, and I refuse to be ordered about.'

'I told you to roll up your sleeves!' the big plain-clothes man said, and one heavy hand gripped Marv's thin arm.

'Hold it,' the shorter officer said.

The big officer let Marv go.

'Marvin Weister?' the shorter officer asked.

Marv nodded, controlling his trembling.

'What do you do for a living, Mr Weister?'

'I write.'

'*A Shadow of Life?*'

Marv blinked his eyes. 'My first novel.'

The shorter officer smiled slightly. 'Good book, Mr

Weister. Better than your next two. But all three were good.'

Marv was too stunned to answer.

The big detective said, 'You gonna let him go, Harry?'

Harry shrugged. 'He was having a soft drink. We can't force him to do anything on that evidence.' He looked at Marv. 'You refuse to let us check your arm for needle marks, Mr Weister?'

'I refuse to do *anything* which humiliates and degrades me.'

Harry nodded. 'Okay.'

Marv took a tentative step toward the door.

'Just a minute.'

Marv stopped.

'Turn around,' Harry said.

Marv turned.

Harry spoke to Mr Elders. 'You know Marvin Weister? You ever sell him dope?'

The heavy, middle-aged man replied, 'I don't sell dope.'

Harry, who had impressed Marv as almost benevolent, drove his fist into Mr Elders' stomach. Mr Elders screamed softly and tried to bend over, but the cop holding him didn't relax his grip enough for that.

'I asked you a civil question,' Harry said. 'Did you ever sell narcotics to this man?'

Mr Elders was still fighting for breath, but he managed the weak 'No.'

Harry turned to the old woman, still rocking and moaning behind the counter. 'Mom, you're up for a good rap. Tell us if this man Weister was ever here for a fix and I'll see you get consideration.'

'No,' she moaned, hands touching her lips. 'No, I never saw him.'

'Goodbye, Mr Weister,' Harry said, and moved to the

big detective. 'Frank, take that back room apart. I want all the horse they've got.'

Marv walked out of the store, pushed his way through the crowd that had gathered, and shook his head when a teen-aged boy asked, 'What's the score, huh?' He reached the subway and rode downtown and got off and walked to his apartment and went upstairs. He lay down on his bed and closed his eyes. The phone rang about ten minutes later. He answered it quickly, anxious to talk to someone, anxious to drive the nightmarish panic from his mind. The strange voice said, 'Mr Weister?'

'Yes. Who is it?'

'I'm Mr Demarco. Mr Elders' cousin.'

Marv wanted to hang up, but he knew he would need this man, soon, despite all the policemen in the city. He waited.

'Got a pencil and piece of paper? Write this number.' Marv wrote it down, and the voice said, 'Ask for me – Mr Demarco. If the person who answers doesn't know me, don't worry. The phone is in a drugstore. I try to be there every afternoon around lunchtime. Twelve to two, say. You call then, you'll get me, and we can make an appointment to talk over old times. Next week I'll be eating in a different place. No trouble that way.'

'How did you get my name?' Marv whispered, suddenly suspicious that this was a police trap.

Demarco laughed. 'I'm not a cop. Mr Elders had a list of his friends. I'm what you might call his substitute. You know what they say about the show, Mr Weister – it must go on. Same here.'

'Yes.'

'Well, so long. I'll be hearing from you, won't I?'

Marv said nothing.

'You can even see me tonight, if you want. Should I tell you where?'

Marv hung up. For the first time since the night last

August that he'd attended a Greenwich Village party and accompanied a self-proclaimed poet to Mr Elders' candystore, he saw himself as a pitiful pawn of sordid criminals. He was ashamed of himself and terrified by his near disaster, but at the same time the need for heroin was coming alive again.

Carefully, he put the slip of paper with Mr Demarco's number into his wallet. He knew he would call that number when the need overwhelmed him; and it made no difference that he couldn't be sure Demarco wasn't a member of New York's narcotics squad. He had no other contacts, no other place to turn. He couldn't go out searching for pushers. He needed reasonable men, moderate criminals, like Elders. Or was Demarco a different breed?

He went to his typewriter but didn't even try to write. He trembled. He sat trembling the entire night, afraid to turn off the lights and lie down.

He got into bed Monday morning, when the sun was full in his windows. Later he washed and dressed and went to a cafeteria. The noise of the place had always annoyed him, but now it pounded in his skull with frightening intensity. Returning to his apartment, he jumped several times, startled by what seemed like tremendously loud sounds – a truck backfiring, a child shouting, a garbage-can cover falling to the pavement.

He wrote one page that evening and slept almost two hours.

He wrote another page Tuesday and slept four full hours.

Wednesday he awoke at seven A.M. with nausea tickling his throat and his entire body itching and burning. He knew he had to have a fix.

But he fought it. He ate a slice of toast and drank a cup of coffee. He shaved and showered and rinsed out two pairs of socks and swept up the place for the first time in over a month. He told himself he had everything under control and sat down at the typewriter. As soon as he faced the blank white paper, his stomach turned over and the itching started and he began to shake.

He went into the living room and picked up the phone and dialed the number Demarco had given him. It was only nine-thirty, but he just had to get a fix!

The man who answered said he didn't know any Mr Demarco. Marv thanked him and hung up. He returned to the bedroom and the typewriter and the clean white sheet of paper, the blank white sheet which, along with all the other blank white sheets, demanded that he justify his existence by filling it with words – entertaining, meaningful and occasionally important words.

The phone rang. He ran to the living room and caught it on the second ring.

It was Henny. Marv almost sobbed with joy.

'Hey, man,' Henny said thickly, 'I've got a bottle of Bols and a belly full of talk. You can share both for free.'

'Come over,' Marv whispered.

Henny paused, and mumbled, 'You sound happier'n me. We'll sing a great duet.'

'Hurry,' Marv said.

'I'll grab a cab. If I drive now, I won't live to enjoy your gay conversation.'

'Hurry.'

They'd sat facing each other, Henny on the couch, Marv in the red armchair, for almost an hour. Henny had drunk steadily; Marv had nursed his one glass of gin and ice water. Henny had talked about Denver and the luncheonette he'd bought for his sister – 'Put an eight-hundred-buck down payment on a four-grand joint; little place, but it'll pay off a hundred a week and more if she works it right.' Marv had nodded and said, 'Wonderful,' and smiled. Henny went on about the lawyer who'd

318

accompanied him and the money he was going to get within a week or two – money to pay off all his debts. Marv nodded and smiled. Finally, Henny put down his glass and leaned forward. 'When're you gonna ask where I'm getting this dough? What'n hell's wrong with you?'

Marv blinked his eyes, smiled weakly, and said, 'Well, I figured you didn't want to tell me about this mysterious business deal.'

'You're right. I won't talk about the deal. But you should've asked, instead of just sitting there. Is it the dope again? Are you trying to shake it? Are you going into the withdrawals?'

'I *can't* shake it,' Marv whispered. 'I'm hooked. I'm lost, Henny.' He looked at his friend, and his eyes filled with tears. 'I might as well be dead.'

Henny shook his head. 'Naw. You never acted like a guy really hooked. I knew a guy really hooked – Walt Machen – used to work out of a studio with me; portrait studio down on Madison when I was first breaking in. He looked different from you. He was all shot if he didn't have it every day. He had different ways, Marv. I don't think you're hooked.'

Marv Weister leaped to his feet. 'Don't talk nonsense!' he shouted. 'If you knew what I've been going through! If you knew the goddam ache, the wanting, the sickness!'

'I know all that, and it has nothing to do with dope. A man can feel all that for lots of reasons. How's the writing coming along?'

Marv stared at him. 'Are you trying to say it's the *writing?*'

'You had more than a fix a week lately?'

'Yes. Hell, yes! I had two in three days last week.'

'What about the weeks before?'

'What difference – '

'You had two shots like that before?'

'No. But I had two shots in a seven-day period before – three times before.'

'At ten bucks a throw, like you told me?'

'That's what the pusher always charged.'

Henny got up and corked his earthenware jar of gin and said, 'Walt Machen used to pay fifteen, twenty bucks a jolt – and that was thirteen years ago. And he paid more just before he was arrested for trying to shoplift a wristwatch to hock. They raise the ante when you're really hooked. Seems to me ten bucks – '

'So I've got a philanthropist for a pusher! So what the hell sense are you making?'

Henny shuffled to the door. 'I don't think you're hooked as bad as you say. I think you've been getting heavy-cut horse, watered-down stuff from an amateur pusher who can't buy enough to give the real thing. I think you're cutting out on the writing, and you want an excuse, and that's it. You're through all right, Marv, if you don't write. You'll have nothing.' He opened the door and muttered, 'Like old money-bags Girado.'

'Wait,' Marv said, coming forward and taking Henny's arm. 'Don't go. Let's talk some more.'

'I don't need another cry-baby,' Henny said, jerking his arm away. 'I'm one myself.' He went down the stairs.

Marv closed the door and put on the snap bolt and said, 'Crazy bastard.' He looked at his watch. Eleven-twenty. He wouldn't call. Not yet.

He went back to the typewriter and forced a few paragraphs out of his tormented brain and checked his watch again. Twelve-ten!

He ran to the phone and dialed the number and a man answered in a flat, nondescript voice.

'Mr Demarco,' Marv said.

'Speaking,' the flat, nondescript voice said.

'I'd like to make an appointment. I was a friend of Mr Elders'.'

'Oh?' the voice said, and it was no longer nondescript. It *was* Demarco. 'And your name?'

Marv didn't hesitate. He had to take the chance. 'Marvin Weister. You called – '

'Okay. Three o'clock. I'll come to your place. Give me the address.'

'But can't you come sooner? I'm quite sick.'

'That's 'cause you had to live on Elders' crap. You won't be sick on *my* mix. It's real horse.'

'What do you mean?' Marv asked, and remembered what Henny had said, and wanted, strangely enough, to disprove Henny. 'I bought – '

'Don't give me that shit,' Demarco interrupted harshly. 'If you think you're going to get it at ten bucks by telling me you didn't know he was cutting it to nothing, you're crazy. Ten bucks wouldn't give me no profit. It's twenty a jolt, and I won't kid you – it'll go higher if the supply runs low, like it sometimes does.'

'Twenty!'

'And higher. Now you want I should come over or not? I got no time to play games with jerks. You're carrying a monkey, so you know you didn't get that way on Elders' milk-sugar mix. So you know you ain't getting it at Elders' price. And lemme tell you he made more dough per jolt than any legit pusher could ever make. That's how he got pinched – a guy needing a fix wandered into his store and then got mad and blew the whistle on him. So if you're sick, you're going to pay. And you'll get the real thing.'

Marv hung up.

Henny couldn't be right!

The itching, and burning, and nausea. Nine months, almost ten, of heroin injections. All right, even *weak* heroin injections! The shot a week, for eight months, and the three or four times of two shots a week, must have done something to his body. He needed the stuff.

321

But how badly?

It couldn't be too serious a habit, if the heroin had actually been cut so severely.

And yet, hadn't he reacted the way he'd read heroin users reacted? Hadn't there been the peace, the utter lack of tension, for an hour or more after an injection? Hadn't there been the nodding-off, the drugged sleep later on, and then the renewed desire for more drug in the days that followed?

Demarco had lied! Demarco was upping the ante and needed an excuse! There'd been enough heroin in those injections to make a confirmed addict out of anyone!

Marv slipped into his unpressed tweed jacket and went downstairs. He walked, and came to a movie theater, and paused. He hadn't seen a movie in almost a year. He went inside and forced himself to watch the picture. Because it was reasonably entertaining, he became interested and began following the story. At the same time he kept one part of his mind free for self-examination.

He walked out on the second feature, but even so he'd been in the theater over two hours. And he hadn't felt nausea, or itching, or been sick or uncomfortable in any other way. Not once in two hours.

He returned to his apartment and as soon as he opened the door he felt the tension rise and his scalp begin itching. He walked to the typewriter. 'Henny was right,' he said to it. 'It's you – not heroin or anything else. It's you.'

That evening he went down and bought the *Daily News* and leafed through it while standing near a lighted shop window. He found the little item on a back page, and at the close of the item, the sentences:

Riccocia, who called himself Elders, was apprehended when an anonymous addict phoned police after receiving a severely diluted injection of heroin. The addict told a police switchboard operator, 'The rat shot me full of milk-sugar.' An analysis of two packages of powder found in the candystore's back room has not yet been completed, but a crime lab chemist stated it appeared to contain very little heroin and a large amount of non-narcotic agent.

Marv Weister hurried back to his apartment. It was getting late, and he didn't want to be caught out on the streets alone.

He didn't go to the typewriter after bolting his door. He took his three novels from the packed bookcase standing near the windows and carried them to the red armchair. He sat down and began reading the first one – something he hadn't done since receiving the galley proofs.

He was going to read all three books, and look at himself, and find out whether he'd ever write again. And because he'd decided on that and didn't have to face the typewriter this evening and probably all of tomorrow, most of the tension flowed out of him, as in the movie house, and he trembled hardly at all.

20

Les Bogen went back to sleep after hearing Sandy leave the house six-thirty Wednesday morning. He was in no hurry to get to the studio. In fact, he preferred that Henny have spoken to his daughter, smashed her dream and saved his own, before he arrived. So he treated himself to a large breakfast, telling Elsie Dudonic to make him bacon and scrambled eggs, oatmeal and strong black coffee. He was on the oatmeal when Louise came down. He greeted her with a robust 'Good morning' and then jumped up and helped her into the chair across the dining-room table. When he was settled in his own seat, he felt her eyes on him. He looked up from the oatmeal and smiled. 'What's the matter? Did I forget to shave?'

'No,' she murmured. 'You forgot to ignore me.'

His smile weakened momentarily, but then he laughed. 'Would you prefer to resume conjugal living?'

She made a face. 'Heaven forbid. Now you've ruined my appetite.' Elsie came in, and Louise asked for juice and coffee, and Elsie returned to the kitchen. 'You and Sandy make up?'

He shrugged. 'Our little difference of opinion is working out.'

'You mean she's not going to see that photographer from your studio – Henny Girado?'

He pushed the bowl of oatmeal aside and raised his cup of coffee. 'I wouldn't know, Louise.'

She stared at him. 'The hell you wouldn't.'

His eyes flashed to hers and his lips tightened.

'You did something to her, Les. You forced her to stop seeing that man. You pulled the strings and made her

324

jump, or perhaps you made Henny Girado jump. But either way, you took her from a man she'd begun to love. That's a cruel and vicious thing.'

He drained his cup and stood up. 'Your imagination can only be categorized as psychotic.'

'You won't talk me out of it this time. I *know* she wouldn't stop seeing him on her own.'

'You're sick, Louise.' He moved toward the living room.

'No, *you're* sick, Les. You aren't normal when it comes to Sandy. You never were. You love her too much, the wrong way. It's *disgusting*, Les!'

He whirled, and only Elsie Dudonic's entry from the kitchen saved Louise from his sudden fury. He would have hurt her – punched her with his fists or perhaps used those devastating holds he'd learned so well from the Japanese master of jujitsu.

As it was, he left the room. Ten minutes later he was racing his Hawk down the driveway. By the time he reached the Taconic, he was telling himself he had no reason to lose his temper so completely with Louise. He knew that she was his enemy, had always been his enemy, and that she sought ways to undermine his equanimity. She didn't actually believe what she said during the times they quarreled; she merely sought for weak spots.

He had to admit she'd found one. The thought that anyone could classify his feeling for Sandy as abnormal, as evoking *disgust*, even now made the blood rush to his head and his fists clench on the steering wheel and the murderous rage pound in his temples!

Yet why should he react that way, he asked himself. The old saw, 'The truth hurts,' certainly didn't apply here. There was nothing abnormal in his feeling for Sandy. He merely loved her and was strong enough to protect both her and himself with direct action. Millions of fathers would do the same, if they had the courage and resources.

He nodded, pleased with his reasoning, and promptly forgot Louise.

It was ten-forty when he reached the parking lot. He stopped on the way out to talk to Jess. 'Henny Girado been in today?'

Jess jerked his thumb at the battered Chevy. 'Came early.'

Les went across the street, up the steps to the second floor and over to Marie's desk. 'Good morning, dear.'

'Morning, Mr Bogen.'

'I think it's time you began calling me Les. Anyone using the studio?'

She smiled and nodded. 'Van Roberts just went in with a model. He brought his wife and little boy. They're such *nice* people.'

'Who's upstairs?'

'Mr Morden, I think. Henny was there earlier, but he left. Laird Drake also left, a few minutes before Henny.'

Les was slightly disappointed. He'd hoped to get some news from Henny.

But then again, Henny would stick to his bargain. He had no choice.

Les opened the studio door. 'C'mon in,' Van called, glancing up from the Graphic View camera. He was shooting a tall, plump, light-skinned Negress named Yolanda Ferris. Yolanda was now tightly encased in a massive corset from upper thigh to bust. She was grunting as she eased herself into a reclining position on a chaise longue but an instant later was smiling, ready to show womankind that Foundation Mold corsets were, as the slogan announced, Light As a Sprite.

'Back a little,' Van said. 'Relaxed. Relaxed . . . yeah.' He shot and straightened. 'You know Yolanda, don't you, Les? And my wife and son?'

326

Les nodded at the model and then at the woman and young boy on the leather couch. Mrs Evaline Roberts hadn't changed much in the two years since Les had last seen her at the studio. She was still small, slender, neat without being prim or dried out. She was attractive, intelligent-looking, but hardly exciting as so many of Van's mulatto models were. And she was considerably darker in complexion than Van.

The boy was dressed in a blue-and-white sailor suit with a small red cap. He sat close to his mother, looking around with huge black eyes. He was extremely good-looking, favoring his father in color and feature.

Les walked to the couch. 'Hello, Evaline.'

'Hello, Les. How've you been?' She didn't meet his eyes squarely, shifting them around his face and then to her son as she spoke; and Les understood that Van had talked about him.

'Fine.' He squatted easily, looked into the boy's face, said, 'And what's your name, young man?'

The boy dropped his head and leaned into his mother and mumbled something Les couldn't make out. 'Al,' Evaline Roberts said. 'His name is Alfred and he's three years, ten months old.' She laughed. 'And he's shy with strangers.'

Van came over, grinning, obviously proud of his family. 'She's taking him to his first movie – a reshowing of Walt Disney's *Bambi*. Wish I could go along to watch his reactions.'

'Wanna go home,' the little boy mumbled, face in his mother's side.

'But first you'd like an ice-cream soda, wouldn't you?' Les asked, and touched his cheek. 'If you come down with me . . .'

The boy whimpered.

Les stood up. 'The usual reaction of children to Uncle Lester. The only child who ever loved me was my

327

own.' He was only making conversation, but he suddenly remembered the first time he'd taken Sandy to a movie – the Roxy, he believed it was – and she was just four, a pig-tailed blonde with the loveliest face in the world. She'd been a perfect little lady, needing the bathroom only once and sitting quietly and whispering her questions into his ear. Afterward they'd eaten in the Automat, because she'd wanted to see how food came out of 'boxes in the wall,' and she'd insisted he buy her four sandwiches and three glasses of milk. They'd returned home as they'd come, by train. She'd sat leaning against him as he read from a book of Uncle Wiggily stories, and then she dozed off. He'd carried her, still sleeping, to the car parked near the Peekskill station and placed her full length on the back seat. She'd awakened as they'd driven up Gallows Hill Road and murmured drowsily, 'I wanna stay with you forever and ever and ever, Daddy . . .' That evening he'd returned to the city by car, telling Louise he had a special assignment, and made love to a girl long faceless and nameless in his memory.

'But she made up for everything,' Les said, realizing he'd been standing and staring at the boy. 'She made some very beautiful moments in my life.'

Van was looking at him, surprised. Les grinned and said, 'That's what happens when you introduce the family unit into a sterile studio. You create sentiment and sentimentality. Pretty soon I'll be weeping.'

They all laughed, and Evaline Roberts stood up and took her boy by the hand. 'We have to be going,' she said. 'I want to make that first feature at eleven-thirty.'

She and Van kissed briefly, and Van swung his little boy over his head and earned a delighted squeal, and then the mother and child were gone. Van resumed shooting, and Les sat down to watch, and Van said, 'How *is* your daughter, Les?'

No one inquired about Les Bogen's family, since he

himself had put up a barrier of silence around them. But now, after having spoken of Sandy, he'd created an opening. He sealed it immediately. 'Fine. How come you're not embarrassed to have your wife watch you shoot a gorgeous creature like Yolanda?'

Yolanda sighed. 'This Van man's not one of us, Les. This Van man's all business.'

Roberts shrugged and bent to the ground-glass finder. 'Hell, why not? Evaline knows I shoot good-looking women with and without clothing. Why shouldn't she drop in and watch?'

'That's not the accepted attitude in the field,' Les replied. 'For example, I don't believe Phyllis Morden has ever been here while Richie was shooting cheesecake or undie stuff.'

'That's *his* business,' Van said shortly, and shot the pose and directed Yolanda into another, and then changed the chaise longue for an ironing board and a kitchen backdrop.

Les had nothing important to do, and he wanted to get Van alone for a few moments. He watched, and Yolanda finally said, 'Excuse, pulease,' and went to the small toilet behind the dressing room. Les walked over to where Van was changing holders in the studio camera. 'Just between us men, Van, how often do you indulge?'

Van finished inserting a fresh holder and straightened. 'You mean extramarital indulgence, I presume. The answer is never.'

Les looked at him, and Van's eyes dropped, and Les said, 'Don't act ashamed of it, if it's true.'

'It's true,' Van said, eyes still elsewhere.

'That means you never want any of the beautiful models you shoot?'

'It means nothing of the kind, and you know it. How could a man help but want some of those women? But

329

I'm married and I take it seriously and so I don't break the rules.'

He still didn't meet Les's eyes, and Les became convinced he was lying. 'You'll pardon my frankness, Van, but I think you're showing discretion where none is needed.'

'I've answered your question,' Van snapped, 'where another man might have told you to mind your goddam business. You choose to disbelieve me. So there's an end to it.'

Les nodded. 'Just trying to justify myself, Van. Still buddies?'

'Still buddies,' Van said.

Les left the studio, smiling to himself. Van had shown every sign of guilt, of shame, and he'd have absolutely no reason to react that way if he'd been telling the truth.

It made Les's answer to Sandy's question a week ago – the one about every man, except the inept and the fanatic, having sexual relations with women whenever he could – that much closer to the truth. Not that it was important to *him*, but it might help in any future discussions with Sandy.

He already knew Henny played the field; and Richie had shown he too had experiences; and now Van. Laird being single made varied sex activity almost a certainty, but with a personality like that, well, he'd have to talk to the man.

Lester Bogen on the American Male. Maybe he could get Marv Weister to do the text.

He was laughing silently as he went past Marie.

Laird wasn't in his office, and neither was Henny. Les sat down at his desk and checked over his schedule book. In three weeks he had a big job of reportage – a forty-eight-hour trip in America's latest atomic submarine – for an electrical-equipment manufacturer's special publication. Twenty-five hundred dollars, plus all expenses, which wasn't bad. Next week he could do what he pleased – work on any of several continuing accounts. As for the rest of this week, Stella Lago's debut as a cheesecake siren was the sum total. And shooting Stella hardly came under the heading of 'work.'

Laird Drake arrived at twelve, and Les called him into his office. 'How's it going?' he asked, giving his voice a familiar tone. 'Any old girl friends you can throw my way?'

Drake lunged at the bait, grinning and settling himself in Van Roberts' chair. 'Don't kid me, Les. You don't need any help. Say, I was wondering who your contact is up at *Life*. I wanted to discuss . . .'

'Mean to tell me a good-looking kid like you doesn't have a few discards for an old man like me?'

Drake looked at him, and Les wondered if he'd gone too far with the familiarity bit. Then Drake smirked and leaned back in the chair. 'Hell, there was a little redhead only last week.'

He told Les of taking a model – nameless – home and being invited to spend the night and having to leave at two A.M. because of her boundless energy.

'That wouldn't be Regina Stouffert, would it, Laird?'

'No,' Laird said quickly. 'You don't know her.'

'But I'd like to. What's her name?'

Laird shook his head. 'Not yet, Les. I've got a long way to go with her.' He launched into another story, and this one was about a girl at his last studio, and it reached its climax in Laird's car parked out on a Long Island estate at midnight.

Les asked questions, and Laird answered them easily; and against his will Les began to believe him. Finally, Laird checked his watch and said, 'Hey, I've got a job to shoot at Coney Island – the opening of a new thrill ride. We'll have lunch together soon, eh, Les? I want to find out about *Life*. I've got some wonderful story ideas.' He hurried out.

Les lighted a cigarette. Even a Laird Drake found women and utilized them. The whole world was that way.

Laird Drake drove toward Coney Island. He was pleased that he'd finally gotten close to Les Bogen. And it had come about through a discussion of women.

Some of his pleasure disappeared. Why did men always react to other men's being successful with women?

And he'd almost made a slip – the time Les had identified the 'little redhead' as Regina Stouffert. If Les ever made out there, he might discover that Regina had indeed been very accessible one evening after an assignment but that Laird Drake, her escort, had been a dramatically unsuccessful lover.

He shrugged away his shame, fear and discomfort. He'd been tired that night. And the possibility that Regina was diseased had intruded. Sure, many free-and-easy girls were diseased.

He thought then, briefly, of all the other situations – the women he'd dated, petted and occasionally loved. And always the quick release for him – the *immediate* release that had a sense of escape about it and which was always highly unsatisfactory to his partners. Lately he'd been backing away, without admitting it, from sexual experience. Lately he'd been aware of Jamie and his 'friends' and how easy it would be to forget his failure as a lover forever.

He blocked further thought, and then remembered how Henny had pulled the scissors from the drawer this morning and of how he had run.

Christ, one of these days he *wouldn't* run! One of these days he'd get Henny without scissors or knives or any other weapons. And then he'd show that grinning bastard, that filthy degenerate with his smooth, confident ways

332

and his women and his good assignments! A man who owed as much money as Henny did should keep his head down and his eyes on work and accept his inferior position – know his place – the way a normal guy would. But Henny had to act like king of the earth; and now there was talk he'd made some sort of big killing and was getting out of debt.

One day he'd knock that king of the earth all over the studio! One day he'd pound him down, beat him into a whining, begging, bleeding mess! Him and his goddam confidence.

Van Roberts finished with Yolanda at one o'clock. As she stepped from the shooting area, she brushed close by him. 'You want to buy me a drink, Van?'

This wasn't the first time she'd indicated she liked him and wouldn't be averse to a little romp. Always before, he'd maintained a coolly proper attitude, ignoring the suggestion in her comments. This time, however, he remembered Les Bogen's questions and without thinking patted her fanny and said, 'Now what would you want with an old married man?'

Surprised, she turned and pressed her corseted body against his. 'An old married time, baby.'

Van felt fire rising within him and stepped back from the big, beautiful model. 'Hey, I was just kidding. I'll buy you that drink, all right, if it's iced tea in Bickford's.'

She sighed and turned to the dressing room. 'You're the damndest nigger I ever did meet.'

Suddenly he was angry. 'It surprises you that a colored man can turn down sex, doesn't it?'

She stopped and faced him. 'What's that supposed to mean? You forgetting I'm colored too?'

'That makes no difference. If a white man was all business, it wouldn't surprise you.'

'I don't know what in hell you're talking about, but

let's drop it right here or else little Yolanda will be out a good few bucks a month. Okay?'

His anger died, and he nodded, annoyed with himself. 'Sure, honey. And don't worry about your assignments. I've never seen anything better in a girdle.' He grinned, trying to re-establish the snappy man-to-woman basis he maintained with all his models, but Yolanda had received quite a shock and merely nodded and walked to the dressing room.

Van went down to Bickford's. He put a sandwich and glass of iced tea on his tray and found a small table against the window wall and sat looking out at the street as he ate. He had nothing to feel unhappy about; he had maintained his integrity, his marriage and his self-respect.

Self-respect.

He put down his sandwich and sipped the cold tea and faced the situation squarely. *Did* he have his self-respect?

He drained the glass and came to the conclusion that he did. Maybe his motives weren't the finest, maybe they would even be considered contemptible by some members of his race, but they resulted in his living the way he wanted to live.

He resumed eating his sandwich. Okay, so he was an Uncle Tom of sorts; he refused to touch any woman besides his wife – even though many of his models aroused him considerably – because whites thought that all Negroes were sexually overactive.

As Van saw it, the American concept of the average Negro was that of a drinking, brawling, lecherous criminal type. (This in place of the old Darky tradition, in which the Negro was seen as an amiable servant-clown who could perform great feats of strength, sing, dance, but never be counted upon in situations requiring either intelligence or courage.) And the American concept of the intellectual Negro was that of a man struggling against a genealogical heritage of being a drinking, brawling, lecherous criminal type, and occasionally succeeding in the struggle, with everything but lechery.

In Harlem, Van had seen much sordid sex play, even among some of his own friends – friends he and Evaline later dropped. It made no difference that the same thing went on in Westport, Connecticut, and Beverly Hills, California. It didn't help at all to know that Bogen was a bigger lecher than any Negro Van could think of. It was a white world, and in order to establish equality a minority group first had to disprove the prejudices of the dominant group. Van Roberts wouldn't touch any woman besides his wife because he wouldn't allow himself to fit the caricature American whites had created of American Negroes, a caricature far more complex than the watermelon-eating, banjo-playing, eyeball-rolling symbol of the past and correspondingly more difficult to destroy. Had he been able to do so, Van Roberts would have punished every Negro – especially the educated – who indulged in adultery, not because he condemned them on moral grounds but because they helped white bigots!

Van Roberts was a man dedicated, as few men are, to conform to the professed moral standards of American society. He occasionally suspected his motives and at those times felt cowardly, but he was unable to think of living any other way.

He left Bickford's rapidly regaining his natural cheerfulness. By the time he'd reached the studio (to pick up a Leica and head for *Ebony* magazine, where he was shooting a Southern Negro business leader), he was wondering how Alfred was reacting to the movie. Evaline and the boy would be home by two-thirty. He'd call at three and get the whole story. If it had worked out well, maybe he'd take Al to another movie Saturday or Sunday. There was nothing like spending time with your child.

A tall, lean colored girl was passing by as he left the studio and came into the street. She had a swinging, sinuous walk, and he automatically registered approval and wondered how she would look without clothing. Good, probably. Exciting. Long, hard thighs and soft hollows in her buttocks.

He changed the mental image, subtly, as he always did, into a critique of a subject for purposes of photographic markets.

Les Bogen sat waiting for Henny Girado. Laird Drake too, he thought with satisfaction. They all do. Henny and Richie and Van and Laird. It's so obvious, even when they try to hide it. So damned obvious. Every man wants it; every man enjoys it; and every man seeks it – some a little more actively, and expertly, than others.

The world was composed of men and women, hunting each other for mutual gratification. And he, Les Bogen, was merely a more honest, more successful, hunter.

In the empty office next door, Henny's phone rang three times during the next forty-five minutes, and Les wondered if Sandy was among those calling. But Henny didn't return, and Les felt it was senseless to sit around waiting for something which was bound to happen anyway, if it hadn't already.

It was a beautiful day. He would go to Rockefeller Center with a Rollei and photograph women, good-looking women strolling in the sunlight. If one asked what he intended doing with the pictures, there might be a pleasant chat over tall drinks in a discreet bar. And from that might come further experiences of the kind that made up half his life. He could concentrate more on that half, now that the other half was again secure.

21

Henny Girado didn't return to the studio after leaving Marv Weister's apartment. He had no assignments lined up until the *luau* on Monday and didn't intend searching for any during the next few days. Whatever turned up through normal studio channels, he'd handle. Otherwise, he was on vacation.

'Celebrating,' he mumbled as he stood on the corner, bottle in its paper bag held in his left hand, right hand rising to signal a cab. 'Celebrating my great expectations.'

He went to a Forty-second Street theater which advertised two films he'd enjoyed very much when they were first shown – *The African Queen* and *Beat the Devil*. He didn't enjoy them now; but sitting in the balcony, far to the side, he was able to sip from his bottle without any of the sparse audience noticing. Somehow he didn't advance further into intoxication but was able to maintain his near-numbness.

At four-thirty he went down to the men's lavatory. There was a phone booth in the little anteroom, and he stopped and looked at it before continuing on to the lavatory.

On the way out he stopped at the phone booth again. This time he called the studio and spoke to Marie. 'You received eight calls, counting the one this morning, Henny. All from that girl, Sandy. On the third call she left a number where you could reach her. Got a pencil?'

'No,' he muttered, but then took pen and matchbook cover and said, 'Shoot.' She gave him the number, and he hung up.

He wanted to leave the booth. He wanted to go back

to the balcony and look at the screen and make believe Humphrey Bogart was still alive and drink his gin and make believe Henny Girado was still alive. But he dug two nickels from his pocket and dialed the number and listened to the ring. A girl answered and he asked for Sandra Bogen and the girl said, 'Just a moment.' And then Sandy was saying, 'Henny. I missed you terribly. Did you have a nice visit with your family?'

The numbness fled. He was talking to Sandy, and he had to destroy the wonderful feeling between them. 'Yes. Great visit. Balled like crazy. You know – old home town and old girl friends and stuff. Lotsa stuff.' He laughed.

She laughed too, but it wasn't real. 'Why didn't you tell me you had to go to Denver?'

'I didn't figure it would interest you, doll.'

'Henny!'

'Uh-oh – the old ball-and-chain tone of voice, heaven defend poor widowers. You gotta realize that one blanket party doesn't make your last name Girado.'

Her silence was full of shock.

'Oops, made a boo-boo, didn't I? Well, guess I'd better hang up and let you cuss.'

'Henny,' she whispered, 'I don't believe – ' She stopped, and he looked out the glass panel into the anteroom and grinned as he might have grinned with a hot poker in his guts. 'At your apartment . . . with Syl . . . the things we discussed. And the way we felt.'

He had nothing to say. He grinned out at the anteroom and wondered how long it would take for the pain to disappear. A month? A year? He didn't think he could stand such pain for a year.

'All right,' she said, her voice steadying. 'We'll sit down somewhere and talk it over. I'm at a friend's apartment in the Village. Can you pick me up in half an hour?'

'Well, I'm busy right now. Maybe we can get together next week.' He marveled at how easily the words came. But then again, it wasn't difficult to pull a trigger or sink a knife into flesh. 'I'll give you a ring.'

'You couldn't be that big a bastard!'

'And you couldn't be that naïve, doll. After all, we did have a beautiful few hours. Without the pretty sentiments, it wouldn't've been anything but a fast – '

The line clicked in his ear. He left the booth and walked into the bright street, already crowding with rush-hour exodus. After ten minutes of fruitless attempts to hail a cab, he began walking the thirteen blocks to the studio, or rather to the parking lot, since he intended to get his car and drive somewhere, perhaps to a movie in Queens, perhaps to a tavern out on the Island, perhaps to the nearest liquor shop and then to a motel. Or maybe Eugenia would like to dance again.

But Eugenia didn't appeal to him at the moment. No woman appealed to him at the moment, except the right woman, and she was no longer available to Henny Girado.

By the time he reached Fifty-second Street, he realized that the gin, and all the other liquor he'd consumed yesterday in Denver and on the plane last night and this morning, had begun taking its toll. His legs were weak, his eyes watery, his mind fogged, confused. He couldn't drive anywhere, except home, and he couldn't think of walking in on Syl and Greta this way. The housekeeper didn't even know he was back; he'd picked up his car at the airport parking lot, put his bag in the trunk, stopped for a few fast drinks at a bar and come to the studio. He hadn't even called her. What was there to say? He'd come home tonight, or tomorrow, or the day after tomorrow. What the hell difference did it make? It was the same old grind again.

He went up to the studio. Marie called to him from her

desk, 'Dennis Parish was looking for you, Henny. Said he had some good news. Try him at home later.'

He nodded and went up to the third floor. Both connecting offices were empty. He went to Richie's office, and that was empty too. He poured himself a Scotch and gulped it down and poured himself another. 'So toss me out again, Richie,' he said thickly. 'Old money-bags Girado doesn't give a damn.' He finished his second drink and poured a third, and only then remembered his bottle of gin. 'Had it when I walked in,' he muttered, and looked around, and then remembered he'd been to his own office before coming here. He carried the glass of Scotch back to his office, and the gin was on his desk. He fumbled for cigarettes and lighted one and sat down. He drank the Scotch and took the earthenware bottle of Bols from the bag and tried to look inside. 'Dark, daddy, dark.' He poured slowly, carefully, and filled Richie's six-ounce low-ball glass to the rim. Then he put the bottle to his mouth and tilted back his head. He got just a sip, and it was empty. 'Dead soldier, go to Arlington,' he mumbled, and tossed the bottle into the waste basket. He leaned back and closed his eyes, and immediately his head spun and he felt himself passing out. 'No,' he said, and stood up and shook his head. 'Dennis got good news. Gotta hear good news.' Still standing, he reached for the phone; and it rang. He raised it, said, 'Money-bags Girado here. If you're a creditor, wait a few days. I'm paying everyone. Everyone.'

'It's Sandy,' said the distinctive voice, the deep and throaty voice, the voice that tore at his chest. 'You're drunk. You must have been drunk before, too.'

'I'm stoned. I'm ready for the screaming heebie-jeebies. I'm having a ball?'

'Shall I join you?'

God, she had it as bad as he did! Dear God, what more could a man ask for?

But he was forgetting.

'Sorry, doll. I got all I can handle in both women and liquor.'

'Henny.' It was a cry.

'I gotta cut out now, doll. I gotta hit a chick's pad. She's got Bob Crosby's "Big Noise from Winnetka" on the machine and I dig that man on that side. She's got the Count and the Duke and Satch, and she doesn't rate sweet talk for more'n it's worth.'

'Henny, I don't believe you! I don't believe you!' She was crying now, openly, heavily. 'You couldn't change!'

'Aw, get off my back,' he muttered. 'I'm sorry I took your cherry. I thought it'd be worth some fast talking later, but it wasn't. Christ, yell rape if you want to, but get off my back.'

'I don't believe you,' she said, but it was only a whisper now, and deep sickness was dominant.

'What'd you think I was, a soph at Columbia? What d'you think I've been doing for the past three years, living in . . .' His tongue grew too heavy then for cutting remarks, or was it the heaviness in his chest? 'See you around,' he mumbled, 'Don't be mad. You want, we'll make it again.'

'Goodbye, Henny,' she whispered, and he knew he'd got through finally.

'Yeah,' he said.

The click sounded in his ear. He sat down, pressed the button on the phone and released it. 'Outside,' he said, and Marie gave him a line. He dialed Dennis Parish's place, no longer thinking, just trying to smother the ache. 'Dennis? Henny. Wha's the score?'

'Sold three pages of your hair-weaving stuff to *Life* for fifteen hundred dollars. And they weren't just buying; they were impressed. You've got an edge now, Henny. I'll bring you up in a few weeks, and maybe they'll talk assignment. Might be a turning point, Henny. Might be a big break.'

'Yeah,' Henny said. 'Yeah, great, Dennis. Yeah.'

'You okay?'

'Sure. Just drank up the wagon.'

Parish laughed. 'Celebrating that hush-hush business deal, huh? Congratulations, Henny, for whatever you've pulled.'

'Yeah. Goo'night, Dennis.'

Parish laughed again. 'Night's come where you are? Well, goodnight then, Henny.'

Henny put the phone down, and put his head down, and the phone made clicking, buzzing sounds. He said, 'Go way, Sandy. Go way, baby, please.' The phone clicked and buzzed, over and over. He picked it up and realized it had been lying on the desk and not in its cradle. Marie said, 'Hello? Hello? Your phone was off.'

'Sorry.' He hung up, carefully and correctly this time, and was out before his head touched the desk.

He woke up later, and it was very dark, and he stumbled to the wall and flicked the switch. He blinked in the sudden glare and checked his watch. Eleven-thirty.

He saw the six-ounce glass of gin on the desk and walked over and drank it. Then he put out the lights and felt his way to the staircase. He went down to the second floor and the studio and put on the lights. He went into the little toilet behind the dressing room and examined himself in the black-speckled mirror. He looked like hell. His clothing was wrinkled, his face dark with stubble, his eyes red and deep-sunk.

He left the toilet and the studio and went downstairs and into the street. He walked to the all-night sandwich shop on Seventh and took a stool near the door, away from a couple at the other end and a lone man in the middle. Jack, the youthful counterman, came over and looked at him. 'Brother, have you been having a time!'

'Sure. You know us gay photographers and our hot models. Buy a Kodak and screw the world.'

'What'd I say?' Jack demanded, flushing.

'I'll have a ham on white and black coffee.'

The counterman's lips tightened and he turned away. He served Henny quickly, coldly, and moved to the coffee urns and wiped them with a rag. Henny ate half the sandwich and gulped the coffee. He put a dollar on the counter and left without waiting for his change.

He returned to the studio. He went to Richie's office and took the bottle of King's Ransom and stopped at his office to pick up the glass and went down to the studio. He dropped into the black-leather couch and poured a drink and sipped it. He put the glass on the floor, took off his jacket and shoes, picked up the glass and sipped again. He finished his drink, looked at the bottle, and then put the glass down beside it. Tomorrow was another day. He'd throw a real one tomorrow. Maybe a party for the whole office. Why not? He was out of the red, and he'd made a fifteen-hundred-dollar sale to *Life*, and even after Parish's 40-per-cent cut he'd have nine hundred left, and he finally had good prospects.

And it was all nothing, less than nothing without Sandy, and he was a crazy square who couldn't shake a nineteen-year-old chick he'd known only a few weeks and seen only three times and slept with only once.

He put out the lights, lay down on the couch and closed his eyes. So he'd cry in his booze a few days; and then he'd shake it and be right again and on the way up.

He'd make it, man. He'd make it big.

He fell asleep, and heard Sandy crying, and then it was Syl who was crying. He wanted to join them but wasn't allowed to. Part of the deal with Bogen.

Someone was shaking him, and he didn't want to get up, and he said, 'Lemme alone, Greta. Lemme alone.'

'Get up, Henny. Sandy didn't come home last night, and she didn't call, and she always calls. Get up.'

Henny opened his eyes. It was Les Bogen, looking his usual dapper, expensive self – except that he was worried. Not too worried, Henny decided after sitting up and looking at Bogen a second time. Bogen knew his daughter would have a reaction, perhaps a violent one. Bogen was prepared for that.

'What time is it?' Henny asked, rubbing his face.

'A quarter to nine. I called your home when I stopped at a gas station in White Plains, but your housekeeper didn't even know you were back from Denver. Did you speak to Sandy?'

'Yes. The bargain's consummated. I've earned my ten grand. Now get out and let me sleep.' He lay down again, rolled over on his face, felt Bogen's hand on his shoulder. 'Listen,' he said into the cool leather, 'don't paw me, Les. I don't like you much. I don't like you at all. I told her it was all a ball, and she cried, and now it's finished. She was at a friend's place, in the Village.'

'Sally Aikers?'

Henny groaned and sat up again and rubbed his face again. Sleep was gone now; the day and its problems had intruded, firmly, and there was no escaping it. Not in sleep. But there was his continuing ball.

'I don't know her name,' Henny said. 'I've got her number.' He looked around for his jacket, saw it had slipped from the arm of the couch to the floor, and leaned over and picked it up. He found the matchbook cover and read out the telephone number.

'Yes, Sally Aikers,' Les murmured, tracing his mustache with a pinkie. 'I can call, as if checking all her friends.' He went to the marble counter at the far end of the huge room and picked up the phone. 'No line,' he said. 'And Marie's not in.' He walked past the couch toward the door, then stopped and turned. 'You say she cried?'

Henny looked up. 'Yes. Feel good, Les?' He tried to grin, and couldn't make it, and whispered, 'Call it off, Les. It's not right.'

'Forget it,' Bogen interrupted sharply. 'If I was going to fold so easily, I'd never have started this. One wrong move from you, and I'll bring every creditor howling.'

'Let's not repeat ourselves,' Henny muttered, head dropping again.

'And you now owe me a thousand dollars, or have you forgotten the check I gave you when you left for Denver?'

'Go gloat over your daughter,' Henny said. 'Go listen to her cry.'

Bogen stepped forward, and Henny looked up, and Bogen's face was tight with anger. 'I'm doing it for her,' he said. 'I'm ridding her of a . . .' He paused, took a deep breath and went to the door.

'What sort of monster am I, Les? Tell me.'

Bogen was his calm self again. 'No monster, Henny. Just the wrong man for my daughter.'

'And what kind of man will be the right man, Les?'

Bogen opened the door. 'I'll know when he comes along.'

'Sure. In twenty years or so. You'll keep her single until you die, Les, if you can. And maybe you can.'

Bogen left, closing the door behind him. Henny found the bottle of Scotch and the glass and poured a drink. He tossed it down, shuddering, and had another, without shuddering. He had a third and went upstairs to his desk and heard Bogen talking through the closed door. He didn't try to make out the words. He got his razor, lather bomb and towel from the bottom drawer and went to the washroom.

* * *

345

Les Bogen called Sandy at her friend's apartment in Greenwich Village. She said she was sorry she hadn't let him or Mother know she wasn't coming home, but it was a last-minute decision. Yes, she was fine. Yes, she'd like to have dinner with him tonight. No, she wouldn't meet him at the restaurant; she would meet him at the studio.

'You know how I feel about that, Sandy.'

'Yes, and *you* know why. But I know about that now, and I'm no longer susceptible to the characters who work there. In other words, there's no longer any reason to keep me away from Morden Photos.'

He refused to analyze the dullness of her voice, the brittle element of pain lurking in the background. And he wasn't going to have her coming to the studio, despite what she'd learned and experienced. 'I still don't see . . .'

'I'm tired of this, Father. What time do you want me to meet you?'

'What time will you be through at school?' he asked, capitulating because it was the only thing to do.

'I'm not going to school.'

'But with exams so close . . .'

'I'm not going to school,' she repeated. 'It's one of the things I'd like to discuss with you. I don't think I'll be going to school again, ever. I'm thinking of getting a job and moving in with Sally. She said she'd be glad to have someone share the rent.'

'We'll discuss it,' he said, and didn't worry too much about it. She was upset now. She might even remain upset long enough to lose this semester; but she'd be back at school after the summer vacation. Time, and Les Bogen, would see to that. 'I have a studio job at two. It should be over by five, five-thirty. Any time after that, honey.' (Actually, the two rolls of 35 millimeter wouldn't take more than an hour, but his subject was Stella Lago, Marie Riposta's juicy friend, and he wanted to insure himself against being interrupted.)

'I'll be there at five-thirty. We can have a drink before dinner. I have lots to tell you.'

'Fine, dear. I think I know . . .'

'Yes, Father. You can say "I told you so."' She paused and then murmured. 'But he was so convincing. I'm sure he meant every word he said.'

'You're speaking of Henny Girado?'

'Yes.'

'Of course he meant every word. He always does, when he's with a pretty girl.'

'No, I don't think he . . .'

'Many men speak of love, and mean it, with many women. But not the kind of love you want, honey. Not the lasting kind.'

She said nothing.

'I'll have a surprise for you, Sandy. Something special.'

'Please don't spend a lot of money, Father.'

'I want to make you happy,' he whispered, and his voice shook. 'I want to do that more than anything else in life!'

She laughed, a harsh little sound. 'Get me Henny Girado.'

Anger welled up in him, and he fought it quickly, successfully. 'That would make you very *unhappy*, in the long run.'

'I guess so,' she said in a small voice. 'Well, till five-thirty then.'

'Yes, Sandy. And don't feel badly. We'll have a wonderful summer together. I'll take a long vacation – four or five weeks. We'll go to shows, and the track, and on trips all through the East. We'll spend weekends at the club, and you'll meet many boys, handsome and educated and sincere. You'll date them by the dozens, baby.'

'And come home to Poppa.'

His heart lurched. 'What?'

But she didn't follow it up, hadn't meant it as Louise

had, as Henny had. 'They'll all bore me, and I'll come home to you and Mother.'

'We'll see,' he said, but he agreed with her. "Bye, honey.' He began to hang up, but she said, 'Daddy, wait.'

'Yes.'

She was quiet a moment. Then: 'I'm sorry I was so childish about . . . your life away from home.'

'Yes,' he said very quietly, afraid to say the wrong thing, wanting her to go on.

'I don't feel that way any more. I need you, Daddy.' He heard the choked-back sob as she hung up.

There was no denying the twinge of pain that shot through him. But the other feeling – the triumphant feeling, the ebullient, ecstatic feeling – overrode the twinge, and then he was standing up, smiling, hands clasped together, seeing life return to its secure and loving pattern.

After a breakfast consisting of pretzels and three coffee royals in the Clover Bar on Seventh Avenue, the idea of a studio party seemed better than ever to Henny. What the hell, he had a hundred twenty some-odd dollars in his wallet – money left over from Bogen's one grand 'advance' on the deal. He would spend most of it on liquor and some on food. He would put the stuff in the reception room later this afternoon and invite one and all to join in. He'd also call a few people – Marv and Eugenia and Eugenia's friend Francie and Dennis Parish. Yes, and Eva Gretz from the hair-goods place and her co-workers and her boss and the Stinker and anyone else who would have a drink and help him ball away the blues. Even Les Bogen. Even Laird Drake. Even his damned creditors, if any happened to show up.

But it was still early, and he would continue his own

private party right now. 'A martini,' he said, and the bartender blinked his eyes and said, 'No olive – right?'

'Right.'

Henny drank the cocktail quickly, then had two more in leisurely fashion, sipping and smoking and reading a newspaper borrowed from the bartender. And when he walked out at ten-thirty, there he was again, back on the merry-go-round, the alcoholic kick which would bring him numbness and lack of thought. And it wasn't just the martinis, and the coffee royals before that, and the Scotch eye-openers before that. It was yesterday's drinking, and the day before yesterday's drinking. Henny Girado was working on a big drunk, a cumulative drunk based upon three days' heavy alcoholic intake. He was aiming for something new, something that had never happened to him before. He walked to the liquor store on the corner and muttered, 'Target for tonight, complete blackout.' He went inside and ordered Scotch, bourbon, gin, vermouth, rye, Canadian, Irish and rum – two bottles of each. The delighted owner assured him the order would be delivered to Morden Photos at three P.M. sharp. Henny paid eighty-five dollars and change. He walked across the street to the kosher delicatessen and ordered ten pastrami sandwiches, ten corned-beef sandwiches, five pounds of potato salad, five pounds of cole slaw and a case of assorted mixers – ginger ale, club soda, collins mix, Coke and quinine water. The owner wrote down the address, said delivery would be at three o'clock, and asked whether a bucket of ice cubes wouldn't be required. Henny said, 'You saved the party, friend. *Two* buckets of ice cubes will be required.' The storekeeper smiled, added them to his list, said, 'I'll have the boy bring up a folding table – you'll need a place to put the food and drinks.' Henny nodded and took out his wallet. The bill was twenty-three dollars, only the table being free.

When he stepped outside, he counted what was left – fourteen dollars and a pocketful of change.

He used the change in a cigar store down the block, making five phone calls, speaking to Eugenia and Marv, leaving messages for Dennis Parish and two editors. Eugenia had squealed with delight and said, '*Crazy!* Just what little Irish needs. I'm your heavy date for the ball, huh, daddy?'

'Sure. And don't forget Francie for Marv. And bring along some of your good records.'

Marv Weister's reaction had been somewhat less enthusiastic, but he'd said, 'I'll be there. Perhaps late.'

'You're sounding a little better,' Henny had interrupted. 'Almost your old ghastly self.'

'I'm reading my own books. I like them.'

'Don't come *too* late,' Henny said. 'I need my only friend.'

He left the phone booth, wondering what movie he would see to kill time until three P.M.

He began walking toward Broadway and realized he had nothing to drink. He stopped at another liquor shop and bought a pint of rye and shoved it into his jacket pocket. He continued toward Broadway. He wanted to see something funny, something to make him laugh.

He knew it would take a damned good comedian.

He was seated in the balcony of a nearly empty theater before he remembered he hadn't consulted Richie about the party. He shrugged, sipped from his pint, and watched the English farce unfold on the screen. Too late now. The party was on, whether or not Mr Morden approved.

22

At two o'clock Henny was back on Fifty-second Street, walking slowly but feeling no pain. The pint was gone and the world was keeping its distance – not a proper distance as yet, but that would be remedied when the party got going.

He stopped at a drugstore and bought a package of chlorophyll chewing gum and put two pieces in his mouth. He was going to call on Eva Gretz, and somehow he didn't want her to smell liquor on his breath.

'My mother image,' he muttered, and nodded, and didn't believe it. He liked her. She was real people. He wanted her to like him.

She was at her table, weaving smoothly, and looked up as he approached. She began to smile, but then he came closer and her smile slipped away and she said, 'You been sick, Henny?'

'Me? Never sick. Just tired. Was out of town and had a rough trip back. But I didn't come here to talk about that. Remember those pictures I took? *Life* magazine's going to publish them.'

She put her hands together in a gesture of delight. 'It's no more than you deserve – such fine pictures!' But she returned quickly to her previous tack. 'You look terrible, if you'll pardon the frankness. You should get into bed and stay a week.'

'Sure. After the big party. You're invited. And I want you to invite all your friends here. It starts at three.'

'Three? Well, there's not too much work this week, so maybe the Stinker'll give in. But you'd better invite him, too.'

'I was going to, Eva. And his father. You coming?'

'Would I miss the chance to see a real studio?' She paused. 'And maybe that colored man – that Van something – will be there and I'll be able to tell him I'm sorry about talking like I did.'

He nodded. 'See you at three.' He went to the tiny office in the rear of the huge room. The father and son were both at their desks but not working. They were engaged in a heated discussion of politics and international affairs.

'. . . sure I want lower taxes, Arnold, but what good'll that do if we end up all alone in the world? The way we kept fooling around with Nasser, and the way the Russians keep getting stronger.' He shook his head. 'No, I'm switching to the Democrats.'

'You're crazy!' Arnold Gernstein snapped. 'We'll have Communism if we let the Democrats . . .'

They saw Henny then, and the old man smiled and said, 'Come in. You can join the big politicians. You a Democrat or Republican?'

'I liked Adlai's jokes,' Henny murmured.

Arnold Gernstein snorted. 'Yeah, that's all he was, a big joke!'

Henny smiled. 'If we go any further, I'll probably never get to invite you to the party.'

'Party?' the old man asked; and Arnold Gernstein lost his angered expression, or as much of it as he ever lost.

Henny told them about it. 'I hope you can let the ladies drop up for a while and that you'll come yourselves. Plenty of liquor and food. It's a celebration for *both* of us – Gernstein and Son and Henny Girado.' He went on about *Life* magazine, and the Gernsteins were pleased – the father openly; the son nodding briefly. The father said he saw no reason not to allow the 'girls' to come up, things being slow. The son looked less pleased at that but said nothing against it.

Henny left while he was ahead.

Upstairs, he told Marie about the party, and she smiled tightly and said, 'I could use a drink or two myself, Henny. But what about Mr Morden?'

'I go beard the lion in his den now,' Henny said, grunting, and went upstairs.

The lion was annoyed but not about the party. 'You took half a bottle of King's Ransom.'

'And I'm returning a full bottle at three o'clock.'

Richie sighed and then nodded. 'Sounds like fun. I'll call Phyll.'

Henny went to the connecting offices. Van Roberts was making a call. Henny waited until Van was finished, and told him about the party.

'Those old ladies wandering around here?'

Henny nodded. 'They're okay.'

'Sure, but Les Bogen's locked in the studio with a new entry – a friend of Marie's of all things.'

Henny now understood why Marie had smiled so tightly. 'That's tough,' he said, and grinned. 'In the interests of good neighborship, or togetherness, or whatever the hell you care to call it, Richie'll have to show them around. I wonder how fast Les can put on his pants?'

Van Roberts laughed, and Henny went next door. Laird Drake wasn't around, and Henny was just as glad. But if Laird came in later, maybe they could patch up the big nothing between them.

On the dot of three the entire Gernstein-and-Son entourage appeared in the second-floor waiting room. Henny was there, expecting the food and liquor, and Richie was there, beginning to relax in the party atmosphere, and Van was sitting on Marie's desk smoking a cigarette. Richie paused for a moment near Henny and murmured, 'I hoped Les would unlock the door before anyone came,

353

but you'd better give him a tip-off. Try the phone.' He straightened his jacket, said, 'Christ, there must be a hundred old ladies here!' and moved forward with a smile. 'Welcome,' he said to the Gernsteins, *père et fils*. 'I've wanted to invite you up for quite some time, but you know how it is.'

The Gernsteins replied they indeed knew how it was and said they too had intended inviting their neighbors in for a get-together party, and at that point Henny saw Eva Gretz winking at him from among the group of some twenty elderly women. He winked back, went to Marie's desk, said, 'Get me the studio, honey. I have to inform Mr Bogen that his day's work – hah! – is going to be interrupted. Richie says the ladies of the chorus are to have access to the studio.'

Marie smiled (rather vindictively, Henny thought) and punched a button on her phone and handed it to Henny. Henny waited, said, 'Ring a few times, good and long.'

Marie pressed the button four times. Henny waited again, then hung up. 'I didn't think he'd answer.' He turned and found that there were ladies all around him and moved through them toward the studio door, and noticed Van Roberts standing at the side, listening to Eva Gretz. Van was nodding, smiling, raising his hand as if to say, 'No, no, please.' Eva was presenting her apologies with obvious effect. Henny reached the studio, nodded at two ladies examining photographs pinned to the wall, knocked hard, and put his ear to the door.

'What is it?' Les's voice called, sounding almost pained.

Henny grinned and put his lips to the joining. 'Les. We've got visitors. Richie says they're to examine the studio and watch you shooting.'

After a moment's shocked silence, Les shouted, 'What?' and there was a frantic scurrying and a girl's voice said, 'But you told me . . .' and Les shouted again, 'You know I never allow anyone . . .'

'Pick up the phone when it rings,' Henny said, and he was laughing now. 'I'll let Richie do the explaining.'

He went through the crowd and got Richie away from the younger Gernstein and brought him to Marie's desk. Richie took the phone and murmured, 'Les, I'm sorry. No, it can't be helped. Our neighbors from downstairs.' He listened a moment and then said, voice firm, 'I can't help it. They expect to be shown around, and what's a photography studio without the studio itself? Just let them watch you shoot the damned cheesecake.' He hung up, shook his head, murmured to Henny, 'Sounds like we interrupted him at the worst possible time.'

Two teen-age boys were bringing in the food and folding table. Before they had reached Henny, who had waved them over, a tall Negro appeared on the landing and set down a cardboard case.

Henny said to Marie, 'Your friend's going to receive an initiation into modeling she'll never forget.'

Marie said, 'I know it's mean, but . . . I could die laughing!' She didn't laugh. She merely looked tense and vindictive.

Henny patted her hand and murmured, 'You'll get there, doll.'

She jerked her hand away. 'Me? Why I'd never . . .' But Henny was moving toward the delivery boys, telling them to set up the bridge table near the desk. He went on to the colored man, told him to bring the case of liquor over to the bridge table and shove it underneath. He then tipped all three and began setting up his party. Eva Gretz came over and said, 'Here, from the girls.' Henny took the bottle of sweet wine and thanked her, and then accepted her help in putting food and liquor on the table. But he kept an eye on the studio door. When it opened, he moved swiftly and was the first to greet Les Bogen.

Bogen's face was white, his usually immaculate clothing

somewhat rumpled, his temper at fever pitch. 'Who's responsible for this?' he whispered to Henny. He waved his hand, and his Rollei – hastily picked up and obviously forgotten – slammed into the doorframe.

'Careful. You'll ruin a good piece of equipment,' Henny said, looking past him to where a flushed Stella Lago stood on the shooting stage, tugging a pair of theatrical leotards into place. She was also wearing a halter.

'I asked who was responsible.'

'Say, the chick's wearing a lot of clothing, Les. *Saturday Evening Post* going for girlie stuff now?'

Bogen glared, and Henny grinned, and Stella Lago said, 'Les, do I hafta?'

Bogen turned, and while his face was white, Henny noticed the back of his neck was red. It made an interesting color combination, he thought. What with his shock-blue lips, the patriotic theme was dominant. 'Only for a few minutes, dear,' Bogen said soothingly. 'This is the first time – '

'And the last time for me,' she interrupted, eyes filling with tears. But she wiped at them, and when Richie led the ladies into the studio, she even managed a weak smile.

'This is the studio,' Richie began in a carny barker's voice. 'We do the actual work here.'

'Some work!' the elder Gernstein said, and chuckled, and gave Richie a friendly elbow in the ribs.

Richie jumped and looked pained. 'Yes, well, you must understand that photographs of women are bread-and-butter in this field.' Still talking, he led the crowd to the studio camera.

Les and Henny remained near the door, and Les looked into the waiting room at the table of food and liquor. 'Why didn't someone tell me there was going to be a party?' he whispered. 'I should have been informed at least a week in advance!'

'Because I didn't plan it until this morning!' Henny replied, and walked past him.

Les caught his arm. 'You did this to embarrass me!' Then he let go, took himself in hand, said quietly, 'You're not going to change a thing, Henny. You're – ' He interrupted himself. 'Sandy's coming here at five-thirty. I'll have to head her off downstairs.'

Henny moved away. He didn't want to hear about Sandy. He didn't want to hear about anything but his ball.

Richie called on Les to shoot a few poses, and Les complied. Stella Lago was too embarrassed to act with even native grace. She moved awkwardly, and anyone in the field would have known she wasn't a model – not yet. But the Gernstein-and-Son troupe watched and murmured appreciatively. They were then led out, on their way to the third floor and the mysteries of the darkroom and the files of photographs which would shock the ladies and delight the two Gernsteins.

Henny followed them, smiling benignly at Bogen. 'They might be back,' he murmured. 'I'd finish up if I were you.'

'I'm already finished!' Stella Lago said, running toward the dressing room.

Bogen closed the door after Henny, and his footsteps trotted across the wooden floor. Henny had to admire him. Bogen never let go of a prospect, no matter what happened.

Henny saw that Eva Gretz was busy at the table. 'Hey, why aren't you upstairs with the others?'

'And who's going to see that twenty sandwiches lasts for twenty-five people now, and maybe more later, from what you said?'

'Yeah, I didn't get enough, did I?'

357

'Sure you did, if you take the *half* sandwiches and mix them around so that most people won't take more than *one* half.' She looked at him. 'But whisky you got. Whisky you got enough for a hundred people.'

'Not the people I know,' he said, and grinned, and suddenly stooped and kissed her cheek.

'Hey,' she said, and colored deeply. 'Poor Eva's in with a fast crowd.'

He laughed, and saw Eugenia Randolph, and waved at her. She came up, threw her arms around him, said 'Daddy, you saved my life! Who else would think of a ball on Thursday afternoon? Who but the greatest? The very greatest! I'm all sniv-sniv about it.' She stepped back and picked up half a sandwich and waved her hand at the desk. 'I got eight great sides in that package. Let's go put them on the machine. You'll flip at the Miles Davis. The horn, daddy, the horn!'

'So now I think I talk a very good English,' Eva Gretz said, and walked away.

'What?' Eugenia asked Henny.

Henny grinned and poured two big gins and said, 'Here. I'm not going to bother mixing martinis. Anyone who wants them can find vermouth under the table.'

They drank, and Eugenia picked up her records, and Henny told her Bogen was in the studio. He described what had happened, and Eugenia bit her lip and murmured, 'Hoo boy! The big man must've bust a gut.'

'Exactly.' Henny finished his drink and had another, and then Stella Lago and Les Bogen were at the table. Henny said to the tall redhead, 'Loosen up, doll. There'll be other days – better days.'

She nodded, still flushed, and took the drink Bogen gave her. 'Just one,' she said. 'Then I'm going.'

'The old ladies won't stay long,' Henny said, feeling sorry for her. 'Stick around. We'll find a nice boy for you.'

Les Bogen said, 'Henny, you're a very funny man.'

'Ain't it the truth?' Henny replied, tossing off his third drink. 'And I'll get funnier as I get older.'

'But *will* you get older?'

Henny grinned and took Eugenia's arm and they went into the studio. A moment later a hot trumpet was blasting, and Henny and Eugenia were dancing. They came out for fresh drinks, and the ladies were back; and then Van Roberts and Richie were moving the table and the case of liquor into the studio proper.

Henny had a fifth drink, and a sixth. 'Hey,' Eugenia said as they began dancing again, 'you're going too strong, dad.'

'Only the beginning,' Henny murmured, and swung her out in a Lindy break and pulled her back. 'Tonight I go all the way.'

'All the way?'

'Fallin' down drunk, baby. Wanna come with me?'

'Well . . .'

'C'mon. Bet you've never drunk yourself cold.'

'I was close to it, once or twice.'

'But never there. C'mon. Let's make a pact.'

She looked at him a moment, and refused to be thrown out in another break, and said, 'You got hit by something, daddy. This is straight out of Hollywood.'

'Sure. But where'n hell you think Hollywood got it? Straight out of life. Nothing like a good drunk to clear the air. By Monday, what hit me won't seem bigger than a flea.'

'A brunette flea?'

'A blond flea,' he answered. 'Let's dance!'

'As long as it's in the family,' she said, and spun out.

Sometime later Henny went to the table – now set up on the shooting area – and Eva Gretz was there and she said, 'Goodbye, Henny. All the girls left, but I wanted to say something to you.'

He took her hands and blocked the pounding beat of jazz from his ears and the answering beat of hysteria from within himself and said, forcing the words to be clear, 'What's that, Eva?'

'Don't drink so much.'

He smiled. 'Mommas are all alike.'

'Don't kill yourself.'

'They all worry, and they all make more of things than they should.'

'And no one listens to them.'

'That's right. That's why the population increases.'

She flushed. 'You're terrible fresh. I shouldn't talk to you.'

He held onto her hands. 'Don't be mad, Eva.'

'Who's mad? I like it.'

He laughed, and she said, 'But anyway, don't kill yourself. Whatever bothers you today doesn't mean beans tomorrow.'

'I'll give that to Mr Bartlett for his quotations.'

She was gone. He had his drink and looked around and saw that all the old women were gone and that the elder Gernstein was gone and that the younger Gernstein, Arnold, was dancing with Eugenia and that Richie was dancing with his wife and that Laird Drake was talking to Les Bogen and Stella Lago. And then Henny was taking Stella's arm and saying, 'Shall we dance, shall we?' and she was nodding and they were dancing. And he held her very close and she said, 'Hey, you're in back of me,' and he said, 'Doll, did anyone ever tell you you're witty?' and she said, 'No,' and he said, 'You've got honest friends.' She laughed and relaxed and her body flowed into his and he wanted to tell her he was too old tonight, much too old, and then his eyes met Laird Drake's and Drake's were hard, like marbles, and then he was looking at the door and the thin little man was there. He let go of Stella

360

and said, 'You'll excuse me, doll,' and went to his friend and said, 'You must be late. Everyone else is here.'

'It's only four-thirty,' Marv said. 'But you're set for midnight.'

'Go drink a bottle or two. Catch up with me. Eugenia says her friend Francie will be here after she gets through with work in a store or something.'

He turned and blinked his eyes and Eugenia was there and she was saying, 'That Arnold character reminds me of the Johns at the Latin Quarter. He kept patting me in the corners and talking about getting out of "this dump" and managed to inform me that he never carries less than one hundred dollars in his wallet. Am I supposed to roll him?'

Henny danced her onto the floor, and the record changed to a female blues singer, and he said, 'She stinks up the joint. She should be on the Hit Parade. She's with Elvis.'

'It's not *my* record,' Eugenia said defensively. 'Some were in the cabinet and Richie put them on.'

Henny stopped dancing. 'Hey. Just remembered. Jess returned my two Bessie Smiths last week and I put them in back of the car and I never took them out. They must be there now.'

'Crazy! Go get them. I'll find Arnold and see if he's improved any. Maybe he'll pat me in the center of the room. Maybe he'll have *two* hundred dollars now.'

Henny went toward the door. As he passed Stella Lago, Les and Laird, Laird was saying, '. . . going to extremes in anything always disgusts me.'

Henny stopped and nodded and said, 'I agree. And that includes long mads. How about shaking on it?'

Laird's lips tightened and he seemed about to turn away, but Les Bogen said, 'Never hold grudges, Laird. Especially with a man like Henny. His little peccadilloes indicate a shaky personal life and, as the song goes, "He's more to be pitied than censured.""

'Which proves,' Henny said to Stella, 'that whatever else you might be doing with Les, you're not robbing the cradle.'

Laird Drake held out his hand as if about to pat a cobra. Henny looked at it, then said, 'I'm sorry. I refuse to be patronized by self-haters. Why don't you lubricate that hand with golden liver bile? You know where your golden liver bile appears, don't you?'

Laird clenched his fists, and Henny stood there, and Laird unclenched his fists. Henny sighed and walked out of the studio. He went down the stairs and across the street to the parking lot. He spoke to Jess and told him the joke about the Midget Martian who landed next to Jayne Mansfield, and Jess responded with one about the Martian and the juke box. Then Henny went to his car, and sure enough the records were in back and he got them and went back across the street. And there was Sandy getting out of a cab. She looked up, and he stopped, and she said, 'Hi,' in a small voice.

His stomach twisted. He lost the beat of the music and the reason for the ball and looked at her lovely face, her wonderful face, and asked himself how in hell he'd ever gotten hooked and told himself Eugenia was upstairs and she had more of everything and was available without strings. And turned away, waving his hand, saying, 'I'll tell Les you're here.' He went up the stairs very quickly and came into the studio breathing hard. Les was just saying goodbye to Stella Lago. 'I'll call you later this week.'

'Les,' Henny said. 'Sandy's on her way up.'

Les Bogen glanced at his watch and said, 'It's not even five and she said five-thirty!' He strode toward the door. As he opened it, Henny saw Sandy passing Marie's desk. Les shut the studio door behind him, and Henny took the

Bessie Smith records to the portable hi-fi on the counter. And that was that.

But that wasn't that. As Henny turned to catch Eugenia's wink over Arnold Gernstein's shoulder, the studio door opened again and Les Bogen, looking much too composed, ushered Sandy inside. She looked right at Henny, and Henny stepped away from the counter and moved to Richie Morden and tapped him on the shoulder. 'I'm drunk,' he apologized, 'but I must dance with Mrs Morden at least once this evening, and in ten more minutes I'll be way, way out. May I?'

Richie laughed and stepped back, and Phyllis Morden said, 'How are you, Henny?' and Henny said, 'You can see how I am, Phyll,' and Richie said, 'Say, there's that girl Norma with Les,' and Henny said, 'Hold tight, Richie, but she's really his daughter Sandra.' Richie paled, remembering the scene in the studio a few weeks back, and said, '*Oy vay.*' Henny nodded and danced off with Phyllis and talked and didn't know what he was saying except that it was clean, as befitted Mrs Morden. Then the record ended and he walked over to Eugenia, and Arnold Gernstein looked annoyed as Eugenia said, 'That Bessie, dad! She's more alive than anyone today! Let's grind, dad! Let's step!'

He was dancing with Eugenia, and then they were walking to the table, and he was drinking, and he saw Marv Weister putting down a huge shot of booze, and he said, 'How's it comin'?'

Marv said, 'I'm doing fine. While I'm here, that is. When I get home . . .' He shrugged and said, 'Say, I heard Les call the little blonde Sandra. And he treats her like his daughter. Isn't she Sandra Bogen? Isn't she the big thing in your life?'

'Forget it,' Henny muttered, and drank and poured and drank again.

'Why don't you dance with her? Why don't you speak to her? What's wrong?'

'Nothing's wrong. I think Eugenia's a better piece.'

Marv looked at him, and Henny turned away, and Francie something-or-other was entering the studio. 'Go live it up,' Henny said, and Marv shrugged and went to Francie something-or-other. Henny wandered around and saw Marie, and she was talking to Arnold Gernstein, and Arnold Gernstein was following Eugenia with his eyes, and Eugenia was dancing with Dennis Parish. And there was Elroy Frankle and another editor from Viewcitement Corporation and they had strange chicks and they were dancing. 'Hey,' he muttered, 'it's beginning to ball.' And Victor Bloom was near the phonograph with Ernie Radish, and Ernie had a girl and everyone was talking and laughing. And he never looked toward where Les Bogen and his daughter stood, and he hoped they'd gone.

Then he saw her. She was dancing with Laird Drake. He was talking to her, and she was nodding and smiling, and Henny turned away and told himself not to be a goddam fool, not to hate Laird and himself and the whole goddam mess. Ball, daddy, ball!

He danced with Stella Lago, and she was all woman against him, and he said, 'Now what has Bogen got that I haven't got?' and she said, 'I don't know, Henny, but he doesn't look at other women when he's holding you.'

He jerked his eyes away from Sandy and said, 'When he holds *me*, he's looking for the short hairs.'

'I thought Les was real easygoing.'

'Sure. Just fooling.' And they danced, and he drank, and he was with Eugenia again, and she said, 'You messed up, daddy. You didn't get any colored girls. Van hasn't danced once all evening.'

'Evening? Is it evening?'

'It's almost ten, Henny. I don't know what's holding

you up – you must've put away two fifths of assorted red-eye.'

'Well, well, well,' he said, for want of anything else to say. 'Well, so why're they still hanging round?'

She said, 'Who?'

He said, 'Let's have a drink.'

She said, 'I know part of that "they" – the little blond Bogen. You refuse to look at her. You work hard at refusing to look at her.'

'Let's have a drink.'

He drank, and then said, 'Say, I never danced with Marie. Poor Marie. Poor scared chick.' But Eugenia was gone, and he couldn't find Marie, and he drank, and it seemed that the next time he looked around there were fewer people in the place. He saw Marv and Francie something-or-other dancing; and there was Richie and Phyll, with Richie looking owlish and putting away a fair amount of booze and Phyll looking disapproving; and there was Eugenia talking to Van Roberts; and there was Laird Drake talking to Arnold Gernstein and both watching Eugenia and Van; and there was Les and Sandy sitting on the couch. No one else. The others had gone.

Sandy's eyes came to his, and he turned away. It was no good. He couldn't pass out and he couldn't look at her and he couldn't go home and he couldn't stay here and he didn't know what the hell to do. Just like that, it was a blue, blue world and he was terrified.

A hand touched his arm. He turned, glad to have someone to talk to, and it was Sandy. He looked at her, and she said, 'I don't believe you, Henny. I've been watching and I don't believe you. You *do* love me. Whatever you're doing, it's stupid and wrong. Dance with me.'

'No,' he said, and was too weary to think of subtle convincers. 'Go 'way.' He looked past her to where Les

365

Bogen had twisted in the couch to stare at him. 'Go 'way.'

She turned and followed his eyes. 'What did my father do? What *could* he do to make you try and get rid of me when you love me?'

'Go 'way,' he said, and she took his hand and he was on the dance floor and they were dancing and she said, 'You're drunk, Henny. You're awfully drunk. You can't hide things when you're drunk. Tell me.'

'Just a game,' he said. 'You and me. Just a game.'

But she was strong and sober, and he was weak and drunk. 'Tell me, Henny. Did my father threaten you somehow? Was it *money?*'

He broke away from her; left her in the middle of the studio and stumbled to the couch and said to Les Bogen, 'Make her lemme alone!'

'Go home, Henny,' Les murmured, but he was white around the lips. 'If you tell her, I'll destroy – ' He stopped, because Henny Girado was crying and stumbling to the door. Les Bogen got up and strode after him and caught him by the arm. 'What's wrong with you?' he whispered frantically, desperately. 'Don't you understand what I've done for you? You're free of debts and worries. I'm giving you almost ten thousand dollars, Henny! Ten thousand! And for what? For not seeing a girl you've known – '

'Make her lemme alone!' Henny Girado said, weeping, and went on toward the door. But something stopped him. Not Les; not Sandy. A shout, and cries, and snapping sounds.

He turned. Laird Drake was still swinging his arms, but Van Roberts was already falling, his face bloody and his eyes closing. He fell straight back, and his head hit the floor with a thump and he lay there. Eugenia screamed and beat at Laird with her fists. He shoved her away and said something to Arnold Gernstein, and Arnold shoved

366

her farther to the side. And then Richie Morden was shouting and running at Laird. Henny couldn't think too well but it seemed he heard Richie say, 'I'm a Negro too! I'm with a white woman too!' And Laird was moving away and Richie grabbed him and Laird suddenly swung and Richie slipped to his knees and Laird kept swinging and Richie slumped over on his side.

Henny began to run at Laird. He didn't know what it was about, but he began to run. He knew he could do nothing to Laird. Laird was big, bigger than anyone there, and he had Arnold Gernstein, and he didn't need Arnold Gernstein. Henny knew something else – all he had to do was grab a bottle and break it and go for Laird, and Laird would fall apart. But he didn't grab a bottle, because he didn't want Laird to fall apart. He wanted Laird to fight. He wanted Laird to be the instrument of Henny Girado's punishment, humiliation and release. He didn't hate Laird. He pitied him. Even when he swung at Laird, and the big man's face lit up with a terrible joy, he pitied him. Not many men despised themselves as Laird Drake did.

But then he missed, and Drake swung and didn't miss, and pity was something for intelligent creatures, not senseless hulks. The fists exploded against his mouth and cheek and neck. He was down, and he had the vague thought that he would get up and Drake would knock him down again and then he would stay down, unconscious, and when he woke up Sandy would be gone and he would be able to go home and sleep.

But Drake didn't wait for him to get up. Drake was a face with a terrible purpose shining from terrible eyes. Drake was a huge body pressing him down and huge fists pounding him and knees digging for his testicles. Drake was doing too much, and a tiny part of Henny's brain screamed for him to fight back, to get hold of that bottle before it was too late.

The fists smashed his face and he was suddenly far away, and still he felt the blow that went deep into his stomach, and the one that followed, and the one that followed that. He couldn't do anything, and he regretted it now that he understood what was happening.

Drake was killing him.

23

Marie Riposta soon lost the vindictively triumphant feeling she'd had when Henny's surprise party – a surprise to all the participants but Henny – had embarrassed and humiliated her friend Stella Lago. She didn't analyze the change in her feelings, but when Stella came out of the studio, flushed and near tears, she found herself ashamed – ashamed of her own smallness, ashamed of gloating (or *wanting* to gloat) over another's discomfort. And, too, it was unimportant. What business was it of hers what Stella or anyone else did?

But her anger, resentment, annoyance at Henny's brief remark – 'You'll get there, doll' – lasted a long, long time. She knew what he meant, all right. He thought she was *jealous* of Stella; thought she wanted men like Bogen. Imagine! As if she would even dream of acting like that!

But then she'd begun doubting herself, and that had made her leave her desk and go into the studio and join the party. It was almost four anyway; if a call came in she'd hear it. If a delivery came, well, either the boy would leave it at the desk or return tomorrow. Everyone else had forgotten that this was a normal business day; why shouldn't she?

She had a terrible time. She didn't feel pretty, and subsequently she couldn't seem to do anything but stand off to the side and hold a drink and watch the others dancing and laughing and talking.

No one asked her to dance. Richie said a few words to her, and Mrs Morden too, and Les asked if she'd like another drink. She accepted his offer, but a moment later he walked away and talked to Van Roberts and she was

369

alone again. Then a man named Arnold talked to her a few minutes, but he stared at Eugenia Randolph and finally went over to her. There were two or three other men – young men – whom she'd never seen before, but no one introduced them to her and they didn't introduce themselves. They spoke to Eugenia Randolph, and to Stella Lago, and later to the blond girl who'd called herself Norma a week or two ago but whom she heard Les introduce as his daughter, Sandra. They just didn't come over to her, and she moved to the corner near the door and sat down in a chair that had been shoved there and felt small and thin and ugly. And began thinking how she'd like to be with her friends Roberta, June and Carrie, telling them what an awful bunch of degenerates this studio crowd was.

But, somehow, that also made her feel ashamed of herself.

She left at five-thirty. She walked into the street and toward the subway. Men passed and she didn't look at them and was sure they didn't look at her.

She reached the subway and put her token in the slot and moved with the mob toward the platform. A Utica Avenue Express came along, and she was right in front of a door, and people behind her began pressing forward.

She didn't want to go home! No!

'Hey, get a move on,' a man behind her said, and she was shoved into the car, and she shoved back, and more people shoved her farther inside, and she turned sideways and said, 'Please! I want to get out!'

'Christ sakes,' a woman muttered. 'Make up your mind, will you?'

'I want to get out. I want to get out!' She was almost shouting now, and tears burned her eyes. It was important that she get out. It was terribly important. Because once the doors closed and the train started, she'd be trapped. And by the time they reached the next station, she'd be resigned. And then she'd go home and come to work tomorrow and send the lamp back to Larry Erlich.

The door began to close.

'Please.'

'Hey, the girl's crying,' a man said, and shoved someone out of the way, and a woman between Marie and the door put her hands on the door's rubber safety edge and it bounced back and Marie was suddenly out on the platform, running toward the turnstiles, and the train was roaring out of the station, and she was saved, saved.

She got to a drugstore and a phone booth and didn't care that people looked at her tear-wet face and didn't stop to think or weigh her actions or do anything but drop the dime in the slot and dial Larry Erlich's store number. She didn't even have to check the card; she remembered the number as if she'd called it a hundred times.

A woman answered, saying, 'Erlich's Fifth Avenue.'

'Mr Erlich, please.' And she was suddenly terrified that he wouldn't be there.

'Who's calling?'

'Marie Riposta.'

There was a wait – an interminable wait for Marie – before the soft voice said, 'Marie?'

She wiped at her eyes with her free hand and said, 'Yes. It's such a beautiful lamp, Larry.'

'You didn't get in touch with me and I thought you didn't want to see me.'

'I *do* want to see you.' She waited, terrified anew – at the possibility of rejection now.

There was no rejection. 'Are you in the city?'

'Yes.'

'Come to the shop. We're open until eight on Thursday nights. I'll show you around, and then we'll have dinner.'

'But your salespeople . . .'

He was quiet a moment, and then murmured painfully. 'You're ashamed because I'm older than you?'

'No! Oh, no.' She'd been thinking of *him* being ashamed! She'd been trying to protect herself from any possible hurt, any situation which would bring the doubts back again.

'Then come,' he said. 'Don't say anything more. Don't change your mind.' Again his voice dropped to a murmur. 'I have thought of you, and thought of you, and prayed.'

She wanted nothing more. She asked for no explanations of motives behind his 'prayers' – demanded no iron-clad assurances of everlasting, romantic attachment as she'd been trained to do and always thought she would do. She merely said, 'It's about fifteen minutes' walk.'

'Take a cab. Please. I'll meet you outside and pay.'

'All right.'

She left the store. She walked to the curb and saw a taxi and, though she'd never done so before in all her life, casually raised her hand. The cab pulled up. She got inside, gave the address and leaned back, crossing her legs. At the next corner, the cab stopped for a traffic light and the driver turned, smiling. 'Real summer weather, huh?' He was young – about twenty-five or -six, she figured. She smiled back at him coolly and said, 'It'll get warmer.' He laughed, as if it were something very clever, and she glanced out the window, but not before she saw his eyes run appreciatively over her legs and body. Then they were moving again.

She didn't know what it was that made her change when Larry Erlich was in her life. She didn't know why she should feel pretty, *be* pretty, when she was with him, on her way to him, thinking of him with acceptance and, if not love, affection and desire. She only knew that it was so, and she no longer wanted to live any other way.

* * *

372

Van Roberts was enjoying the party. He talked to Ernie and Richie and Mrs Morden, and then he had a few more drinks and half a sandwich and listened to the good jazz records Eugenia and Henny had brought up. He'd called Evaline and explained about the party and she'd said, 'I can't leave Al with the Johnsons – they've got company. And I can't ask Momma.' She explained why not and finally said, 'If you want, stay a while. I don't mind, honey.' He asked if she was sure, and she laughed and said, 'I know you, Van. Even if they weren't all white girls, I'd trust you.'

And they *were* all white girls. And so he felt no necessity to ask anyone to dance – which he disliked and did badly – or circulate too heavily, and was able to be himself: calm and quiet and happy with the food, drink and music.

Dennis Parish discussed the shrinking cheesecake market, made a few suggestions for speculative jobs, and then drifted away. Elroy Frankle of Viewcitement Corporation came over and they talked and Elroy said something might be coming up on a jazz festival and he'd see if he could throw it Van's way. Elroy left the party with a strange redhead and so did the other Viewcitement editor, and Van had another few drinks and really felt good. Not drunk, but good.

Then Eugenia came over, and she was sky-high. 'Daddy, I'm all alone and you're all alone and can't we get together?'

It embarrassed him. He didn't want anyone being noble – not with *him* as the subject. 'I'm having a great time,' he said, smiling. 'This is exactly how I enjoy a party. Anyway, Henny'll be jealous.'

'Henny can't see me, he's so busy not seeing the little blonde. And Bogen can't see me, he's so set on being a perfect square for the same little blonde. And I can't stand Drake or his new friend Arnold. And Richie's got

373

a wife with him.' She waved her hand. 'I like you best of who's available, and you're alone too.' She leaned up against him. 'Don't be narrow-minded, Van. Dance with the white girl.'

He grinned, no longer embarrassed. 'I'm a bad dancer, Eugenia. I'll get you a drink and we'll talk.'

'Well, *one* drink and then we'll dance. Okay?'

He nodded, turned to the table, and saw Laird Drake staring at him. The stare was cold, unfriendly, and he suddenly remembered his suspicion that Laird was a bigot and quickly told himself not to jump to conclusions. Just because the man was looking at him . . .

He winked at Drake and smiled. Drake's lips tightened and he looked past Van, and Van knew he was looking at Eugenia.

Van felt sudden rage. He mixed two drinks and returned to Eugenia and said, 'Here's to Bessie Smith. May we listen to her another hundred years.'

'Amen,' Eugenia murmured, and drank, and put her hand on his wrist. 'You know, I've danced with colored men only twice in all my life. And I've never been kissed by – '

'Let's make it three times,' he interrupted, uncomfortable, yet unwilling to leave Eugenia now that he knew Drake was critical of his being with her.

They began to dance, and almost as soon as they did, someone tapped him on the shoulder. He stopped and turned. It was the surly guy from the hair-goods place, Arnold Gernstein. 'Mind if I cut in?' he said, but didn't wait for an answer, stepping between Van and Eugenia and taking the blonde in his arms. She shoved him back angrily and said, 'I don't know if he minds, but I do! We just stepped out. Go back to your friend.'

Arnold Gernstein paled and looked at Van and murmured, 'Just because she's drunk doesn't mean you can take advantage . . .'

Van saw red. For a moment he thought he'd hit the man; but then Eugenia was laughing, saying. 'Hey, Van, he's protecting *me* from *you*!' She laughed and laughed, bending over and gasping for breath. 'It's the other way around, Cunnel Arnold, suh. It's way the other way around. Go count money with Laird Drake.'

Van stepped around Arnold Gernstein, and Eugenia did too, and they came together, and both grinned at Gernstein. Eugenia's grin was authentic; Van's was full of rage and hate and despair. *Even here. Even where he was known and liked. Even in his own studio.*

Someone else tapped him on the shoulder; tapped him very hard, so hard that he grunted as the fingers jabbed into the spot close to his neck. He turned, saying, 'What the hell's going on?'

'Leave that girl alone,' Laird Drake said, voice dramatically deep and soft. 'If you continue bothering her – '

Eugenia squealed, wordless for a second. But then the second was over and she shoved at Laird and shouted, 'Oh! How lousy can a guy be! You, playing the part of white savior, white gentleman. You *hit* me! You slapped – '

Van was bringing up his fists and listening to Eugenia. He expected that he'd have to fight this tall, heavy bigot, but he didn't expect it would be before Eugenia had her say, and Richie and the others came over and they all had a say. He didn't understand Laird Drake. Laird had to stop the talk right here. Laird had to retain his justification for hating Van.

Laird brought his right hand up from his side in a clean uppercut. It caught Van deep under the chin, and he was immediately out of action. As he staggered and slumped, Laird hit him again, on the temple. Van's knees stiffened; he was unconscious as he fell.

Eugenia screamed and tried to pummel Laird. He shoved her away and said, 'Arny, get her.' Arnold

Gernstein, acting as if he were policing a brawl, said, 'Right,' and grabbed her hands and shoved her to the wall, even though she kicked at him and wept with rage.

Van Roberts was unconscious only two or three seconds. But when he focused his eyes, he felt drugged, without strength, helpless. He saw that something was going on. He saw Richie Morden falling. He tried to move, to help his friend, and blacked out for a moment. When he saw again, it was Henny who was up there and Drake slugging him and Henny falling. He began to push himself up, and shoes came into his field of vision, and Arnold Gernstein's voice shouted, 'Stay out of it! You started the whole thing! Goddam it, you knew you shouldn't bother a white girl! Stay out of it!'

Van couldn't move his arms, and so he tried to bite Arnold Gernstein's leg. Arnold hit him once, twice, three times on the back of the neck, and this time Van went to sleep for a long, long time.

Richie Morden hadn't minded Henny's throwing the party, even at half an hour's notice, because he was fed up with himself, his thoughts, his fears and his inability to regain his natural zest for life. The party – any party – was welcome because it would give him a chance to drink and be with Phyll and perhaps shake the depression which had been mounting within him during the past three weeks.

And that's exactly what happened. He had a great time. He enjoyed the collector's-item jazz records Eugenia and Henny provided, and danced with Phyll almost steadily, except for Henny's one cut-in, and congratulated himself at least a dozen times on his return to normalcy.

Even learning that the 'Norma' who'd been present in the studio when he and Van had been kidding about Les Bogen's love-life was actually Bogen's daughter failed to dampen his spirits for long. He was having fun. He wasn't thinking and worrying about the past. He was himself.

But at about ten o'clock, while he and Phyll were at the bridge table having a drink, he noticed Van Roberts standing alone, and Phyll noticed it too, and she said, 'It's too bad Van's wife couldn't come. I'm surprised he decided to stay without her.'

And just like that the fears returned. And he understood that they had never left, would never leave, had been in his mind all his life and would be there until he died. 'Why?' he muttered. 'He's having fun. And he can dance with anyone here, can't he? If he wanted to, I mean?'

'I can't speak for the other women . . .' She shrugged. 'Let's not discuss it, Richie. I'm having a wonderful time. Let's dance some more.'

He wanted to pursue the discussion, and didn't want to, and said, 'You'd certainly dance with him if he asked you, wouldn't you? I mean – after all, it's Van Roberts, someone you know and like.'

'Knowing and liking him doesn't mean I'd feel comfortable dancing with him.'

He began to sweat. 'But if he asked you.'

'I guess I'd be forced to say yes.' She sipped her drink. 'But I wouldn't like it, Richie. I'm an old Reb at heart.'

He changed the subject. He danced with her, and pressed his lips to her cheek, and loved her, and hated her, and more than anything else feared what she would do if she found out.

She would never find out. There was *nothing* to find out!

The same old thing, the same crazy thoughts and fears, the same attempts at reassurance and the temporary failures and the just as temporary successes. And it would go on this way.

'What's the matter?' Phyll asked.

He looked at her. 'Matter? Nothing.'

'You looked so . . . sad for a minute.'

He laughed, and they danced, and they talked, and they danced some more.

And while they were dancing near the marble counter and the phonograph, they saw Van and Eugenia move out onto the center of the floor. Richie didn't want to comment on it, but he knew Phyll would, and he wanted to head off anything critical. He said, 'Eugenia is a fine girl.'

'I'm sure she is,' Phyll murmured. 'I admire her, in a way.'

He was about to ask her to clarify that statement when the younger Gernstein walked up to Van and Eugenia and cut in, and Eugenia sent him on his way, and then Laird came up and was much too physical about his cut-in.

Richie stopped dancing. Phyll said, 'This was bound to happen.'

Richie said, 'Shut up.'

She looked up at him, mouth hanging open in shock.

Laird struck Van, and Van began to fall, and Richie said, 'God!' Laird struck Van again, and Van fell straight back, and Richie heard someone bellowing insanely. The words were: 'All right! Hit me too! I'm colored too! I've got a white woman too! All right! Hit me too! I'm a Negro too!'

And he was grabbing Laird's arm and Laird was trying to get away from him and he punched at Laird with his free hand and hit him on the shoulder and Laird turned and said something about Richie's being drunk and Richie shouted, 'You goddam moron. You lousy bigot. You . . .' He searched his mind for words, insulting words, and came up with two or three more, and came up with, 'You fuckin' fairy,' and wanted to go on with others just as wild, as long as they were insults. But one found Laird

378

where he lived, and he paled, and his big fists pumped efficiently. Richie was surprised at the tremendous power of the blows crashing into his face and body, and he wondered through the pain that Laird had never acted with the assurance of a man so superior at fighting, a man so eminently capable of handling other men.

'Damn you,' he said, or thought he said, and the blows stopped. Then he felt something slam into the side of his body, and he blinked his eyes. Out of the corners, he saw a dusty, yellowish brown surface and realized it was the floor and couldn't seem to do anything but lie there and blink his eyes at it.

Marv Weister drank with Francie something-or-other and ate with her and danced with her, but he wasn't really in her company. He was thinking of the reading he'd done most of last night and a good deal of today, and of the questions that continued to plague him.

He'd liked his three books. He'd been amazed at the range of his thoughts, at the clarity and depth of his terminology, at the honesty, the refusal to dilute realism with plot gimmicks. But he'd also realized he wasn't a 'writer' – not as he'd always defined the word. He wasn't a *novelist*. And that was the only thing in the world he wanted to be.

Up until very recently he'd used a typewriter and marveled at being published and gone on putting words down on paper. And gone on writing about Marv Weister – not Marv Weister spread thin over a dozen or more characters but Marv Weister as the protagonist in each of the three books; Marv Weister as he'd actually lived his life, sometimes physically and sometimes as he'd lived in his mind. But always Marv Weister.

He'd written three books, and they'd called them novels, and he'd thought himself a novelist. But it was wrong. He'd written three autobiographies. And on this fourth book he had run out of Marv Weister material, without being aware of it, and was writing – or trying to write – about *other* people, characters in the legitimate, fictional sense of the word.

Knowing it now, at the party, didn't solve anything. He still didn't know if he'd be able to *create* people and situations – perhaps not out of whole cloth, but inventing much of what was to be tacked onto people he'd known – combinations of the real and the imaginary. This was the novelist's business, and it was a tough business, not (despite certain popular conceptions) for weaklings, cowards or dope addicts.

If he was a weakling, a coward and a dope addict, how could he possibly endure the months, perhaps years, of day-by-day struggle to create living people, situations and ideas on paper? If he was a weakling a coward and a dope addict, how could he hope to *sustain* thought, and the ambition necessary to create thought, for those long months or years?

He realized, with a certain amount of bitter amusement, that he yearned to return to short stories. For even the most erudite, sophisticated and meaningful of short stories required only the *talent* of their creators. The relatively brief periods of time necessary to evolve these works – either of commercial value or of art – made no such demands on strength and endurance as did writing the novel.

But returning to the short story would be another indication of weakness and cowardice; another running away from a fight, as he'd run when Drake had slapped Eugenia in his apartment, as he ran whenever he saw a group of Puerto Rican boys on a stoop.

So he was stuck with being a novelist who hadn't yet written a novel: a novelist who knew he was a weakling and a coward, and possibly a dope addict.

Knowing these things, he was left with the vital questions:

Can I change?

Can I write ('write' being synonymous with 'survive') *while changing?*

Just how deeply tied to narcotics am I?

And a final question – one which made him shake inside:

If I can't change and am a true drug addict, can I end the misery, can I destroy myself?

And he was also left with the on-and-off, now you-feel-it-now-you-don't craving for a fix. However little actual heroin he'd been taking into his system, he now felt it had been enough to create a legitimate physical need, and he didn't know if he could resist this need over any length of time.

Just thinking of it set up the ache, the want, the deep, deep hunger.

He was standing with Francie, feeling the ache spread out from the pit of his stomach, when Laird Drake knocked Van Roberts to the floor. Francie gasped, and Marv turned slightly to face the scene, and the thought came that this was a miracle, a visitation of events specifically tailored to his problems, his questions. If he could discard his physical weakness, his physical cowardice, it would be a step toward proving to himself that he could eventually change on a wider basis.

But in the next split second he was backing up, paling, telling himself it was ridiculous to think in terms of a fist fight at a heavy-drinking party; a fist fight in which he didn't know whose side to take.

And in the instant after that, he called himself a liar. Laird Drake had knocked Van Roberts to the floor and was now beating Richie Morden, and Eugenia Randolph had tried to stop Drake. Drake was big, and he had the medium-sized dark man named Arnold Gernstein on his side, and he was wrong, had to be wrong, because he was what he was, a frustrated, frightened, bitter, envious man.

As Francie said, 'Marv, do something!' he saw Henny shuffle by and come at Drake, and he whispered, 'Henny, no, he hates you!'

But it wasn't Drake's hating Henny that brought the tortured whisper from Marv. It was Henny's involving himself in the fight. It was Henny's being Marv's friend and therefore robbing Marv of any possible moral basis for staying out of the fight. Now Marv would run, and know he was too weak for life and therefore too weak for the business of the novelist – creating life on paper.

Henny was on the floor, and Drake was on top of him, and Henny was being beaten, terribly beaten. And Marv Weister was still shuffling backward, away from the violence, still proving he was weak and cowardly and unfit to do the thing he most wanted to do, the thing he had to do in order to survive. Every tiny step backward was a huge step away from writing.

Henny made a strange little sound – a high-pitched, agonized, pathetic little sound. Laird Drake had slugged him in the stomach and was doing it again. As he drew his big fist back for still another vicious blow, Marv Weister echoed Henny's agonized little cry and went to help his friend. But Arnold Gernstein appeared before him, his face sure and unafraid as he looked this puny opponent up and down. 'Go back before I take you apart,' Gernstein said sternly.

Marv Weister had all the arguments in the world on his tongue. He had all the convincing explanations, all the indignant reproaches, but instead of using them, of using reason, he said, 'Idiot! Don't you know a Jew must always be on the side of the angels?' And as Gernstein's eyes registered surprise and the beginnings of doubt, Marv Weister hit him as hard as he could as far below the belt as he could. Had Marv been a reasonably strong man, Gernstein would certainly have fainted. As it was, he doubled over, gasping, and Marv Weister hit him as many more times as he could, in the face and neck and body. Arnold Gernstein stumbled aside and said, 'No.' He kept stumbling until he bumped into a chair and then sat down and rocked back and forth.

Marv began turning to Laird Drake, knowing that there he would find no chance for victory. But someone brushed past and said, 'Get off him, Laird. Right now. And if you throw one punch at me, I'll hurt you.'

Les Bogen suffered continuously from the moment he ran out of the studio at four-thirty and saw that Sandy had already arrived in the waiting room. He tried to tell her that the party was a boring affair, that they'd have a much better time in a good restaurant, and even extended the bait of a four-week cruise of the Caribbean – 'That's the special surprise I mentioned on the phone. We'll go to a travel agent right now.' But she'd merely shaken her head and murmured, 'I want a drink,' and moved toward the studio door. Again he had no choice. Again he tried to make the best of it.

As soon as they entered the studio, she found Henny with her eyes. She sat down, and Les went to the bridge table and mixed her a highball – a very weak one – and poured himself a straight Scotch – a very stiff one – and brought both drinks to the couch. They sat, and he talked. He talked smoothly, brightly, in a steady stream, until Laird Drake came over. He introduced Drake, and Drake asked Sandy to dance, and Sandy stood up, and they danced.

He was glad of that. Maybe now she would stop watching Henny with fixed, pained eyes.

But she didn't stop. Somehow, little as she was, she maneuvered the big Drake so that she was almost always in a position to watch Henny and Eugenia. And when the music stopped, she walked away from Drake with nothing more than a nod. Les could see that Laird was hurt. Les could see that Laird knew she'd been watching Henny; it was obvious, from the way he turned and looked at Henny, his lips tightening.

Sandy sat down again, and Les talked again, and Sandy said, 'Yes,' every so often and kept watching Henny.

Les suffered. Sandy's eyes were sick, and so he suffered.

But he told himself this situation, this party, was just a bad break. Otherwise, she'd never have seen Henny again. And even seeing him now, it would change nothing. Henny was acting the way Les knew he'd act. Henny was drunk, but Henny was a man of his word. Not even with a glance did he recognize the fact that Sandy was in the room. But Sandy kept watching him.

Les kept talking.

Time passed. Hours. Les talked.

Phyllis Morden came to the couch. He introduced her and asked why Richie didn't come over and she said he was discussing business with Van. He'd be over shortly. But she left a moment later, and Richie never did come over. Neither did Van Roberts. And so Les understood they were embarrassed by what they'd said to 'Norma.'

Sandy danced with Elroy Frankle of Viewcitement, and with Arnold Gernstein, and came back to the couch. She didn't smile – not once. Her eyes followed Henny around the room, all around the room.

At six-thirty, seven, seven-thirty, eight, eight-thirty and nine, Les made the suggestion that they leave. Each time Sandy said, 'No, Father. I like it here.' Her eyes followed Henny.

He wanted to ask her how she could feel so much for a man she'd known so short a time. He wanted to shout that question at her and slap some sense into her and rock her in his arms with all the love – the *real* love – he felt. He merely talked, on and on, hoping to drag her eyes from Henny.

At about nine-thirty, Henny was having a drink, and he finally looked at the couch. Sandy paled, swiftly enough for Les to see the transition, and then Henny turned his back and danced with Stella Lago, whom Les had pointedly ignored since Sandy arrived. Les began describing an Italian sports car he felt Sandy would like. 'Maybe we'll make that twentieth birthday a memorable occasion.'

At that point she turned her head and fixed her eyes on him and said, 'I can't prove anything, Father, but I believe *you're* responsible for Henny's actions.'

It took him a moment to accept what he'd heard. It was the one thing he'd least expected to hear and least *wanted* to hear. 'Henny's actions?' he asked, in order to gain time.

'Yes. His changing toward me so completely. Except that I've been here four hours or more and I've watched him and I know he *hasn't* changed. He can't look at me.'

'My dear child, I can't see where that – '

'I've also been listening to you those same four hours. I wish I had a tape recording of your monologue, Father. It's, well, *frantic* is the only word I can think of. You're afraid of something, Father. And Henny is afraid to look at me.'

'I'm not aware of anything unusual in my manner of speaking. And if Henny doesn't care to be reminded of an indiscreet – '

But his throat was dry and his voice weak, and when she interrupted him he fell silent.

'I've also been *thinking* during these four hours, Father. I wish you'd tell me now, while I still might be able to understand, whatever it is you did, and your motives.'

'I did nothing,' he said, and looked her straight in the eyes, hoping it would convince her.

'Though I believe I know your motives,' she said, as if he hadn't spoken. 'And I *pity* your motives, Father.'

That he couldn't tolerate. He turned away from her, crossed his legs and shook his head. 'You've had only two drinks, but I must have made them stronger than I thought. You're talking utter nonsense. And I don't want to hear any more! If you can't make sense, let's leave!'

'No'. She kept looking at him, and he refused to face her again, and she said, 'I'll never believe he gave me up of his own volition.'

'Really?' he said, voice cold, almost hard now. 'How many times have I heard that before, from discarded young ladies.' He laughed. 'It's the very best salve for egos, though it generally wears thin in a week or two.'

She said nothing. He said nothing. They sat there.

And then she stood up, and he looked at her. She was walking to Henny Girado, who had his back to the couch. She touched Henny's arm, and he turned, and even from halfway across the room Les could see the greeting of shock and pain and longing on Henny's face. They talked, and Henny seemed to be telling her to go away. Then Henny looked right at him. Sandy turned, also looking at him, and Les Bogen cursed Henny for being too drunk to control his eyes. Sandy took Henny's hand and made him dance with her, but Henny broke away a moment later. Les could have shouted his anger when Henny ran right to the couch, right to him.

'Make her lemme alone,' he said.

Les kept his face and voice calm because he knew Sandy was watching and told Henny to leave. Henny began to cry.

At that point Les Bogen felt that even the strongest man would despair of the cause. But in the next instant he reminded himself that he wasn't just a strong man; he was a man fighting for half his life. And so he moved swiftly after Henny, grabbed his arm, tried to drive home a few important words to make the fool see what he'd gained by giving up Sandy. The tears kept running down Henny's cheeks as he pulled free and went to the door.

At least he was leaving. At least this evening would be ending soon.

And then they both heard the shouts and cries and turned to see the fight. And Henny ran toward it.

Things happened so quickly, it took Les a few minutes to decide how he felt about them. First, Van fell under Laird's blows; and immediately afterward Richie. And even as Les was feeling surprise at Laird Drake's clean, powerful, almost professional punching, Henny went down.

Laird went down after Henny. And the look on Laird's face was a look Les had seen only once before: on the face of the brother of a girl he'd been seeing some five years ago, a girl who'd refused to accept the casual termination of the affair. The brother had tried to club Les with a section of iron piping, tried to kill Les. Only Les's skill at jujitsu had saved him. And a promise to continue seeing the girl had ended the threat forever. (He had, of course, disenchanted her completely within three weeks, by which time she wouldn't have risked her brother's spending a night in jail, not to say a lifetime, over Lester Bogen.)

Les stood where he was. He decided this was a good thing. Because Drake was hitting very hard, and he might kill Henny, and that would certainly put an end . . .

But even as he thought this, his stomach lurched at the blow Laird Drake sent into Henny's. And Sandy was running to him, crying, 'Daddy, help him. Please, Daddy.'

Marv Weister had surprised Arnold Gernstein with a sudden attack and actually seemed about to turn on

Drake. But Les Bogen had seen his daughter's face, tear-streaked, terrified, and she had come to him, called on him for help, as she had as a child. 'Daddy, a boy pushed me off my bike and hit me and my knee's all bloody.'

He'd run all the way down to the road that time, and found the twelve-year-old, and slapped his face, and told him to send his father up immediately. And when the father had arrived, big and loud and full of anger at the slap, Les Bogen had told him to shut up and listen, and had dressed him down, and the man had seen that there was danger here, not the normal angry-father danger but something more, something indicated by the hands held stiffly open at the sides, ready to chop in deadly opposition to any simple fist attack.

And it was the same now, even though Les Bogen felt he might be destroying half his own life by saving Henny's. It was the same tone of voice and the same ready-for-combat stance that he directed at Laird Drake. He expected Drake to understand.

Except that Laird Drake had tasted, for the first time in his life, his own strength, his own prowess, and realized that the gym instructor had been serious when he'd said Laird had the makings of a heavyweight slugger. Laird Drake had knocked three men to the floor and was getting even with the third for a lifetime of insecurity, rejection and failure. Laird Drake wanted to continue battering at Henny Girado, no matter what the cost. But of all the people at Morden Photos, he most wanted Les Bogen to respect, admire and like him.

However, he also knew he would no longer be at Morden Photos – not after having slugged the owner, Richie Morden. And perhaps the best way to gain the respect, admiration and even liking of men such as Les Bogen was to show them they were inferior – at least physically – to Laird Drake.

He got up, and Henny rolled his head a little and

groaned. Laird Drake looked at Les – a full head shorter than him, and not nearly as broad, and very obviously in his forties. 'I have nothing to lose any more in this studio, Les. Take a good look at Henny and then mind your own business.' He smiled, to show he was perfectly willing to let it go at that. He tried to add warmth to the smile, to show he was also willing to accept future friendship.

Les Bogen said, 'Get out of here. I don't want to hurt you.'

That tone of voice. That damned authoritative tone of voice! 'Where the hell do you get off talking that way to me, you little jerk?'

Les Bogen jumped in and slapped Laird Drake's face and jumped back. He did it so quickly, Drake barely had time to blink his eyes before Bogen was standing in his previous position, about three feet away, arms at side, seemingly relaxed.

Suddenly Laird Drake lost the triumphant, invincible feeling and was his normal, frightened self.

'Get out,' Bogen repeated.

Everyone was watching, and everyone was against him. Arnold Gernstein had his head down and was moaning to himself, but Laird felt he was faking. Still, it made no difference. He was alone in this thing now. Alone.

But he fought the fear. Only Les Bogen was threatening him. Only that middle-aged little man.

He clenched his fists, and Les Bogen said very softly, 'The harder you punch, the worse you'll suffer. Remember that. It's your own strength that'll be directed against you.'

Laird Drake wanted to leave. God, how he wanted to leave! But he wanted to leave head up, with his victory intact. He had started all this not so much to stop a Negro from dancing with a white girl – though he firmly believed he was right in that, too – but because he wanted to show them, to show everyone here, that he was a man, a real man, more man than anyone they knew. And also because he'd hoped Henny Girado would be drawn into it.

Everything had worked out, and now the entire victory was being threatened, and everyone was watching.

It was hearing Eugenia Randolph sob that decided him. He wouldn't be humiliated a second time in front of that slut!

He crouched and moved forward and threw two punches, in combination, putting everything behind them, even more than he had against Henny. And as he threw them, he felt sure again. How could this little man possibly defeat him?

The next instant he was off-balance, and there was excruciating pain in his right elbow. As he cried out, his feet left the ground and he was hurling through the air, turning completely over. He crashed into the wall near the bridge table, his neck wrenching badly. But he tried to get up. Then he saw Les Bogen's gray flannel trousers approach, and something knifelike jabbed into a point between his chest and his stomach. He immediately gagged and vomited.

'I'll ask you again,' Les Bogen's voice said. 'Get out.'

It was a struggle, but Laird Drake got to his feet. He stumbled to the door and out, and all the time he thought he would die of the pain – not the pain in his right arm, which felt broken, nor the pain in his neck, which was definitely sprained, nor the burning pain in that spot between his chest and his stomach. It was the pain of shame, the pain of defeat. He smelled his own vomit, and reached the stairs, and stumbled down them.

Always defeat.

Why? Why should it be so? Didn't men win victories? Didn't they come away with their victories intact?

Why not he? Tonight he'd had a great victory.

But then he knew it wasn't so. He hadn't had a victory.

390

He'd been defeating himself all along. He'd created a situation and tried to create a victory. But one didn't *create* such victories. They were *forced* on one. They came along. Otherwise, it was like fixing a prize fight. He'd fixed the fight tonight. He'd taken on men far under his size and weight; men who'd been drinking heavily while he hadn't; men he'd surprised one way or another.

And then the policeman had arrived. Justice. The law. Les Bogen. But anyone else with the strength or the skill would have served as well. And the criminal had been punished.

He went across the street to the parking lot, dark and unattended. He found his Dodge convertible and got inside and said, 'Christ in heaven, help me.'

He wanted to rest, but the thought that others would soon be leaving the studio, coming down here for their cars, made him reach for his keys. He sobbed aloud with the pain of his right arm, and dropped the keys, and picked them up with his left. He got the car started and, using only his left hand, backed up and pulled out of the lot. He'd go to his family physician in Washington Heights.

But even with the pain and the fear that his arm was broken, he couldn't stop thinking of his defeat, his criminal victory and shameful defeat.

And what if he'd hurt Henny Girado badly? He'd hit him and hit him, and maybe he'd ruptured something and Henny would be hospitalized, or even die.

He shook his head, trying to shake the thoughts.

And what if Van and Richie and Henny got together and found him and took vengeance? Or what if Van got some relatives or friends, and they came to his home one night, angry black men with knives?

He shivered with fear and pain. He said again and again, 'Christ in heaven, help me.'

Just before he reached the doctor's, he decided he

391

would take a two- or three-week vacation, starting tomorrow morning. He'd go down South. He'd shot the road company of a successful musical in Alabama recently and liked the town of Birmingham, where he'd met another photographer, Wallace Jerreson, who owned a portrait studio and who also did a brisk business in confirmations, weddings, conventions and an occasional free-lance job. Jerreson had said he could use a partner.

He'd definitely leave tomorrow – early. And he'd definitely contact Jerreson and look around for other prospects, too.

Sure, lots of people were settling in the South people sick of the racial pigpen the East was fast becoming. He would never have gotten into a fight of this sort in Birmingham. There'd never have been a Negro in an equal position with whites there – certainly not at a party with whites . . .

Doctor Neilson said he'd given his elbow a nasty wrench, but nothing had been broken. He taped it, applied a leather brace to Laird's neck, and found nothing but a red welt at the sensitive spot between chest and stomach. He took fifteen dollars – because of the brace – and, looking pointedly at Laird's spattered clothing, suggested Laird drink less and in less 'excitable' company.

Laird went home. His mother was reading in the living room. She gave him one cold glance and said, 'Before you begin your explanations, clean up.' She returned to her reading.

For a moment he wanted to scream insults at her. She hadn't even asked about his neck, plainly encased in the brace. She hadn't voiced any worry about him; hadn't offered any sympathy.

But then again, that's the way she'd always been. Cool. Very cool, except as regarding her *own* sacred entity.

He decided to leave tonight.

He showered, changed clothes, went to his room and

began packing two large bags. His mother finally came in to see what was keeping him. 'Well?' she asked, glancing at the bags. 'Aren't you going to explain your shameful appearance?'

He continued packing. 'It wouldn't interest you, Mother.'

'I believe you're right, since it probably concerns those people you work with. Probably too sordid to repeat.'

He closed one bag. His arm still hurt like hell, but his mind was clear. 'I'm leaving town for a few weeks,' he said. 'A big assignment came up and I've got to drive to Birmingham, Alabama. I want you to send a messenger to the studio for my equipment. I may wire you to ship it out to me in a few days.'

She stared at him.

He put his Rollei and a Leica in the second bag, added clothing and toilet articles, turned to his bureau for more.

'Jamie took me to dinner tonight,' his mother said. 'He asked when I thought you'd tire of working in that cheap studio. I replied that it would be very shortly.' She paused. 'I think it's right now.'

Laird kept packing.

'I also told him you'd certainly accept his offer when the time came. That should be immediately after you return from Alabama.'

Laird didn't bother contradicting her. He no longer doubted he was man enough to last among men; and among women, too, for that matter. But not here, not in New York. He had to get away, find his own kind, become secure.

The South.

He didn't even kiss her goodbye.

He stopped at an Esso station for maps and, as the attendant selected them from a rack, he looked out the plate-glass window at the city and began to wonder if he was doing the right thing.

For just an instant he saw into himself, glimpsed the truth: wherever he went, he would find people more or less the same, despite the presence or absence of certain minority groups in business and social situations. He would also find himself lacking in relation to other men – as he always had – and this would build up his resentments and hatreds to the point where he would again try to prove himself. And that would mean another fight. And one day he would either hurt someone badly or himself be badly hurt.

The attendant came over with the maps, dispelling the flash of insight. Laird paid for twelve gallons of gas and drove off, using his right arm as little as possible. He put on the radio, got some music, and a few minutes later began to feel good.

Yes, he'd needed a change for a long time. He'd needed to get away from Mother and Jamie and the studio and the entire city of New York. '*Jew* York,' he muttered, remembering some cracks Wallace Jerreson had made. At the time – eight months ago – he'd resented them slightly. Now, however, he agreed wholeheartedly. He'd tell Jerreson plenty when he got to Birmingham! And perhaps there was still a chance to buy into the portrait studio.

Yes. The South. He knew he'd be happy in the South.

24

Marie was surprised at the size of Larry Erlich's establishment. It was a large store, opening up from its modest Fifth Avenue frontage to a wide interior and a wider second floor. It had between twelve and fifteen employees, about a third of them attractive women in Larry's own age group, and everyone called him Mr Erlich and seemed to like and respect him. And he treated Marie as if she were something special, calling over a salesman or saleswoman every so often to explain fully the make and worth of an item. There were beautiful lamps, and tables, and paintings, and all sorts of things for the home – the *expensive* home.

They left and had dinner at a restaurant on Third Avenue she'd heard Les Bogen mention as his favorite – the Chambord. The food was the best she'd ever eaten, and Larry chose a wonderful bottle of wine, and she smoked gold-tipped cigarettes in different gay colors.

She saw the bill. It was enormous. She'd never dreamed two people could spend twenty-eight dollars for a meal, without drinking themselves silly.

And then he leaned back in his chair, waiting for change of his fifty-dollar bill, and said, 'The last time we sat and ate together, you told me you thought I was about to ask you to come to my apartment. I asked if you were disappointed that I hadn't, and you said, "No, relieved." Would you be relieved if I failed to ask again?'

She knew she should say yes, but all she did was light another gold-tipped cigarette and blow smoke across the table and smile.

An answering smile touched his lips, but briefly, uncertainly. He wasn't sure what reply he'd received.

'Then it won't offend you if I *do* ask?'

'Try,' she said, and suddenly knew that she wanted to experience everything tonight.

'All right. I would like to show you my apartment.' He said it as if offering a tour of St Patrick's, and she found herself giggling.

'It can't be *that* impressive,' she said, and giggled again.

'Oh, no, it's a very nice, a very *warm* place.'

'I'm sure it is,' she said, and nodded.

'Then you'll come?'

He was so delighted, so obviously amazed at his victory, that she found herself touching his hand and saying, 'I'd love to come, Larry.'

They left a moment later. Standing in the street, still bright with day, she watched Larry trying to hail a cab and wondered if he could be as *youthful* as all that. Had he really been so surprised at her answer? Had he really been so uncertain of himself? After all, he'd picked her up smoothly enough in the bar and had certainly done all right later on.

She felt tension rising and wanted to leave, and then thought of what *that* would mean. Back home to Brooklyn. The TV. The talk about baseball and fights. And she, always alone.

In the cab he drew her close and murmured, 'Are you happy, Marie?'

She said, 'Yes,' but it was no longer true. She was confused.

He lived in a five-story building, not large but very fine looking. There was a doorman and a cool, dim lobby and an elevator, but she didn't really see them. She was churning inside, terrified; and yet, at the same time, she wanted, wanted everything.

His apartment was on the third floor – two huge rooms,

and a kitchen unit tucked away behind a partition. There was a fireplace in the living room, and three sections of beautifully covered bench couch drawn up as three sides of a square, with the fireplace the fourth side. 'It is real,' he said, standing behind her as she examined the cut-stone frontage. His hands touched her forearms and pressed them, and his lips brushed her neck. 'It burns large sections of log, and in the winter I keep it going for hours.'

She'd sensed a change in him as soon as they'd entered this lovely place, a change she wasn't sure she liked, but which she knew was necessary if anything was to happen. He had begun acting the part of an expectant lover. Gone was most of the fumbling boyishness. In its place was a growing excitement.

She turned, looking at him. 'Will I be able to sit and watch the fire this winter?'

'Of course, dear.' He tried to draw her to him, but she shook her head quickly. His lips tightened a bit, and she wondered if he were getting tired of playing the kindly young-old man. And then she wondered at herself for seeing all this and realized he had already helped her to grow in understanding.

He would help her more, much more!

'Why should we know each other this winter, seven or eight months from now? Why should we know each other so long?'

His eyes blinked. 'I would like to know you the rest of my life.'

'You mean marry me?'

His eyes fell away from hers, and he laughed too long and in too gay a manner. 'What a girl! Give us a chance to say hello.' He laughed again.

She also laughed; but there was still the old Marie, and the old Marie was very perceptive, very raw to the slightest indication of rejection, and this was more than slight. This was a man shocked by something he'd never considered. This was a man avoiding a return to the romantic hints that had been part of his first approach; a man beginning the retreat from formal man-woman relations; a man covering himself because of what he hoped would soon take place.

There was no denying it, she felt pain, and some anger, and almost moved toward the door.

'Let me get you a drink,' he said, worried by her silence, her changing expression. 'What would you like?'

'Champagne,' she said quickly, almost sharply, thinking he'd have to go down for it, wanting to make him run for her, work for her, sweat for her.

'I have a bottle in the refrigerator,' he said, smiling, trying to make her smile. 'Wonderful Mumm's *brut* that ends all thirst with just one swallow.'

She nodded then, fighting the old Marie, telling herself she must expect nothing but what he offered. As he began to move away, still worried, she stopped him with a hand on his arm. He turned and she looked at him; and she wanted him, despite everything the old Marie tried to do, despite the conflict in her own mind. She wanted him and refused to go through the *why's* of it.

She stepped close and tilted up her face. He kissed her on the lips, gently, as if still afraid she'd retreat. She leaned into him, and his arms tightened, and she began to move her body as she had never moved it before. Her erotic fantasies had done little to prepare her for the preliminaries of love-making, having concentrated on the physical act, but she returned his caresses with an instinctive expertise. She *wanted* to give herself to him, and that somehow seemed to give her the knowledge of what to do.

She felt his tongue probe between her lips, exploring her mouth, and the sensation made her head swirl. Her arms tightened around him, her breasts crushing against his chest, her hips grinding against his loins. She moaned deep in her throat, a cry of pure longing, of pure need. Larry responded by taking his mouth from hers just long enough to steer her gently into the other room. It was dominated by a huge double bed. Marie stared at it, then at Larry. In the shadowy bedroom he looked younger, his face electric with desire. Marie found the expression arousing; she was not used to men looking at her in that way, and she enjoyed it.

Larry reached for her again, and she went into his arms with a strange new confidence. His obvious need of her gave her a strength she had not known before, a certainty that was at the same time very calm and wildly excited. He kissed her hard, his hands roaming over her body, and before she was fully aware of what he was doing, her dress was unfastened and he was slipping it from her shoulders. Marie wriggled her hips to help him, and the sudden intake of his breath was a delight to her ears.

'You're lovely,' he murmured, swallowing hard.

Marie smiled and unsnapped her brassiere. Her breasts were not large, but they were well-shaped and firm, and excitement had hardened the nipples. She enjoyed the way Larry's eyes gazed at them. Enjoyed even more, the touch of his hands. She was dimly aware of tumbling onto the bed with Larry's mouth covering her bosom with kisses. Then she was helping him remove his own clothing, and his body was hard against her. She was shocked by his erection, but at the same time aroused and delighted. *She* was responsible for that! She found only pleasure in his kisses as he pressed his lips to her breasts, her neck, her mouth. His hand moved between her legs, and she spread her thighs, opening herself to him, hungry for his touch. It was less adept than her own, but the very fact that it was a man's finger, not her own, made it better. She moaned, and drew his mouth to

399

her lips as she reached down to touch him. He was big, and very hard, and he groaned with pleasure as Marie enclosed him in her fingers. She was not sure what to do next, but her touch alone seemed to be exciting him, because he murmured, 'Oh God, I want you, darling.'

Marie smiled against his mouth, knowing that she wanted him, and that it was a good feeling, devoid of any guilt. All that seemed so silly now, unimportant in the fact of the glorious rush of raw desire she felt. She shifted onto her back, drawing Larry with her so that he lay on her, his weight an excruciating delight against her breasts and hips and thighs. She drew her knees up, making herself as big as possible as he reached down and began to insert his penis.

For an instant, she felt afraid. Larry believed her a sophisticate, and she was a virgin. Suppose there was blood?

Then the fear was gone as he slid into her, smoothly and easily, and a great soaring flood of pleasure filled her and lifted her to a place she had never known before. Her eyes closed, and her head arched back against the pillows, her hands moving down his body to cup his buttocks and drive him harder into her. She could feel his lips on her neck, his hands strong on her shoulders, but mostly she could feel his swollen manhood driving into her. Her body moved of its own accord, answering his strokes with a counter rhythm that took him deep into her, filling her until she cried out, and began to shudder. Larry's strokes quickened, matching her urgency, and they climaxed together, the strange, wonderful flood she felt pouring into her driving her to a peak of ecstasy that made her scream.

She didn't get her *brut* champagne until almost an hour later.

Lying across the large bed, she watched Larry leave the room. He moved slower than before, his long silk robe flapping about his stockinged, gartered calves. She laughed silently and looked at her body, white, firm, young. She felt different. So very different. She felt *alive* and capable of many things.

She jumped up and ran to the mirror over the dresser. There were heavy shadows in the room, but she could still see herself, every part of herself, and she was beautiful.

No doubt now. No doubt ever again.

But then a horn blew outside, and she was reminded that this room was not the world, and that Larry Erlich was not the end goal in men. She went to the window and raised a venetian blind slat and peered into the darkening streets. Down there, the young men walked. Down there, the young men who would need much convincing.

Larry Erlich returned with the champagne and glasses, and he stopped and looked at her. She smiled. 'I guess I should put on some clothing.'

'No, please don't.'

She smiled again. She hadn't intended to do so anyway. (And she marveled that she felt so clean, so at ease, so completely without shame or fear or sin!)

They sat on the edge of the bed and drank. He kept looking at her, and she put her nose in the chill bubbles, in the unsweet liquid that still managed to convey the essence of all the goodness and sweetness of the grape.

His hand reached out and stroked the curve of her hip, and his eyes blinked at her. 'What you asked me before, Marie.'

She knew what he meant, and her smile deepened. He was remembering her question about marriage, and he was beginning to wonder if perhaps he might not want to reconsider that question some day.

She changed the subject by kissing him with champagne-wet lips. He breathed heavily, and his hand lifted and came to her breast. She kissed him again.

'In a while,' he said, and seemed angry at himself, and she understood. He wanted youth. He wanted strength.

She understood so many things now. She was learning so fast. And it was all good, all real, all *life*. She understood that he didn't love her but wanted her very much, and that he might soon begin to love her because of that and because of his wanting youth and strength. She also understood that she didn't love him, not even a little, and never would, and only *needed* him.

He would continue to want her, but she wouldn't need him much longer. Only until he had taught her what he knew and given her the confidence she was looking for. Only until then, when she would go down into the streets and convince some young man; convince him of her beauty because she would feel beautiful, convince him of her purity because she would be pure in her mind and her heart – as she could never have been with the memory of the shower.

She laughed, amused and delighted with herself, and he smiled and said, 'Now I know you are happy.'

'Yes.' She laughed again, and felt cruel, and didn't care. She would give him pleasure, for a short time. And he? He would eventually make her inaccessible to aging gentlemen such as himself.

Van Roberts got home about forty-five minutes after he'd been knocked unconscious. He'd examined himself carefully in the studio washroom and was surprised to see that he bore no obvious signs of the fight. Of course, the underpart of his chin was tender as hell, and when he moved his jaws his right temple ached. But no swellings to speak of.

Yet as soon as he walked into the living room Evaline dropped her book and jumped out of her chair and said, 'Van, what happened?'

402

He grinned ruefully. 'Is the back of my head split open?'

'You look terrible.'

'Oh. Just my expression, huh?'

'You were in a fight?'

He sat down and told her about it. And, strangely enough, he was no longer angry, no longer vengeful, as he'd been all during the drive home, when he'd made and discarded half a dozen plans for inflicting horrible wounds upon the person of Laird Drake. Now he saw the fight as an isolated incident, the work of a sick-minded bigot, a bigot who would no longer be around the studio to bother him or anyone else.

But Evaline was enraged. She walked back and forth, back and forth. 'I'd like to *kill* him! Of all people to attack for bothering white girls! Of all people! You, Van! You!'

'Yeah,' he said, and asked her to make him a bite.

He had cold chicken and chocolate milk and kidded about the whole thing, and little by little she loosened up. Finally, she went to the living room, and he heard her crying. Then she came back and smiled. 'Just as long as you're all right. Just as long as it didn't bother you too much. He's through in the studio, so the hell with him.'

That's exactly how Van felt, until they were both in bed and she was sleeping and he was trying to sleep. Then something began to bother him. Not Laird Drake. Not the fact that he'd been knocked unconscious. Not even something he vaguely remembered Richie shouting – something about being part Negro – but which he knew couldn't be right. Even if Richie *had* said such a thing, he'd done it because he'd been boozed to the ears and because he'd wanted to get in on the fight.

No, it was something much more important personally.

As Evaline had said, 'Of all people to attack for bothering white girls!'

Yes, of all people. He'd spent a good part of his life resisting the very *thought* of extramarital sex, and that with members of his own race! He'd denied himself even fantasies, not to say the many lovely women who'd been available.

He turned over on his side, fighting the insidious thought. But it became stronger each minute.

He'd fought the caricature of the Negro as a lecher, as helpless in the grip of sexual passion, as perhaps no other Negro had – certainly as no other Negro of his acquaintance had. And this was how much good it had done him!

So it was all for nothing.

So he might just as well have enjoyed himself occasionally with the women he'd wanted, the women who'd wanted him. He might just as well have taken Yolanda Ferris right there in the studio, as Les Bogen took his women. He might just as well not have denied himself all these years.

But he didn't want that.

He looked at Evaline and then got up and padded into the second bedroom, where Al slept in his new 'big-man's' bed. No, he didn't want anything more than his wife and his son. He didn't want to feel *dirty*. He wanted the self-gratification of being *right*.

His reasoning about fighting bigotry by remaining true to his wife had helped immeasurably. Now he was stripped of that reasoning.

That's where Laird Drake had hurt him.

He returned to bed, and lay flat on his back, and put his hands together on his chest. He prayed silently, fervently. He asked God to help him remain as he was, at peace with himself in that one important way. Then he turned on his side and closed his eyes, and wondered what the next cheesecake shooting would bring, and all the cheesecake shootings after that.

He would try. God, he would try to remain *right*. But he'd lost his armor.

Richie Morden was helped to a chair by Marv Weister and Phyll, and kept saying he felt all right, and felt horrible. Not physically. He had a tender nose and a growing lump on his right cheek, but they were nothing compared to what he felt when he looked at Phyll and saw her pallor and knew that she'd heard what he'd said about being part Negro. Others must have heard, but he didn't care about them. They'd either put it down to the liquor or to his desire to align himself with Van. But Phyll – she would remember the discussions he'd forced on her.

He stood up and said, 'I'm fine now.'

Marv Weister said, 'Well, if you're sure,' and moved across the room to where Henny was lying on the couch, with Les and his daughter and Stella Lago and a dark little girl hovering around him.

Richie was left facing Phyll. 'How's Henny?' he asked, and tried to think of what to say, and could only think of what he'd already said.

Phyll remained pale, terribly pale. 'I didn't go over there,' she said, voice too high. 'But he was all bloody. They'll take care of him. I want to go home.'

'Yes.' But he was afraid to go home now, and still couldn't make his brain function properly. He saw Arnold Gernstein sitting in a chair watching the people around Henny. Richie walked up to him. 'I'm surprised someone hasn't kicked you down the stairs,' he said.

Gernstein got up and began saying he'd been drinking and wanted to apologize and please, please not to mention this to his father. Richie wanted to kill him for being part of what had ruined his life.

And it was only then he fully grasped what he'd done.

405

He turned, and Phyll was moving toward the door, and he said, 'Phyll, wait.'

She stopped. He felt it was against her will that she stopped; felt she wanted to keep going, out of the studio and out of his life. He stood still, and she stood still, and he saw it all now, so very clearly now. He'd presented as fact something that was nothing more than a childish, childhood fear!

How could he have done it? How!

All these years he'd worried about what couldn't be more than an unfounded suspicion. Seeing her pale face, her agony, and what he was sure was a withdrawal from him, he understood he'd allowed an obsession ride him and finally destroy the best thing in his life – his marriage.

And yet he also knew that he would never have seen the situation for what it was until he'd done just this – tell Phyll. It was inevitable – stupid and terrible and wasteful – but inevitable.

She began walking again. He knew he had to go after her and convince her that it wasn't true, hadn't a chance in a million of being true.

As he tried to think, she went out the door. He put his hands to his head and tried to form the words – the words that would convince her he'd been obsessed by a foolish fear, an untruth, or at least something that had no more than a chance in a million of being true.

There! There, again, the chance in a million! If he admitted even *that* slim chance of his being colored, how could he make their life what it had been until now? And any change from what it had been would be a change for the worse, and he couldn't stand to have his marriage change for the worse!

He had to convince her it was all nonsense. He had to get her back.

He ran out of the studio and started down the stairs, and then he heard someone upstairs. He turned, took the steps two at a time, reached the third floor and opened the door. 'Phyll?'

'In your office,' she said, her voice trembling.

He went down the hallway, walking slowly.

She was sitting on the couch, under Bogen's prize-winning portrait of a woman and a baby. He looked at it, afraid to look at her, and felt something he hadn't felt before.

'All right, Richie,' she said, and took a deep breath.

He moved his eyes to her, too frightened to speak. She was going to end their marriage.

'I understand a lot of things now,' she said. 'I remember things you said, and I understand them. I'm sorry if I ever hurt you by what I said. But before it was just Negroes I was discussing. Now it's you.'

He could have tried explaining then but decided not to. He decided to wait.

'It's *you*, Richie. And I love you. That makes quite a difference. Whatever you are, it's you, Richie, my husband for nineteen, almost twenty, years. Whatever – ' She bit her lip, and looked at him. 'Richie.'

He didn't go to her – not yet. He'd received a reprieve, the most wonderful, the most unexpected reprieve. And yet, as he heard it, he wondered that it should be unexpected, that he'd ever thought she'd have acted differently. How else could he have loved her if he hadn't known – or sensed – she'd be capable of acting this way? But he wanted to hear it all; prove it all.

'Would you have a child, Phyll?'

She hesitated, then nodded. 'I think we'll almost have to, now.'

'Why?'

'I don't know why. I just think we'll have to.'

He knew why, and he was so happy he could barely contain himself. She meant she'd have to *prove* what she'd said about loving him as before, loving him as her husband.

'And if it weren't white?'

'It would still be my child, as you're my husband.'

'But . . . a colored child, Phyll?'

She clenched her hands. 'Do you think I could feel anything but love for my own child!'

He had no more questions. He came to her, dropped to his knees and put his head in her lap. He said, 'Thank you, Phyll. And forgive me. I haven't any evidence that I'm colored. None at all. It's just something that I built up in my mind. But you're right about the child. We should have had one.'

She was very still, and he looked up at her face. She was blinking her eyes, as if stunned. Then she stood up, throwing him back on his haunches. 'Was this some stupid drunken game? Was this some cruel test? Was this another of your question-and-answer – '

'No, honey. Honest! It's been eating at me for years.'

She was crying now, shouting, 'I'll never forgive you for this, Richie! Never!' She ran out of the office, and he got to his feet and ran after her, anxious to explain, anxious to end her suspicion and her hurt and her anger. But even as he sent the pleading, frantic words after her, laughter rose in his throat and joy overwhelmed him.

'Phyll, wait, it wasn't a game.'

He caught her on Seventh Avenue, and people stopped to stare at the man who was laughing and trying to stop his laughter and trying to talk, all at the same time. And at the woman pushing at him and crying and shouting she hated him. One girl wanted to call a cop, but by the time she'd convinced her escort it was the thing to do, the laughing man and crying woman had started down Fifty-second Street together.

* * *

Henny Girado opened his eyes or, rather, one eye since his left was puffed so badly it refused to open. There were four or five people looking down at him, and hands were applying damp cloths to his face and head, but he saw only Sandy, felt only her hand wiping his mouth and heard only her voice. 'Please, Henny. Please.' Then she saw his open eye and stopped speaking.

'How do you feel?' Les Bogen asked.

Henny tried to nod, and the world filled with flashes of light. He closed his eye, afraid he was going to be sick all over himself. 'Okay,' he said, and was surprised at how weak his voice was. He looked at them again and saw the handkerchief in Sandy's hand – red with blood. 'Guess I'd better see a doctor.'

'Try to sit up,' Bogen said, and put his hand under Henny's arm.

Henny sat up, and the flashes of light came again, and he fought sickness. He also felt the sharp pains in his side and chest. 'Did he work my body over?'

'Yes,' Bogen said. 'Feel any broken ribs?'

'I think so. Just help me to my car.'

'You can't drive yourself,' Sandy said, and he saw she'd been crying.

Marv Weister appeared, and Henny said, 'You know how to drive, don't you, Marv?'

'Well, it's been two years, but I can get you to a doctor.'

'Okay. Let's go.'

Marv got on one side of him, and Les on the other, and they helped him to his feet. He grew faint. 'Wait.'

He was sitting again, and Eugenia's voice said, 'We should call the police! It's too much. Drake tried to kill him! And he would have, if Les hadn't stepped in.'

Henny looked at Les Bogen and couldn't find a scratch; not a hair out of place. 'Thanks,' he said. 'But then again, a man has to protect . . .' He was going to say that a man has to protect his *property,* but he saw Bogen's eyes narrow and stopped himself. Nothing had changed. The deal was still on.

He moved his tongue around his mouth, found the raw spot, and sighed. 'I always liked that upper incisor. We had fun together.'

There was salt on his lips, and he licked them, and Sandy leaned forward and dabbed away blood with her damp handkerchief.

'Thanks,' Henny said. He pushed himself erect, with Marv Weister's help. 'Made it. And now, dear friends, adieu. I doubt if I'll see you for a few days. I'm going to throw another party – just me and a bed and a bottle of aspirin.' No one answered his painful grin. He and Marv moved slowly toward the door.

Sandy came up on his left side as they stepped into the waiting room. 'Henny, may I come along?'

He waved his hand and said, voice sharp, 'How about letting me die in peace, huh?'

Marv murmured, 'Hey, take it easy.'

Sandy nodded calmly. 'You can't get rid of me, Henny.'

'No?' He tried to move faster and almost fell, and she grabbed his free arm. He shook her loose. 'I'm going to try like hell!'

She stayed behind. He and Marv reached the landing and began the long trip down the stairs.

When they reached the street, Henny said, 'She coming after us, Marv?'

'No. But you're too obvious, Henny. You and that girl are a team. She knows it, and anyone who spends five minutes with the two of you knows it.'

'But *I* don't know it.'

'We'll discuss it some other time. Is your car in the lot across the street?'

'Yes.' They moved to the curb. Henny said, 'And Les Bogen doesn't know it.'

'He will.'

'Yeah, but when? At the age of ninety?'

'I rather think he'll know it tonight, if he doesn't already.'

Henny looked at the small, thin man, his one eye blinking rapidly.

Marv took a firmer grip on his arm. 'Watch the curb. Okay, no traffic coming, but try and move faster.'

They reached the other side of the street. Henny's stomach turned over, and he said, 'Watch out.'

Marv stepped back, bracing him from behind. Henny threw up, heavily, painfully. He finished, and accepted Marv's handkerchief and wiped his mouth. He laughed a little and said, 'That solves my hangover.'

Marv took his arm again. 'You're beginning to sound like yourself.'

They walked through the darkness and reached the Chevy. Marv helped him into the front seat, on the passenger side, and Henny said, 'Let's just sit and talk a while.'

'But the doctor?'

'It's nothing that won't keep a few minutes. I want to hear your reasons for thinking Les Bogen will give me his daughter with his blessings. And remember, you don't know what's stopping me from going to her, and you don't know how much trouble Les went to . . .' He waved his hand weakly. 'You can't possibly be right, but I always loved comforting fairy tales – the ones in which the wicked witch was turned into Jello or something.'

Marv got behind the wheel and peered at him. 'Try the handkerchief on your mouth again.' Henny dabbed at a trickle of blood and winced as he touched his now swollen lips.

Marv said, 'I can't understand why you shouldn't see it. She cares for you and isn't foiled by your brush-off, so what's to keep you apart?'

'*Me*. I won't allow us to get together.'

'Why?'

'Never mind why. I just won't. But let's say Bogen has me on a string. Only if he says, "You can see my daughter," will I see her.'

'Okay. So he'll say that. She'll make him say that.'

Henny laughed. 'You don't know Les Bogen.'

Marv shrugged. 'He's only people. You're too close to the situation to realize how hopeless any resistance on his part is. She'll be contacting you again, soon.'

Henny said nothing, and Marv tried to make out his face in the darkness. 'You okay, Henny?'

'I will be,' the still voice answered, 'if you're right, Marv.'

'I'm right.'

'How can you be so goddam sure of something you don't know?'

'I saw her. And I saw you. And I saw Les. I know it all, buddy.'

'Give me a cigarette.'

'I think we should go.'

'Just one cigarette.'

'A few minutes ago you were passing out.'

'A few minutes ago I was dead.'

'I'm not sure I understand that.'

'Forget it. Let's have the cigarette.'

They lit up. Henny fixed his one good eye on the glowing end and waited. If Marv was right . . .

He hadn't taken more than three or four drags when a sound made him look toward the street. A man and woman had entered the lot.

'That's Les and his daughter,' Marv murmured.

'Don't jump to conclusions.'

'Me? I've got troubles of my own. I only meant that if you both continue to feel the same way, sooner or later . . .'

'Yeah,' Henny muttered. 'I guess it'll be later. They're going to Les's car.'

The two figures passed behind the Chevy and continued deep into the lot where Les had parked his Hawk. A moment later an engine roared and back-up lights flared.

Henny flipped his cigarette out the window. 'Okay, genius. Let's go see the doctor. And remind me never to believe you.'

Someone got out of Bogen's car and ran across the pebbled lot. Then Sandy was at the driver's window saying, 'Henny.'

'He's on the other side,' Marv Weister said. 'A genius is sitting on this side. But don't bother going over there. I'm getting out. *You* can drive him to the doctor.'

Henny began to protest, but very weakly. Marv got out and walked away. Sandy got in. Henny said, 'Does your father know?'

'My father knows everything, Henny. How to fight good guys and how to fight bad guys. He can beat both, too, but only if his daughter isn't involved. He doesn't know how to fight me, Henny.'

She leaned toward him, her hand moving slowly, carefully, to touch his face, to stroke his cheek. 'You're both a little stupid,' she said.

He still wasn't sure. He wasn't going to let himself go and then take another beating – the worst beating of his life, emotionally. 'Really? And did your father admit that he could destroy me, my family, everything?'

She shook her head. 'He only said, 'Tell him he owes me a thousand dollars. Tell him he's back where he was, and doesn't that make him happy.' I know he did something to make you drop me, Henny. And he's ashamed to tell me what it is. And you're ashamed too, aren't you?'

He wasn't. Not really. He'd been forced into a corner, and he'd had no choice. Despite everything the

413

romantic poets wrote of love, there were the obligations, the overpowering necessities of providing for one's dependents.

But he was beginning to feel happy.

The dunnings would start again and the scrounging for dough and all the rest of his troubles. And he'd have to try and get back that deposit on the little luncheonette in Denver. There were all the old problems and a few new ones; but there was also Sandy and her plan to save him eighty a week.

He fought the happy feeling. He refused to move toward her. He had to be sure.

He got out of the Chevy painfully and said, 'I'll be right back.' He heard the car and moved a few steps away from the Chevy. The headlights swung toward him and slowed and stopped. He came up to the driver's window.

'How are you feeling?' Les Bogen asked.

'Lousy. But I want to know –'

'You do know.' Bogen's voice was tired. 'And you owe me a thousand dollars.'

Henny began to smile, lips hurting like hell. 'You'll have to get on line, Les.'

'The *front* of the line, Henny. Don't you forget that.'

'I'll pay, Les.' His lips were killing him, but he grinned wider and wider. 'Just give me some time.'

Les Bogen said, 'Yes,' and raced his car's powerful engine, and Henny took the hint and stepped back. But Les didn't drive away. He looked past Henny, at the Chevy. He seemed to be trying to make out his daughter in the blackness. Then he murmured, 'Good night.'

Henny wasn't sure to whom Les was speaking, but he said, 'Good night, dad.'

Bogen's face twisted.

Henny laughed. 'I didn't mean it that way.'

Bogen drove off.

Henny returned to the Chevy, got inside and put his arms around Sandy. He said, 'If I pass out, throw cold water on me,' and pressed his swollen lips to her cheek. Afterward, he was content to let her kiss him.

25

Marv Weister took the subway home. There was no one to give him a lift; he didn't want to spend the dollar or more for a cab, and the subway *was* handy. But none of these reasons was the real one. None of them would have made him take the subway at eleven P.M. and then walk three long blocks through a neighborhood which had known muggings, a neighborhood which held the groups of Puerto Rican boys he feared so much. None of them would have sufficed, before tonight.

But tonight he'd taken a step toward manhood. Or so it appeared to him; and if it appeared that way, it *was* that way. Tonight he had to smash as many ikons in the dark temple of his mind as he could.

He left the subway at eleven-forty and began the three-block walk. It was dark. The streets were deserted. He kept his head down and moved as quickly as he could and told himself over and over that nothing was going to happen. But by the time he'd completed one block, he was sick. And the second block had two broken street lamps and a long stretch of absolute darkness, and he had to fight the desire to break into a run. The third block was his, and the worst of the three.

He was halfway to his building, already congratulating himself on not having met a single person, when he heard the snicker and then the voice whispering, the words unintelligible but definitely Spanish.

He raised his head and glanced to his right and there, not five feet away, were eight or ten teen-age boys clustered over the stoop of a brownstone, sitting on the steps and on the stone railing, smoking and whispering and looking at him, faces dark and foreign and hard; the dispossessed, the second-class citizens, looking at and hating him.

He could have screamed.

But this was more than a group of tough, dangerous boys, just as the fight at the studio had been more than a fist fight. This was opportunity. This was another choice between the hell of the past and a hope for change.

'*Buenas tardes*,' he said, wondering if that were correct for Puerto Ricans on a stoop near midnight. Prep-school Spanish was a long way back.

There was no immediate answer, and he kept walking, thinking he heard them moving, coming up behind him, thinking they were taking so long.

But he wasn't more than two steps past the stoop when the answer came – a mumbled chorus of '*Buenas noches*.'

He reached his building and climbed the three flights and opened the door. He put on the lights and sat down and lighted a cigarette. He trembled. His underwear was soaked with perspiration. His stomach churned and his hands hurt from hitting Arnold Gernstein and his head ached from all the convulsions it had contained.

And he still wanted that fix; began wanting it more and more by the minute; began knowing he *had* to have something before too long or he'd die.

He got up and went into the bedroom and put on the light. He sat down, jacket and all, before the typewriter. He touched the keys and told himself it was stupid to think of writing tonight, after all he'd been through and as sick as he now felt. He'd had enough victories for one day.

But the thought that anything could be a victory without a correspondingly positive result on this typewriter made no sense. He took off his jacket, picked up the last few pages he'd written two days ago and read them over. Lord, they stank!

He put them aside, inserted a blank sheet in the roller and began copying the first line of the material he'd just read. He began to change it.

Two hours later he got his cigarettes and smoked one. He smoked it standing over the typewriter, afraid to walk away, afraid he'd lose the mood. Then he sat down and went back to work.

He had to stop again in half an hour because of nausea.

A fix. One fix and he'd be okay for a week, two weeks, maybe longer. One lousy fix! And he had Demarco's number.

He couldn't reach him until tomorrow afternoon.

All right, tomorrow afternoon.

But he thought it through, and he was strong – perhaps because of his two small victories; perhaps because the time had come for him to be strong. He went to the phone, dialed, waited a long time, and then said, 'Dr Bernstein? This is Marvin Weister. I'm sorry to wake you.' He listened. 'Oh, I'm glad – or should I be sorry you're forced to keep such late hours?' He laughed, forcing the sound. 'Yes, it *has* been a long time. You did? I'm glad you liked it. No, I wrote two before that. I'll bring copies when I come to your office tomorrow morning.' He listened, and his face grew gray, and he said, all pretense of flippancy and laughter gone, 'I forgot about your not having office hours on Fridays. I need immediate help, Doctor. I think I've become a dope addict.'

The doctor asked for details.

Marv explained, and the doctor said he'd see him at nine the next morning, and Marv thanked him. 'Are there ways to cure it?' he asked, hoping there'd be a miracle drug or something, yet knowing there was only one way – self-denial.

The doctor said there was only one way – self-denial. But, he added, there were methods of *helping* the patient who was willing to deny himself, especially if the addiction were partly psychosomatic, as it might be in his case. There were placebos and substitutes. And, finally, if the patient was a trusted friend, there were times when actual heroin could be used to 'ease extreme pain' – in complete confidence, of course.

Marv needed no more. He thanked the doctor and hung up. He returned to the typewriter. He wrote a total of eight pages by four A.M., and read them over, and wanted to beat his head against the wall. He threw away three, and revised the rest, and felt exhausted and depressed. But then he read his five pages and was comforted.

He went to bed. He'd had a long day. He'd struck a man, and said hello to a group of boys, and called a doctor.

He and Superman.

He smiled a little. If life didn't get any worse, he'd make it.

Les Bogen watched Marv Weister lead Henny from the studio. He glanced at Sandy and couldn't read her face. She looked calm enough now; had looked that way the last part of the evening, except for the few moments it took for the fight to run its course and immediately afterward when Henny had been brought to the couch.

Les was beginning to regain a little hope.

He'd get Sandy away from here, back home, and perhaps . . .

But then she ran after Henny and took his arm in the waiting room, and Les wondered what Henny would do.

When Henny shook her off, Les knew he'd made his deal with the right man. Sandy wouldn't break him down, no matter what the circumstances, no matter how many fights, tragedies, and co-incidental meetings took place. *Nothing* would change the situation.

Sandy stayed in the waiting room, and Les said good night to Eugenia and her friend Francie, offering to put them in a cab. They thanked him and said they could manage themselves. He then looked around for Stella Lago. Eugenia said, 'The new one's having a crying fit in the dressing room. She's not tough enough for us, Les – not yet.'

He couldn't muster a smile to answer Eugenia's. 'Guess I'd better wait.'

'Go on, take your daughter home,' Eugenia said, and Les refused to admit he read something like pity in her eyes, something like sympathy in her voice.

'We'll take a cab together,' Francie said.

Les insisted on giving them ten dollars, explaining that Stella lived in Brooklyn, and Eugenia said, 'Hey, dad, so this is what the call-girls mean by "cab fare". Good deal!'

He joined Sandy in the waiting room and took her arm. 'Let's go home, honey.'

She didn't look at him; she didn't answer; she merely allowed him to direct her to the landing and the stairs. There he stopped. 'Tell you what, we'll forget about going home tonight. We'll drive out to Montauk and find a motel. Tomorrow morning we'll buy toothbrushes and bathing suits – '

She looked at him. 'I'm not going anywhere with you, Father, ever again. Tonight, when you take me home, will be the last time we'll do *anything* together.'

He believed her. There was no doubting the coldness in her voice, the *dislike* in her eyes. But he started down the stairs, saying, 'You'll feel differently tomorrow.'

'No.'

'Then the next day, or the next week.'

'Only if you undo what you've done to Henny.'

He stopped and turned. 'Me? I saved his skin.'

'Don't, Father. No more. It's played out. You've managed to change my life, and Henny's, for a few unhappy hours, but it can't last.' She came down the four steps separating them and looked into his eyes. 'I won't be your darling daughter any more.'

He laughed shrilly and turned away. 'Sounds like an old English folk song.'

They went into the street. He took her arm, and she went with him to the parking lot. They both saw Henny's car – Les almost immediately, Sandy when they were passing behind it. They kept going.

She got into the Hawk as Les held the door. He went around the other side and opened his own door and saw her face in the interior light. She was still calm, quiet, assured. And completely lost to him.

He knew that now, but it took another few seconds for him to accept it. He got into the car and put the key in the ignition and started the engine. He threw the lever to reverse, then cut the ignition and said, 'I'm not sorry I tried to stop you.' His voice shook very badly. 'I'm not sorry I fought to have you for myself a few more years.'

She turned, her voice coming alive as she saw him breaking. 'A few more years, Father?'

'Let's say that, Sandy. Please. I wasn't really aware of wanting more.'

'All right. Let's say that. Can I go now? Can I tell him it's all right now?'

He hadn't finished. He wanted to tell her of his love, wanted to justify himself and explain whatever Henny might tell her – though, at the same time, he felt Henny would never tell her the details, the ugly details of her father's blackmail. He wanted to take her hands, and talk himself dry, and perhaps even allow his bitterness, his loss, to come out in tears.

But he'd made her wait too long, and there was no way to explain or expiate or alleviate. 'Yes,' he said. 'You can go. Just tell him he owes me a thousand dollars. Tell him he's back where he was, and doesn't that make him happy.'

'I'll tell him.' She got out of the car and ran to the Chevy. Les sat a moment and then backed the Hawk and swung it around. His lights hit Henny, walking away from the Chevy. He drove up and stopped, knowing Henny had to be sure. He made him sure, and drove onto the street; and suddenly he didn't want to go home, couldn't tolerate the thought of home.

He parked in front of the studio and went upstairs. Eugenia, Francie and Stella were sitting on the couch having a drink. Stella's eyes were red. 'This looks pleasant,' Les said, and poured himself a Scotch.

Eugenia said, 'Did you throw your daughter to the wolves?'

'Not plural, dear. Singular. Henny's only *one* wolf, you know.' He smiled at Stella Lago, running his eyes over her long legs, wanting her in an instant, wanting her newness, her freshness.

Eugenia said, 'Well, it seems we're standing in the way of progress.' She nudged Francie, and they both stood up.

Stella Lago said, 'Oh, no. I have to get home.'

'I'll drive you,' Les said, and sat down beside her. 'I want to explain what happened tonight.'

'Eugenia already explained,' the tall redhead muttered, face sullen, apparently disinterested in anything he had to say. But she didn't get up to leave, and Les Bogen said a prayer of thanks. He needed her tonight.

When Eugenia and Francie left, he assured the suddenly timorous girl he would take her home after 'just one more drink.' Before he mixed that drink, he locked the street door and put out the lights all over the studio, except for one dim goose-neck section on the marble counter far in the rear. He sat down beside her, took her hand, and began talking.

'I'm terribly sorry about this afternoon.'

He put his heart into every word, revealing his need, his desire, his love – temporary, but still love. And since she'd been willing during the afternoon, it didn't take much to bring her to complete compliance. When he put a hand on her knee, she made no protest, so he slid an arm around her shoulders and drew her closer. Her mouth opened when he kissed her, and he brought his hand from her knee to her breast. She sighed, straining against him, and he reached round to find the zipper of her tight-fitting dress. He tugged it down, and eased the dress from her shoulders. She was wearing a pale blue brassiere that lifted her heavy breasts. Les bent to brush his mouth over the cleavage, at the same time putting his arms around her and unsnapping the catches. Stella said, 'Oh, Les,' as he removed the brassiere and began to kiss her nipples. Les teased and sucked until she began to moan, and pushed his coat down. He pulled away then, undressing swiftly, with economic, practised movements. Stella rose from the couch to slide her dress off and remove her panties. She stood before him, wearing only dark stockings and a black garter belt. She began to remove the stockings, but Les stopped her, pulling her down onto the couch.

'You look wonderful just like that,' he murmured.

'Good enough to photograph?' Stella asked, striking an erotic pose.

She had a good body. Slightly fleshy about the buttocks, her suspenders indenting the flesh there, her thighs bulging fractionally over her black stocking tops, but otherwise smooth and youthful. 'Later,' Les said huskily, reaching for her.

She came into his arms eagerly, her mouth red and hungry. Les kissed her, one hand about her shoulders as the other explored the contours of her waist and hips and thighs. Stella moaned again, taking his hand to push it between her parted legs. She was already wet to his touch, and as he inserted a finger in her vagina, she took him in her hand and began to stroke him gently.

Les let her arouse him, then disengaged her hand and pulled away. 'Kneel in front of me,' he whispered urgently. Stella looked at him doubtfully for an instant, but only for an instant, then drew her long legs up onto the couch. Les guided her into position, adjusting her body as though for a photographic session. When he was finished, she was on her knees, her bottom towards him, the globes of her buttocks white against the black lines of her suspenders and the dark nylon of her stockings. Les bent forwards, running his mouth over her buttocks and the cleft between. Stella gasped, pushing back against him. Les smiled, studying the pinkish-brown ring of her anus. It was too soon for that, he decided, and let his hand wander over the puckered opening to the parted lips of her vagina. He moved forwards on the couch, stroking her buttocks and thighs, excited by the contrast of white flesh and black nylon. He placed the tip of his penis against her womanhood. Stella said, 'Oh, Les,' again, and reached back to touch him and guide him into her. Les put his hands on her waist and the swelling curve of her hips. As he pushed forwards, Stella rammed back, letting out a little scream as he drove into her. Her vagina was tight, gripping him, and he closed his eyes, luxuriating in the sensation of her buttocks slapping against his stomach and thighs as he brought her expertly to climax.

He needed her at that moment. He needed to pound against those seductive, fleshy buttocks to find the oblivion he sought. The thrust of his rampant penis into her wet, eager vagina promised forgetfulness. A dimming of all the disappointments and loss he had suffered, a respite from the knowledge that he had lost Sandy. As he came, and Stella screamed, pounding against him of her own accord now, he loved her for the relief she gave him. Just as he loved all of them. And always would for that brief instant.

He drove her to St John's Place in Brooklyn, and it was three A.M. as they pulled up before the red-brick apartment house. He kissed her good night, and she responded nicely, and he was sorry they'd left the studio so soon. Then she said, 'Gee, Les, I can hardly believe you have a daughter my age. Funny, isn't it?'

He nodded, smiling vaguely.

It was five-fifteen when he parked his car in the garage and went up to his room. He got into bed and fell asleep immediately, and dreamed he and Sandy were in the Automat and she was four and kept saying, 'I wanna stay with you forever and ever, Daddy.'

He woke up, and his eyes were wet, and his body was damp and uncomfortable. He looked at the windows facing the terraced back. The sun was there, and from the angle of the rays he guessed it was noon. He got up and checked his watch – twelve-twenty. He'd guessed pretty close. Sandy would be interested.

Sandy . . .

He slipped into a bathrobe, went out in the hall and knocked at Sandy's door. From downstairs, Elsie Dudonic called, 'No use doing that, Mr Bogen. She ain't home. Called late last night to say she was staying with a friend.'

'I see.'

He went to the bathroom, showered and shaved, and took a long time combing his hair, brushing his teeth and putting talcum on his body. He examined himself in the mirror: still cleanly muscled, still firm and strong.

For how long?

He didn't pursue that thought. He left the bathroom and dressed in Bermuda shorts and a polo shirt and went down for brunch. He ate well, and asked Elsie where Mrs Bogen was.

'Outside, playing with them bushes.'

He nodded, had a third cup of coffee, and couldn't rid himself of a baby voice: 'I wanna stay with you forever and ever, Daddy.'

He got up and went into the living room and looked out the window over the valley. Sandy had always loved the view.

He remembered telling Henny he'd have to pay back the thousand dollars. He winced and admitted to himself that he'd known, even then, he wasn't going to collect that money, was going to see that Henny's sister got the luncheonette so that Henny – or rather Sandy – had a chance to live decently.

What was it he'd begun to say to her one day last week and stopped because he'd been ashamed of his own perfidy? *'I'll give you the biggest dowry.'*

Maybe not the biggest, now. But there'd be the lunch-eonette. And another few thousand in cash that he'd put aside with her in mind – for trips, for school, for a car, for whatever she needed or wanted. She'd get her forty-five hundred; more, if she ever asked for it.

She would never ask. He would have to come to her, urging her to accept his gifts. She would never ask, and Henny would never ask, and neither would fully trust him.

Not that he wanted their trust or even Sandy's watered-down love. He'd wanted *all* her affection, her deepest feelings, and failing to get this wanted none of it. Sure, he'd see her once in a while.

He began to feel nervous, hemmed in. He went outside, and it was another bright, warm, summery day. He found Louise cultivating the ground around the climbing red pillar roses at the north side of the garage. 'Japanese beetles,' she said, by way of greeting. 'If we cultivate from early spring until late fall, their larvae won't have a chance to survive.'

He nodded. She wore a work dress of brown, denimlike material, and her hair was tied back with a thin yellow ribbon. She moved lithely and made quite an attractive picture holding the long rake. And yet, she lacked the one thing a woman most needed to be desirable to men – the inner asking, the inner need, the always present invitation to love.

'Sandy called,' she said, still raking away. 'She sounded very happy.'

'She's going to marry Henny Girado.'

'Yes, she told me.' She was smiling, and he realized it wasn't the cold, vindictive smile she usually showed in his presence. She was happy for her daughter. 'I'm glad you let it happen, Les. You'll help them along, won't you? Every young couple needs help.'

'Yes, I'll help them along.' He changed the subject. 'Sun feels good. I'm going to take off my shirt and get a tan.'

She nodded, and continued raking.

He hesitated, and then said, 'Why don't you join me?'

She looked at him. 'Are you lonely already, Les?' And then, quickly, 'I didn't mean that as a criticism of any sort. I was just commenting.'

He was sorry he'd asked her. He didn't really want her company. She could never be a woman – a real woman – for him, no matter how lonely he got. He turned away without answering.

He took a contour chair from the basement and put it outside the dining-room door, facing the multiflora hedging. He stretched out, closed his eyes and tried to doze. Later he checked his watch, thinking several hours must have passed. He was shocked to see it was only one-thirty. He'd been sitting less than twenty-five minutes!

He got out of the chair and stood rubbing his hands together. It terrified him, that slow passage of time.

He went into the house and made himself a gin fizz and

took it to his room. He read a collection of short stories, and they bored him. Then he got out the picture album and looked at Sandy as an infant, a six-year-old, a high-school co-ed, a college sophomore.

He felt the crying deep inside him, closed the album and went back to his book of short stories. Time passed slowly, slowly.

He wasn't sure how long the thought had been with him. It may have been lurking in his mind since last night, or perhaps even before then, if he'd glimpsed the inevitability of his defeat. But as he sat in his room, it emerged clearly. He laughed at himself and then shuddered. But the thought remained.

After a while he went downstairs and found Louise, still cultivating her rose bushes. She looked up at him, and he said, 'Yes, I am lonely.'

'What?'

'You asked me a question before, which I didn't answer. I'm answering it now.'

She blinked her eyes – stupidly, he thought. But he made his voice warm. 'I've been sitting out back. Why don't you join me?'

She looked at her bushes. 'Well, I'm just about finished anyway.'

He got the chairs, and they sat in the sun, and he began speaking on a topic he knew would interest her. 'I've been thinking of what to plant on the upper terrace – the rim where we've got so much clover and assorted weeds.'

When he asked if she'd join him in a drink, she said, 'Yes. I'm thirsty after all that cultivating.'

He brought out two gin fizzes, and they drank together, and she murmured, 'My, it tastes strong.'

'Only the usual amount of gin,' he said, but he was lying. He'd put more than three full shots in hers.

Over her protests, he insisted on a second round, and

by the time she finished that she was laughing at every-thing and stopped only long enough to say, 'Why'n't we have another drink, Les? It's so *pleasant* out here.'

He went into the house with the empty glasses. Elsie said, 'When're you two gonna have something to eat?' She obviously took a dim view of such goings-on between a husband and wife who hadn't said more than a coldly polite word to each other in years. He almost expected her to accuse him of 'indecencies' – and the funny part about it was that she'd be right! Lord, he felt as indecent as a man could!

'You can go now,' he said.

'Go?'

'Go.'

'I wanta tell Mrs Bogen about dinner.'

'Go. Take the next seven days off. With pay. Starting tomorrow.' He nodded to himself, planning a call he'd make to Richie Morden. He was going on vacation, starting right now. A seven-day vacation.

She stared at him. 'You're not drunk?'

'Elsie, do as I say.'

She continued to stare at him, and he smiled, and she shrugged.

When he came out with the tray, Louise was sitting up in her chair. 'Whose car went down the driveway?'

It wasn't time to let her know Elsie had left. 'Some salesman or other. Now for our drinks.' He handed her the glass and sat down on the ground beside her. They sipped, and he put his hand on her bare leg, and she said, 'Lester!'

He talked quickly, about anything that came to mind, and drained his glass. This time his drink had even more liquor than hers. This time he wanted a degree of nirvana for himself.

They had yet another drink, and Louise lay back in her chair and giggled at everything he said – things such as:

'I dislike clover because it attracts bees with its white summer flower.'

And:

'Those rose trees from Stern's certainly turned out to be a fine investment.'

He was sure she'd laugh even if he said, 'I've got a razor blade here and I'm cutting your wrists.'

She was ready.

'I've been thinking,' he said, and began working his hand along her leg, under her dress, watching the way her eyes flickered drunkenly and her color mounted.

'Yes?' The word was thick in her mouth.

'We really ought to try getting closer.'

She laughed a long time, and shook her head, and laughed again. 'Silly, silly, silly.'

He smiled. His hand was stroking her thighs, and he raised himself so he could kiss her face and neck.

'Silly, silly.'

He wasn't worried about resistance any longer. She'd had more than twelve shots of gin in an hour, and she'd never been much of a drinker.

He stood up and drew her out of the chair and kissed her hard. She mumbled something about its being 'a crazy business.' He agreed with her and led her into the house. One week of this would be all he could stand. If it didn't happen by then . . .

He refused to accept that possibility. He wanted a child, and he knew they could still have one. He only hoped the shock wouldn't kill Louise when she found out.

Monday evening Henny and Sandy went to the *luau* at the West Side Hawaiian restaurant. Henny shot the proceedings in somewhat less than two hours and then sank down on the rug- and cushion-covered floor. 'Momma,' he muttered, 'that Drake man sure packed

430

a wallop. I feel the ribs more today than I did last Thursday.'

'Is the tape in place?' she asked, worried.

'Sure. Don't fuss. I was just making conversation. Now put some of those yummies on a plate and serve them to Poppa. And let's have a coconut.'

The 'coconuts' were filled with potent rum and gin concoctions, and after two of these Henny felt fine. He put his arm around Sandy and drew her to him. She resisted, murmuring, 'Henny! People will see.'

'Since when did you get so sensitive?' he asked, grinning. 'You're not forgetting where you've been living the past four days? Greta certainly bounced out fast.'

'That's because you didn't tell her.'

'She'd have bounced out anyway. Marriage next week's no excuse for gutchie-goo tonight – not with Greta.'

She laughed and kissed him, and then said, 'I'll call home next Monday, when we get back from Maryland. I . . . hope Daddy's all right.'

Henny shoved a coconut at her, and she drank, and he began to eat. There were fried shrimp, barbecued spareribs, lobster bits, and piles of soft white rice. There were rum drinks and gin drinks and wine drinks. And it all tasted so goddam fine that he forgot everything but the feeling of good food, good drink and a good woman. And the feeling of a good life, which was his.

'I wonder what he's doing right now,' Sandy murmured, visualizing a bent, aging figure sitting in a darkened room.

Henny didn't try to answer that, because he had a damned good idea. The only question was – with whom?